PRAISE FOR THE CAREYS

"The Careys nest smaller tales within the larger story and often jump around in time; it's a good approach, backed by fast pacing and great characters . . . [*The Steel Seraglio* is] a thrilling tale."

—*Publishers Weekly*

"*The Steel Seraglio* brings its alternate world of struggle, politics and magic very much to life, transcending the more labored construct of symbol and metaphor in a fairy tale or fable retold only to make some kind of point."

—*Locus*

"With remarkable elegance, the Careys have enriched metafictional allegory into furious pop entertainment—full of sex, passion, violence, and magic. *The Steel Seraglio* is razor-sharp, cutting straight through the bullshit of bigotry to tell a fun, resonant story."

—*Slant Magazine*

"*The Steel Seraglio* is not a work of feminist or utopian theory. Nor is it a historical fantasy, a romance, a thriller, a poem, an allegory, or an epic. Rather, somehow, it is all of these things, mixed with a handful of gnomic utterances, a generous splash of the comic, and permeated by a deep understanding of what it means to weave a fairytale through with vision, to tell stories as a way of making meaning and making change, and to let those stories hang and fall . . ."

—*Neon Magazine*

"*The Steel Seraglio* is a masterful, engaging and utterly fascinating story by three wonderful writers. One can only hope they will collaborate again, as this project has proven how well they work together. The reader is really the winner here."

—*SF Revu*

THE HOUSE OF WAR AND WITNESS

MIKE CAREY, LINDA CAREY & LOUISE CAREY

CZP

ChiZine Publications

FIRST NORTH AMERICAN EDITION

The House of War and Witness © 2015 by Mike Carey, Linda Carey & Louise Carey
Cover artwork © 2015 by Erik Mohr
Cover and interior design © 2015 by Samantha Beiko

First Published in the U.K. by Gollancz

Distributed in Canada by
Publishers Group Canada
76 Stafford Street, Unit 300
Toronto, Ontario, M6J 2S1
Toll Free: 800-747-8147
e-mail: info@pgcbooks.ca

Distributed in the U.S. by
Consortium Book Sales & Distribution
34 Thirteenth Avenue, NE, Suite 101
Minneapolis, MN 55413
Phone: (612) 746-2600
e-mail: sales.orders@cbsd.com

Library and Archives Canada Cataloguing in Publication

Carey, Mike, 1959-, author

The house of war and witness / Mike Carey, Linda Carey, and

Louise Carey.

Issued in print and electronic formats.

ISBN 978-1-77148-312-4 (pbk.).--ISBN 978-1-77148-313-1 (ebook)

I. Carey, Linda, 1959-, author II. Carey, Louise, 1992-, author

III. Title.

PR6103.A72H68 2015   823'.92   C2014-907356-9

                                            C2014-907357-7

Shelfie

A **free** eBook edition is available
with the purchase of this print book.

CLEARLY PRINT YOUR NAME ABOVE IN UPPER CASE

Instructions to claim your free eBook edition:
1. Download the Shelfie app for Android or iOS
2. Write your name in **UPPER CASE** above
3. Use the Shelfie app to submit a photo
4. Download your eBook to any device

CHIZINE PUBLICATIONS
Toronto, Canada
www.chizinepub.com
info@chizinepub.com

Proofread by Tove Nielsen and Sandra Kasturi

Canada Council Conseil des arts
for the Arts   du Canada

We acknowledge the support of the Canada Council for the Arts which last year invested $20.1 million in writing and publishing throughout Canada.

ONTARIO ARTS COUNCIL
CONSEIL DES ARTS DE L'ONTARIO
an Ontario government agency
un organisme du gouvernement de l'Ontario

Published with the generous assistance of the Ontario Arts Council.

Printed in Canada

THE HOUSE OF WAR AND WITNESS

MIKE CAREY, LINDA CAREY & LOUISE CAREY

1

There was a border up ahead, though the trees were so thick here that no sign of it could be seen. The forest stretched for many miles in all directions, and the trees were the same ahead of them as behind. Nevertheless, the border was there. Not half an hour ago the ground had risen and the trees with it, and through the trunks they had all seen the flash of the river. On the other side of it was Prussia.

The men were too hungry and dispirited to celebrate much at the sight, though it meant their long march was almost at an end. Not so much a march, Colonel August had to admit: there had been no road for two days, and the officers had been leading their horses more often than riding them. It wasn't possible to maintain an orderly column among so many damned low-hanging branches, not with an infantry company more than two hundred strong. But at least they'd all kept up, and after his threat to cut the rations of the next man who complained, the grousing no longer reached his ears.

"There's a great house here? Really?" Lieutenant Klaes said. He looked again at the map, hand-drawn for them by the landlord of the last inn they had stopped at, three days ago. It was crude, but better than the official map, which showed a swathe of beautifully depicted trees with a single cross at the edge and blank space beyond.

The colonel—newly promoted from lieutenant colonel for the purposes of this assignment—didn't bother to look at either document. "It'll be where command says it is," he pronounced with easy confidence. "The family hasn't used it in years, apparently. I think we're still trying to find someone to accept the requisition papers."

"And the village: Narutsin? Outlandish name."

"Outlandish place, no doubt. But this close to the border, what do you expect? There's a small detachment there already: local forces. Their captain can fill us in on the peculiarities of the natives if he's halfway competent. And if it's really a backwater, so much the better in some ways. It'll discourage the men from fraternising."

"It's not so much the men I'd worry about," muttered Klaes as a burst of girlish laughter reached them from far back among the trees. The women—that is, the respectable women—were all in the rear party, together with a couple of the older sergeants for protection, the pack-mules and the baggage. They were the officers' wives, who were too delicate to travel at a soldier's pace and would arrive later in the day, following the trampled path left by the company. But a few of the camp followers, mostly washer-women and whores, had managed to tag along with the men. They kept to the back of the column where their presence was not too obvious, but Klaes could not ignore them: giggling and flirting and disrupting every attempt at good order. One of them, the gypsy girl Drozde, had a laugh that could drown a church bell. He turned to glower over his shoulder at the noise.

A cry from one of the scouts brought his attention back to the road ahead. Klaes glimpsed a straight edge through the trees and the grey of stone: a building. Only a few more minutes' walk confirmed it. The trees thinned, and through them the soldiers could see the gables of a house.

It stood on a rise too insignificant to be called a hill, the trees straggling around it on three sides. On the fourth were the house's grounds, maybe a dozen fields' width. Part might once have been laid out as lawns and herb beds, but all that could be seen there now was scrubby grass and a tangle of the same bushes they'd been pushing through for the last few days in the forest.

The house and its grounds were surrounded by a stone wall that might once have kept out intruders but was crumbling now in several places. Beyond it were the villagers' fields, jealously reclaimed from the forest and still more jealously guarded from each other with partitions of ditches or stick-fences. In the distance they could just make out the village itself: low, grey-brown buildings topped with a haze of cooking smoke.

After two miles the road crossed a bridge. It was yet another landmark that did not appear on their inadequate map, but the garrulous innkeeper at Kastornya had told them to look out for it. "It's a bridge over nothing! You'll see for yourself. It's where the river ran—not the big river, the Oder, but the small 'un. Mala Panev, I think they call it. Only then they dammed Mala Panev as she comes out of the hills—trying to make some good pasture, I reckon, but there's none to be had up there. So now there's just this big cut in the land. This big dry cut, see. And they call it the Drench."

This was a concern to Colonel August, and he stopped to take some measurements—or rather to allow Klaes to do so. It was not the Drench itself that troubled him. That was, indeed, only a dip in the land, five or six feet deep and no more than twenty wide at this point. It was dry at the bottom apart from a thin trickle and some standing pools, and even if there had been no bridge the officers would not have had to dismount to lead their horses down the gentle slope.

But the guns, which were a day behind them, were another matter. Lieutenant Dietmar needed well maintained roads, and given how few there were to choose from, would almost certainly be obliged to take this one. So it was of some moment to determine whether this wooden bridge would take their weight.

Klaes drew out a tape and stick that he kept about his person and solemnly did his calculations. His original posting had been with the corps of engineers, and he had learned a great deal there about the mechanics of this and that. Fortification, transport, sapping and undermining. Intellectually, it had suited him well, and he still evinced a fascination with such technical minutiae, but he had turned out to have little willingness to get his hands dirty, and so had found his way into a regular regiment by the quickest way.

But now Klaes inspected the bridge and pronounced it sound. And his commander accepted the verdict, knowing that if there was one thing Klaes could be relied on to do well, it was to weigh and measure.

Once over the bridge they halted at the edge of the trees while August gave orders: Sergeant Janek to run and take word to Lieutenant Tusimov in the rear, while the other sergeants relayed the order to halt along the rest of the column. The main body of the company would remain where they were, awaiting further instructions. A smaller group, headed by Klaes, was to accompany August into the village to meet the burgomaster.

"He won't be expecting us," Klaes observed. "It's clear your message miscarried, sir, or else he would have sent someone to meet us along the way."

"Still, he will come out to us," said August. "We're marching over two hundred men onto his land. If the mayor's not the first to greet us, he's not the one we should be dealing with."

In fact, it was not the burgomaster they met first. The season was late autumn, the ground still boggy from the first rains of the season, and the company were concentrating on their feet as they crossed the fields. They had been keeping to a narrow track between two harvested plots, but the hedges which served as boundary markers here had been allowed to grow straggly and wild. Privates Leintz and Rasmus swerved to avoid a bush in their path and ran into a man hiding behind it.

He started up from them like a pheasant, flapping his arms. His eyes were wide with terror.

"It wasn't," he said, high-voiced. "I didn't. I don't know a thing about it!"

He stood for another moment goggling at them. Then he turned and ran off across the field, his boots picking up fresh clumps of mud with each step.

"Local dullard," said Leintz, watching the man's lumbering retreat. "There's always one."

"More than one, I'll bet," Rasmus said. "Place like this, it's probably their main crop."

The company usually looked forward to their arrival in a new town. According to the archduchess's edict, soldiers of the empire were to be given food and lodging wherever they stopped along their route, provided free (or at a reduced rate at least) by the grateful populace: a small gesture to the heroes who defended them from the Prussian threat. In practice this mostly meant that the enlisted men under August's command were given a flattish field to pitch their tents, and could supplement their rations at their own expense from the town market. The arrangement worked well enough for a week or two, so long as they kept Taglitz away from the drink and restrained Pers in his target practice. But the day of their arrival, that was generally a high point. The towns out here, at the edge of the empire, were small and scattered and might not see a visitor in months. To most of them the arrival of a troop of soldiers—whipped into marching order by their colonel as they approached, uniforms as smart and swords as bright as could be managed after months on the road—was as good as a circus.

Not here, though. In fact, the town seemed almost deserted, nothing but a few chickens pecking around on the muddy track of the main road to show that people lived here at all. No pretty young girl waved or smiled; no old wife threw them the look of interest that might mean a free meal. The detachment, which had marched in briskly enough, began to slow. Some murmuring arose from the ranks. August frowned. It looked as though they had been stationed in a plague town.

But when they reached the town square—though this was too illustrious a name for the flattened patch of earth which terminated Narutsin's main street—the burgomaster was waiting with a cluster of men, just as the colonel had predicted. A squat little church, the town's only stone building, lay to their left. From its doorway Klaes heard the sound of low voices, and saw a crowd shifting about in the shadows. This accounted for the whereabouts of the townsfolk, but why on earth they were all in church on a Wednesday was a mystery to Klaes. He was at a loss to know how to respond to this turn of events. Perhaps these yokels were unaware of whose forces they were receiving and had hidden out of fear? If so, reassurances were in order. But August seemed determined to ignore this witless game of hide-and-go-seek, so the lieutenant did too.

The little group of men gathered in front of them filled the road, from the cattle trough to the gate of the biggest house. All of them seemed to be old, and all dressed in waistcoats or jackets, which probably passed for formal wear here. At their head the burgomaster stood stiffly, shoulders back in the manner of a sergeant at attention. His red-grey hair bristled and his collar was fastened high beneath his chin. He might have been bursting with pride at his own importance, receiving the ambassadors of the archduchess's army outside his home, but his face was guarded.

He and August bowed formally to each other while Klaes advanced a little awkwardly, holding out the letter of commission. The mayor took it and scanned it—he appeared to know how to read, Klaes noted with faint surprise. After a moment, he looked up and inclined his head to both men.

"It is all in order," he said. "I am Meister Berthold Weichorek. You and your men are welcome here, Colonel."

He turned from them before they could answer and held out the commission to the old men behind him.

"This says—" he raised his voice, possibly for the benefit of the listeners in the church "—the archduchess suspects some of her enemies might want to try how safely she sits her throne. These men are here to defend us should any of them think to strike here. So we're to give them lodging and food while they're with us, and make them welcome."

There was a collective shuffling from behind him. The greybeards in his retinue did not seem particularly pleased at the news. The older ones rarely were, in Klaes's experience: they tended to think more of the cost than of any diversion the company's presence might occasion. They began to wander off, each one nodding to the mayor as he left. One of them disappeared into the church, and the whispering from within intensified.

August cleared his throat pointedly. "We won't require lodging," he said. "I have requisitioned the mansion house three miles up the road for our officers, and the men will camp in the grounds. I understand that the owners are absent, and there is only a small force stationed there at the moment? There should be room for all of us."

Weichorek turned back to them with a look of puzzlement. "Another force, Colonel? My apologies, but what do you mean?"

Klaes stepped in fast: nothing tried the colonel's patience like block-headedness. "The soldiers who are here already," he explained. "The ones who arrived here last summer."

The mayor's face clouded. "Oh, the militia men," he said. "Yes." For a moment he said nothing more, but only gestured as though his position could be made clear by a mummers' show. "But they left months ago. They were moved on somewhere else where they were more needed, I understood." He wilted a little under August's glare. "I am sorry, sirs," he stammered. "This is a small town, and unimportant."

August's expression did not change. "As loyal subjects of the archduchess," he said, "you deserve her protection as much as any city. And now we are here to give it. Lieutenant, the great house will not be prepared for us: take your men there now and see to it. You can tell the rest of the company to begin making camp in the grounds." The irritation in his voice was for Klaes too.

Weichorek seemed to realise that he had given offence in some way and was clearly anxious to repair the damage. "You are welcome here, Colonel," he said again. "My wife and I would be honoured if you would share our table at supper tonight."

Klaes, heading off to muster his men, permitted himself an inward smile. It was only sensible for the officers to stay on good terms with local dignitaries, of course. But boiled eggs and small beer at a provincial's table! Colonel August would certainly not relish that prospect.

The great house's owners had named it Pokoj—Peace. Klaes assumed that this reflected their romantic expectations rather than the actual experience of living in these uncivilised borderlands. The name was worked in imposing letters amidst the ornamentation of the wrought-iron gates. Klaes could easily have led his men through one of the gaps in the surrounding wall, but, deserted or not, the house was private property, so he had Edek and Rasmus heave apart the great gates on their rusted hinges, so they could advance down the carriage path like visitors. Even from here they could see the house's dilapidation: the moss on the pale stone walls, the cracked windows and the missing roof tiles. This was not the only abandoned mansion hereabouts, of course: all along the border the nobility had fled their country retreats at the first threat of an invasion the previous year. But Pokoj had the look of a place that had been empty for much longer than that.

The carriageway was uneven, its gravel spotted with weeds. On each side were spiny bushes, some of them the height of a man. Above them, some way off to their left, rose a ruined building of some kind, its stone a darker grey than the house, with an arch and a ragged tower.

The house itself had clearly been designed on the model of the great ducal palaces, though less than half their size, with a pilastered frontage and two wings flanking a courtyard. It looked out of place here against the background of forest, as if its builder had imagined himself living somewhere more cultivated, closer to the heart of things.

The front door was massive, iron-chased and stuck fast in its frame. The burgomaster had found them the key, but even once Klaes had managed to free the lock it took three of them, straining their shoulders at the damp wood, to get the thing open. Inside was darkness and a powerful whiff of mildew. Lighting their lanterns, they found a cavernous hallway big enough to house a stable. The floor was marble and the walls studded with mould-flecked statues. Corridors led off to each side, and ahead of them a great staircase curved up into the dark.

Exploring, Klaes found the interior as ramshackle as he had feared. The roof had fallen in on the north side and the rooms on the upper level had spongy floors and stank of fungus. Downstairs, the ceilings dripped and bulged ominously. The south wing was a little better, and here Klaes set the men to work, driving tribes of mice out of the cupboards and shaking the dust and beetles from the curtains. Everywhere the wallpaper was peeling and the carpets alive with roaches. The owners had taken most of the furniture with them, but in the billiard room a heavy oak table stood alone, facing a marble fireplace with a picture above it too blackened for its subject to show.

It took some time for Klaes to find suitable rooms for the officers. By the time he had identified the four or five best upstairs, with the fewest holes in the walls and floors, the majority of the company had finished setting up their tents and were sitting around outside, leaning on their packs and dicing or playing cards. Klaes was gloomily overseeing his men as they swept floors and laid out pallets—he did not trust the remaining beds—when he heard his commanding officer's voice over the buzz of conversation from outside.

"Klaes! Where is the man?"

Klaes hurried to obey the summons. August had clearly recovered his temper: he greeted his lieutenant with some cordiality, strode past him into the house and, not seeming to notice the dank smell or the scrofulous walls, pronounced that it would do very well.

"I have another job for you," he told Klaes. "The mayor has invited me to sup with him this evening. I had to decline, of course; my presence is required here to oversee the encampment. But we need to maintain good relations with these people. I've told him that my place at his table will be supplied by my lieutenant, a young man of great acuity who will be able to tell him all that is needed about our stay here. You're to be there at seven."

Klaes prided himself on his discipline: he did not show his dismay by so much as a twitch. He suspected that August saw it anyway.

"Very well, Colonel," he said. "I'll go and change my clothes."

"No need to wear dress uniform, anything like that." August gave a small snort of laughter. "But you might go on horseback; that should impress them."

Klaes bowed and made to withdraw.

"And while you're there," August said before he could go, "find out what they're hiding."

"Sir?" said Klaes, taken aback.

"There's something going on here. The people are too sullen and the mayor too eager to please. You saw how they all hid in the church when we arrived. They have some secret they think they can keep from us, and that's bad for morale."

He did not say whose morale, Klaes thought. The colonel could well be right—he recalled the sideways glances between the old men and the unaccountable desertion of the town—but the thought of involving himself in the villagers' petty intrigues filled him with such deep disgust that he risked a protest.

"It'll be some provincial matter, no doubt. Someone taking in someone else's sheep, that went the wrong way on the mountains. This close to the border, sir—"

"This close to the border," August repeated heavily. "And maybe *ignoring* the border, where it suits them. Treating the dispositions of Her Imperial Highness as though they were dainties at a meal, to pick and choose from. You think that a small matter, Lieutenant?"

Klaes was mortified. "Not at all, sir!" he said, drawing himself to attention.

"It's really a matter of discipline," August said. "It may be some entirely trivial matter; most likely it is. But they think to conceal it from the officers of the empire, and that cannot be permitted. So you will find out their little secret, discreetly and by whatever means you choose, and report it to me. I'll decide then what action is required."

Klaes saluted. "Yes, Colonel."

"They must be made to understand that they cannot lie to us," August repeated. "See to it, Lieutenant."

2

The gypsy girl Drozde (who in truth was neither a gypsy nor still a girl, but a travelling entertainer who had fallen in with the troop for want of something better) was enjoying herself for the first time in days. Her man among the soldiers, Quartermaster Sergeant Molebacher, was no doubt nettled by her absence from his side. He had been kept behind in the rear party, and she had taken the opportunity, while he was busy arranging supplies in the back of one of the carts, to slip away and seek out the company of pleasanter companions. Libush and Alis had both worked in the brothels of Legnica before taking up with the company, and their stories could surprise even Drozde. Her feet ached, and she suspected that Molebacher would have something to say to her when she saw him next, but still she was laughing.

"And he stuck like that! They couldn't get him out, front or back. We had to cut him out at the finish. It took, I swear, the whole night. . . ."

"You're lying."

"No, I promise you. The sun was rising. If you'd only seen how fat he was . . ."

Libush's voice faded into silence as the three women came through the last stand of trees and saw the house properly for the first time. It was huge, bigger than any building Drozde had seen up close before. It had been even larger once, she could see: there was a broken-down structure over to one side, like the ruins of a church. *What sort of rich family keeps their own church and lets it fall down?* she wondered. But most likely it had been damaged in one of the wars. There had clearly been a good deal of fighting around here. She could tell by all the ghosts.

She noticed them as soon as she passed through the house's gates. They were everywhere—more than she'd ever seen in one place. She told herself it made no difference: she'd long ago learned how to ignore them, and it wasn't as if they bothered her—or at least no more than flies in summer bothered her. Still, she couldn't deny it was off-putting to see so many of them so densely clustered.

She turned away deliberately from the two grey figures she had just noticed hovering behind the spiny bushes lining the carriageway and tried to put them out of her mind. She had enough to think about right now. The house was more than a little dilapidated: even from here she could see the sagging sections of roof, the gaping holes where windows had been. That meant damp and mould, not a good environment for her puppets. She could keep them in her tent, of course, but it would be cold and windy, and if the rain came back they'd be better off indoors. And anyway, there was Molebacher to consider. If he wanted her in his bed every night, that was where she'd have to be.

The thought of Molebacher made her quicken her pace. His party was not far behind: they might be here before the day's end, and there were things she needed to arrange before then. The first group of soldiers had already reached the house and were standing at an approximation of attention in the courtyard, receiving their orders from Lieutenant Tusimov. Drozde bid goodbye to Alis and Libush with a promise to find them again in the evening and left the gravel drive, trampling weeds and pulling her skirts in against the thistles to overtake the men in the rear of the column. There were some curious glances at her, but the men were used to Drozde's quirks by now; besides, after a three-day march, small wonder if she was impatient to reach the end of it.

Tusimov dismissed most of the men to make camp in the grounds to the south of the house. They'd need an hour or more to clear the ground first, Drozde thought: she caught some disgruntled looks as they streamed past her. But a small party was also deputed to help the young lieutenant, Klaes, prepare the officers' quarters. Excellent! They were headed by Sergeant Strumpfel, who was slow and elderly and would give her much less trouble than Tusimov if she were caught. Drozde joined the men unobtrusively on the far side from the lieutenant and accompanied them through the mansion's great wooden door.

It was gloomy inside, and as damp-smelling as she'd feared. Men's voices came from overhead, and the sound of shifting furniture. Strumpfel halted his party in the great entrance hall and began to give ponderous instructions. Drozde quickly slipped away into the closest side passage and made her way along it, keeping to the wall and watching her feet. The kitchen would be at the back. They usually were.

It was so dark she had to feel her way much of the time. The walls were clammy and alive with a sort of buzzing. God alone knew what creatures infested them. But after listening intently for a while, Drozde decided that the sound was not in the walls; it was perhaps not even a sound, but more of a restlessness in the air around her. It made her skin prickle, as if she were being watched. *More ghosts*, she thought irritably. Though in fact ghosts rarely seemed to watch her. Sometimes, it was true, groups of them would gather at the back of the audience at her puppet shows, although she could never understand why. Perhaps they were drawn to any crowd. With this exception, however, they usually paid her no attention at all. Even the ones she'd seen in her childhood, the ones she'd known when they —— were alive, had mostly seemed not to recognise her, and if they spoke to her, said nothing that made much sense. It was one of the ways she'd learned to tell a ghost, even the most solid ones, from a living person: that inward look; the feeling that whatever occupied them, it was nothing she could see.

The wall fell away beneath her hand: a cross-corridor. At the same time, the buzzing intensified until the air in the hallway seemed to crackle with an indefinable energy. An excitable ghost, or maybe more than one. Whatever it was, she hadn't time for it now; the supply party might be arriving any time. She felt around for the opposite wall and pressed on, and the charge in the air abruptly subsided.

She found the kitchen at the back of the house as she had expected. It was a huge room, filthy and decked with cobwebs but clearly serviceable. Two half-glazed windows let in some light through their covering of dirt; through them Drozde glimpsed an overgrown garden and a well partially obscured by creeping ivy. The larder was wide and mercifully empty. There was copious shelving, a small but solid table and a monstrous fireplace. None of these details concerned Drozde overmuch, except perhaps the fireplace, but a spacious kitchen to work in would certainly sweeten Molebacher's temper and so make her life pleasanter.

The only downside to the room in her eyes was the ghost stretched out across the middle of the floor, an issue which would not inconvenience Molebacher at all. Normally Drozde would not have minded either, but it was an ugly thing, no more now than a black stain, though it still held the vague contours of a man. Again and again it moved to cover the remnants of its face with one attenuated arm—the same movement of shame or shielding each time, like an echo that never faded. For some reason the sight of it disconcerted Drozde, and she gave it a wide berth.

But she found what she had been looking for, at last: a staircase in the corner of the kitchen led down to a storeroom, which was cool and relatively free from damp. A tall cupboard against one of its walls would make an ideal place to hang her larger puppets: it even had hooks at the top, and there was plenty of space beside it for her trunk. Molebacher was fat and hated unnecessary exercise. He would be in no hurry to spend time down there, and would be happy to depute any fetching and carrying up and down the stairs to her.

Humming to herself, Drozde went back up to inspect the nearby rooms, where Molebacher's patronage would require her to spend much of her time. In his absence, she risked a whipping for wandering about here without leave, but she was not unduly worried. All the sounds of activity were from the rooms above, and even if one of Strumpfel's men discovered her, she reckoned she could sweet-talk the old sergeant. Klaes was a trickier proposition, but although he was stiff and humourless, the lieutenant had a painstakingly scrupulous air about him: she doubted he would order a woman to be beaten.

The next-door scullery was open to the outside where a back door had fallen in. There were puddles on the floor and orange mould on the walls. Beyond it was a large cupboard that had served as a game-hanging room; Drozde shut the door hastily, wincing at the smell. The rooms to the other side were more promising: a smaller kitchen with a bread oven, and a furniture store containing benches, more tables and a high-backed wooden chair with arms. She looked around with satisfaction. These would be Molebacher's quarters: fair-sized, close to his domain and already furnished. The chair, with its generous seat, might have been made for him. And sharing his pallet in here would be more comfortable than lying on the stone floor of one of the kitchens—or in a tent, for that matter.

It was time to leave: she'd done all she could here for the time being. The passage outside seemed less forbidding now; perhaps her eyes had grown used to the darkness, but she found her way back without needing to feel the walls as she went. She paused as she reached the side corridor that had demanded her attention on the way in. It was silent now. Wasn't it? She listened and thought she caught an echo of that strange buzzing.

A ghost was like a fly in the room, Drozde told herself. You couldn't reason with it and you couldn't get rid of it. Best just to ignore it and hope it went away on its own. But on the other hand . . .

No, she decided. *If it's in the house, I'll run into it sooner or later. Might as well see what I'll be living with.*

This passage had a smoother floor and taller doors than the other. As she made her way down it she could still hear a faint trace of the disturbance from before, less a sound than a vibration in her head. It led her to a door about halfway down, rising sharply as she laid her hand on the handle.

The room inside seemed almost untouched by the decay of the rest of the house. It must once have been used for dancing: the floor was of closely laid wooden tiles, scuffed but undamaged, and in the middle of the far wall was a platform, its ornate and spindly railings still touched with gold, where musicians would have played. The silk tapestry wallpaper was discoloured and tattered now, and the marble fireplace choked with dust. It was empty, but something about the quality of the air suggested to Drozde that it had been full only moments before. The shadows at the edges of the room seemed to squirm in the dim light. She closed the door carefully and walked away. She did not run. She was not a child any more, to start at shadows. But she could feel her heart beating uncomfortably fast as she gained the entrance hall and slipped out through the half-open door.

The sky was darkening with the threat of rain, and she was alone outside the house. From within she heard heavy boots on the marble floor and the voice of Colonel August shouting orders. She hastily moved away from the doorway. The men must be hurrying to finish making camp now, with Tusimov overseeing them. She should really head over there: Alis and Libush would be wondering what had become of her.

The wind had picked up with the onset of evening. Drozde pulled her shawl more tightly around herself and ran across the courtyard, suddenly aware of how tired she was. As she plunged into the weeds and thorns of the grounds, she heard something approaching from the road beyond: a low rumble which resolved into men's voices, the clopping of hooves and the trundling of carts. The supply party had arrived.

3

Choosing his moment with care—the men of the detachment busy erecting their tents and pavilions, his wife no less engaged in the retrieval and sorting of her wardrobe—Colonel Jander August retired to a room with a serviceable table in it (it was a billiard table, but that didn't trouble him) and wrote an entry in his journal.

The hour was perfect. The windows, thrown open, let in the slanting light of late afternoon, and the fresh scent of earth awoken by the rain which had just started to fall outside. The autumn sun was not profligate, but it was no miser. He needed neither candle nor fire as he set out ink and pens and blotting sheet, found the page, chose and fitted a nib.

With a profound sense of peace and rightness, he dipped the pen and began. He had no illusions in this. He knew that he wrote for his own posterity only, not for the future generations of humankind. But his own posterity was not a small thing: Augusts not yet born would know him through these pages, and his thoughts would become their thoughts. It was dizzying. It was, in a complex and bounded way, immortality.

In the business of empire, he wrote:

As in many other businesses, great care must be given to borderlands. A border is where the logic and cohesion of your endeavour will be tested. It is where, if there are loose threads, the processes of unravelling and wearing into holes will be seen to begin. Rome was sound at the centre but rotten at the edges, and so Rome fell. If our empire unravels, it will unravel from the east.

I have been set at the head of a small detachment—two hundred regular infantry, together with a hundred artillerymen who bring ordnance of every size up to the very largest. No cavalry, alas, but that is because of the nature of our orders.

We are to fortify a section of the border and guard it with unceasing vigilance. Similar units are being stationed even now at intervals along this whole contested front of two hundred miles or more, in the first place to discourage the Prussian monarch from pressing his absurd claim to Silesia and in the second place, should he venture a foray across the Oder (or its tributary the Mala Panev, which marks the border where we are), to make him understand how costly any such adventure would be to him.

Is it an honour to be chosen for this assignment? No. It is not. My general does not think, and nor do I, and nor does any man of sense, that Prussia will presume. It would be as if a small, fierce dog should bite the tail of a lion. Of course, if circumstances changed and the lion was beset elsewhere by tigers or bears, then the dog might take his chances. But for the moment it is unlikely we will be too much troubled—and certainly not before the spring, for what fool would invade with all the worst of winter to come?

Still, I do not regard this posting as a waste of our time. Far from it. Given my remarks above on the subject of borders, you will easily understand that I interpret my role here more broadly than my official letters of commission would suggest.

If the centre is to hold, the extremities must be reinforced with pillars of stone and columns of men. While the Prussian hangs back and waits his moment, we must shore up the house

of Habsburg, the seat of our archduchess, with stout timbers.
And any timbers that are rotten we must cast into the fire.

The colonel sat back and read over what he had written. It started well, but this last section would not do at all. He had talked of pillars of stone in one sentence, but in the very next he had switched from stone to wood. And rotten timber wouldn't burn well: if it were rotten on account of damp it would spit and sputter and resist the fire.

With the edge of his penknife, using the cover of another book as a rule, he carefully excised the page and began again. To be forgotten and ignored by those who came after him seemed to him a terrible thing, but to be remembered as an imbecile would be worse still.

4

Afternoon gave way to evening.

Once more within the walls of Pokoj, Drozde sat on the table, her tired feet dangling, and watched Sergeant Molebacher build his kitchen. As she'd expected, he'd been pleased by the facilities and by the storeroom which would be his new quarters. Whether he was glad to see her too, and had forgiven her for disappearing that morning, she could not tell. His face was impassive as always, his only greeting a nod and an order to follow him inside. Drozde had taken care to give him her sweetest smile before going to check on her trunk: to her enormous relief, it was still where she had placed it, squarely on the bed of the largest cart, wedged between sacks of grain and extra bedding. After that, her main concern had been to get the puppets safely out of the rain and into their new resting place, and she followed the quartermaster willingly, allowing him to make his own way to the kitchen. The orderlies lit the way for him with torches, and if there was any strange sound in the corridors, it was drowned out by their excited voices, loud with good cheer at the prospect of a cooked meal and a night indoors.

Drozde waited until Molebacher had set the men to work and departed for a closer inspection of the other rooms before vanishing downstairs with her trunk. Though she knew that it was of no interest to him, she was always careful to avoid drawing Molebacher's attention to where she kept her theatre. He had a prodigious memory, both for details and for grudges, and Drozde was never entirely certain which impressions would sink through his mind without a trace, and which resurfaced to be used to his advantage when time and opportunity served. So she erred on the side of caution, reasoning that it never hurt to think ahead. She was prepared to stay with Molebacher for a goodly while, but if she ever had cause to rethink that position, she wanted to leave him no opportunity to take hostages.

In the basement she allowed herself a few minutes to check on the puppets' condition. They had mostly survived the journey undamaged: there were some scuffs and cracked limbs, a little flaking of the paint, but nothing she couldn't fix. The only real casualty was a coquette, which had somehow been trapped beneath the theatre. Her nose was broken and two long, deep scratches scored her face. She must have become wedged against a loose nail, Drozde reasoned, though she could not see one, either on the bottom of the trunk or protruding from the wooden framework of the theatre. The scarred coquette was a real blow, but she would have time to repair her later, and she shouldn't stay down here any longer than she had to. Swallowing her dismay, she went upstairs to tend to her more troublesome charge.

Molebacher had his advantages. As a sergeant—and a quartermaster sergeant, at that—he had a higher status than her previous lover, a mere private named Janut Frisch. Combined with his physical size and strength, this made Molebacher far better able to protect her on the occasions when she was unable to make shift for herself. That he was unprepossessing didn't trouble Drozde overmuch. True, a big man working in a hot kitchen will tend to sweat a great deal, but Sergeant Molebacher was morbidly conscious of this fact and washed more often than most of the men Drozde had known. She approved of this. Rutting with a dirty man increased the risks both of disease and of pregnancy, since the atomies of nature would swarm on such a man, and nobody knew what they might quicken.

Underneath a blanket, Molebacher was no worse than any of

Drozde's previous companions, and better than some. He only occasionally forced the issue on nights when she was not inclined, and she was gradually training him out of this habit by lying like a plank whenever he tried it, which usually made him lose interest. Granted he was rough and had no interest in pleasing her, but these were failings so common as to be almost expected, and Drozde took them in her stride.

Private Frisch, by contrast, had been inclined to raise his hand to her, and had stuck fast to that religion through all her efforts to dissuade him. He beat her when he was in his cups, which was at least one night in two, and whenever he saw her talking to another man. When Drozde had raised the possibility of ending their relationship, he beat her again and assured her that she was his property until the day he died.

So Drozde had applied her best efforts to hasten that day, the weapon of her choice being a puppet show.

Frisch was a Pomeranian—the only one in the company, so far as Drozde knew. Bearing this in mind, she included in one of her Sunday night revues a comedic item about the propensity of Pomeranians to fuck livestock. Her marionette hero started with a goat, but being unable to satisfy the goat with his incredibly small manhood, he reduced his ambitions by gradual degrees until he finally found his soul-mate in an unfastidious mouse.

Most of her audience loved this conceit and cheered the puppet on lustily. Frisch, on the other hand, took exception both to the content and the presentation. He tore the blanket behind the toy theatre down to get at Drozde and commenced to beat her with the butt of his musket.

The rest of the audience wanted to see the end of the sketch, not to mention the still more obscene and scurrilous material with which Drozde usually concluded her performances. They hauled Frisch off her and gave him a drubbing from which he never fully recovered.

It wasn't intended to be so severe—each soldier landed no more than two or three kicks. But a man receiving the frustrated aggression of forty or fifty other men will not often come out of it intact. Frisch lost an eye and the use of his right arm, alongside a number of other injuries that were less easily classifiable. He was cashiered at the next town they came to and turned loose to fend for himself. He assumed that Drozde would come with him, and was astonished when she told him that she was staying with the company.

Frisch bellowed threats at her and called her whore. Drozde shrugged. She reminded him that she'd given him the choice of letting her go of her own free will. If they'd stayed together, there was no doubt in her mind that one night he would have gone too far and left her either dead or crippled. She gave him just so much mercy and consideration as he would have given her.

And she didn't rob him, though she could have done so very easily, of the seven silver *groschen* that were his severance pay. She only took one of Frisch's two tobacco pipes, made of white meerschaum turned rich orange from age and use, and a purse of Spanish tobacco, which she used to worm her way into Sergeant Molebacher's favours.

At the time she considered it the best bargain she'd ever made. She was puzzled, in fact, that a sweet billet like Molebacher had not been snatched up long before. The quartermaster's doxy got a free pass to the quartermaster's kitchen, after all. Bread and cheese and butter, eggs mashed with potatoes, beet soup, chicken and fried parsnips— and small beer, at the very least, with every meal. The food was good, and it was plentiful.

And Molebacher himself didn't seem so bad: in his good moods he could be convivial and open-handed, and even when angry was not one of those men who went from words to blows without marking the difference. Yet for all this, she had never seen him with another woman. It was said that Alis had dallied with him for a time, but that had been over a year before Drozde joined the company, and the other woman never spoke of it now. Drozde was aware of the rumours that circulated about the quartermaster's dark moods, but she had never given them much credence. Molebacher traded on his image as a fierce and irascible taskmaster, and being a performer herself, she knew the importance of maintaining a reputation.

It wasn't long, though, before she realised that the rumours were true, though not in the ways she had expected. Molebacher's viciousness manifested itself in small, stinging ways, more like the bites of flies than the heavy, inevitable impact of Frisch's fists. He had a sense, sure and unerring, for what would hurt her. Once he had tripped on his way into the kitchen and Drozde had laughed at him. That evening he made a double portion of stew and ate it all himself, slowly, while she watched.

Though far less dangerous, these little cruelties exhausted and frustrated her more than the beatings had ever done. At least she had known where she was with Frisch: she had known when he was in a rage, when to hide from him, when a few well-placed words would be enough to soothe him. More importantly, she had known how to escape him when she needed to. Molebacher was an altogether more uncertain quantity, and his small acts of spite, arbitrary and unpredictable, weighed on her in spite of herself.

Living with him wasn't easy. But still, Drozde felt, Molebacher's advantages outweighed his drawbacks, considerable though they were. Until that changed, she was content to stay with him. Being a realist, however, she knew well enough that the yea or nay was unlikely to lie with her. Charles of Austria was dead; his daughter Maria Theresa ruled now, and in spite of her father's best efforts during his life to cajole, bribe and browbeat the rest of Europe into allowing an archduchess to fill an archduke's place, there were murmurs from Prussia that such an arrangement defied both law and decency. Everyone said war was coming—if not with Prussia then with Naples or Turkey or Russia or even England (although the English seemed an unlikely enemy, unless they found some way to sail their ships over the Beskid mountains).

If war came, the company would move again, probably to fight on foreign soil. The wives would be sent home or to lodge at Oskander barracks outside Wroclaw. The camp followers could follow or not, as they saw fit, but armies on active manoeuvres moved quickly and moved far. If the women were separated from the company inside Prussia, they would have to sink or swim by themselves, unable even to speak without their burring Vilamovian or *Sudöster* German betraying their origins.

In those circumstances Drozde would probably detach herself from the army and go back to civilian life, with all that that implied. She certainly wouldn't miss Molebacher, though she would be sad to lose his kitchen. But she had never been sentimental in such matters: hold on to a man past his usefulness and you let yourself in for all sorts of inconveniences.

The quartermaster was fully occupied when she returned, so she sat on the table, keeping her feet out of the way as three of his orderlies—she didn't know where the other three were—cleaned the floors and surfaces of the enormous room. Under Molebacher's cold eye they swept, then scrubbed with stiff brushes, then rinsed with washcloths dipped in water to which lye had been added. Finally, they sluiced with pure water from the well outside. Drozde moved from one quarter of the room to another in order to stay out of their way as they worked. They stepped through the ragged ghost on the floor many times, without noticing. Sometimes their doing so coincided with its repeated gesture, so it looked as though it was flinching away from them. It was an unpleasant sight, and Drozde turned her eyes resolutely in another quarter.

Molebacher, with the complacency of ownership, ignored her, but one pair of eyes followed her wherever she went. They belonged to Private Fast, one of the orderlies. He was clearly smitten with her. His glances at Drozde were sidelong and flirtatious. He was a well-built lad, with pleasingly symmetrical features, and since Drozde would have been saddened to see that pretty, thoughtless face flattened against a wall, or against the sergeant's fist, she turned her back on the private and snubbed him utterly.

After the cleaning came the unpacking. The big tureens and bowls first, stacked up beside the fireplace on a monstrous frame like a gun limber that Molebacher had designed and built himself. Then the smaller cooking pans and baking racks, the pewter plates and tankards favoured by the officers and the wooden trenchers used by the enlisted men. No knives, apart from those used in preparing the food. If a man wanted to cut his meat and bread, he provided the knife himself. Most did.

The amorous Fast took care to set down most of the loads he carried very close to Drozde, and although she gazed resolutely in the opposite direction, she was certain he was still making eyes at her. It was annoying. The only way of avoiding this coming to a violent head would be to absent herself, and she still hadn't eaten.

Panniers of dried herbs were brought in too, in considerable numbers, for Molebacher was a great proponent of the French and Italian styles of cooking, which used flavoured sauces to hide the imperfections of other ingredients. The trend had reached Silesia some time ago but was still a rarity in military cuisine. Drozde liked it and encouraged Molebacher's wilder experiments.

She got to her feet at last and headed for the door. "Perhaps you'd like an escort for your lady, Sergeant," the incautious private offered, "to see her safe back to the tents."

Molebacher sighed. "You stupid little fucker," he said.

And to Drozde, "Bring me Gertrude."

Drozde was content to do so. If Molebacher had meant to chastise this stripling with actual violence, she doubted that he would have raised the issue now. The quartermaster had the bulk and solidity of a glacier, and his reactions could be similarly sluggish. People who didn't know him well often made the mistake of thinking him phlegmatic. In fact, he just put more thought into his score-settling than most men, and the longer the reckoning took in the coming, the worse it generally was. But Gertrude, a cleaver with a fourteen-inch blade, was for showing off, not for using. Drozde took it down from where it had just been hung, on a nail over the fireplace, and brought it to the sergeant like an offering, in both hands.

Molebacher took it from Drozde and stropped it, ostentatiously, on his forearm. Private Fast blanched a little. His two colleagues stepped hastily away from him, not wanting to be too close to the monstrous thing if it should be swung in anger.

"You see this?" Molebacher asked the young man.

"Yes," Fast offered in a slightly tremulous voice. His hands twitched. He was clearly wondering whether to draw his pocket knife, the only weapon he carried that would be remotely of use in this situation (his musket requiring a minimum of twenty seconds to load and fire).

"Her name's Gertrude. And she'd like a kiss."

A few seconds of silence followed as the implications of this sank in with all present.

"What?" the orderly asked.

"She wants you to kiss her. But she's not a whore. She's only just met you, and she wouldn't dream of letting you get your tongue on her sharp end. Just give her a little kiss on the flat, there. Like you kiss your mum."

Fast looked at Molebacher to see if he was joking. Molebacher clearly wasn't. And the other two orderlies were studiously looking elsewhere. There was nothing else for it. Knowing that this would be the talk of the camp before nightfall, he puckered up and did his duty. For the rest of this posting he'd be known as the man who kissed the sergeant's chopper.

"Now bugger off," Molebacher told him, giving Gertrude back to Drozde. She hung the cleaver back up on its nail. When she turned around, all three of the privates had vanished.

"Too many men in this camp who can't see past their own swollen balls," Molebacher muttered.

"Shall I cut you some bread and cheese?" Drozde asked him. He took the hint and handed her one of the sacks that he had brought in himself. It contained three small loaves, a roundel of goat's cheese and an earthenware tub of butter wrapped in muslin.

Filling her belly for the first time that day, Drozde considered her man with a more complacent eye. Still, there was something wrong with him this evening. She was getting better at reading his moods, and something in the set of his shoulders or the way that he ate—turned slightly away from her—warned her that all was not well. He was probably still angry with her for running off earlier that day. She sat and ate without speaking for a while, working out how best to proceed. If she confronted him directly he would only brush it off, and resent her still more for challenging him. If she did nothing, he would continue to brood until he eventually found some way to make her suffer down the line, long after she had forgotten that she'd ever offended him. No, the best response, she decided, was to try and placate him now, before he had too long to contemplate revenge.

"I should have stayed in the back with you," she sighed, laying her hand on his. He shrugged off her touch, but she affected not to notice. "Well, I was punished for my thoughtlessness. The cart jolted my trunk, and my best coquette was ruined."

Molebacher turned to face her now, his expression unreadable. "Leave your pretty things lying around and they will get broken, Drozde," he said with something of satisfaction in his voice.

Drozde couldn't decide if this meant that he was prepared to let things lie or not, but she did not raise the issue again, and they finished their meal in silence.

5

Lieutenant Klaes was a man of punctilious habits, and made no distinction between large and small commitments. The colonel had told him he was expected at the mayor's at seven of the clock, so at ten minutes before the hour he was trotting smartly towards Narutsin's main square.

He noticed as he rode that the suspicious glances and dark frowns which had greeted the detachment's arrival earlier that day were more pronounced now that he returned alone. Men scowled behind their hands as he passed, and any children who ran out to stare were quickly pulled back into doorways. Klaes realised that to these people, who probably had no more than one horse between them, his entrance must look like a deliberately ostentatious display of power, and he began to regret his decision to ride into the village.

The mayor's house was scarcely any bigger than Narutsin's other dwellings, although the walls were made of clay bricks clad with plaster rather than clapboards, and the shutters on the windows still had most of their paint. Someone had built a yard in front of the house, extending a little way out into the street and surrounded by a low drystone wall. There were gateposts, but no gates; in the absence of a stable, he tethered his horse to one of the posts, wishing the poor beast a quieter evening than he anticipated for himself. A dozen or so chickens scratched in the dirt, watched by a single beady-eyed rooster.

A slovenly and aged servant, without livery, answered to Klaes's knock and admitted him into the meister's presence, announcing him as "a soldier from them at the big house." Then he withdrew, without taking Klaes's greatcoat.

The situation was somewhat ridiculous from the first. The mayor was awaiting Klaes's arrival in an infinitesimal drawing room whose walls were a vile green decorated with flowers painted directly (and without skill) onto the plaster. With the mayor were his wife and son, and all three of them were dressed as if for church, coats included. They stood as Klaes entered, and though the officer gave a precisely executed bow, it was not mirrored by the mayor, who seemed to expect a handshake or shoulder-clasp of some kind instead. They manoeuvred around each other inconclusively. Then Klaes had to request to be presented to the lady.

"Oh, yes," the mayor said, making a show of slapping his own head with both hands. "My manners! Forgive me. This is my wife, Kethe. And Jakusch, my oldest son."

Klaes ignored the son as he paid proper compliment to the mother, taking her hand and bowing low. She curtsied reasonably well. Perhaps she had passed some of her youth in more civilised parts. To the son, he nodded perfunctorily. Then he addressed the meister again. "I am pleased to meet you all," he lied. "And I'd like to thank you for this kind invitation. It's good of you to open your doors to us so hospitably."

He put a subtle but definite stress on the "us," making the point that he was there not as a private citizen but as an officer and representative of Colonel August's detachment.

"The pleasure is all ours," Dame Weichorek assured him. Klaes almost asked her what pleasure she meant, since this enforced socialising was as far removed from pleasure as anything he could imagine. But he stopped himself in time. If a man set down among boors gave himself permission to be boorish, civilisation would not last long.

A serving girl entered the room just then. She was a mousy creature of perhaps twenty years, in a linen bodice and skirts the colour of a rain-washed potato sack. A woollen waistcoat, dyed blue, provided the only leavening of colour. All the same, in this unassuming peasant garb she was considerably better dressed than her mistress. At least she didn't look as though she was aping her betters.

While the maid hovered, waiting to catch her master's eye, Klaes took off his greatcoat and handed it to her. She seemed startled, but bobbed and retreated with the coat, returning a moment later without it. Out of the corner of his eye Klaes had seen her hastily toss it over the newel post at the bottom of the stairs. Presumably she had been coached but recently in how to receive formal company, and he'd thrown her off her stride.

"Shall I serve the brandy now, Meister Weichorek?" she asked.

"Thank you, Bosilka," the mayor said. "Please do." Brandy? Before the meal? And the lady of the house drinking with the gentlemen? Curious. But this wasn't Vienna. It wasn't even Wroclaw. Klaes was not so impolite as to let his surprise show in his face. He accepted a glass of brandy from the girl—she brought them in one at a time, so presumably the useful item known as a tray had somehow not won favour yet in these parts—and offered a toast to the archduchess.

It was dutifully echoed all round. Then the mayor downed his brandy in one gulp, as though it were schnapps.

When Klaes took a sip of the liquor himself, he received his first pleasant surprise of the evening (or perhaps his second, for the serving girl had a tolerably pretty face). It was not schnapps. It was a truly fine distillation, and burned on his palate with an agreeable heat.

They drank standing up because the lady had not taken her seat again and that meant that Klaes couldn't either. The mayor asked where the company had last served, and Klaes was able to phrase his answer—Beograd, which he called Belgrad after the manner of the French—without revealing that he had not even joined August's muster until eight months after the end of the Turkish debacle. That sat ill with him, still. He had been cooling his heels at Ledziny, waiting for his transfer from the engineer corps, while that crucial action played out a day's ride away.

They talked about the rout of the Turks and the glory of the late emperor, stretching the facts of that wretched campaign as far as could be done by men and women of Christian conscience. Then the topic somehow shifted to the impressive achievements of the

Weichoreks' many children (Ingela could ride a horse, though she was not yet seven, Huls knew all his catechism by the German rote, and so on) until the serving maid came in again to tell them that dinner was served, saving Klaes from incipient despair.

The dining room, at least, was of a reasonable size. After the cupboard they'd just left, it seemed cavernous. All the same, it was not quite big enough for the dining table, which abutted the far wall and so turned the room into a passageway with two elbows in it. They took their seats to either side of the great barricade, the meister and Klaes facing the wife and son. More brandy was served with the soup, and was a welcome distraction from it.

Above their heads while they ate, a wooden chandelier as big as a cartwheel creaked and shifted frequently. It was suspended, Klaes noticed, from a single rope of no great girth. As it moved, dust and occasional flakes of encrusted wax were dislodged from it. He was genuinely afraid that the wheel itself would at some point follow them down.

As yet Klaes had seen no sign of the suspicious behaviour that August had told him to watch for. But that came in due course, as soon as the conversation turned to the reason for the company's arrival. "Surely," the mayor said, "a commander such as yours, who gravelled Sultan Selim on his own ground, should not be spared from the front lines to come down to a quiet place like Narutsin."

"Well," Klaes replied, happy enough to lay down his spoon, "the front lines must change when the enemy changes, Meister Weichorek. The Turks have had a taste of Austrian mettle and they'll remember it. King Frederick is another matter."

The three faces presented to Klaes shared a single look of blank incomprehension.

"Frederick II," Klaes expanded. "The king of Prussia."

"The *duke* of Prussia," Dame Weichorek hazarded. Klaes laughed and nodded, thinking for a moment that this was a patriotic sideswipe at the house of Hohenzollern's outrageous ambitions. But then he saw that it wasn't. Astonishing as it seemed, these people had somehow failed to notice Prussia becoming a kingdom, even though this had happened practically outside their gates (outside their gateposts, rather, since gates were a commodity they seemed to lack).

"No, I mean the king," he said. "King Frederick. Your neighbour across the river, whose kingdom now consolidates western Prussia and Brandenburg, along with Cleves and the county of Mark. Doubtless the list runs even longer now, for the Hohenzollerns have the charming habit of snatching up any small fiefdom that's left unattended. And now he conspires against your archduchess."

Klaes paused to allow his hearers to voice their outrage at the presumption of the Prussian ruler, but the three faces remained serene and mildly questioning. "Frederick of Prussia has declared that he will not honour the Pragmatic Sanction," he said bluntly.

"Will not honour it?" the mayor echoed. "Really? That's troubling, to be sure." After which silence descended.

"You . . . do know what the Sanction is?" Klaes demanded. The mayor waved his hand in a circular motion. "Not in . . . all of its details and ramifications. The broad outline, yes."

"The broad . . . ?" Klaes's reserves of diplomacy suddenly petered out. "By God, sir, it forms the basis of your allegiance to your archduchess! Surely your priest, if nobody else, will have explained to you . . ." Klaes stumbled into silence. Of course, that was the nub of the matter. Maria Theresa's succession to the thrones of her father had a direct and critical bearing on who would become the next Holy Roman Emperor, and in Catholic Austria, where Klaes had been raised, the clergy had been preaching nothing but the Pragmatic Sanction throughout Charles's last sickness. But these Silesians belonged to the Protestant communion, like Klaes's own family. If they went to church at all (a doubtful enough proposition in a place of this stamp), they'd hear no sermons about the Sanction. Its importance to the Holy Roman Empire was a hundred leagues outside their experience and as far again outside their interests.

Klaes breathed hard. He was tempted, albeit briefly, to conclude that the mayor and his family, and by extension this whole benighted village, deserved the ignorance in which they wallowed, that in this instance sin and punishment came all wrapped together in one package. But he was a man who revered learning—more, if truth be told, than he loved either God or country. He could not allow himself, even for a moment, to be on ignorance's side.

He tried to explain.

"You surely know that the marriage between His Imperial and Royal Highness Emperor Charles, and Elizabeth of Brunswick, produced no sons. Under Salic law, a daughter cannot inherit the crown, so our late emperor issued an edict, the Pragmatic Sanction, which suspended the rules of succession and provided our beloved archduchess with a means of obtaining the throne.

"Charles VI devoted his last years to securing agreement to the terms of this edict. Why did you think he entered the Turkish campaign with Russia in the first place, if not to guarantee Russian support for his daughter's claim? The majority of the European powers signed it in the end, but since his death there are some who seem all too ready to break their word.

"This was two months ago," Klaes concluded, unable to hide his impatience. "In October. You didn't hear of this?"

"Obviously we heard of the emperor's death!" the mayor exclaimed. "God rest him. Eorlfrit Schander—he's the town clerk over in Stollenbet—read the funeral orations out to us in church, just as they were declaimed in Vienna, and only two weeks later. He rode to Wroclaw and back to collect the pamphlet, along with an urn containing some of the emperor's ashes, for which we paid by public subscription."

The emperor had been buried, not cremated, so heaven alone knew what was in the urn these yokels had bought. Ashes raked from a fire, no doubt. Klaes was trying to think of some tactful response when the serving girl, Bosilka, came in with the main course, a side of pork from which she carved at the table. It smelled good and proved to be excellent, with crisp crackling and very tender flesh. Bosilka leaned over Klaes to serve him potatoes, then again to serve him shallots and a third time to spoon gravy over his meat. He was conscious of her proximity, and very conscious of her scent, which was compounded both of strong cooking smells and of lily of the valley. She smelled like a banquet in a meadow. Tallow candles were in the mix too, however, and Klaes's imagination rebelled against the image of a meadow with a candelabrum in it.

"Frederick's father," he persisted, "then king of Prussia, signed the Sanction along with everyone else. Yet now the son, this new Frederick, claims that it's illegal, and that his father's pledge is annulled *de ipso facto*. He declares that Maria Theresa can stand as neither queen nor archduchess. He has encouraged France and Britain to forswear their own oaths and go to war to restore the true line of succession—which reveals his motives more clearly than anything."

"Why?" Bosilka asked.

Klaes was nonplussed. He turned his gaze on the serving girl, who blushed deeply. "What?" he demanded.

"I meant . . ." the girl faltered, "why does he want other kings to go to war too? Will that help him?"

Klaes glanced sidelong at his host. The spectacle of a servant venturing to speak while waiting at her master's table was somewhat astonishing, but it was for the master rather than the guest to take her to task. The burgomaster, however, seemed to be waiting for him to answer.

"Well . . . it provides a diversion," Klaes said. "If Her Highness's armies are engaged with a major power to the west, they'll have fewer resources to spare if there's a simultaneous incursion here in the east."

"Thank you," Bosilka said, curtsying to him. "I'm answered." She took up the bowl of potatoes hastily and retreated to the other side of the table, keeping her eyes lowered as she served Dame Weichorek and her son. Klaes could not forbear from staring at her, and she was clearly aware of his gaze. He was outfacing her, without meaning to. With a conscious effort, he looked away.

Bizarre beyond words, he thought. As though distinctions of social status and degree meant nothing here, and the limits of the empire were the limits of the civilised world. And yet the question the girl had asked had been a pertinent one, and she wasn't pretending, as the meister and his wife were, to be already fully conversant with matters that had only just been brought to their attention.

"So you think that there'll be war?" the son, Jakusch, asked now. "That Prussia and Austria will fight?"

Another pertinent question. "No, I think they won't," Klaes said, gratified to come at last to the crux of the matter. "Because France and England will ignore King Frederick's exhortations and stand firm to their oaths. They would be shamed to do anything else. And Prussia will not provoke us without that cover, because without that cover she would be crushed."

Klaes downed the last of his brandy, and waved the empty glass at the serving girl to get it filled. It took a moment or two to get her attention, but once he did she curtsied and left the room at a rapid trot.

"Nonetheless," Klaes said, turning a solemn frown on the mayor, "Her Highness is not complacent, nor is she unaware of what is at stake for the most vulnerable of her subjects. She has sent us here—and other units like us, up and down the frontier—precisely in order to ensure that Prussia makes no hasty move against Silesia. A show of strength, if you will. To remind King Frederick that the imperial lion has both teeth and a temper. You must see us as a ward, or a prophylactic. Our presence *precludes* war."

Which was exactly one half of the truth. The other half was that the archduchess knew very well how negotiable loyalties became at the borders of the empire. Austria adhered to the Catholic communion; both Prussia and Silesia were Protestant powers. A few soldiers on their doorsteps would remind these people who they belonged to, in case they should be misled by the accidents of geography or religious conscience. But it would do no good at all for Klaes to rehearse such matters unless his host raised them first.

Tactfully, he changed the subject. "Certainly none of us are complaining about our posting," he observed with false cheer.

"Pokoj," Dame Weichorek said, misunderstanding him. "Yes, it's a lovely house. Such a shame that it's fallen into neglect these past years. When I was a child, the family was constantly in residence. There were thirty servants then, all coming in either from our village or from Stollenbet. And it was all we could do to keep them supplied with meat. Do you remember, my love?"

She touched her husband on the arm, smiling. He grimaced slightly and looked away. As well he might, if Klaes had understood this exchange correctly.

"To keep them supplied?" he queried. "Why did this task fall to you, Dame Weichorek?"

The woman shrugged her shoulders. "Why, who else would it fall to? My Berthold was the butcher. The best in all these parts for pig and calf meat, and an expert slaughterer besides. He used to do the markets in Stollenbet and Grünberg, didn't you, my love? Until the old mayor died and we decided to go into politics."

The meister blushed deeply. Klaes almost laughed at his discomfiture. The great tree of his pretensions was planted in no more than an inch of earth. No wonder he let his servants talk back to him!

The girl, Bosilka, was at Klaes's elbow again, with a decanter. He nodded his thanks as she poured for him, wanting to show her that he was sorry he'd embarrassed her earlier.

"It's a shame," he said blandly. "Where is the family now?"

"Oh, in Pozdam," Dame Weichorek said, rolling her eyes. "This is their country seat, but Baron Oppenberg's wife—his second wife, I mean—is Posener born and bred, and can't live without her Polish friends and her Polish fashions and her Polish theatre. When Ilsa was alive, she loved Narutsin and wanted nothing better than to spend all her time here. But now . . ." She sighed mournfully. "I think it's more than ten years since they came back even for so much as a weekend in the hunting season."

It must be far longer than that, Klaes thought, judging by the decay and disorder at the house. "Well," he said, "the colonel and his wife will probably need another maid to shop and cook for them. And we've three married lieutenants, whose wives will quite likely take on help for their toilet now that we're in quarters for the winter. It's a good opportunity for . . ."

He faltered into silence. Bosilka's shoulders were heaving, and tears were running down her face. She'd moved on to refresh the mayor's glass but now stood frozen, the decanter at half-mast like the flags at Schönbrunn on the day when the public was finally admitted to the royal family's grief.

Damning us to that fucking woman, Klaes's father had cursed. And wept as Bosilka was weeping now.

"I'm sorry," Klaes said, speaking to the mayor though his words were meant for the girl. "If I've said anything to cause hurt or offence, it was unintended."

"It's nothing," Dame Weichorek said. "Silly girl. Go on, Bosilka. You're excused."

And the talk passed to generalities. From whence did Klaes's family hail, and how did he come to be a lieutenant in the army? Was August his first commander? Had he left a sweetheart at home?

And so on, and so forth.

Klaes answered as best he could, ate his pork and kept his counsel. Nothing that was said after that bore directly on the detachment's presence here or the Prussian threat. And yet was not that very reticence odd in itself? A village of less than three hundred souls that had suddenly had a troop of soldiers the same size or greater move in next door might be expected to be very exercised about any number of practical matters relating to their feeding and watering, their entertainment and their general impact upon the local economy. The mayor and his wife had asked about none of these things, even though the mayor's background in the dressing and vending of meat made it all but inevitable that mercantile considerations had come to his mind.

It was curious. Perhaps, as Colonel August seemed to think, it was suspicious.

And then, there was the girl. As he rode the three miles back to Pokoj, Klaes reviewed that portion of the conversation repeatedly in his mind, but was wholly unable to identify the word or phrase that had distressed Bosilka enough to make her cry. Something about the house, certainly. Perhaps the thought of having to serve there, with the soldiers quartered so close by. But she already had a position, and it was evident that the Weichoreks valued her. She was in no danger of having to sue to Colonel August for employment.

It seemed there *was* some secret here. Klaes was inclined, however, to believe that the secret related in some way to Bosilka herself. And if that were so, then its substance, if it were ever brought to light, would no doubt turn out to belong to the realm of confidences, promises, fancies and fallacies that made up young girls' lives until they married.

He would say as much to the colonel, and advise him to take the matter no further. He wanted no more suppers with the Weichoreks.

6

Drozde lay on Molebacher's pallet and stared into the dark. She couldn't sleep, even though the bedding was softer than she'd lain on for months. She was still alone. After feeding August and the other officers, Molebacher had decided it was too late to make a general issue to the men, even though that was the tradition on the first night in a new billet, and had fobbed them off with travel rations of black bread and weeks-old sausage. But he had softened the blow by sending the orderlies out with three casks of the good beer. And naturally he then joined them to help drink it.

The rain had set in heavily shortly after dark, and no one was in any hurry to return to their tents. They had commandeered one of the largest rooms towards the front of the house, with a solid floor and no obvious leaks, and dragged in benches for the sergeants; the rest of the men sat on the floor. Drozde could hear voices and laughter from there now, even a snatch of song. She was a little surprised at Molebacher: after the long march, the colonel might give the men some latitude, but they'd do well not to rely on it. The quartermaster was usually careful to keep on the right side of the officers. As if he had plucked the thought from her head, she heard Molebacher's sharp voice, and the noise subsided.

It must have been near midnight when a general commotion in the corridors told her the enlisted men had been dispatched back to the camp. When the last of them had gone, she heard low voices in the passage outside her room, punctuated by Sergeant Strumpfel's hoarse cough, and then the sound of another cask being trundled from the racks. Molebacher could don the persona of the convivial quarter-master like a second skin when it suited him, and whether disposed to carry on drinking for pleasure or indulging the other sergeants for reasons of his own, Drozde guessed that she wouldn't see him again till morning. Relieved, she rolled over and closed her eyes.

She was woken by a pressure on the bedclothes at her side. She opened her eyes quickly and pulled herself up: Molebacher would expect her to be waiting for him after so many days apart, and when he was drunk was not a good time to thwart him. But it wasn't Molebacher sitting on the bed. It was one of the ghosts.

She must have imagined the pressure. But this ghost was so distinct, so vividly present, it was easy to imagine that she had substance. Drozde had never seen a ghost of such solidity. She was young, maybe nine or ten years old by the look of her, and outlandishly dressed, as so many ghosts were. In fact the colours of her jacket and stockings—clashing pinks and reds—were so bright they hurt the eyes. Drozde wondered how she was seeing them when the room was so dark. But most astonishing was the child's face. She was looking at Drozde with clear recognition—and with such unaffected joy that for an instant it caught at Drozde's heart. She could make nothing of it. She stared at the little girl dumbly.

The child seemed to be waiting for her to speak. After a moment's silence she laughed, as if they were playing a game, and laid her small hand over Drozde's own. The slight warmth of it hit Drozde like a thunderbolt.

"Hello, Drozde!" the little girl said. "What shall we do now?"

7

Drozde was no stranger to ghosts. She'd lived with them since before she was even old enough to know what they were. Once she did, it was far too late for her to fear them. She associated them with many things, some of them melancholy and some merely curious, but none terrible. And they caused no confusion, because for the most part they were easy to tell from the living. They were paler, the colours of their bodies and their garments washed out to a near-uniform grey. In fact, so many of the details that would have identified them as human were missing, and so seldom did they move or speak, that it was easier for the young Drozde to see them as features of the landscape—outcrops of mist or cloud in the same way that mountains displayed outcrops of rock or bushes in summer outcrops of leaves and branches.

When they did speak, the sounds most often failed to come together into words. Or else they did, but the words made no sense or merely repeated themselves. In the kitchen of her parents' house in Trej there had been a ghost that looked something like a woman. It was silent mostly, but two or three times in a month would say in a low voice, "Let it sit by the door a while, it won't harm." The words were always accompanied by the same gesture, a hoisting of the shoulders and a ducking of the head as though she was trying to hide her face. But she had no face to hide, only a stipple of near-translucent grey, like the film of ice on a water barrel on a winter morning.

Once, when she had maybe ten years on her back, Drozde had made the mistake of asking her parents about the dead who stood or sat with them wherever they went. She was even reckless enough to speculate on their possible identities. Since they rarely strayed far from a single spot, perhaps they were the ghosts of people who'd died in those self-same places and now were doomed to spend eternity there, like markers for their own graves.

Her father had beaten her for being fanciful, and her mother all over again for her lack of respect for the dead. The dead looked on, never asking for respect or acknowledging it. Drozde learned her lesson, and though it was probably not the one her parents wanted to impart, it was nonetheless of great value. She learned to keep her own counsel.

Since then she had had many lovers and more than a few friends, but she had never indicated to any of them that her sight went beyond theirs. Perhaps it didn't. For all she knew, there might be many like her. It might even be the rule, rather than the exception, to see dead and living alike. It didn't matter. She had taken the habit of silence, and it agreed with her. She needed no reassurance that her situation was common. She suspected that everyone's experience, in the end, was unique. That each lived alone in the world of their own flesh, their own thoughts, looking out from time to time through their eyes but never stepping across the threshold.

But this strange dead child *did* frighten her. She was anomalous in too many ways. Her expression was lively, her voice vivid and inflected. The colours of her clothes were brighter than Drozde had seen on most living people, not at all like the bleached uniformity of the dead. And she had used Drozde's name, although Drozde was certain they'd never met before.

The first question that came to her lips was both banal and unanswerable. "Who are you?" There was no point in expecting a ghost to answer that. *Who were you?* would be more to the point, and even then most could not say—could not turn air into sound, memories into words, the past into the now. They were trapped in their death like flies in spilled beer.

She tried again. "How do you know me?"

The girl laughed delightedly, as though Drozde was playing a clever trick on her. Placing her hands over her eyes, she first covered them and then exposed them again—the game which all mothers play with their children before the children can even talk, usually accompanied by the cry: *Peepo!*

"I'm serious," Drozde said sternly. "How do you know me?"

"You're my friend," the girl said. Her joyous enthusiasm waned just a little, a note of doubt creeping into her voice as she added, "You're my Drozde."

"I'm my own Drozde, not yours. Where have we met before?"

The girl looked around her, very expressively, and pointed. "Here."

"I've never been here before," Drozde said. "You're mistaking me for someone else."

The girl smiled a tentative smile. "I don't think I'd ever mistake you for anyone else," she said. "If I heard your voice from the bottom of a well in a deep, dark wood in the middle of a storm, I'd know it was you because I love you so much. And you love me too, best of anybody. Better than Anton, even. You know you do."

"Who is Anton?"

The girl looked long and hard at Drozde.

"Oh," she said at last, with a tinge of what sounded like hurt or bitterness. "All right. I'm not supposed to say that to you. I'm going to get into trouble now. But really, I don't know who it's meant to be a secret from, when nobody else can even see us!"

"No," Drozde agreed guardedly. "I don't know either." She had never met a mad ghost before, or thought it possible there could be one. She got up out of the bed, wrapping the blanket around her. The proximity of the dead girl was unnerving her, as was this impossible conversation. The ghosts she'd seen in the past had no use for words, but clearly the spirits of Pokoj were different.

"I think you should go now," she said. "It must be almost morning. Ghosts don't walk in the daylight."

The dead girl rolled her eyes. "Yes, we do," she said. "Don't be silly. We walk whenever we want to. It's just that people can't always see us in daylight. And you said daylight might be bad for us because the light wears us thin like old sheets. But then you said no, it was only that we're like whispers in a room and the sun is like a big shouty voice that drowns us out. But it doesn't stop us being there; it only stops other people seeing us and us seeing each other. It doesn't hurt or anything."

She smiled brightly, as if she was a little pleased with herself to have delivered this long speech so faultlessly. Drozde felt cold stone against her shoulders and buttocks. She'd drawn away from the child without realising it, until she was backed against the wall of the small room.

"Anyway," the girl said into the strained silence, "it's not going to be morning for ages yet. Can we go for a walk?"

"A walk?" Drozde echoed.

"Yes. It will be nice. We can watch Amelie come." Drozde hesitated. The house seemed very forbidding in the dark, and the chill air on her skin did nothing to make the prospect of a midnight stroll more inviting. But there was a perversity in her nature that made her advance towards what frightened her, and there was no denying that this precocious child with her senseless assertions frightened her badly. She felt there was something here that she needed to understand, and she wouldn't achieve that understanding by hiding from it.

So she rose and dressed—which just meant slipping her smock and shirt back on and lacing up her boots. She hadn't taken off her stockings or her shift. "Show me, then," she said, and the girl clapped her hands in delight. She led the way, her movements as natural as those of a living girl. Most ghosts drifted like flotsam, but this one moved purposefully and her feet seemed to touch the flagstoned floor at each step rather than stepping through it or hovering above it.

The candles had all guttered in the kitchen, but the fire had been built up well and was still filling the room with a faint red glow. Molebacher and some of the other sergeants had drawn chairs up to the fire and drunk until they passed out. Drozde could see their outlines against the firelight and hear the rumble of their snores as she threaded her way through the room, still following the dead girl and avoiding by unexamined instinct the other ghost she'd seen earlier on the kitchen floor.

Once they left the kitchen behind them the great house was almost entirely silent. The officers and their wives were meant to be sleeping here, Drozde knew, but she saw no sign of them. It would be difficult for her if she did, for if one of them heard her and awoke then she could make no ready explanation for her presence.

She had the moonlight as a lantern, there being no curtains on any of the high windows. And the little girl was her guide, showing her stairways and passages that took her deeper into the house, away from encounters and explanations. This aroused mixed emotions in Drozde. She had no desire to be where the house's living occupants could see her. On the other hand, to trust herself to the dead ones seemed just then a questionable strategy. The girl was amiable enough, and certainly not threatening in the least. She had called Drozde by her given name, and asserted the warmest of feelings for her. But how could those feelings be genuine when the two of them had never met until this moment? In spite of herself, Drozde felt uneasy, and the feeling heightened when they reached a servants' staircase that was narrow and lightless, panelled in on both sides.

"I won't be able to see in there," she pointed out.

The little girl frowned. "I think there may be candles," she said. "There were candles once. There. In a big bucket." She pointed to the wall at the foot of the stairs. There was no bucket to be seen. "Well, take my hand," she suggested instead. "Just until we get to the top. There are windows in the gallery, so you'll be able to see up there."

"Take your hand?" Drozde repeated. "How is that going to work?"

"It's easy. We did this, remember? You taught me." The girl reached out, and the tips of her fingers brushed Drozde's bare forearm. There was a definite sensation, as of a faint breath very close against her skin.

Tentatively, she reached out, palm open. The girl put her small hand inside Drozde's, and Drozde closed her fingers slowly. It was like holding on to a sigh.

They went up the stairs in this manner. The ghost's touch was palpable, but not of very much use. Still, the direction was straight up. Drozde used her free hand to feel her way.

At the top of the stairs there was, as the girl had promised, a gallery or walk. There were windows all along one side looking down into a well of shadow that must be a courtyard, and on the other wall hung great numbers of paintings. They seemed all to be landscapes, or at least those that were touched by the moonlight were so. All were in much the same style, too, with hills and cypress trees and the occasional waterfall, as though someone had painted them all at once, with one brush and one pot, in the same way as you'd daub a wall with roughcast to keep out the damp.

The little girl clearly liked them, though, and walked down the gallery counting off each in turn. "Saw that one," she muttered, more to herself than to Drozde. "And that one. And that one. Not that one."

"Saw them?" Drozde enquired. "What do you mean?"

The girl turned to face her again, all seriousness. "In the collection. When I came here. I like to remember that time. Do you want to see Amelie? See her come, I mean? Tonight is when she comes."

"I think I'd like to know who you are."

"Yes." The girl nodded. "I know it's important to remember, Drozde. Every night and every day. And I do. Honestly. But can I not tell it tonight? I don't think it's my turn, and Arinak keeps count. You know she does. And so does Mr. Gelbfisc."

Every word this strange creature spoke seemed only to add to Drozde's feeling of disorientation. "I have no idea who those people are," she said, "or what it is you're talking about. Just tell me who you are. Where you come from. Did you live here in Pokoj before the family moved away?"

There was an awkward silence. The girl seemed as false-footed by these questions as Drozde was by her bizarre soliloquies. "Come and see Amelie," she said at last, stepping around the impasse.

She beckoned to Drozde and ran ahead down the length of the gallery. At its further end, under a shuttered window, there were several stacks of pictures and picture frames of various sizes, which had been leaned against the wall there at some time in the past and forgotten.

"There," the girl said, pointing down.

Drozde knelt and leaned in close to peer into the narrow recesses behind the frames. In one of them something moved. She started back in surprise, but a mewling cry from the interior darkness told her what it was that was in front of her. In the gloom she could barely see it at all. She undid the shutters on the window and threw them back, letting the moonlight in.

It was a full moon, huge and perfect. The little girl seemed pleased to see it. She looked from its face to Drozde's, smiling broadly as though the moon was a joke that they shared. She pantomimed reaching up and taking it down out of the sky, then tucking it into the pocket of her skirt. "You won't miss it," she said. "It was never yours in the first place."

Drozde was mystified all over again. "What?"

The girl raised her eyebrows and repeated the words, her face full of exhortation like a teacher asking a child to recite. When that didn't work, she coaxed: "What Mr. Stupendo said. When he did his trick."

Unable to sound the depths of this nonsense, Drozde decided that the simplest course was to ignore it. She squatted down to look at the cat, since that was what the girl had brought her here for.

The cat was not very much illuminated, her fur being jet black, but Drozde was able to see now how very big and round she was. Pregnant, clearly, and about to drop her litter. She hissed and gaped her mouth to show her sharp teeth, not at all appreciative of her audience.

"We should leave her to it," Drozde said.

"No, no." The girl wrung her hands. "Please. I love this part. You have to see."

Drozde sighed heavily. "It could be hours before she—" The cat shifted her weight and thrust one of her hind legs vertically up into the air, at the same time bending her head into her own crotch. Pale against her fur, a tiny half-liquid thing was trembling there, like a teardrop or a pearl. The cat miawled once, and the kitten was squeezed out onto the floor. Streamlined by the birth canal and the birth juices that drenched its fur, it was as blunt and smooth and shiny as the brass pendulum of a clock. The cat commenced to lick it into shape, even as a second head crowned between its legs.

One by one, five tiny shreds of life emerged and were delivered by their mother's tongue. As soon as they could move they sought her teats, some of them squeaking like bats, others intent and silent.

Then came the sixth. It moved once but afterwards fell still. The mother cat sniffed at it, nudged it with her nose and licked it tentatively. But when it did not respond, she turned to her living offspring.

"That's Amelie," the little girl said with proprietary pride. "She's mine."

"And what will you do with the kittens?" Drozde asked dryly. She didn't bother to point out that a ghost couldn't own anything.

The girl shook her head. "No. *That's* Amelie." She was pointing at the sixth kitten, which lay a few forlorn inches away from the meal its siblings were enjoying—the bounty that it would never taste.

"She's dead," Drozde pointed out.

"No, she's not. She's going to be, but she's not. This is when she was alive. Just watch."

The forlorn little object, which had seemed as lifeless as a nail or a splinter, stirred and shook and uttered a thin, all but inaudible wail. Its mother leaned over its five siblings, now all securely locked onto teats, to nuzzle it briefly with her nose. The kitten arced its little body into the movement, like a flower following the sun.

Drozde's skin prickled. The ghost girl's words still made little sense to her, but it was clear that she'd known the kitten would revive. Perhaps she had some additional sense, an instinctive feeling for the edges and corners where life and death butted up against each other.

"What's your name?" she asked the girl again.

"You call me Magda," she said, after a slight pause.

"Do I?"

"Yes. Because my name isn't a name where you come from."

"Well, it's been very nice to meet you, Magda, but I think I have to go and sleep now. It's late."

The girl looked startled, her arms half-rising in a gesture of dismay. "But the others . . ." she blurted.

"What?"

"They're waiting for you. They won't like to miss a night—especially not this night. You have to come, even if it's only for a little while! You have to come and talk to them!"

"Another time," Drozde said. "Not tonight." But the girl would not abandon her pleas, and in fact became more and more importunate, hanging at Drozde's shoulder as she descended the stairs.

"I have to sleep," Drozde repeated.

"But not until you've talked. Silence is what breaks us, you said. You don't want us to break, Drozde, you don't. And the other one went away so you could come, so it has to be you that listens tonight or nobody will and it won't count and everyone will just stand there and look at each other until—"

"Enough!" Drozde hissed. "Enough, Magda." Now that she was back on the ground floor again she was reluctant to raise her voice in case she woke Molebacher from his slumbers, but she had to stem this torrent. "Who went away? What are you talking about?"

"I'm not to tell."

"And why does it have to be me that listens? Listens to what?"

"The stories, of course. The tellings."

"It's too late for stories."

"No! It's too late for anything else!"

The ghost girl's face was so earnest, so full of anguish, that Drozde had no choice in the end but to relent. "All right," she said. "All right, I'll come. But this had better be something more important than a cat dropping her litter."

"It is," Magda promised, virtually bouncing up and down in the intensity of her eagerness. "It's very important. It's the most important thing ever!"

This time she took Drozde to the ballroom that she'd visited earlier in the day. Drozde wasn't keen to enter. She felt she knew, now, who the others were going to be.

But the same stubborn streak, the need to prove herself unshaken and unshakable that had led her to follow Magda in the first place, made her step forward now into the cold, echoing space.

"I'm here," she said.

The echoes answered her. But not only the echoes.

8

As though Drozde's words were a signal, the shapes coalesced from the darkness on all sides. They clustered around her, much more densely than any living crowd could because their immaterial nature allowed them to overlap and interpenetrate. They were not like the ghosts she'd known before. They were like Magda, entirely human in appearance and as animated in their manner as any living people Drozde had met. And like Magda, they called her name as they advanced, hailed her, wished her well.

She braced herself for their touch, but they did not touch her. They stopped a few feet away from her on all sides, respectful of her person, and smiled in welcome. It seemed that Pokoj had its own population, its own economy. It was a republic of the dead, and it was offering her citizenship. She wasn't minded to accept.

"Who are you?" she demanded. "And how do you know me?"

"We are as you see us," one dead man said. "Poor souls left shipwrecked here when the boats that were our bodies foundered. As to how we know you, that might be a question better left until later. The way we see these things . . . It's not easy to explain to those who haven't experienced it for themselves."

"I don't understand," Drozde said.

"No."

"I mean, I don't understand how it can be hard to explain. I don't know any of you, but you all seem to know who I am. So tell me where we met before. Or have you spied on me without letting me see you? Did you follow me here?"

She knew as she said it that it couldn't be true—that it was no explanation at all. She saw the ghosts as well as they saw her, so how could they have watched her without being noticed in their turn? And in any case a dead man didn't move about. He stayed where he'd died, as though his death was a stake driven into the ground and he a dog tied to the stake.

"We wouldn't watch you if you told us not to," a woman said, her downcast eyes full of reproach. Though she had already seen it in Magda, Drozde was amazed all over again at this—that the faces of the phantoms were clear enough to show expressions. Most ghosts looked like freshly painted portraits left out in the rain, the details running together into abstract splotches of colour.

"But you won't tell me the truth?" she demanded.

An unhappy murmur passed through the crowd.

"You," Drozde said to a handsome man of middle age with a forked beard. "Do you know me?"

"We are all friends here," the man said.

"Answer my question."

"Yes. I know you. Everyone here knows you, as everyone here knows everyone here."

She gave him a warning look. "Are you going to tell me that I'm your Drozde?"

"Lady, I would not presume to such intimacy."

"Good. Tell me this, then: who are you?"

This time the question got a very different answer—perhaps because this time Drozde addressed it to a single person. There was a quickening of excitement among the ghosts as a whole, while the one she was speaking to seemed to draw himself up a little higher and to come into an even clearer focus.

"You want to hear my story?" he asked, with more emphasis on the *my* than seemed to Drozde to be warranted.

She wanted no such thing, but she felt by this time that she was in a situation she didn't fully understand, and it troubled her. So, "Yes," she said. "Go on. Tell me your story."

The ghosts shifted and reformed, like the glass beads in a kaleidoscope. Abruptly, they were facing the bearded man and turned inward upon him.

"My name," the man said, "is Samuel Gelbfisc."

I was born a Jew, in the city of Koszalin in Poland, under Casimir Jagiellon but before the Nieszawa statutes (may the paper on which they were written run with boils like diseased flesh!) deprived me and the rest of my race of so many of our rights and freedoms. In that time it was still possible to be a Jew in Poland and to pursue a trade—as I did, working and learning under my father and then upon his death inheriting his thriving business as an apothecary.

I was born a Jew, I said, and in many respects I am a Jew still. Not in respect of religion, however. I renounced my faith when I was twenty years old. This was out of love for a woman, and I learned from that experience how little such loves really mean. Also, how inveterate is the hatred of some people for anything that is different from themselves. Her parents did not accept me as a putative son-in-law, for all that I had kissed the feet of Christ. They sent my Josie away to school in Tarnow, and when she returned she was betrothed to another.

Enough of that. I make no complaint, for I was too young then to understand what I desired and we were unlikely to have made each other happy. I found love enough later, with women and men alike, but never stayed long with any of them. That early disaster with Josie had made me mistrustful of human affections—at least, of their durability. I preferred a fire that burned very hot and died all the quicker for it.

It might be supposed that I had reverted by this time to the faith of my forebears. But it was not so. The God I believed in cared nothing for the vestments, the trappings of religious ritual. He was to be found as easily in the droning Latin of the Catholics as in the ecstatic swayings and intonings of the Chassidim. In fact, I found Him most often in solitary prayer, and went to church only because it was expected of me.

But church was, I must admit, a boon in business. I met many customers in chance conversations at the church gates, and was often recommended to others through acquaintances I'd made in the course of what was only nominally an act of worship. I wasn't alone in this. Jesus may have chased the moneylenders from the temple, but I guarantee you they crept back again as soon as His back was turned. That's the way of it, and always has been.

In 1492, just after John became king, I decided to go on a pilgrimage to see the scarred Madonna at Jasna Gora. Again, this wasn't primarily a matter of piety. It was a pleasance first, and after that a commercial speculation. The Nieszawa statutes were law by then, and it was harder now for a Jew to trade from fixed premises. As an apothecary I was able to adapt to this better than most, but by consequence I'd become an itinerant, seldom staying in one town or city for more than a few days at a time. A pilgrimage suited me nicely, allowing me to visit suppliers and former clients in many places across the country.

My fellow pilgrims presented a great diversity and variety, from the very amiable to the very aloof. I made no secret of my origins, since my name—which I had not changed—already marked me out as a Jew. To those who asked, I told my story. To those who stood by, purse-lipped and hard-eyed, I said nothing.

With one group in particular I became close friends. They were the Lauzens, a family of four from Kalushin. Alojzy Lauzen was a merchant, most of whose trade was in wines and spirits. He enjoyed life and liked those around him to enjoy it too. He had come on the pilgrimage for the sake of his wife, Etalia, who had been unable to conceive again after the difficult birth of their first child—Tomas, now twelve—which had lamed her. She thought that the icon of the scarred virgin, which was said to be particularly responsive to the injuries of women, might restore her and make her fertile again. The fourth member of the family, and the most recently acquired, was a cow, Erment. Her presence on the pilgrimage was explained by Tomas's weak constitution and a recommendation from a physician in Kalushin that he should drink a great deal of milk.

I liked Alojzy and Etalia very much, but I liked their son better than either. Tomas was a child of uncommon intellect and open, ingenuous spirit. This was his first experience of the world outside his hometown, and he was devouring it as a monkey eats fresh fruit. To see a humpbacked bridge with Tomas, or a campanile, or even a haywain, was to see it for the first time. He took such pleasure in the unfamiliar, he made the banal lading of the world into gaieties and festivals.

It goes without saying that Tomas was fascinated by the apothecary's art. He was fascinated by everything! When I began to explain to him how I worked, mixing minute amounts of potent pharmaca with exquisite care, he besieged me with a thousand questions. From where did I source my potions and powders? How did I know what concentrations to use, and which simples had which effects? Since the relative volumes were so crucial, what about the metal of the vessels I employed, or the mortars and spoons I ground and stirred with?

I answered all these questions as well as I could, and also showed him how certain rudimentary tinctures could be brewed. Under my instruction he made a simple from andrographis, poplar and bee balm, which he mixed into the milk of the cow, Erment, and served to his mother to ease the pain in her hip. It gave her a great deal of relief, and the boy no less pride.

Our southern progress was leisurely, to say the least, and my friendship with Tomas grew each day. I demonstrated for him a great many minor mysteries of the art—such as are not profound but produce a great spectacle when they're performed. I showed him the fire that continues to burn when submerged, the kettle that pours potions of different colours on command, the sea-stone that flows like water and yet becomes still and solid at a touch. These things are really no more than the tricks of mountebanks, but their explanation touches on deeper truths, and Tomas would not rest, after seeing each such marvel, until he had learned all the whys and wherefores of it.

I have said we made a slow and casual progress. I should say, besides, that we broke our journey each night in conditions of relative comfort. Only seldom—two or three times, perhaps—did we sleep by the road, at risk from footpads and at the mercy of foul weather. More usually our guides contrived to stop in the evenings at a post inn or hostelry, or if none was close enough they would beg lodging at a monastery or abbey, pleading the pious purpose for which we travelled.

And so we came here to Pokoj, not by design but by chance. It was an abbey then; we passed it on our way to the village of Narutsin, where we intended to seek a place to stay. It had rained heavily for some days before, and as sometimes happened the rain had made the Mala Panev break her banks at Ortzud. The spate cut us off from Narutsin, and although it might have been shallow enough to ford, we didn't want to take the hazard. We turned back to the abbey, which lay just half an hour behind us, and asked for shelter there.

The monks of Pokoj were Benedictines, and they gave us courteous but cautious welcome. The lay brothers would see to our needs, of course, but the abbot himself, one Father Ignacio, came into the refectory to greet us. We were introduced to him one by one, and when he came to me and heard my name, his nose wrinkled as though at the smell of a fart.

"A Jew?"

"Yes," I said. "But converted, Father, to faith in the Messiah."

"You can't change a Jew," Father Ignacio said, his face still twisted into a caricature of disgust like a carved gargoyle. "If you could, Christ would have made his ministry to them."

Historians know, of course, that this is exactly what Christ did. It was only after His death that Paul took His teachings out to the Gentiles. But I did not say this. I only smiled and reminded the father abbot that Jesus had counselled the forgiveness of our enemies.

"It's not *my* forgiveness you stand in need of," Father Ignacio growled. And having thus identified himself as my enemy, he walked on down the line to speak with the other pilgrims. He did not stay with us for the meal, but only said once again that we were welcome to such hospitality as his house could offer. He looked at me as he said this, as if he would dearly have liked to make an exception, and then he retired. I hoped that this would be the last I saw of him, but alas something happened that night that brought us into disastrous contact with each other.

The boy, Tomas, fell sick. He retired early, complaining of a malaise. Something he had eaten, he said, must have taxed his stomach. I was the last—apart from his mother and his father—to say goodnight to him. Afterwards, before I retired myself, I gave Etalia a digestive powder, which I told her to give to her son if the gripes worsened.

The next morning Tomas was not at breakfast. I asked Meister Lauzen how the boy had passed the night, but he shook his head and turned away without a word. Grief and fear sat heavy on his brow. Tomas had not slept well, Etalia told me. The pains in the boy's stomach had persisted—if anything, they'd worsened. She'd mixed my powder in a little milk and given it to him shortly after the abbey bells rang for lauds. It had not seemed to help. This morning Tomas had barely stirred. He seemed sunk in a terrible lethargy from which he woke only to moan and whimper and then fall back at once into fitful slumber.

I asked if I might be permitted to examine him. "Certainly," Etalia said. "We would be grateful, Meister Gelbfisc." She led the way to the room that had been assigned to them, close by the calefactory. I knew the acuteness of the boy's affliction as soon as I entered the room, first by the sharp smell of his sweat and his vomitus and then by his pale, sweating face.

I knelt beside his bed and put a hand on his throat. Etalia yelped in alarm—the gesture is a strange one, and easy to misinterpret. I explained to her that I was feeling the movement of his humours, whose vigour is a broad indicator of health or sickness. And I reassured her that the passage of vital spirits through the canals of the boy's chest and gorge seemed promisingly rapid and forceful.

I might have suggested a phlebotomy, but forbore to do so. I had read widely among classical sources, if not deeply, and was aware of how contentious bloodletting had been to the ancients. Only in our own day had it become unquestioned orthodoxy.

Instead, I examined the vomitus more closely. I found black threads there, in among the remains of food and the boy's natural effluvia. Melancholia must be the natural diagnosis, and yet that tended to progress over a period of weeks or months. The violence, the sudden onset of the boy's symptoms suggested some other, more proximate cause for his current crisis. I asked Etalia what Tomas had eaten the night before, and she gave me a most exact account. Only what everyone around the table had eaten, she said. The bread and the smoked *oscypek* cheese and a small bowl of barley groats. And what had he drunk? Only water. Not even the small beer that was on the table, though Alojzy had offered him some.

At this point we were interrupted by the arrival of two of the lay brothers. They entered in haste, and told us that the abbot required our presence in the great hall. He had heard of Tomas's affliction and wished to speak with us about it.

It was apparent from the first that Father Ignacio had an agenda, and that it concerned me. He asked the Lauzens how much contact I had had with Tomas both on the road and then once we had arrived within the abbey itself. He took particular interest in the digestive powder I had given to Frau Lauzen to administer to Tomas, and raised his eyebrows when he heard that I was the last to say goodnight to him.

In short, as you've probably guessed, he accused me of poisoning the child. When I asked him why he thought I would do such a thing, he answered that I was a Jew. A Jew would commit any vileness against Christian folk for no other reason than innate wickedness and perversity.

I appealed to fact and to reason—two crutches that would not carry me. I reminded the father abbot that I had renounced my religion. And I pointed out that Tomas had begun to show the symptoms of his illness before I gave the nostrum to his mother. Before I said goodnight to him, for that matter.

"But you sat opposite the boy at table," the abbot responded, glaring down on me from the eminence of a joint stool set on a wooden dais. It was a pathetic throne indeed, and I almost laughed at his pretension, but the threat to my person was far from amusing. Father Ignacio had already sent word to the local landowner, Count Kurnatowski, requesting that one of the count's reeves come to Pokoj to sit on the matter. At such a hearing the abbot's word would carry a great deal of weight, and mine none at all. And against the reeve's arrival, he ordered me confined to one of the monks' cells with the door barred from the outside.

Here at least I was able to assert myself against his authority, by reminding him that it had limits. He was a functionary of the church, not of the state, and though his influence was vast his temporal power was circumscribed. If I had sworn myself to the order, he would have power over my body and my soul. I had not, and he did not. I refused to surrender myself into the brothers' hands, and being mostly aged men of a peaceful and meditative bent, they did not press the point.

Yet I was conscious as I walked from the hall of my fellow pilgrims' eyes upon me. There was a muttering where I passed, and some two or three spat upon the ground as men do when a hearse goes by to make Death look the other way. Even the Lauzens wouldn't meet my gaze, and when I tried to speak to them they turned away.

I have said that I had little time for the doctrines of the church, or indeed any religion. Common sense prevented me from seeing the hand of God in a world so disordered and arbitrary as the one I saw around me every day. That same common sense told me now that there was no good way for this to end. Even if Tomas rallied and made a full recovery, the wheels of church and state had been set in motion. They were unlikely to stop until they'd run their course.

I had been thinking about the boy's sickness, coming so soon after our arrival at the abbey. Its abrupt onset suggested food poisoning, but he had eaten nothing at table that had not also been eaten by others. Unless—which was always a possibility—his mother had lied to me.

I made a circuit of the abbey grounds. They were not extensive, and I had a clear sense by then of what it was I was looking for. In a secluded corner, close to the stable yard, there was a patch of weeds whose flowers grew in tight, white clusters like the explosion of sparks from damp wood when it finally catches fire. *Apocynum*. Dogbane. Dimly, I began to see a way of saving myself. Not with the innocence of the dove—though I was free from any taint of blame—but with the wisdom of the serpent.

I lingered in the stables a little while longer. Then I returned to the abbey and gave myself into the hands of the brothers, saying I was ready to be judged.

But they were not ready yet to judge me. For all that he hated me, Father Ignacio wished to adhere to the forms of law. He had me committed to a cell to await the reeve's arrival. The door did not lock, but two men guarded it constantly in case I should change my mind and attempt to leave.

Several hours after my incarceration I heard shouts and running footsteps, which persisted for some time. It seemed that a further outrage had been committed. Erment, the Lauzens' cow, had been slaughtered in her stall. The guards outside my door were questioned as to whether I had left at any point, but they were able to say that I had not. Possibly, they hazarded, I had killed the cow in the afternoon before I surrendered myself into captivity.

In the morning I was brought before the reeve, Meister Ruprecht Ganso. It was in the refectory, the largest room in the abbey. The space was needed in order to accommodate the audience, which consisted of most of the brothers and all of my fellow pilgrims. The tables had been removed, the benches set out in rows. Tomas was there, in the front row between his parents, wrapped in a frieze blanket. The stare he bestowed on me was full of fear and uncertainty.

The reeve set out the terms of the accusation. The Lauzens and others testified that I had sat close to the boy on the night when he fell ill, and had plentiful opportunities to add poison to his food. Etalia added that I had given her a powder (she said *sold*, not *given*, which perhaps hurt me most of all) and that she had stirred this simple into a glass of milk and given it to Tomas in the course of the night.

The reeve asked me whether I denied any of this. Not a word, I assured him.

"Then have you any evidence to offer in your own defence?" he demanded.

"None."

A babel of voices arose in the wake of this word, most of them demanding a judgment. The reeve raised his hand to stem the tumult, and I spoke again into the silence that followed.

"I ask for an ordeal."

"An ordeal?" The reeve was somewhat scandalised. "How will an ordeal serve when your guilt is already clear?"

"If I'm guilty, it will serve me not at all. It will merely remove all doubt."

"There is no doubt!" Father Ignacio proclaimed. But other voices called out for fire and water to be brought. Some of the pilgrims were on their feet now, shaking their fists and stamping their feet upon the floor. The reeve saw which way the wind was blowing and gave order for a fire to be lit and a cauldron set upon it.

This being the refectory, the order was swiftly obeyed. The fireplace, indeed, was already set for the evening and only needed the stroke of a tinderbox. An iron trivet was brought by one of the cook's boys, and then a cooking pot big enough to make pottage for a great multitude. As they set the trivet on the fire and the pot on the trivet, the audience moved the benches around to face this new spectacle.

Then this same serving boy filled the pot with water from the well in the abbey grounds. I stepped forward before I was even told to, and took my place before the fire. But before I put my hand into the water, I turned to look at the Lauzens. The parents, first. And then the boy.

"Tomas," I said. "Do you believe I tried to harm you?"

"It matters nothing what the boy believes," Father Ignacio cried, perhaps genuinely indignant or perhaps trying to drown out any answer.

Tomas Lauzen shook his head, his eyes on mine.

"Your faith will give me strength," I said. "And in the face of your innocence, all evil will find itself abashed."

I thrust my hand into the pot. My hand and half my forearm, for it was very deep.

"The water has not boiled yet!" Father Ignacio sneered, as though I was trying to cheat in some way.

"Then let us wait it out," I said.

A watched pot, they say, never boils—and surely no pot was ever as closely watched as this one. Yet it warmed quickly enough, and steam began to rise from it. I swirled the water around with my hand, as though I was stirring a bath, and let my gaze travel across the faces of my accusers. For by then, with one exception, there was nobody in the room who doubted my guilt.

They began to doubt, perhaps, as the steam started to rise from the water and my face remained calm.

When the water boiled, people gasped and cried out. But I kept my hand in the fire for a good while longer, not moving at all—except for my eyes, which now found the father abbot. He was staring at me in fear and consternation.

Finally, I withdrew my hand from the roiling water and displayed it to the crowd. It was whole and unburned. It was not even red from the heat.

"Am I innocent?" I asked.

"He needs to be fully immersed," Father Ignacio pro-tested. "Not just his hand, but his whole—"

"Whose court is this?" I bellowed over him. "My question was for Count Kurnatowski, represented here by his reeve, Meister Ganso."

Sensible of the abbot's slight, the reeve nodded. Sensible of the abbot's status, the reeve made answer to him, not to me. "You agreed to the rite of ordeal, Father Ignacio, and so you must abide by it. The Jew is found innocent, and these proceedings are concluded."

There was a great noise and perturbation in the hall, which rose to a crescendo and then subsided as I raised both hands—the wet and the dry—and shook my head. "It is not concluded," I called out. "Unless the count's law says it is enough to exonerate the innocent. What of the guilty?"

"What of them?" the reeve asked me testily.

"They must be found," I said, "and punished. Someone tried to poison Tomas. Whoever this was, they sat at table with him and broke bread with him. Someone in this room is—by will and intent—a murderer. God forbid we should rise before we find him."

Murmurs of assent came from the pilgrims, and even from some of the friars.

"I can't question everyone here," the reeve protested.

"No," I agreed. "But the fire can."

The reeve gasped. "You suggest . . . putting everyone to ordeal?"

I shook my head emphatically. "Not everyone. Only until one is found to be guilty."

The reeve and the father abbot looked at one another. It could easily be read in their faces that they felt they were losing control of these proceedings. "Masters," I said, "hear me out. These others"—I gestured to the pilgrims—"are little versed in matters of law and religion. They see a fire, and a seething cauldron, and they fear it. But you're different. You know that God finds out the truth and makes it manifest."

"Indeed he does," the father abbot agreed, nonetheless giving me a look forked with enmity.

"Then put your hand into the fire," I told him, "and show them the way."

The abbot was stupefied at this suggestion. "My innocence is not in question!" he yelped. "It does not need to be tested!"

"No?" I said. "What of your faith, Father Ignacio? Does that not need to be tested either? I would have said otherwise. If I, a Jew, didn't fear the flame, why should you?"

"I do not fear it!" the abbot roared.

I took a step back from the fire, and with outspread arms invited him to approach it. "Show us," I said.

I meant only to humble him, but I had reckoned without the stern and stony virtue of the man. Full of hate he might be, but he was full of belief too. He hated Jews for scriptural reasons he thought impeccable.

Ignacio rose, and stepped down from the dais.

He rolled up the sleeve of his gown with finicky care, staring the while into the steam that rose from the rolling water.

Having exposed his flesh, he stood where he was for a few moments in total stillness. Everyone in the room seemed seized with the same paralysis. Nobody even breathed.

Then Ignacio thrust his hand into the pot.

I watched the face rather than the hand. I know too well what boiling water does to flesh. I saw the shock on the father abbot's face—the realisation, blossoming in sudden agony, that his faith was not strong enough nor his innocence unblemished.

His shriek as he wrenched his hand back rose every echo of that ancient room in appalled protest. His sleeve, flopping down again, caught the rim of the cauldron and upended it, so that those nearest had to retreat hurriedly from the boiling water that slopped across the floor.

Two of the lay brothers led Ignacio—carried him, almost—away to his rooms. He was hugging his hand to his chest and his face was slack with shock. The reeve, almost as shaken, declared the proceedings at an end, but forbore to pronounce on the abbot's guilt or innocence. There are, of course, two different dispensations for Christians and for Jews—and for the church and the laity.

There's little else to tell. I parted company from the pilgrimage that day and took another path. I did not speak to the boy Tomas again or even see him, although he wrote to me some years later and we entered into a brief correspondence. His mother I did see, when I went to fetch my horse from the stables. She was washing with well water the pail in which she had formerly collected the milk of the cow, Erment, for her son's libations.

I gave her a nod, which she returned, and it seemed we would leave each other's lives with no more said than that. But as I led my horse out through the doors she called out to me, and I turned. "I'm sorry, Meister Gelbfisc, that I suspected you," she said, "and that I spoke out against you. It was wrong of me."

I shrugged. "It was your grief and concern for your son that spoke. You don't owe me any apology."

She wiped her eyes with a trembling hand. "I thought . . ." she said. "I didn't know what to think. Was it the abbot, then? Did he try to poison Tomas so as to have an accusation to throw against you?"

"Is that what people are saying?" I asked.

Her answer was only a look, but it was an eloquent look.

I might not have spoken even then. But there was such misery in her face. I could not leave her in a world like that when I possessed the truth that would free her from it. "There is your poisoner," I said. And I pointed to the patch of weeds beside the stable wall.

"I don't understand," Frau Lauzen said.

"That's dogbane, madam. It's a very potent pharmacon. The oil of dogbane twists the entrails and blinds the eyes. And it collects in the milk of those animals that feed on it, becoming even stronger through the titration of the animals' own guts. It would have killed Erment eventually—my slaughtering her was a mercy in more ways than one—but until it did, her milk was killing Tomas."

Frau Lauzen's face became a mummers' show in which many different emotions were successively portrayed. "Would have killed . . . ?" she echoed me. I made no further answer but left her to her musings.

"And that's the story?" Drozde demanded. "It seems unfinished." Gelbfisc held up a hand as if to entreat her patience.

It was seven years later that I received Tomas's letter. I had all but forgotten these events, or at least I did not think of them very often. Its arrival surprised me for many reasons, not least because it must have taken him some effort to find my address.

He told me in the letter that his father and mother were both thriving. His father, not so young as he was and failing in strength, had taken Tomas on as an apprentice, but it turned out Tomas had no head for trade. He had entered the church instead, and was prospering there as the priest of a small parish in the municipality of Reshen.

But science, and chiefly chimick, was his hobby. Was it not true, he asked me, that certain oils, themselves boiling at higher temperatures than water, might when combined with water produce an immiscible compound that boiled at a much lower temperature? He had heard that the oil of indigo, for example, had this property. And, this being the case, was it not also true that if a man secreted up his sleeve a cake of such oil, and thrust his arm into a cauldron, the water might reach a full boil without ever becoming hot enough to hurt him? But that afterwards, the oil being sublimed away, the water would reach its proper temperature and the natural order of things be restored?

I wrote back, briefly, to wish Meister Lauzen joy and good fortune in his chosen career. The church, I told him, needs prelates of open and enquiring mind, and I was sure he would do much good in his life and bring credit to his family.

Yes, I said, in answer to his query. Such tricks could be performed—not with indigo, which would make a difference of only a few degrees to the boiling point, but with other tinctures not dissimilar. But

I reminded him that God watches all, and will not permit base stratagems to prosper unless it be his will.

I added that I was only sorry for the cow, which was a dumb beast and guilty of nothing more than pursuing its natural appetites. Father Ignacio, being a man and therefore possessed of wit and conscience, deserved no such consideration.

A divine irony: I have told you how, during my stay in Pokoj, I outfaced the threat of death with nothing but brazen rhetoric and parlour tricks. Yet it was in this very same abbey that I met with death again, and this time in a form which I could not avoid. It was much later in my life, and I was passing through Narutsin, a common enough occurrence on my commercial journeys, when on the sudden I became grievously ill. There being no hospital nearby, the monks took me in for the second time, to tend to me in what (it soon became clear) was my final illness.

Ignacio had passed away long before; the father abbot presiding in Pokoj upon my arrival was none other than Tomas Lauzen, now risen in the church and much loved and respected. My second stay in the abbey was brief, and Tomas remained with me constantly, nursing me with simples and soothing balms just as I had once nursed him. He tried on several occasions during those last days to take my confession, uneasy at the thought that I might die with that old sin on my conscience, but I could not repent and therefore saw no point in confessing. Perhaps that is why I remained here after death—in this house that now stands where the abbey used to stand, instead of journeying on to God's house.

But God's house stands everywhere. Who knows?

There was a respectful silence after the ghost finished his story. His voice, which had been growing in animation throughout the telling, had swelled to fill the room and seemed to have woven his audience into a state of enchantment.

Then as the applause broke out—soundless, because the hands of ghosts can't disturb the air—he bowed deeply, pleased at the impression he'd made. Some of the dead now looked back over their shoulders at a gloomy shade who seemed somewhat less pleased. He was a tall, gaunt man in the robes of a monk.

"I don't think it was clever or honourable how you tricked me," this one muttered.

"I wouldn't have been able to trick you if God had taken your part," the Jew retorted.

The other man—presumably the father abbot of Gelbfisc's tale—seemed inclined to argue further, but the little girl stepped between them. "You know Drozde's rules," she said sternly.

"No arguments between us," the shade of an elderly woman took up. "No taking the teller to task for the facts of the tale. It's not in the facts we live, but in the memories."

"Like birds in the branches of a tree."

"That any loud noise might scatter us."

The words came from all quarters, like the words of a liturgy. The abbot subsided at once. Several other phantoms had come between the two men, giving warning looks to both, but they had turned from each other and retreated from the confrontation. And by ones and by groups the other members of the strange assembly faded back into the shadows in the corners of the room, until all were gone saving only Magda and Drozde herself.

"They get so carried away sometimes," the ghost girl said with childishly exaggerated annoyance.

She laughed, made a face at Drozde, and then began to dance. The twists and turns of the dance were bizarre and extreme, and ended with the girl dropping to the floor, one leg stretched out in front of her and the other behind. She arched her back to look at Drozde with her face upside down.

"You had to come," she said. "You had to let there be a telling. But I like it better when it's just the two of us."

Once again Drozde had no answer to this. It was late and she was tired, and none of the ghosts had come close to giving her the explanations which she sought. The unreality of the last few hours had left her feeling frayed and irritable.

"Good night, Magda," she said bluntly. "I'm going to bed."

The girl made a sour face. "Do you have to? All right, I know you do. But it's so nice to see you like this!"

"Like what?"

"You know. Like *this*." She swept her hand up and down, gesturing emphatically to the whole of Drozde, from her head to her boots. "This is a special time, and it's so short. Please come and talk to me again soon. Promise. Promise you will."

Drozde considered. She could avoid the ballroom entirely if she wanted to, but she was bound to run into Magda again, and she could already imagine the look of reproach and sadness on the girl's face if she simply ignored her. Besides, it wasn't as though she disliked the child. it was just that this whole situation was unfathomably strange.

"Soon," she said, keeping her face neutral.

The girl hugged her. Another first for Drozde, to be embraced by a spectre. The feeling was again like the passage of air across her body, but the girl smiled beatifically as she wrapped her arms around the woman's waist. "I love you," she murmured.

And was gone.

Klaes waited on Colonel August early the next
morning, although he knew the report which he had
to deliver would be found deeply unsatisfactory.
He held to the principle that the more unpleasant
a duty, the more important it was not to delay in
performing it, and accordingly he rapped on the
heavy wooden door of the colonel's quarters at 8
A.M. sharp.

His assiduity was to no end, however. A
messenger had arrived at first light from
Opole, where Henrik Dietmar, the fourth of the
lieutenants under August's command, had been
assembling the detachment's artillery. The big
guns, and the final detachment that would bring
the company to its full muster, were less than a
day behind him. The messenger, a self-important
artillery sergeant named Jursitizky, had much to
relate on the subject of the guns and their possible
deployment, and August remained closeted with
him for most of the morning, pausing only to send
out the adjutant with orders for Tusimov to set
up a second camping-ground to the north of the

house, and for Klaes to prepare another room upstairs for Dietmar and his new wife.

The wives, Klaes remembered. They would all be here now. He had been at the mayor's house when they arrived: the colonel's lady and those of two of the other lieutenants. Of all three now, of course. He sighed inwardly. He already had to suffer a certain amount of ribbing on account of his youth—and also, from Tusimov at least, because of his father's position as a small-town magistrate. The arrival of the wives would remind the other officers of another of their favourite reasons to mock him: the fact that he was the only one among them who was still single. And here he was, once again given the job of chamber-master for the married men.

Heading for the main staircase to try to find another dry bedroom upstairs, he ran into a couple of privates squabbling in the hallway: Standmeier, he thought, and Fast, two of the quartermaster's orderlies.

"We have to bring an extra donkey!" the older of the two was insisting. "He wants a hundred turnips and five sacks of oats. How else are we going to get that lot back here?"

"How are we going to control three of those brutes without help? Toltz can come with us—or Janek; he'd go if we asked him."

"You going to charm him like you did Molebacher's chopper? You're a whore, Fast."

"Fuck off, Standmeier!"

They stopped abruptly when they saw Klaes, and the older of the two saluted. The younger, slower off the mark, hung his head, red to the ears.

"Private Fast, keep your voice to civilised levels. This is not a fish market," Klaes said to him. "And you," he snapped at the other man, his tone considerably sharper. "I don't tolerate name-calling, nor baiting people for your own amusement. You've been given your orders: go and carry them out."

Klaes was pleased to see that Standmeier lost his swagger and even looked a little abashed. Both men saluted and marched smartly out of his sight. It was not really his place to reprimand them: they were not in his unit. But today of all days, exercising the authority of his rank went some way towards relieving Klaes's feelings. He watched Privates Fast and Standmeier retreating in the direction of the stables, still arguing. If they were hoping to buy that many turnips—that much of anything—in the town, he wished them luck. The current quartermaster was efficient, Klaes would grant him that, but even so the man would have his work cut out providing for all of them in a place like this. He fervently hoped they wouldn't be here long.

As he made his way somewhat cautiously upstairs (the treads were faced with marble, but he could feel the creaking of the wooden structure beneath) he heard women's voices: the ladies were still up there. Most of the enlisted men never got to see them at all, and Klaes himself was not usually required to mix with them much; still, the atmosphere of a posting was subtly different when they were present. It wasn't that they were demanding, exactly. Dame Osterhilis, the colonel's wife, was well accustomed to the privations of military life, and she kept the other two in line. But there was always a certain awkwardness when they were around. Klaes himself was never quite sure how to address the ladies. He often thought Dame Osterhilis and Tusimov's wife, Konstanze, looked down on him for some reason: his provincial accent, perhaps, or his Protestant origins.

It was Dame Margarethe who met him in the upstairs corridor: Lieutenant Pabst's wife, the youngest of the three, a thin, pale lady with freckles and a hesitant manner.

"Oh, Lieutenant," she cried as soon as she saw him. "There is a bird in Konstanze's room. We cannot get rid of it. Would you be so kind?"

It was a starling which must have got in through the roof somehow and was nesting above the beams. They had discovered it, apparently, when it flew into Dame Konstanze's coiffure. She sat on the bed, grimacing and patting at her high-piled hair while Klaes chased the bird around the room and Margarethe watched from the corner with little cries of warning and encouragement. By the time he had wrestled open a window and shooed the starling through it (he would have to send someone up to deal with the nest later), Konstanze was asking if he could find her a looking glass. Klaes began obligingly to search through the closets and chests in the empty rooms, whereupon Dame Osterhilis appeared with a request for more blankets. Klaes had considerable respect for the colonel's wife: he had never heard her complain in the face of discomfort or hunger, but she would not tolerate dirt. It appeared that some of the bedding she had been given had fungus growing on it.

Klaes took on this new duty with good grace. Bowing low, and with heartfelt apologies, he took the offending blankets and escaped downstairs with them, promising to return in due course with better ones. The kitchen was empty except for Private Hulyek, Molebacher's third orderly, who was sweeping the floor listlessly with a threadbare broom. The quartermaster had gone into the town to make some special purchases for the officers' supper, the man said. Klaes gave the dirty blankets to Hulyek and ordered him to fetch some clean ones from the officers' stores. Then he hurried back upstairs.

He'd have to make over his own bedroom for Dietmar and his wife, he decided, and find a different billet for himself further down the corridor. He swept the floor and brought in another pallet, involuntarily checking his movements whenever he heard any of the ladies' voices in the corridor outside. When he was finished he went back down for the clean blankets Hulyek had brought and was assailed by more female voices, chief among them the raucous laugh of the puppet girl, Drozde—there seemed no way of containing the woman! She was gossiping loudly with a group of camp followers, clustered around the well outside the kitchen. Klaes opened the door to issue a general reprimand, and recognised Dame Osterhilis's maid, Carla, among the noisy group. His appearance broke up the party at once: the maid started upon hearing her name called and ran to him, curtsying nervously, while the others scurried about their business.

"Take these to your mistress for me," Klaes told the girl, thrusting the blankets at her. He watched her go with the closest thing to satisfaction he had felt all day and, finally released, headed once again for the billiard room, which the colonel had designated as his headquarters.

Jursitizky was leaving as he arrived, and he and Klaes met in the doorway. Looking past him into the big square room beyond, Klaes saw that the billiard table was scattered with papers, gloves, cups, even a punch ladle, set out to show the positions of town and river, the most likely points of approach of the Prussian army and the possible placement of the guns.

"Let them come!" August said to Jursitizky's departing back, ushering Klaes in with an expansive gesture. "With a hundred pounds of cast iron at our backs, I don't give much for their chances."

The colonel seemed to be in a genial mood. He insisted on sitting the lieutenant down while he heard his report, and listened attentively, nodding when Klaes mentioned the burgomaster's near-total ignorance of national affairs as if this confirmed everything he had suspected. Klaes was as full and circumstantial as he could be. At the end of his recital the colonel looked at him with a raised eyebrow.

"A very clear summary of the conversation," he said. "And now?"

Klaes was confused. "Now, sir?"

"By your account, Lieutenant, there is more to discover. The maidservant burst into tears, you say, and was dismissed from the room. And the mayor didn't so much as ask how long we would be here, which is suspicious in itself. He used to be a butcher. He could have sought favour—and profit—by offering to provide us with meat. He could have tried to offload his neighbours' clapped-out oxen on us. He did neither. Depend on it, the man is keeping his head down."

"I cannot imagine that any of them have suspect intentions, sir," Klaes ventured. "Their very ignorance, surely—"

"—would not prevent them from trying to deceive us if they have something to hide," August interrupted him. "Go back to them, Klaes. I suggest you start with the girl; she seems the most likely to give something away. Sweet-talk her, man! Make love to her if you need to. She certainly won't be a virgin." His lips twitched. "And your sabre will need to lose its edge somewhere."

Hot-faced, Klaes gave a stiff nod and got to his feet. "I'll pursue the matter further, sir, as you instruct." He stalked out of the room, barely waiting to be dismissed. It was almost insubordination; he half-expected to be summoned back and rebuked. But it seemed nothing could dent August's good humour today. As he carefully closed the door behind him, he could have sworn he heard the colonel laugh.

Klaes was at least spared the need to go back into Narutsin immediately by the announcement only a few minutes later that the artillery party was approaching. The guns could be felt before they were seen or heard: the weight of the gun carriages and the drumming hooves of the horses pulling them made the ground shake.

Their arrival was far more momentous than yesterday's. August himself came out to see them: Lieutenant Dietmar galloping ahead, and in the lead cart, against all precedent, his young wife, cushioned and parasoled, attended by her maid and followed by a guard of ten men marching in step. Behind them came the guns. There were ten of the smaller cannons, six-pounders, and four impressive twelve-pounders, each with its own cart and an escort of a dozen men. And finally there was the monster, the thing that had caused the earth to shake.

"This is Mathilde," Sergeant Jursitizky said with pride as the outsize cart rumbled to a halt. It had taken six horses to pull it. "She's a twenty-four-pounder; you won't find a bigger."

It was more like a siege engine, Klaes thought. He couldn't imagine what use it would be here, out at the edge of the forest. But Dietmar wheeled his stallion and came up alongside the great cannon, patting its black iron barrel with affection. "She'll see us right," he said. And August, standing to attention as the guns were arrayed in front of him, nodded in heartfelt approval.

The great guns, it became immediately clear, required more attention than the ladies. Dietmar's new wife, Dame Feronika, was handed over to Klaes to be taken to her quarters while everyone else, Dietmar included, clustered around the cannons. The young lady chattered to Klaes all the way to the house, mostly about the hardships of the journey and her concern for a silk robe that she feared had been damaged in transit. She had a high giggle and suspiciously golden hair. Klaes found himself comparing her unfavourably with the maid at the Weichoreks', who at least had something rational to say, even if she spoke out of turn. But that thought, recalling his new instructions, plunged him into gloom. Luckily Dame Osterhilis appeared to take charge of the new wife, who fell silent at the sight of her—in awe, Klaes supposed. He wished he could inspire anything similar.

By the time he returned, the smaller guns had already been brought inside the house to a makeshift storeroom. The twelve-pounders were being housed in one of the stables, opposite the donkey stall, and Mathilde stood imposingly next door, a team of privates already hard at work building a shelter around her.

"What are we meant to do with a gun that size?" Klaes asked Lieutenant Pabst, who was supervising the building. He found Pabst a little more approachable than the other two; at least he didn't routinely twit Klaes with his lack of experience. But the lieutenant could not give him an answer.

"They do some damage, I can tell you that," he said. "I've seen twenty-four-pounders in action: a single ball from one of these could most likely level that old church in Narutsin."

"But as we're not planning to level it, what use is the cannon?" Klaes persisted.

The older man shrugged. "Who knows? Never question the commanding officer, lad."

Klaes received an answer of sorts at supper that night. The colonel had instructed Molebacher to cook a special meal for the officers and their wives, and Molebacher had excelled himself: fennel and mushroom soup, veal with cream sauce and chestnuts. Even the wine was good, although not remotely comparable in quality to the brandy he had been served at the burgomaster's house the previous day.

"So, Dietmar," Tusimov said over the veal. "What's the story with your new mistress?"

Dietmar, whose temper was uncertain at the best of times, turned scarlet. His wife went pale. Tusimov addressed her before Dietmar could speak.

"Don't fear, madam! It's just my rough tongue; the rapscallion loves you too well to stray! But for all that, he has another love. Big girl. Made of metal. Name of Mathilde?" He laughed uproariously, joined by Pabst and August. Dietmar seethed for a moment, then subsided and gave a reluctant chuckle. The ladies politely echoed him, Dame Feronika's giggle sounding somewhat forced. Klaes tried to look entertained.

"But in all seriousness," Tusimov said to Dietmar, still sounding anything but serious, "why such a great lady? What walls do we have here to blow down?"

If Klaes had asked such a question, there would have been laughter at his naivety. But Dietmar nodded, acknowledging the point.

"It's to show them we mean business," he said, and tapped the side of his nose as if to say there were deeper reasons he could not reveal.

August cut in impatiently. "Its purpose is to crush the enemy before they start," he said. "You were never in the Turkish campaign, Tusimov."

"Deployed too late," Tusimov said. Klaes thought he caught a note of satisfaction in the man's tone; the Turkish defeats were still recent enough to sting.

"It wasn't pretty," August said. "Pabst, you remember the attack at Grocka?"

"I'll never forget it!" Pabst assented.

Molebacher, coming in with a small apple cake and a jug of cream, deposited both on the table with an unnecessary clatter and said, "Grocka, sirs? That was a hellhole and no mistake!"

Usually such a brazen attempt at familiarity from a sergeant would be met with cold silence, if not an outright rebuke. But Molebacher too had served against the Turks. August turned towards him, his expression animated.

"Of course!" he said. "You were our quartermaster there too, Mole."

No one but August was permitted to call Molebacher that. If one of the lieutenants tried it, he would refuse to hear them. But now he nodded vigorously, drawing himself up a little straighter. "Not that there was much time for cooking, as I recall. I never saw such a shambles, if you'll excuse the freedom, sir."

"We lost at Grocka because we were not sufficiently prepared," August said flatly. "That won't happen this time."

August's face was full of fervour, and it was mirrored in the expressions of the other officers and Sergeant Molebacher.

"By God, we will!" cried Dietmar. "A toast, gentlemen! May the Prussians get here fast—so we can drive them away even faster!"

They all rose to acknowledge the toast. "Tails between their legs!" Molebacher shouted, and he poured himself a glass of the table wine and downed it in a single gulp. August clapped him on the back.

"Well spoken, Mole!" he cried.

Klaes could hear the drink in his commanding officer's voice, and he was a little taken aback by it. This sort of jingoistic rapture came over his fellow officers with moderate frequency, and it was a sentiment of which August heartily approved. But the colonel had a certain reserve which set him apart from those under his command, and he did not often join in with their brazen rhetoric.

The lieutenant shifted awkwardly in his seat. The atmosphere of celebration around the table did not sit well with him. It was all so thoughtless: the praising of big guns to high heaven, the talk of cold steel and hellfire. To men like Tusimov, Dietmar and August, it was what war meant. Klaes could not help but feel that there was more to it than that. But the whole table now was in a blaze of triumph, as if somewhere in the darkness outside the Prussians were already fleeing. Even the ladies were flushed and laughing, and the colonel was loudest of all. So Klaes raised his own glass, and joined in the cheering.

10

The following day, since the weather was still mild, Drozde decided to put up her theatre and give a performance.

She'd already been asked a dozen times or more when the next show would be. It was a reasonable question. The company had just moved house in the middle of October, when it would normally have expected to be settling into winter quarters, and there was every expectation of fighting in the spring. Add to that the arrival of Lieutenant Dietmar, bringing with him not just the cannons but his new wife, and there was almost too much material to deal with. If Drozde didn't perform all this, the news would grow stale, and her reputation for saying what was in everyone's minds would be tarnished. Reputation was crucial. Of all the stories she told, the most important was the story that her stories were indispensable. Without that, she was just a grown woman who'd never put away her dolls.

The site she chose was the ruins of the old abbey, which stood in the grounds in front of the house and slightly to one side of it, close to a pear orchard that was so overgrown that the weeds were as high as the trees. For the most part, the ruins were now little more than the outlines of the abbey's foundations. The nubs of stone that projected had been worn as smooth as glass. But one wall and part of another still stood, covered so thickly with ivy that they looked like some mad gardener had sculpted them out of the surrounding greenery. They made a natural windbreak, an effective backdrop and even a spotlight: through an arched window close to the ragged apex of the intact wall, pale sunlight spilled down onto the grass like the ghost of summer. That thought reminded Drozde of the other ghost, Gelbfisc, and the story he'd told her. This had been a place of power and influence once, only a few generations ago. Time buries everything, she thought, like an avalanche moving so slowly that you can't even see it.

She fetched her trunk from the storeroom below the kitchen, put it down on the grass in the shadow of the wall and began to unpack it. The theatre itself had suffered a little damage in transit, despite the trunk having been wedged in securely at the bottom of Molebacher's cart, so she addressed herself first of all to that—knocking in a few more nails to secure a loose board and re-attaching the curtain where it had come away from the iron hoops that held it. Then there were the damaged puppets to consider. Some of them would require no more than a new coat of paint, but for the others she would have to go into the village and see if there was a carpenter who could sell her some wood. Good solid beech, seasoned and cut into cylinders, would be ideal. Using green wood, which would warp as it dried, would only mean doing the same work twice.

For now Drozde set the three most damaged puppets aside. They were a soldier, a nobleman and the ruined coquette. She had plenty of soldiers to spare, and nobles didn't figure in her sketches very often. The coquette had been her best one, though, and she'd been intending to use her for the new Dame Dietmar. The blonde hair was a good match, and the face—rendered grotesque now by its long scars—was one of the finest she'd ever painted.

She made do, turning a little girl doll into a coquette by changing her clothes and repainting her eyes and lips. It's only what happens in real life, she reflected with a mixture of amusement and chagrin.

Private Taglitz wandered up while she was working. He stood over her for a while, watching in silence while Drozde pretended to be too absorbed in her preparations to notice him. "Will you need me?" he asked at last. She looked up, shielding her eyes from the sunlight shining over his shoulder.

"That depends," she said.

"On what?"

"On whether you plan to stay sober this time."

Taglitz squared his shoulders and thrust out his chin, aiming for a pugnacious look that his soft face couldn't carry. Drozde noticed that his paletot overcoat, which he wore open despite the cold, had soup stains on it. The uniform was usually a good indicator with Taglitz—it went before the rest of him did. "A man's got a right to a drink," he pointed out.

"Yes, Tag, he has. He has a right to two drinks, or ten, or fifty. So long as he has them when he's done with his work. If you can promise me you'll be able to find the stops, you can pipe for me. Otherwise, I'll get Drisch."

"And sing to *drums*?" Taglitz was scornful.

"Drums can beat out a rhythm. I'd rather have no tune than the wrong tune."

Taglitz seemed to have run out of arguments. He folded his arms across his gaunt chest, as though he meant to wait her out. Drozde turned back to the little girl puppet and resumed the task of primping her into a siren.

"All right," Tag said to her back. "I won't drink until after."

"Then you shall have a *grosch* for your pains," Drozde said, like a mother promising a treat to her child. "And a pottle of beer when you're done."

"A white *grosch* or a brown one?" Taglitz demanded warily.

She reached up and tapped one of the buttons on his greatcoat. "What are these made of?"

Taglitz was bewildered. "Pewter."

"And your flute?"

"I don't know. *Kupfernickel*, I suppose."

"Right. There's no silver about you, Tag. So don't be pulling your hopes up higher than your socks. We'll stick to brown *groschen* until you make colonel and I marry a duke."

"All right. But small beer or real beer?"

"Real."

"The light or the *dunkel*?"

"The dark."

"And when you say a pottle . . ."

"A tankard, Taglitz! A thumb stein, with a handle and a lid to it! Bugger off and let me work!"

She shooed him away, and he was happy enough to go, all smiles now that he'd won his point. A *grosch* wasn't much for an hour's work, Drozde knew, but Tag loved to play for her. And it would hurt his pride, besides, if she let him go. Especially if she let him go for the loud and sneeringly confident Drisch, a Lusation from the northern Berglands who exaggerated his already thick accent in the hope of getting people to pick fights with him.

Drisch wasn't a viable option in any case. He wasn't the sort of man to do what he was told by a woman, and that was the sort of man Drozde needed as her accompanist. It mattered that he should have some sort of an ear for music, but it mattered a lot more that he should let the puppets be the centre of attention. The piper she'd had before she found Taglitz had played over her dialogue and killed some of the jokes. And he wouldn't be told, so she'd had no choice but to send him packing.

She decided on four o'clock for the performance, and went round the camp announcing it. She took her time and allowed herself to get drawn into conversations, because this was an important part of her preparation. In gossiping about stories they'd heard, and in asking Drozde whether she was going to refer to this piece of scandal or that outrageous rumour, the soldiers and their doxies helped to shape the entertainment they were about to see.

Four o'clock was early, but Drozde was constrained by the sun, which would be down before five. She could play through twilight with the aid of torches, but in full dark too much nuance was lost.

After she'd told the soldiers, she went up to the house and passed the word along to the officers too. Not directly, of course—she couldn't knock on the doors of the lieutenants, and she'd be even less welcome to speak to their wives. What she could do was to tell Carla, the colonel's lady's maid, and to extend her usual invitation. Most likely the lieutenants would come, with or without their ladies, and Drozde worked up her material based on that assumption. If they didn't appear, she just had that little bit more latitude with the bawdy parts. August usually stayed away, although he surprised her every now and then by putting in an appearance. He would stand rather than sit, and he never cracked a smile. Possibly he thought that he was showing solidarity with the men under his command, but actually his solemn church face cast a pall over proceedings that she had to work hard to dispel.

After she'd finished her rounds she still had some time left before the performance was set to begin. She debated with herself whether she should walk into the village and try to find that carpenter. But the walk was a good three miles each way, and she couldn't afford to be late. It was probably better to put it off until the next day.

So she visited Molebacher instead, and ate with him. He was cooking pottage for the officers, his two big cauldrons bubbling side by side in the fireplace. Hulyek and Fast were with him, chopping onions and yellow turnips, while Standmeier moved between the pots and stirred them, sweat pouring from his face. All three of them studiously avoided looking in her direction.

The meat in the pottage was beef, but for himself Molebacher had made a rabbit stew with carrots in a tin pannikin, tucking it in against the stones at the side of the fireplace to let it simmer slowly until it was done. He shared it with Drozde, and she listened to his complaints about the kitchen's shortcomings. Too many draughts, too many doors, not enough surfaces for preparation, cracked flags on the floor and a ceiling that would certainly leak at the first rain. He didn't need her to respond to this litany. Her role was to listen and shake her head while she ate her allotted portion of the stew.

"What about the lords and ladies?" she asked Molebacher when a suitable pause in his monologue presented itself. "Are they giving you a hard time?"

She was always cautious about asking Molebacher for gossip, especially about the officers and their wives. His reactions to such questioning were unpredictable: often he would simply say nothing, but he had been known to forget to save her a portion of dinner when she pressed him too hard. Today, however, he seemed to be in a loquacious mood.

"They're fine," Molebacher said, shrugging his big shoulders. Then he amended that blanket endorsement. "The colonel's fine. The others . . ."

A pause. Drozde waited him out. If he had any specific stories to tell, they might find their way into the puppet show. Obviously she couldn't say anything that actually criticised the officers, but she could dress up their foibles as satire and rely on their delight at being noticed outweighing their embarrassment at being named. Molebacher was usually the soul of discretion when it came to his betters—August permitted him a greater degree of familiarity than he allowed most of his lieutenants, and he wasn't about to sacrifice that hard-won licence through incautious talk—but occasionally he let something slip.

He did so now. "The new one . . ." he said.

"What, Dietmar's lady?"

"Yeah, her. She wants Lipisher *torte*."

Drozde arched an eyebrow. "Cake in brandy?"

"With hazelnuts. And cream. Lots of cream. Well, I'm not going to go wandering around the woods gathering fucking nuts, am I? Dietmar says he'll slip me a couple of *cruitzers* if I make her one. I'll believe that when I see it. But if I don't deliver and she goes whining to him about it, I'll never hear the end of it."

"I'm going into the village tomorrow," Drozde offered. "I'll see if I can find some hazelnuts there."

Molebacher didn't thank her. Thanks weren't in his repertoire. But he nodded as though he was pleased that she'd seen her way through to this obvious solution.

"So," Drozde said, still fishing. "Pottage. With beef. Any chance you'll tell me where the beef came from?"

"Any chance you'll keep your nose where it belongs?" Molebacher countered. But he grinned as he said it. He loved to tell tales of his own resourcefulness, and since a large part of his job was legally sanctioned piracy, he usually had plenty of stories to tell.

"Those fields we passed on our way here," he said. "About ten miles back. With the big dairy herd. Did you notice Swivek and Rattenwend weren't around yesterday? Yeah? Well I'd sent them back there, hadn't I? They picked out seven or eight of the biggest cows and painted a letter M on their arses. Not in paint, obviously. I didn't have any paint. It was blackjack gravy, from the barrel I made before we rolled out of Vostli. Then they went round to the farm and told the farmer they were looking for some stolen cattle belonging to Count von Molebacher and marked with his sign. Put the fear of God into the poor bastard. Serious business, stealing from the nobility. 'All yours? Well let's just take a little look, shall we? Oh dear oh dear.' And of course the man's swearing blind that it's a mistake, he's owned the cows for years, they're practically members of the family. 'All right then,' says Swivek. 'We'll just take a couple, and show them to the count, and if he says they're yours we'll bring them right back.' Of course, by then he thinks he's going to lose all the bloody animals, so he's very happy to settle for a couple, and off they go."

Molebacher was laughing uproariously throughout this speech, hugely enjoying his own joke. Drozde smiled too, even though she didn't really see how it was funny to rob a man of his livelihood.

"Got the turnips from the next farm along," Molebacher added. "Nobody in sight, so just grabbed those and kept on walking. Plenty of meat to keep the brass and lace happy for a few days, and what's left I can parcel up and sell off to the enlisted men. Fresh meat goes faster than anything."

Armies lived off the land, Drozde knew. What else were they going to do? The alternative—keeping them supplied from some distant point where provisions would first be stored and then doled out—had been tried, and it didn't work. It was both expensive and fragile. As soon as your enemy waltzed across your supply line, you were well and truly buggered. Better to help yourself to what was around you—so long as you didn't care who you antagonised or ruined. But this was an Austrian company on Silesian soil. Colonel August had been ordered to tread lightly where possible, and he'd passed the same order on to Molebacher. This was Molebacher's way of squaring the circle.

"I'm doing a performance," Drozde told him now. "Tonight."

Molebacher grunted but said nothing. Drozde wasn't sure of his position on her shows. He never attended them and on the whole was inclined to dismiss her puppets, and indeed anything she did besides warming his bed, as profoundly unimportant. She suspected, however, that he enjoyed the social visibility she gave him, though he would never admit it. And he couldn't argue with the money she was putting by from the shows, which was considerable.

Drozde gave the money to him for safekeeping, which was a tactical manoeuvre. There was nowhere in her tent or on her person where she could safely keep it. But she knew where *he* kept it—in a strongbox at the bottom of a sack of potatoes that he topped up daily so it was always full—and when she parted ways with the company it was going with her, not staying with him. The money represented the next stage of her grand plan. It would pay for the rent and the stock of a small shop in Ledziny or Imielin, or some other town in the far south that basked in the twin blessings of good climate and being a million leagues away from where she was born.

Drozde rose from the table, gave Molebacher a kiss on the cheek—
for the benefit of the three privates he fended her off as though this
was an unwanted irritation—and took her leave.

She still had an hour or so left. She used it to practise some of the
sketches she had in mind and to work up a song to one of her favourite
tunes—that of a hoary old ballad called "Bären Gässlin." The original
song was a grim screed about ghosts and vengeance, but its simple
rhythms were very easy to compose to. Drozde had taught Taglitz to
play it fast and light, and she used it regularly.

Soldiers began to wander over to the ruins in twos and threes as
she worked. Most of them were content to sit and enjoy what was
left of the sunlight, but some wanted to talk and Drozde (already in
persona as the mistress of ceremonies) had to talk back. It was just
chaff, flirtatious on their part and outrageously insulting on hers.
They expected it and she had to deliver, even though she could have
used a few minutes more to prepare.

When Taglitz came, she ran through the songs with him quickly
and then, as the ruins filled with men and women, she retired into
the tent-like space behind the theatre where the puppets were laid
out ready. She watched through a worn patch in the fabric, judging
her moment. Dietmar arrived (with wife) and then Pabst (without).
Klaes came last of all, talking to the adjutant, Bedvar, and staying
right at the back, where he could leave early if there was anything he
disapproved of. There usually was.

When she judged by a quick count that two-thirds of the
detachment was sitting on the grass in front of the theatre, she got the
proceedings underway with a ragged fanfare that she played herself
on an old, battered trumpet that probably had more tin than brass in
it. The sound was awful, and she made no attempt to stay in tune, but
the soldiers and the women greeted that raucous, untempered squawk
with their usual cheers and applause.

Drozde started the show, as she did all her performances, with a
short speech from General Schrecklich. The general's puppet had a
huge stomach, gin blossoms on his cheeks and so many medals on his
uniform that they stood out further than his shoulders. "Pay attention,
you men," Schrecklich rumbled. "Entertainment's an excellent thing.
Takes your mind off other things. Like getting your heads blown off.
All to the good, what, what? Watch the nice puppets. Give the puppet
lady your pennies. And don't think about the Prussians. We won't be

seeing any trouble from them. Sticklers for good manners, you know. They won't shoot you if you don't introduce yourself."

The general said several more things in a similar vein, ostensibly trying to improve morale while dwelling in insensitive detail on the imminence of war. The soldiers, for whom this was no laughing matter, laughed until they pissed themselves.

The next item was broad slapstick—Molebacher's liberation of the cows. Molebacher himself barely figured in the piece, whose heroes were Privates Swivek and Rattenwend. The farmer they swindled was belligerent and suspicious. He chased the soldiers away three times before they finally succeeded in tricking him out of his livestock. Finally they took the cows back to Molebacher, who ennobled them as Sir Swivek of the beef stew and Baron Rattenwend von Cowpat. The piece ended with the first song, a hymn of praise to beef sung by Molebacher and the two privates to a lilting skirl from Taglitz's pipe. This was the song that Drozde hadn't had enough time to work out, so it wasn't very funny until, in a moment of pure inspiration, she had the cows join in, singing off-key. Tag played off-key too, as though there was a cow piper piping for the cow singers. That went down pretty well.

After that she enacted the piece she felt most confident about. The coquette came on along with a second puppet who played the role of her mother. "What ails you, Feronika?" the mother asked as her daughter languished prettily.

"I need . . . Lipisher *torte* !" the coquette sighed. "If any man should bring it to me, oh, what I should give to him! How my heart would swell with love and tender feeling for him! How pliant and willing I would be in his masculine arms!"

There was a yelp from the back of the audience. Drozde risked a quick glance through her peephole and saw the newly minted Dame Dietmar with her hands clasped to her mouth, eyes wide at the outrageous dialogue. But she was thrilled, not scandalised. She turned to her husband, shaking her head in wonder, and he chucked her under the chin as he kissed her. *Look at this*, his smile said. *You married me, and now you're famous.*

Enter an officer puppet, much to the two ladies' astonishment. Drozde put a swagger into the soldier's movements as he introduced himself as Lieutenant Dietmar and swore himself into the coquette's service like a knight of old. He would never return, he said, until he had found a Lipisher *torte* and brought it back to her.

"From Lipish?" the coquette hazarded. "It would take you no more than half an hour to ride there."

No, the soldier said, not from Lipish. From the den of the ice dragon in the far north, who was known to keep a stash for his own use. Nothing would prevent the brave lieutenant from finding the dragon's lair, slaying the beast and bringing back its hoard for the maiden's delectation.

This was greeted ecstatically by the audience, as Drozde had known it would be. She kept the joke going through a series of comedic encounters, with the Dietmar puppet braving more and more absurd dangers to find and bring back the cream cake, and then in due course getting his reward—the love of the coquette, who married him with the ice dragon officiating. Drozde loved the dragon puppet, which had taken her three days to make, and lost no opportunity of bringing it into the show.

Another song, then—the "Bären Gässlin" one, with the coquette singing about the many reasons why she loved Lieutenant Dietmar, referring back to a great many of his exploits from former times, all well known to Drozde's audience. She was careful to avoid any reference to Dietmar's sexual conquests. They were a theme she'd visited often, but in front of Dietmar's wife it would be perilous to cause him any real embarrassment. Instead, the jokes she retold in the song turned on drunken excesses or narrowly averted disasters.

The Dietmar piece was the longest in the show. Drozde went on to a series of short vignettes about the village people and the brief interactions that the company had had with them thus far. Most of these were harmless in the extreme, turning on the villagers' mistrust of the soldiers and their ignorance of current affairs, but she'd saved (as she often did) a sting in the tail to end the performance.

The Schrecklich puppet, without his medals and standing in now for Colonel August, brooded silently in a dungeon-like room. A second officer entered, marching with such vigour and energy that his boot came up above his head with each step. He saluted his commanding officer, then bowed for good measure. When the colonel failed to notice him, he went out and came in again, saluting all the way.

"At ease, Klaes," the colonel said. Drozde had to pause for a moment here, as this simple line caused such hilarity that it was a minute or more before she could make herself heard again. The rules were subtle here, but what it came down to was that Klaes was fair game because he was the youngest officer in the company, required to show good-natured tolerance rather than take offence when he was lampooned.

The colonel gave Klaes a secret mission—to spy on the villagers and see what secrets they were keeping. Klaes went on to do an appallingly bad job of this, spying on milkmaids while murders, thefts and wholesale debauchery went on all around him. The real Klaes had already left by this point, but Drozde couldn't tell whether this was before the piece or in response to it. She wasn't afraid either way. Klaes wasn't a brute like Dietmar, and even if he were offended he wouldn't stoop to act on his hurt feelings. It was sad, but it was so: the more pretensions a man had to good manners, the more liberties she could take with him. The vicious cleared a circle around themselves that she had better sense than to enter.

She wound the show down with a final song that was more sentimental and maudlin in nature. Then she came out from hiding and stood with her skirts hitched up to catch any coins the soldiers might give her as they filed out from her makeshift auditorium. Most gave a copper, or perhaps two. The women generally gave nothing, which wasn't surprising. For them, as for Drozde, money was a matter of survival. Dietmar gave her a *cruitzer* and a condescending nod. From the smirk that tugged at his lips, she guessed that Dame Feronika had enjoyed *The Quest for the Torte* and the spotlight it put on her.

Once everyone had left, Drozde began to fold away the puppets. Taglitz knelt down to help her, but she shook her head and shooed him away. She had her own method of looping the strings so that they didn't tangle in the box, and he'd never been able to learn it. To forestall any more well-meant but unneeded assistance, she paid him off.

Taglitz stared at the coins in the palm of his hand, counting them twice before he spoke. "There are five *fenings* here," he said.

"Yes. So?"

"That doesn't add up to a *grosch*. It adds up to a *cruitzer* and a *fening* over."

"You had a good idea. Going off-key for the cows. So you get a little extra."

"And I still get my beer?"

"And you still get your beer."

"*Fielen danken*, Drozde."

"You're welcome. But don't talk Schönbrunner, Tag. Not even bad Schönbrunner. Someone might mistake you for an officer, and then where would you be?"

Clouds had begun to scud in from the north as the sun retreated to the horizon. Tag cast a suspicious glance up at their black bulk. "Sleeping up in the house," he sighed, "instead of in a tent with a fucking hole in it."

Drozde hefted the first of her boxes onto her shoulder. If it was going to rain again, she had to get them inside quickly. "Everything has two sides to it, Tag. The secret to staying happy is turning things around so only the good side faces you."

Taglitz didn't look convinced. "Even getting soaking wet and chilled to the bone?"

"Even that. Isn't Swivek in your tent?"

"Yes, he is. Why?"

"If he farts in the night, the hole will save you from suffocating."

The first drops were starting to fall as she walked away.

11

Drozde began to think that this might not be such a bad billet for the winter. The puppet show had made a good profit, and Molebacher seemed pleased when she turned over the coins. She'd go into town tomorrow, get some supplies and, just as importantly, start talking to people. With luck the village would turn out to be a rich source of stories for future performances.

For now she was free. Molebacher planned to drink with the sergeants again tonight and had dismissed her to her own devices. She had some idea of spending the night in the camp: the other women would certainly be happy to see her and talk over the show. But it had started to rain heavily, as it had the night before, and the tents outside looked bleak and uninviting under the louring sky. Almost without intending it, Drozde found she was heading towards the old ballroom where she had met the ghosts on that first night, as if they might still be there. It would be stupid to expect such a thing, of course. These spirits did not stay put like most, and she had seen them in other places since. But even before she turned into the side passage, she felt a light pressure against her hand, and looked down to see the little girl, Magda.

"It was a funny show," the child said. "We all liked it a lot."

"I didn't see you there," Drozde said, somewhat startled. "We stand at the side," explained Magda. She beamed at Drozde. "But I'll sit right out in front next time, because you said that."

When Drozde opened the door of the room, the ghosts were waiting. They clustered around her, murmuring their congratulations on her performance. Several even touched her arm as she passed in a kind of greeting. Drozde was expecting their welcome this time around, and so she was ready for it. She did not flinch at their proximity, nor draw back from the feather-light contacts. The unease that she had felt so strongly before was fading now. She knew that the ghosts respected her, though she couldn't work out why, and it felt somehow churlish to snub the open and ingenuous goodwill that she saw in their faces. Still, there was a lingering sense of wrongness to all of this, a strangeness that set her on her guard. And in spite of their frank welcome, she knew that there must be things the ghosts were keeping from her. She noticed that a few of them—maybe only one or two—held back from the press, even turned away as she came in. But their shyness was no more accountable than the friendliness of their fellows.

She had no way of making them explain these puzzles—ghosts were immune to bribes and threats alike. But perhaps, if she was patient, they might give her the answers she wanted without her having to ask.

"Can we have another story?" Magda asked, while the ghosts were still milling around her. The talk stopped abruptly, and faces turned to Drozde in expectation. Magda put a wheedle into her voice. "You've got some time now. Pleeease, Drozde?"

Drozde shrugged. "If you like," she agreed, and rolled up her shawl so she could sit comfortably on the floor, leaning against the rail of the old orchestra stand. Many of the ghosts copied her. As Magda had done on the first night when she climbed the stairs, they acted for all the world as if they had substance, as if walls and floor were real to them. A young man stretched out long legs with an audible sigh of pleasure; an older one hooked one arm over the rail. This all seemed a perverse pantomime to Drozde, but if this mimicry made them happy, she thought, then why not? She had to admit that the ones closest to her really did look comfortable—and remarkably solid, as they had the day before.

"Well?" Drozde asked. "Whose story shall we hear?" She addressed the room at large, but Magda darted forward before anyone else could speak.

"Thea!" she commanded. "Tell Drozde what happened in the house when you lived here. I like that one!"

The ghosts parted, and a little knot of women came forward, their wide skirts interweaving with each other. They were severely dressed, with high collars and hair pulled back, but their expressions were eager. One of them, taller than the rest, took a further step towards Drozde, and in doing so came into sharper focus. She looked around the room as if assuring herself of her audience, and as she began to speak, Drozde saw the lines in her face, her grey eyes and shy smile.

"I was born in this house," the woman said, "the only daughter of the family, and in my own mind the only child."

My brother Franz-Augustus was eight years older than me: I only saw him when he came back from school at Christmas, when he already seemed like a man. Our family was rich, though I had no way of judging that we were different from anyone else. One of my earliest memories is of sitting with my mother, looking at engravings of furniture. She pointed out a curly box with legs, which she said was a pianoforte, a musical instrument. She showed it to my father, and three days later a pianoforte was delivered to our house, all the way from Leipzig. It took two men to carry it in. I was much older before I knew that this was at all unusual.

I grew up against a background of war, in a family that had made war their living. Our grandfather was the distinguished general Gebhard von Schildauer. My mother told me once that the "von" in his name, and the house itself, had been rewards for his service in the wars against the French. So of course my father was a soldier too, a major in the 6th Regiment, and my brother would be a soldier in his turn. But for me, as a girl, the surname meant very little. My mother called me Dorothea, and so did my brother, when he was home. I don't remember my father calling me anything but "child," or sometimes, when he was in a very good mood, "little lady." But he did not talk to me often: he was not comfortable with children. He must already have been over fifty when I knew him, and he was away a good deal with his regiment, leaving my mother to manage the house, which she did well. I was raised mostly by my nurse, and then by my governess, both of them women of spotless reputation and strict principles. They taught me to revere God, the empire and my parents, to uphold my family's honour, do my duty and tell the truth. Since then, I think I have broken all those commands.

I was a solitary child, but not discontented. The house was full of books that no one else ever read; I could wander where I liked, and make up my own stories to keep me company. And twice every week I had another companion. In the village nearest the house, which was called Puppendorf, there lived a glassblower who was famed locally for his skill. In the early days of my childhood, when my father came home from fighting the Danish, my parents used to entertain guests in the house. The servants were clumsy, so there was always a need for glassware. When I was about seven, the glassblower's daughter came to the house with my mother's latest order: six wine glasses, packed in a basket of straw as if they were eggs. My mother saw the girl pick them out and set each one on the kitchen dresser, noted how delicate-handed she was, and engaged her to come in on Mondays and Thursdays to clean the china. So I met Cilie.

She was a revelation to me. She was a year and a half older than me, but looked younger. She laughed readily, and cried to see a mouse die; her hair was always escaping from her cap, and she never stopped talking. Her given name, Cecilia, was too long for her taste, and so was mine, so when I was with her I became Thea. If my mother or the housekeeper was by, to be sure, she kept her eyes down and hid her smiles and called me Fräulein as a respectful servant should. But in the afternoons my mother took a nap, and Cilie was left alone in the little storeroom with her cloths and spirits of vinegar. At first I just slipped in and talked to her. Later I started doing half her work, to give us time when we could play together outside. The grounds were wide in those days, with many trees, and if we stayed in the orchard no one could see us.

Through Cilie's stories I learned about the lives of her friends in Puppendorf: Sanne, who minded her little brother and sister while her mother was at our house doing the laundry; Jens the baker's son, who rose at five every morning to help his father, and Irmal, who sewed clothes with her mother every day until the sun set. I had not realised before that other children, the same age as me, had to spend their days working. It troubled me. I had never before questioned the world or my place in it. But now it seemed wrong that Cilie, who was so clever, and so pretty with her black curls and dark eyes, had never been taught to read, and had only two dresses. She willingly learned her alphabet from me, but when I tried to give her a dress I had outgrown, which would have fitted her well, Cilie shook her head.

"They'd laugh at me at home if I wore something so fine," she said. "Or else think I stole it, and have me whipped." That thought appalled me so much that I never suggested such a thing again.

My mother valued Cilie's work and gave her more to do, until she became a part of the household. But all too soon I lost her as a playmate. My mother fell ill with a nervous complaint which confined her to bed; I was needed to sit and read to her every day when my lessons were over, and had no more leisure to wander around the house. Then my father left us to visit my brother, who was about to leave school and join the regiment. We had no one whom my father trusted to manage the house while my mother was sick, and after a struggle with himself he invited his cousin Gottfried and his wife from Westphalia to stay with us.

This Gottfried was my father's nearest relative: a big, red-faced man and a soldier, like all the men in the family. His father had been a brother of our famous grandfather Gebhard. He had a great regard for family honour and tradition, and he looked around our house with awe, as if every wall and piece of furniture was a sacred relic. My father disliked him, considering him an upstart from an inferior branch of the family who had no right to affect the full name of von Schildauer. But his wife, Eugenie, was young and fashionable, and my father hoped she would be a welcome companion for my mother while he was away.

My mother, though, did not take to her. Eugenie had a view about everything, and began her stay in our house by taking my mother's physician to task about her diet and medicine, and instructing her to exercise every day. When my mother pleaded exhaustion, she turned her attention to me. She put my hair into curl papers and tried to teach me French. I had sometimes been able to enjoy a few minutes' talk with Cilie when she brought my mother her medicine, which she was trusted to mix herself. But cousin Eugenie, seeing us together, scolded me for time-wasting, and after that made a point of watching the preparation every day, whether because she doubted Cilie's competence or to prevent us talking, I could not say. She had a sharp nose for any activity of which she disapproved, and sharp eyes which seemed able to seek me out wherever I was.

I had hoped that Gottfried might take up some of her attention, but while my father was away our cousin spent most of his time hunting or fishing in the woods around the house. He was an excellent shot, and the cook was kept perpetually busy preparing the grouse and hares he brought back. I was allowed to take my supper with my mother in her room, but one night, bringing our plates down early to save the maid the trouble, I overheard the two of them at the table.

". . . could live here very happily," Gottfried was saying.

"But the child has been sorely neglected," Eugenie complained. "She has had hardly any education and is far too familiar with the servants. It would be a sad task to take her in hand as she requires."

"I'm sure you are equal to it, my dear," Gottfried replied with a laugh.

I must have learned discretion from Cilie, for I got by the doorway and into the kitchen without them noticing me. I used the back staircase to escape to my room, where I stayed awake until morning, praying that my mother might not die.

Perhaps God heard my prayer, for only a few days later we received news that Franz-Augustus was fairly settled with the regiment and my father was returning home. I greeted him with more joy than I ever remember feeling in his presence, and my mother gained heart enough to rise from her bed for the first time in weeks. Shortly afterwards our cousins returned to their home in Westphalia. But they had taught me a useful lesson: how quickly my home might become my prison. I began to look around for some means of escape, and the day after my cousins departed I went to my father and asked if I might be allowed to learn to ride.

I owed this idea to cousin Eugenie herself, who had proposed it as one of the measures needed for my improvement. Before she left she had said as much to my father, and now he agreed that I looked pale and had been too much indoors: a little healthy exercise would be good for me.

I did not enjoy the learning. It was hard to balance on a sidesaddle, and the pony my father found for me was a stubborn little beast. But I persevered until I could canter around the park. In a few months I was allowed to ride through the woods or into the village, with Cilie behind me on a donkey as chaperone.

I had been to Puppendorf before, of course: we attended church there at harvest, Christmas and Easter. But then we always travelled by carriage, and apart from the responses in church and some how-do-ye-dos, I hardly needed to speak to anyone. Now I had to give an account of myself. Cilie's friends, when I met them, were clearly as curious about me as I was about them. They were cautious at first: over-respectful to the young lady from the great house. I was shy and awkward, fearful with every word of revealing my ignorance. Their homes seemed dreadfully cramped to me. I did not know where to sit, or what to do if I was offered food. But as the weeks went on, we grew accustomed to each other. Sanne sold me cherries, and showed me how to pick the best ones. Casper, at the forge, gave me advice on how to manage my wilful pony.

And at last I saw Cilie's home, and her father, whom I had never met. He was Bruno Mander, a wiry little man with a famously short temper, though I never once heard him shout at Cilie. Her mother had died when she was small, and she was his treasure. He was invariably mild-mannered with me as well, most likely out of respect for the great house. Maybe, too, he was flattered by the interest I took in his work, which seemed miraculous to me. The workshop behind their house had been set up by his great-grandfather and great-great-uncles, and he still kept some greenish jars and bowls from that time, which he called forest glass. At one time, he said, his family had employed as many as ten men from the village; now it was just two. When the furnace was stoked, the heat in the workshop was overwhelming, but the three men, with their shirts open to the waist, walked through it unconcernedly, holding between their paddles, or on the ends of tubes, little globes of pure light. I never tired of watching them blow a shining bead into a balloon, twisting handles or stem with fine pincers until the shape was a recognisable object—but luminous, transformed.

These were years of contentment. I was growing up a sad disappointment to my mother: tall and gawky, with hair that would not curl and no aptitude for either embroidery or the pianoforte. But Cilie was as beautiful as ever, and as she grew more useful to my mother she came to the house more often. When I was thirteen, she became my maid, which meant that she had a new suit of clothes and two marks more each month from my mother, and I was able to see her every day. She was walking out with Jens the baker's son by then, and putting away money for a wedding some time in the future, but we did not think much about the future in those days. I was newly released from my governess, and allowed more freedom than I had ever known. Every morning I would read with Cilie, and almost every afternoon, while my mother slept, we would ride to Puppendorf together. I was at peace, and had forgotten that peace does not last.

The next war was already growing in the north, and it sent its upheavals ahead of it. When my father was next at home, I heard him telling my mother that his regiment would be moved before long: the Danes were once again laying claim to Schleswig and there must soon be fighting. Then a decree came that all single men below forty-five were to be conscripted. For once I heard this news before my mother did: the village was in a panic about it. And Cilie and Jens called the banns for their marriage the next Sunday.

Cilie wept to be parted from me, and I shed tears myself, but we both knew they had done wisely. When the recruiting men came round later that year, Cilie was already pregnant with their first child, and Jens was spared for a time for her sake as they had hoped he would be. But Casper, and Henek, and some thirty others, were marched away for three years of service.

Puppendorf became a different place. Without the young men's labour, roofs went unmended and drainage ditches choked. It took frantic effort to cut, bind and safely store the crops before the rains set in. The following year the harvest was poor, and the year after that. People's clothes began to get ragged. No one turned down my old dresses now: they took them with thanks, and my mother's too. One dress might make skirts for two children and a jacket for a third. I once saw a girl of no more than eight or nine dressed from an old morning gown of mine, leading a troupe of smaller children, two of them clothed in the same material. After little Katya was born, Cilie looked after the young children of neighbours who now had to do their husbands' work. And Bruno, who had lost both his helpers, kept his workshop open only with Jens's help, and had no customers but my mother and me.

So when the formal declaration finally came—it was in winter, more than a year after the men were taken—the war had already started for us in all but name. All that was added was a heavier burden of anxiety. Our family had more luck in one respect than the villagers: my father and brother were given a short leave of absence before the fighting. My father had been made colonel, and he was more animated than I had seen him for some time: proud of his new command and delighted that Franz-Augustus would be in his own regiment. I had not met my brother for two years, and saw him now almost as a stranger, trim and brave in his blue uniform, with a moustache and newly wide shoulders. He kissed me and declared I had not changed, but I thought he looked at me differently too.

I had a chance, after supper that night, to talk to my brother as I never had before. I asked him about his training and his friends, about the causes of the war (which it seemed he understood little better than I did) and about life in the army camp. I did not dare ask him how he felt about the killing that lay ahead of him. I remembered that he had liked sketching when he was younger, and turned the talk to that instead: might he have chosen to become an artist, I said, if he had not been a soldier?

Franz-Augustus seemed puzzled by the question. "This was always my duty," he said at last. "We don't choose what we do."

"It's not so bad," he continued, after a pause. "I have good comrades, and we're well trained. We'll stand together and fight for each other. In a battle, you know, that's what keeps men strong."

He had never been in a battle then. I don't know who told him that piece of wisdom; I doubt it was my father. I hope it held true for him. A few days later they left together for Schleswig, my father as colonel of the regiment and Franz-Augustus as its newest ensign. And that spring we received a letter from the town of Sonderborg to say that my brother was dead. He had taken part in the storming of a fortress, the letter said, and had been hit by a musket ball. The assault had been a success, and the letter was full of words such as honour, triumph and heroism. It was not from my father.

My mother put the letter away in a drawer. I never saw her look at it again, though sometimes she would shut the door to her room and I heard her crying. She told me that she had begged my father to keep Franz-Augustus away from the worst of the fighting, and he had only said he would do what he could.

That war came to an end with the end of summer, and it was not till then that the wives and mothers in the village had their news. Eight of our men had died in the fighting or from wounds or disease afterwards. Five could no longer fight, and were brought back to us. The others had been sent to the barracks at Liegnitz to serve out the rest of their period of duty.

My father came home only once that autumn, to attend a memorial service in the village church for Franz-Augustus and the others who had died. He left us almost at once, saying that he was needed to oversee the training of the recently conscripted men. I suspected he could not face my mother and me. When he was gone again my mother seldom spoke of him, but left her room and came with me on my visits to Puppendorf, doing what she could to help the other bereaved women there.

The next war, two years later, was with the Austrians, who had been our allies against the Danish. The conscripting officers came round again to find the few men they could pick up: three boys who had been too young last time, and four married men. One of them was Jens. Cilie and I pleaded for him: he had two young children now. But Katya was a big girl of four, and Little Jens was nearly two and already running around. The officers said that Jens must go, that his country needed him. Cilie's need seemed to weigh nothing in that balance. I wrote to my father, begging him to intervene, but he replied that there was nothing he could do, and that all of us must make sacrifices in times of war. I knew then that he was thinking of his own sacrifice, and that far from waking any fellow feeling in him, Franz-Augustus's death had hardened him to the plight of others. In any case, by the time his letter arrived, Jens had been signed up and marched away.

He never came home, and nor did my father. The Austrian war was as short-lived as the one before, but it was enough to kill ten more of our men. Jens lost a leg to an artillery shell, we heard later. A surgeon cauterised the wound, but he died the same night. As for my father, we received a letter from the field marshal himself expressing his condolences for his death. His rank and age had made it impossible for him to fight in the front line—he was over seventy—but he had insisted on staying with his regiment and had died of cholera from an infection then raging in the camp. My mother, when she read the field marshal's letter, turned very pale, but nodded her head, as if it were news she had long expected.

When the worst has happened, there is a kind of peace. Cilie became my maid again. Without his helpers, her father had been forced to shut up his workshop, so she was supporting him now as well as herself. We found work for two other widows from the village in the kitchen and laundry, and all their children came to the house to play in the sculleries and the garden under the eye of Sanne's eldest daughter.

We lived half a year like this, in calm if not contentment. And then, one summer morning, a young man presented himself at our gates and begged admission. He was a captain of the 6th named Hildebrand Eckert, handsome in a swaggering way, with great moustaches and a martial air. He said he had been my father's adjutant, and had been with him at his death. He had letters from him to give us, and begged our pardon for his delay in bringing them.

He handed my mother a slim packet: my father had never been a great writer. Since Herr Eckert showed no inclination to go, she rang for Cilie to bring him a glass of wine, and retired to the parlour to read the letters, taking me with her. When she had finished she was whiter even than when the news arrived of my father's death. She said only that she thought Herr Eckert might stay with us for a while, and gave me two of the letters to read.

In the first my father described Eckert as a very good fellow: of indifferent birth (as indeed, he said, his own father had been) but a fine soldier and devoted adjutant, who had been a support to him in difficult times. He went on to speak of the man's exploits in battle. I turned to the second letter. The writing here was shaky, but the words had a fervency to them that I had never heard from him in life. He was ill, he said, and thought he might die. Eckert, whom he called Hildebrand now, nursed him with a son's tenderness, and declared himself ready to do anything for him. He would ask Hildebrand to give his protection to us, his widow and orphan, should the worst happen. He commended us to God.

I looked up at this point. My mother was reading over my shoulder, her eyes full of tears. "Why should we need protection?" I demanded.

"Dearest Dorothea!" my mother said. It was a remonstration, and I fell silent.

So a guest room was made up, and Herr Eckert came to live with us. He behaved himself well. He was charming and attentive to my mother, and polite to me. At first his presence did not even constrain me much: I was managing most of the household by now, and had developed a routine that kept me out of his way. But I could not avoid seeing him as he wandered around the house. He looked at the walls and furnishings, I thought, rather as my cousin Gottfried had once looked: with admiration and longing; also with a sort of calculation. I never spoke with him except in the presence of my mother or Cilie, but sometimes I thought I saw the same calculation in his face when he looked at me. My mother, though, seemed happier and more at peace than she had been since my brother died, so I made no protest as weeks turned into months, and Herr Eckert remained with us.

I discussed most of my affairs with Cilie, but on the matter of Herr Eckert we said nothing to each other. I think loyalty to my mother kept us both silent, but I felt that Cilie did not like him any better than I did. I had been with her once when Katya and Little Jens, running in the garden, had nearly collided with Eckert as he took his constitutional. Nothing was said, but we both saw his recoil and the curl of his lip as he walked away.

He spent more and more time with my mother. He took over the handling of my father's business affairs. He read to her and even mixed her medicine. And one afternoon I was startled to hear her call him by his Christian name.

"Dear Hildebrand has already done so much for us," she said. "I could not continue standing on ceremony."

And Eckert smiled at me kindly. "I hope I may be allowed to address you as Dorothea," he said.

He did so from that day; it seemed to me that he made a point of it. For my part I tried to avoid addressing him at all.

My mother's afternoon naps were becoming longer; often now she would not rise until nearly supper time. I noticed that on some of these occasions Eckert would entertain two guests in the drawing room or walk around the house with them: men of business in sober suits who took notes in books. He was concluding some affairs of my father's, he explained when I asked him who they were: debts left unpaid at the time of his death. My father had had a horror of debt— it was a rule of his neither to lend nor borrow money—but I did not contradict Eckert; only asked him whether he had told my mother. He flushed a little, and begged me not to trouble her with the matter. I might not be aware, he said, how delicate her health was. The next day he asked me to marry him.

It was not entirely unexpected, and I had my polite refusal already prepared. He received it with equal courtesy, saying only that he hoped, in time, my feelings towards him might change. It felt like the first incursion of a campaign.

He had more guns on his side than I had imagined. That evening my mother took me aside and told me she knew what had passed between us. She said that she gave her consent to the match and begged me not to be cruel to poor Hildebrand. His lack of title did not matter at all. She spoke of my famous grandfather, who had risen from obscurity by his own excellence. She spoke of Hildebrand's valour in battle, and of his kindness to us. She could not in honesty talk of his passion for me, and she scrupled to point out the obvious—that I was already twenty and plain, and unlikely to find a better suitor. But she feared that if I rejected him he would leave us, and she had come to think of him almost as a second son. I said I did not think he would leave so readily, that his attachment was to the house and grounds, not to me. I told her that he invited speculators to look around the house behind her back. She grew angry with me then, and said that she trusted Hildebrand to manage her affairs: how he went about it was his concern and not mine. She was in tears when I left her.

I went to find Cilie. She was alone, for a wonder, mending the children's clothes while they played elsewhere. She smiled to see me, but her greeting was polite rather than warm. I thought: *We have drifted apart*, and the thought made me cold.

"Herr Eckert has proposed marriage to me," I told her.

She was silent and still for a moment. "And what did you tell him?" she said at last.

"Tell him!" I burst out. "Cilie, what do you think? How could I marry a man like that?"

"Oh, thank God!" Cilie cried, and dropped her sewing to jump up and embrace me.

She had mistrusted Eckert from the start, as I had. He had given my mother laudanum, she said, and poked around the house while she slept. But my mother would not hear a word against him—and from their conversations Cilie had believed that he was courting me, and that I liked him.

Now, at least, we could share our fears. But we were no closer to a solution: my mother loved Eckert and would not change her feelings for anything we could say.

"Send for your cousin Gottfried," said Cilie suddenly.

I stared at her. "Gottfried?"

"He's a von Schildauer, and a man. He'll hate Herr Eckert, and Madame will have to listen to him."

God forgive me, I did it. I did not even need to summon Gottfried or ask for his help. I simply wrote to tell him that my father's adjutant had come to stay with us and had offered us his protection. Gottfried arrived a bare week after I sent the letter.

He was bigger and redder even than I remembered; but of course he was angry. His first act was to forbid me to marry Eckert, though I had said no word of any such thing. I tried to assure him that I had no intention of marrying anyone.

"Of course you'll marry!" Gottfried roared. "It's your duty. But it must be a man worthy of the name."

It seemed to me that our duty as a family had only ever been to fight as soldiers or to produce them. I wanted no part of that. But I only repeated, as mildly as I could, that I had met no man whom I wished to marry. At that he calmed himself a little and gave me an appraising look.

"We'll need to find you someone soon," he said, and added a little doubtfully, "Eugenie has a brother you might meet."

I escaped on the pretext of telling my mother he was here. I wondered if our solution might prove to be as bad as the problem.

His interview with my mother went badly. She insisted that Hildebrand was her protector and friend; that he had deserved only well of us and she would never throw him off. Gottfried shouted that she needed no other protector now that he was here. Eckert, who had been with my mother when Gottfried arrived, gave me a sharp look at the start of the meeting, but after that he was all gentleness, sighing to hear Gottfried traduce his birth and character but refusing to retaliate. In the middle of it, Cilie came to the door to summon me to some crisis in the kitchen. I was very glad to go.

She took me, to my surprise, not to the kitchen but up the stairs, and stopped outside Eckert's room. He had locked the door, but my mother had a set of master keys and Cilie knew where they were kept.

"I've been doing my own poking around," she said, "Since I knew you were worried about him too. Have a look: my reading's not as good as yours."

She showed me the box in which Eckert kept his papers. There were his army documents, one certifying his enrolment as adjutant in the

6th, and beneath it a second in a different name, as a junior lieutenant in the 3rd. There were surveyors' reports on our house and a lawyer's letter with a valuation of the property. And at the bottom of the pile, new and freshly creased, was a will, drawn up in a fine clerk's hand, making Hildebrand Eckert the executor of all my mother's property and my legal guardian for as long as I lived.

She had not signed it yet. She loved Hildebrand, but she had loved me longer.

Cilie opened a cupboard to show me an apothecary's jar of laudanum and measuring spoons of different sizes. By then I had seen enough. I put everything back as if it burned my fingers, and hurried downstairs to the drawing room, where I could hear my mother sobbing. As I put my hand to the door it opened violently and Eckert pushed past me, his face white as snow. A moment later Gottfried came out, redder than usual, if that were possible, and strode off in the other direction. My mother, when she could speak, told me that he had struck Hildebrand, and challenged him.

I might have tried to stop them. But after what Cilie had shown me there seemed only one thing to do. I went in search of Eckert and asked for a few minutes' speech with him. He was still very pale, but he had recovered himself enough to agree.

"Herr Eckert," I said. "Hildebrand. I know we have not always agreed in the past. But my mother loves you dearly, and I would not have either one of you hurt. It grieves me more than I can say to hear of this challenge."

There was a flash of malice in his face, just for an instant. Then he smoothed it over. "The Christian thing to do, dear Dorothea, is to turn the other cheek," he said.

I must admit, I was surprised. Though I knew what Eckert was, I hadn't thought him a coward. I suppose, growing up in the family that I did, I had never encountered a man who was. But my mother would forgive, even praise, a decision to disregard Gottfried's challenge, and he would be as welcome in our home as ever. I could not allow that to happen.

"You'd do that? Bear the disgrace, to spare my mother? But then—" I stopped, as if checked by a sudden fear.

"Dorothea, what's wrong?"

"Oh, Hildebrand, my uncle is such a violent man! Though he is a von Schildauer, he has none of my father's honour." I looked at the ground. "I do not wish to impugn my family's good name, but—"

He waved my scruples aside with a motion of his hand. "You have my word that I will not reveal a word of what you say to another soul. I beseech you, if you have information about your uncle that concerns my person, tell me." He added, after a pause, "I could not bear the thought of leaving you and your mother friendless and unprotected."

I put a tremor in my voice. "Gottfried is so vengeful, so easily angered. Even if you declined his challenge, I do not think that would assure your safety. He would attack you when you were unarmed, or worse, suborn some masterless man to—I can hardly speak it!—stifle you while you slept. No, you must face him. I cannot think of any other solution."

Eckert was good with words. He had surely used them to defraud and deceive many times before he met us, and he planned to acquire our house and my hand by the same means. But I saw him swallow my story the way a fish takes bait, and I knew that I was better at this game than he. It was a good feeling, but I did not have time to revel in it long. Quickly, before he could reply, I leaned in, as if imparting some great secret.

"I can help you a little," I told him. "You know that my cousin is a descendant of Gebhard von Schildauer, and like him he is fearsome with a sword. He trained in the French style, as well as the Prussian, and did not stop until he could confound all his teachers. He has never been beaten. Please be on your guard: it would distress my mother so if you were harmed."

They fought the next morning. Eckert, as the challenged man, had the choice of weapons: he chose pistols, and Gottfried put a ball through his forehead at twenty paces. I knew nothing of my cousin's swordsmanship, but I had seen him shoot the head off a grouse when it was almost too far away to see.

There's little else to tell. Duelling had long been against the law, and Gottfried had to leave quietly for Westphalia the next day—he had not even had time to unpack. We gave Eckert a decent funeral, making up a gun-cleaning accident as the cause of his death. He is buried in the village churchyard under a granite stone that my mother paid for. At first she grieved more deeply for him than she had for my father. When I finally persuaded her to look over the document box her grief was lessened, but the pain of his betrayal was nearly as great. It took her a long time to overcome the effects of the laudanum Eckert had given her, but longer still to forgive me for having revealed her dear Hildebrand as a deceiver.

She lived seven more years, tended by Cilie and me. She rewrote her will to name me as her only heir, to make certain, she said, that Gottfried and Eugenie would never get hold of our house.

After her death I contacted my father's lawyers and did some travelling myself. I invited sober-suited men of my own to the house. And in a year we had built a glass foundry in the courtyard by the south wing, and turned the rooms behind it into painting and packing workshops.

One of Bruno's assistants had returned from Austria, and the two of them trained Henek as a helper, as he had lost a leg and could no longer farm. They made jugs and glasses first, which we sold to the daughters of my mother's old dinner-party friends, and later, vases and fancy-ware with painted designs. There was work for the women whose sons and husbands had died: painting, gilding, making crates and packing our wares in them with straw, like eggs. Several learned to blow glass themselves; Cilie's girl Katya was one of Bruno's first apprentices.

And after some years I followed Gottfried's instruction and found myself a husband, though not one he would have chosen. I married Bruno, Cilie's father. He was horrified when I first suggested it, but I persuaded him in time. We married in the village church, with two notaries present in case Gottfried tried to raise objections, and afterwards drew up our wills so that the workshop and the house would belong, at our deaths, to Cilie, Katya and Little Jens. Bruno found it hard at first to be the master of the great house, but he was respectful and kind to me, and our friendship grew with time. We had, after all, the most important thing in common: we both loved Cilie more than anything.

Thea bowed her head, as if embarrassed to have spoken for so long. For the first time Drozde noticed the woman beside her, smaller and slighter, with dark eyes and still-black curls. The two of them were holding hands, and they smiled at each other before turning back into the crowd.

There were many details in this account that puzzled Drozde, not least the fact that she had no idea where Puppendorf was; the nearest village to Pokoj was Narutsin. Perhaps, in the distant past, there had been another settlement closer to the great house.

She didn't ask. As she knew from the day before, there were rules in this house about challenging a storyteller. And in truth she was content for once to be the receiver rather than the maker of the tale. It gave her a curious sense of freedom.

12

Narutsin came to life on market day, more so than Drozde had expected. She had taken care to arrive early, as the stallholders began setting up: the best time to start an idle conversation was while they were waiting for the rush to begin. Not that she'd really thought there would be much of a rush. She was amazed to find the place so busy already.

She had been hoping to garner some interesting stories for her next show while she bought the things she needed, but the stallholders she chatted to eyed her with suspicion and met her questions about the village and its people with sullen silence. Perhaps the housewives and daughters of Narutsin had an instinctive distrust of women who threw in their lot with soldiers. Or maybe they just didn't like strangers.

Eventually she stopped at the stand of a clothier who seemed more cheerful than the others she had encountered. Her stall held a few bales of heavy material and some promising-looking ribbons, and Drozde was pleased to see that the woman stocked needles and reels of thread too—the puppets' garments were always in need of darning, and the curtain at the back of the theatre was growing decidedly ragged around the edges. Drozde introduced herself and showed the puppet she had brought with her. This often made it easier to start a conversation, she'd found, as well as helping to drum up business for her next performance. Today it was the newly made coquette. She held up a ribbon against the doll's bodice and asked the stallholder if she had any lighter cloth, muslin perhaps.

"Wrong time of year, dear," the woman said. "But come back in a couple of weeks and I'll see what I can do."

"Two weeks!" It seemed a long time to wait for a sale, Drozde thought. "Do you live hereabouts? Maybe I could buy from your house."

The woman laughed. "Not unless you have a boat. I'm from over the river. And I can't come every week, the ferryman charges a fortune." She looked at Drozde curiously. "You're not from this area yourself, I'm guessing."

Drozde gave her the edited version of her life: a village childhood in the north; an early marriage to a travelling puppet-master whose death left her with a livelihood but no home. She always wore a ring for these trips. Being a young widow got her more acceptance from most of the women and less unwelcome attention from some of the men. If necessary, she could make his death be no more than a month ago. Tears were always a last resort for Drozde, but they were useful for getting rid of unwanted suitors. It was true, too, that her memories of the old puppet-master were fond ones for the most part, though there had never been anything so formal as a marriage contract between them. He had beaten her much less than her father and had fed her whenever he had food himself. And, of course, he had taught her. True, the puppets were better dressed now than they had been under his ownership, and certainly better voiced, but it was old Vanek who'd shown her how to carve, how to attach the strings and how to work them, and for that she would always be grateful.

She told the tale well, and the stallholder was suitably impressed. In return, as Drozde had hoped, the woman told her own story. She was Hanna Kasturas, one of several traders who lived in the villages over the river and came here regularly. Narutsin had a good market and was prosperous by the region's standards: some of her neighbours were here every week. For her part, on alternate Thursdays she lent her patch to her cousin, who had married a Narutsin man and sold his milk and cheese here. It was a useful arrangement which avoided leaving the spot empty. Hanna knew all the local people, and could point out who would give Drozde a good bargain, who sold two-day-old milk and who was known to put his finger on the scales.

Drozde laughed at the woman's jokes and thanked her for her advice. Before she left she asked the way to the local carpenter, and bought the ribbon and a couple of needles. They'd always be useful, and Hanna could prove a valuable contact, happy as she was to gossip about the lives and characters of her more tight-lipped neighbours. The carpenter, she learned, was Jorg Stefanu; Hanna thought him an honest man and a good craftsman, but somewhat above himself in his ambitions. His daughter was fully twenty, and instead of helping the girl towards a husband, someone with a trade to his name, he'd sent her to work as maid to the burgomaster, as if she might catch Meister Weichorek's son, perhaps. Poor Dame Stefanu would turn in her grave at such foolishness, said Hanna. Drozde shook her head and laughed with her at the delusions of fathers. But the market was filling up; a girl with an outsize basket came up to ask for pins, and Hanna stopped laughing abruptly. Drozde took her leave, cordially promising to seek the stall out again in a fortnight.

It was the carpenter she most needed to visit. The supplies she'd promised to find for Molebacher could wait till last: the less she had to carry around the better. But her puppets needed mending and she would not be easy in her mind till she had seen to them. Hanna had described the workshop as being only a little way off the main road, but Drozde had seen too many small towns to believe it would be close. In fact the side road went on for half a mile and petered out into a muddy track before it reached Stefanu's workshop.

The shop itself, when she finally reached it, surprised her by being sturdy and well built; made of wood, of course, but far from the shack she had expected. The joints were dovetailed, the walls straight and smooth, sealed against the weather with some preparation that had turned the planks a rich chestnut. The windows had overhangs to keep out the rain, and the door opened smoothly. Hanna had been right to praise the man's skill.

The inside was less neat but had the same look of substance and purpose. A bench along the back wall was strewn with works in progress and lined with tools crammed together on hooks. The floor was full of shavings and the air thick with motes. A man was bent over a long table in the centre of the room, planing a length of pale wood from end to end. He nodded briefly as Drozde entered and bent over his work again. It was a full two minutes before he completed the job to his satisfaction and looked up.

"Sorry to have kept you, lady," he said. "The trick is to keep a steady hand all the way along; I didn't want to stop halfway. How can I help you?"

He seemed young to be the master carpenter: no older than Drozde herself, a wiry, alert-looking man, as clean-cut and brown-skinned as one of the carvings on the bench. "Meister Stefanu?" she hazarded.

He laughed. "Not me! The master works at home most mornings. I'm Anton Hanslo, the journeyman here. But tell me what you need, my lady, and I'll see if I can help." This time the glance he gave her was one of frank appraisal, and Drozde sighed inwardly. If the detachment was to spend the winter in Narutsin, she might have to patronise this workshop regularly, and she could do without complications. She put both hands on the work table so he could see the wedding ring and told him crisply what she needed: cylinder shapes of ash or beech wood, a dozen of finger-width and eight more in varying, wider thicknesses. She marked out the widths she needed in the sawdust on the tabletop and had him note down the dimensions on his slate, which took him some time.

"Or if that's too difficult," she added, when he didn't answer at once, "I'll take thin slats, the same width. Four each for the bigger sizes and forty of the little ones. Can you manage that?

"You'll get your rounds," Hanslo said quickly. "No trouble at all there. But I'm curious, is all. You going to work these yourself? What are you making, if I might be so bold?"

He'd dropped the "lady," Drozde was pleased to see, and was looking at her now with a certain respect. She allowed herself to unbend a little. "I make puppets," she told him, and produced the coquette. "This one has an older sister who's been scratched up a bit and needs a new nose."

His eyes widened in surprise. He reached for the little doll, and after a moment's hesitation Drozde handed it to him. "She's well made," he said, turning the puppet over delicately in his calloused hands. "So you'll copy her head to replace the other?"

"Just the nose."

He whistled softly, studying the detail of the coquette's unpainted hand. "Tricky job. You'll need a fine-grained wood: I'll try to match up this one. And how do you fix it on? A peg, or glue?"

They talked for a while about finishes and varnish, the price of nails and the relative merits of knife and chisel for detail work. Drozde found she was enjoying herself. It was pleasant for once to be treated as a fellow craftsman. She told him something about the shows she put on and heard in return about his work: very little fine carving, he said sadly; mostly house repairs, door hangings and coffins, though sometimes one of the better-off villagers might commission a table or a new set of chairs after a particularly good harvest.

"But carving, now, that's what I like the best," he said, his tone warming. "I never had much learning; can't write much, as you see." He looked down ruefully at the numbers he had scrawled on the slate. "But I can do fine work if there's a call for it. Have a look at these."

He led her over to the workbench and showed her a row of carvings pushed to the back. An angry goose, beak open, with her gosling pressed against her feet; two boys fishing, their backs against a stump; a girl scrutinising a limp chicken at arm's length. It was skilled work, and Drozde said so.

"It's my record," Hanslo said, reddening a little but clearly pleased. "Sometimes you see a thing that you remember." He picked up a smaller, unfinished carving; a skinny cat, sitting expectantly with its head to one side. "Like this one. She used to come to the door for scraps when I was a boy."

Drozde was looking at the girl with the chicken. Her face, with its look of deep suspicion, was so well captured that she had the feeling she had met her before. "That's Bosilka, the master's daughter," Hanslo told her. "It was a few years ago when that happened. A feast day. She got to the market late, and there was only the one chicken left. She wouldn't have it in the end; we had to eat fish, and the master wasn't pleased." He laughed. "I think that's why he won't keep this one in the house."

His face was younger when he smiled, cheerful and reckless. The carpenter was good company, no doubt about it, Drozde thought, and not at all bad-looking. But of course it would not do. She thanked him for his time and arranged to come back and pick up the wood in a few days. "How much will it be?" she asked, reaching for her purse.

"Oh, as to that," Hanslo said, "it's a small job, and as much a pleasure as a chore. If you'll take a drink with me when it's done, and maybe show me your work afterwards, we'll call it quits."

"I'll pay what I owe you," Drozde said firmly. For an instant the man looked almost comically downcast, but he recovered himself quickly and asked for two *cruitzers*, a reasonable enough sum that she felt no need to haggle. As she counted out the coins he painstakingly wrote the amount on a slip of wood.

"Thank you," he said, handing it to her. "That's to say you've paid in full."

There was something a little hurt about his formality; Drozde felt inclined to laugh. "I'll be glad to show you the other puppet, though," she said. "When I've mended her."

He brightened up at once. "That would be good! And then we could have that drink."

I didn't say anything about a drink, Drozde thought. It was not a good idea to get into a man's debt, however pretty his smile. But the carpenter seemed well-meaning, and she held her peace for the time being.

As she went to collect the puppet from where Hanslo had left it on the table, the door opened and a girl came in. Drozde recognised the big basket on her arm, now full of parcels: she was the one who had come to the clothier's stall as Drozde left. A moment later she realised why the face was familiar. She was also the girl in Hanslo's carving, the master carpenter's daughter who had gone to work for the burgomaster. No wonder Hanna had stopped her gossiping so suddenly when she appeared. The girl certainly didn't have the air of a husband-hunter: she was small and slight and demure, her light brown hair neatly braided beneath a cap and her dress fastened at the throat.

"Silkie!" Hanslo greeted her. "Won't your mistress be wondering where you are? It's nearly midday."

"You can run up there yourself, Anton, if you're so worried," the girl returned, with the quizzical look that Hanslo had captured in his carving. "I'm sure you could polish the candlesticks better than me."

"Ah, no." Hanslo shuddered theatrically. "Have you bought something good for our suppers?"

"For father's supper," Bosilka told him pertly. "You'll get yours if you behave yourself." She saw Drozde and dropped her a quick curtsy, then turned back to Hanslo. "Eggs, good large ones, and some bread," she told him, removing each item from her basket as she named it and laying it on the table. "Onions, a leek and a cabbage. And I found some nuts too."

Nuts, Drozde remembered: she'd promised Molebacher to look for some. She was about to ask Bosilka where in the market they'd been on sale when the girl gave an exclamation.

"When did you make this, Anton?"

She was looking at the coquette, running a finger over the painted face. "She's beautiful. You should make more like her."

"Not mine, Silkie!" Hanslo said. "This lady is a puppet-maker."

Bosilka turned to Drozde, her face alight. "You carved her! May I pick her up?"

She handled the puppet reverently, stroking the material of her dress and admiring the detail of her face and hands. She asked Drozde how the joints were made, and what sort of paint she had used. She clearly understood the tools of the carpenter's trade: her father ought to have made the girl his apprentice, Drozde thought, rather than sending her off to clean the burgomaster's candlesticks. She glanced at Hanslo, wondering if he resented the loss of Bosilka's attention, but he was looking at the girl with an expression of kindly indulgence.

"Give the lady her puppet back, Silkie," he said. "She has somewhere to go, and so do you."

The spark left Bosilka's face. She curtsied again with lowered eyes, returned the puppet and busied herself with her groceries. Drozde felt a sudden irritation with Anton Hanslo. She raised a hand in farewell and left the workshop to do her own shopping.

It was late afternoon before she returned to Pokoj. She had made a half-dozen more useful acquaintances, learned some gossip which was mostly too trivial to be of use to her, and worn out her shoulders. The haversack Molebacher had given her was too small for all the foodstuffs he'd told her to get, and she had bought herself a basket almost as big as Bosilka's, which bumped painfully against her leg on the long walk back.

Molebacher was satisfied with her haul. When she gave him the hazelnuts he grunted, and rewarded her with a full half-share of the mutton stew he had made for their supper. He was serving the officers and their wives again tonight, he told her, and drinking afterwards with the artillery sergeants, who were much in demand. Jursitizky had promised to show them all the great gun Mathilde, he said, and explain how she worked.

She! Drozde thought. Gertrude. Mathilde. Why was it that whenever a man had a murderous tool, be it a cleaver or a big gun, he insisted on turning it into a woman? But she swallowed her irritation, smiled, and left Molebacher to his chopping. She had gifts for the other women in the camp: mushrooms and fresh plums that had sold cheaply as the market closed, and willow bark to make tea for Alis, who was suffering her cramps. She spent a pleasant half-hour regaling them with some of the filthier tales she had heard at the market. But then Ottilie and Libush were called away by their corporals, and Sarai gathered most of the others around her for a card reading. Drozde often enjoyed the readings—she had no faith in the predictions, but Sarai was a good performer. This evening, though, she didn't have the patience. She was tired of company, she told herself.

When Molebacher left the kitchen to attend to the officers, she slipped downstairs to visit her puppets in the kitchen cellar. If he was going to have more of these gunnery nights, she might use the time to whittle a new puppet or two: another little girl, perhaps. Her paints and glue were fairly fresh, and she still had some ends of cotton material as well as the new ribbon. She sat down with her sharpening stone and put in some time restoring the edges on her chisels, promising herself that she'd borrow Molebacher's leather strop tomorrow for the knives.

By this time it was dark. Drozde sighed, and acknowledged to herself that she was bored and lonely. She went upstairs and wandered through the house until she could no longer hear the buzz of conversation and clatter of cutlery from the officers' dinner. Then she stopped and closed her eyes.

"Magda," she said aloud.

The child was there. She felt the light pressure of her hand before she had finished speaking, and opened her eyes to see her ecstatic smile.

"I knew you'd come!" Magda said. "Do you want to play a game?"

"I'm tired tonight," Drozde said. "Let's just sit and talk, if you don't mind."

Magda was serious at once. "In that case," she said, "you should hear someone else's story."

Drozde had listened to too many stories today. "Not now," she began. But the girl was already pulling her down a corridor. She couldn't understand how a touch so nearly non-existent could be so compelling.

"It's like you always say," Magda told her. "We've got all the time in the world, but that still might not be enough."

"I've said I'm tired!" Drozde protested. But Magda only tugged harder.

"That's all right! You only have to sit and listen. And the stories are important. You *said* that!"

Drozde gave in and let the child lead her. They went to the ballroom, as she had known they would—clearly it was a part of the ghosts' ritual, as necessary to their tellings as she herself now seemed to be. Perhaps, Drozde thought, they congregated here every night, in the hope that she or someone else who could fulfil her function would turn up. But when she opened the door, they had never once looked surprised to see her. They knew that she would come, just as Magda had known that the kitten would live. And she saw again a couple of figures who withdrew as she came in, almost as if they had only waited for her arrival to go about some other business. She could not fathom their behaviour: not how they could expect her so confidently, nor why those few seemed to flee her, nor—especially—why most of them received her with such pleasure. And she felt a sudden desire, stronger even than her tiredness, to sound the bottom of this mystery.

As she reached the centre of the ballroom, the murmured conversations of the ghosts ceased, and there was an expectant silence. She turned in a slow circle, meeting the gazes of the ghosts immediately around her. "Whose story shall we hear tonight?" she asked, and she felt now the subtle weight those words carried, a ritual significance which gave the atmosphere in the room a different quality, as hard to define as the difference in quality between the air in the evening and the morning.

The figure who came forward this time wavered for a moment as if approaching from some great distance. Drozde could not see it clearly at first, but the voice she heard was a woman's, though deep and strangely accented. Then the speaker was fully there: very short, with long tangled hair, wearing a shapeless tunic that reached no lower than her knees. Her feet were bare, but there was a glint of gold around her neck and a matching glitter in her dark eyes.

Drozde leaned against the rail, surrounded by shadows, and listened with growing amazement to the day's last story.

13

It is hard to say when my time was in relation to your time. It was a handful of handfuls of handfuls of years ago, and probably some years more. My people lived on this ground, and we called it Khethyu. We called ourselves Khethyu also.

It was very hot and very humid, with warm winds coming all the time from the east. Like living inside the chest of a man who is snoring, or in a bread oven when the bread is rising. It was a blessed place. The earth teemed with life and the possibility of life, so that if a man chewed tree bark and spat on the ground a tree grew in that place. And if a woman squatted to piss, the stream became an oasis and deer came there.

The blessings came from the river goddess, Panafya. She loved the Khethyu as any mother loves her children, and wanted all good things to come to us. We gave her our love and worship in return. We promised never to drop stepping stones into her body: the proper way to cross a river is to wade or to swim, trusting the goddess not to take you, though she always could. And whenever we dipped so much as a foot in her waters, we felt Panafya's caress and knew her love for us.

We had no other gods, but there was one devil who we were compelled to acknowledge. His name was Shin and he lived in the great well that he dug out with his claws in the before times—the well that gave us water even in the dry season. It was Panafya's water, of course. She gave water freely to everyone. But sly Shin never drank his water. He hoarded it at the bottom of his well and counted the drops the way a farmer counts his goats.

So when the dry season came and the only water to be had was from Shin's well, we Khethyu came to borrow it. But we placated the devil with prayers, and we always paid him back in the spring when the river flooded.

We placated him in another way, too. Every year a boy and a girl were chosen to dance for Shin on the great flat stone beside his well—a very difficult and complicated dance. They danced naked, and afterwards they fucked with all of the Khethyu looking on and singing a praise. In this way they dedicated both their skill and the beauty of their bodies to the devil.

But one year the girl who was chosen for the dance was Arinak, a vain and empty-headed thing. It is no spite or envy in me to say this, because Arinak was me. I had no thought in my head beside the thought that I was cleverer, more beautiful and more admirable than any woman had ever been. I thought the devil was lucky that I'd been chosen to dance for him, and the boy, Dimut, was lucky that he would get to fuck with me. I thought the sun was lucky to shine on me and the earth to bear my feet.

And those were the thoughts that were in my heart when I danced.

It was a glorious day, a wild dance, and a joyful lovemaking. I had never been so happy. When we were done, Dimut asked me if I would walk under the marriage tree and pick a fruit and eat it with him. I kissed him—because his admiration made me happy—but I told him no. I wanted an older man with more than a single handful of goats to his name. I was sure that plenty of older men would come to court me.

But that was not how things fell out.

The morning after the dance I pushed my friend Venni in play and she fell the wrong way, so that her leg broke. Her furious family demanded half our herd and half our honour stones in compensation, and the elders agreed it. They were right to do so. The leg healed thwart and Venni was crippled.

Then my mother fell ill of a fever that would not abate, until in the end her wits left her and she could no longer talk. Only sit in the fire pit and run her fingers through the warm ashes as though she had lost something there.

Then five of our goats died in five nights, one after another, with no sign of sickness. They just fell to the ground as though someone had hit them with a stone.

So many disasters in so short a time caused people to ask what curse had fallen on my family, and what sin it could have been that had brought the curse down. My father, made furious by such wicked gossip, told them to mind their own affairs. And so they did. A circle cleared around our house, as though there was plague within it.

Dimut was the only one who still called on us, and still greeted us when we walked abroad. What's more, he proposed to me again. He didn't mind, he said, if I was cursed. He'd rather be cursed with me than blessed with some other woman.

I'm ashamed to say this, but I took his kindness badly. It looked like pity to me, and I told him sharply to take his nonsense to someone who had the time to listen to it.

But his words set me thinking. Up until then I had thought of these troubles as belonging to us all alike—to my mother and my father, my sisters and brother as well as to me. Only when Dimut said "if *you* are cursed," meaning me and me alone, did I begin to wonder if this could possibly be true.

And once I had thought that thought, I had to know the answer. I asked my great-uncle's wife, Ghuda, what steps I should take to find out a curse, and she told me a very powerful finding spell. I can't tell it to you because it belongs to my people and isn't mine to give, but I can tell you it involved the blood of the moon and the shadow of a cat that had eaten its own kittens.

At this point a wail of protest rose from Magda, who was sternly shushed by the other ghosts. "Drozde's rules!" they whispered, and the dead girl subsided with bad grace.

I bled the moon, and walked the outline of the cat's shadow. I did ten other things besides, and as the thirteenth thing I turned in my own footsteps to see what was behind me. If there was a curse on me, it should have been standing or lying there upon the ground, plain to see. But there was nothing. Nothing at all that I could see.

I laughed with relief.

And then stiffened in horror, because another voice laughed alongside mine.

"Who's there?" I cried.

"Who do you think?" said the other voice. And the cruelty in its tone made me shake like a spider's web in a rainstorm.

"The devil from the well," I said, because somehow I knew that that was who it was.

"Give me my name."

"Shin!"

"Yes. I am Shin, and I will hound and torment you until you go mad and die by your own hand."

"But why?" I wailed. "I danced for you!"

"Ah, but you danced with stupid, skittish and disrespectful thoughts in your mind. The dance is meant to be tribute to me. Yours was mockery."

"I didn't mean it as mockery!"

"All the same," the devil said, "that was how I took it."

I was aghast. I knew now what I'd done, and that all the terrible things that had happened were due to my transgression. I had already blamed myself for Venni being maimed, and for the loss of my family's wealth and honour, but the dead goats were my fault too. And worst of all, I had visited madness on my mother.

I spent the night on a bare rock over a precipice. I was dazed with guilt. A hundred times I thought to cast myself down into the abyss, I hated myself so much—and Shin encouraged me to do it, telling me that I would never know any peace in this world until I was dead.

But I endured, somehow, and in the morning I went before the elders. I told them what I had discovered, that the demon from the well was persecuting me and all the people I loved. I begged them to allow me to dance before the well again, or failing that to try to appease Shin with some other offering.

They refused outright. As far as they could see, they said, the sin was mine and the punishment was also mine, which was right and good. Since Shin hated me, he would probably not be happy to see me dance again. And if they offered further sacrifice, Shin might come to expect it in future years, which would be a burden to all the people forever. Better to let things run their course.

They told me that I was banished. They told me to expect no help or welcome from the people, then or ever.

I was weeping with grief and rage when I left the elder circle. I almost walked into Dimut, who had been waiting for me the whole time. He told me again that he loved me and would be happy to marry me, even with the demon's hatred and the banishment thrown into the bargain.

The boy was clearly mad. But his bravery and his devotion warmed and cheered me. And Goddess, I was cold and miserable then! It would have been easy to fall into his arms. But it would have destroyed him. I could feel Shin's breath on my shoulder. If I showed any fondness for Dimut, I would only be teaching the demon where to strike next.

"Don't you have anybody else to bother?" I shouted at him. "Do you have to be crawling around my feet all the time? A dream told you that you loved me, and you believed the dream. Wake up, and see the truth. I won't be yours until the river wets the treetops!"

I left him there and turned my steps towards home. But I heard the demon's steps echoing mine, and my loathing of him rose in me like a flood. I began to run.

I ran into the forest, where the thorns are thickest. They tore my skin to ribbons, but it did not avail me. "I'm still here!" Shin chuckled. "Nothing you can do will shake me loose."

I ran into the desert, where the sun beats like a hammer. I pushed on through the heat of the day, letting it burn my skin red and black, but it did not avail me. "I'm right at your side," Shin gloated. "You're wasting your time."

I ran to the cliff edge where I had sat the night before, and jumped from rock to rock over drops so steep they made the breath stop in my throat, but it did not avail me. "I like it here," Shin sighed. "It's very cozy when it's just the two of us."

I stopped running then, and sat me down and thought. Was there any place in the world that would be easier for me to bear than him? Any place where I might cast him off? At first I could think of none. But at last a strange inspiration came to me. Blasphemy and disrespect had brought me to this terrible situation. Perhaps they could save me too.

I jumped to my feet and began to run again. I ran to the flood plain, which—this being high summer—was an endless wasteland of cracked mud. I sought a place I knew, and when I found it I stood my ground.

"What did that achieve?" Shin jeered. "It was barely a stroll to me, while you seem to have used up the last of your strength."

It was true that I was exhausted, but I defied him anyway. I spat on the ground at his feet. "You are nothing!" I shouted. "Your power is so weak, a baby could topple you!"

That seemed to anger him. "You little animal!" he growled. "Your mind isn't big enough even to imagine my power! There is nothing like me in the world!"

"Nothing like you," I agreed. "But many things greater than you."

"No! Nothing! Nothing greater!" His voice was right in my ear now, as though he stood at my side and leaned his head forward to disgorge his answer at me.

"Yes there is. There is the goddess!"

"Panafya? That dull-eyed cow! I'd smack her head right off her shoulders if she ever dared to cope me! I'd rip her heart and lungs and lights out if she so much as—"

"IF SHE SO MUCH AS WHAT?"

The voice that cut across Shin's was so vast and loud it was like a mountain falling on us—and yet so musically beautiful that my arms, which I had raised to cover my ears, remained frozen in the air halfway.

Panafya rose before us, a tower of water with a face that frowned down on the demon and on me from the zenith of the sky.

This was her place. The place where the river flows in autumn and winter and spring. But in high summer there was no water there to show where it ended or began. When I had spat, I had prayed a summoning—water of any kind being a right offering to the river goddess. I had brought her there so that she might hear Shin's blasphemy against her, if he could be coaxed into uttering one.

"Panafya!" the demon gasped. "Great one! I . . . I meant no insult!"

"THEN WHY INSULT ME? WHY DRAG MY NAME THROUGH YOUR STENCHING MOUTH AT ALL?"

I saw Shin now for the first time, as the goddess's gaze stripped him of all his protections and disguises. He was not as impressive as I had imagined him. He was a good deal taller than a man, but his limbs were gangly and pocked with sores, and the splintered teeth in his grimacing mouth stuck out in all directions like sticks of kindling on a bonfire.

But water, not fire, was his nemesis.

Panafya raised her hand—she had not had a hand until then, but she had one to call on when she wanted it—and brought it down. A great wave kicked us, as hard as a wild horse kicks, and knocked us off our feet.

I heard Shin wailing and begging as he was dragged under.

I saw river weeds wrap around his arms and legs and throat to still his struggles.

I saw the silt of the river bottom swallow him like a mouth.

Then I saw only sparkling lights and encroaching darkness, because I was drowning.

But strong arms embraced me, and lifted me to the surface, where I gulped and wriggled like a fish on a line. It was Dimut, of course. We rode out the flood tide, he and I, each in turn giving strength to the other when the other seemed ready to give up and slip under. We held each other more tightly than we had in our lovemaking.

When the deluge abated, we lay in each other's arms in the clinging mud, so spent that for a long while we could not even speak. When we could, Dimut asked me again to be his wife, and I said yes. We did not need a marriage tree.

"We'll go away," he said, "and find another people who will take us in. We're young and strong, and we can work. Someone will want us. Or else we'll start our own tribe, somewhere in the hills where there's a lake for the goats to drink from and wood to make a house."

It was a pleasant dream. But I liked the river plain, I loved my family, and I had a better idea.

I went back to Khethyu. To my people. I told them Shin was dead, by my hand. I told them the goddess had risen at my bidding, even in the bone-dry summer, and shown her winter face.

I told them that Dimut and I were to be numbered among the elders now, and that anyone who said no had better be a strong swimmer.

We lived long here. We had thirteen sons and daughters, and ten of them lived. So many were the generations of my children that they called me Arinak Imat Basya—thousand-times-blessed Arinak.

But they called me Demonslayer too, and I liked that name better.

After the story was done, and the ghosts had thanked Arinak with their silent applause, Drozde felt compelled to ask the question that was uppermost in her mind. But she was conscious, too, of the etiquette she was gradually learning.

"Thank you, Arinak, for your story," she said. "It was well told, and though your world seems very far from mine, you brought it closer to me."

The pale spectre threw out her arms and ducked her head in a strange, exaggerated bow. "That was my only wish," she said. "*Ia*, Drozde. *Ia*, Pokoj and my new tribe. My death tribe."

The cue fell convenient to Drozde's purpose, and she picked it up with alacrity. "You said you lived on this ground," she said. "Did you mean right here?" She pointed at the faded wooden tiles that made up the floor of the ballroom. "Did you live and die where we're standing now?"

Arinak seemed uncertain of how to answer. She thought for a moment, then made a circular gesture with both hands. "We lived all through the valley," she said, "and in the hills on both sides of it. Panafya was our life, so we stayed close to the river. My home when I was wife and mother was quite far from here, on the western bank by Scowling Brow. But Shin's well was here." She pointed towards the rear of the house. "It still is, of course, though he's long gone. And this was where I died. I fell down one day—the day of my fifth granddaughter's naming—and I died where I fell."

"And was buried here?" Drozde ventured.

Arinak shook her head emphatically. "No indeed. We Khethyu buried our dead close to where the river rises, at Six Spring. The running water . . ." She seemed to grope for a word. "It makes things clean. All sorts of things. Even souls."

"The river still followed its old course through the Drench in those days," the ghost of Meister Gelbfisc observed. "She probably means Zielona Góra."

At the mention of the river being moved from its place—presumably a terrible sacrilege for Arinak—she covered her eyes and fled. Meister Gelbfisc was widely censured under the rules of Drozde, which were recited again with as much gusto as before.

"Why do you name your manifesto after me?" Drozde demanded. She had held her peace through the tale, but felt free to speak now. A thought occurred to her. "Was it my puppet shows that gave you the idea for this game of storytelling?"

The ghosts seemed shocked and perturbed. "It's not a game!" Magda exclaimed. "Drozde, don't say that, not even as a joke! It's everything!"

"How we live and who we are," another ghost confirmed. He was a slight but very handsome man in a military uniform that—Drozde saw now—was quite different from the uniforms of the soldiers in the company. Was he, like Arinak, a warrior from a long-ago time, or a soldier from another country who had fought and died here? Because dying here, she had come to realise, was the crucial requirement for membership of this group. Pokoj was home to those who had breathed their last breath within its grounds, whether they'd lived there formerly or not.

"But still," she persisted, "why do you say I made it up?"

All the dead faces looked uncomfortable, and Magda's most of all. "It's easier to say that," she ventured, "than to explain. Explaining is hard, and you . . . someone . . . It's . . ." She pursed her lips, frowning with a child's ferocious seriousness. "We're not supposed to tell it yet," she said.

"When, then?" Drozde asked.

"After you know some other things."

"And you can't just tell me the other things now?"

Magda shook her head.

With a loud tut of impatience, Drozde turned her back on the group and walked away; she had no more energy for these intrigues tonight. Their pleas and protests and frantic apologies faded quickly behind her.

14

Lieutenant Klaes made his observations, and then his plans.

The girl Bosilka's employment in the burgomaster's household seemed to involve no regular hours. She went there most mornings and stayed through the serving of the midday meal, but after that each day was different. She might leave immediately or stay to do some other work, whether cleaning floors, washing clothes or feeding the chickens in the little yard in front of the house. On market days (Thursday in Narutsin and Tuesday in neighbouring Stollenbet) she did Dame Weichorek's shopping. On Sundays she herded the younger children to church while the parents and the oldest son walked ahead in solemn state.

Klaes planned to make his approach on market day, taking advantage of the crowds and the general atmosphere of openness and holiday. But when it came to it, he found he couldn't commit himself to an exploit that was so open to a dishonourable interpretation. Despite August's suggestion, he had no intention of paying court to this woman. She was young and naïve and, although he knew the colonel thought otherwise, he was convinced that she had never been wooed before. Attentions of that sort from him, an officer in the Austrian army, would probably turn her head, and he drew the line at breaking a country girl's heart for the sake of his commission. Yet if he accosted her on a market day, anyone watching would assume at once that his mind was set on some sort of dalliance.

So he waited until Sunday, and went to church. None of the other officers in the company would be there, because this was a Protestant church in which the anti-papist revolutionary Jan Hus was thought of as a third Saint John alongside the Evangelist and the Baptist. Klaes suspected Hus had been more rogue than saint, but he held to his parents' faith insofar as he held to any at all. Low church was good church, wherever you found it.

The little stone chapel was full to the brim with the stolid citizenry of Narutsin. As Klaes walked in, he felt rather than heard the shift in volume which indicated that a dozen conversations had been halted by his entrance. He was the only soldier there. He knew he had a few co-religionists in the detachment, but clearly that morning they were not feeling devout—or else, perhaps, they were more fiercely partisan. Whatever the reason, it left Klaes as a conspicuous flash of military green in a sea of homespun greys and browns. He hurried to an empty pew at the back, desperate to escape the collective gaze of the townsfolk. Nobody seemed inclined to join him there.

Bosilka was in the front row along with the burgomaster's family, and she noticed him at once. She seemed surprised to see him there, and perhaps a little curious. She stole several glances at him before dropping her gaze each time back to her hymnal, which she was surely holding for propriety's sake only. It was vanishingly unlikely that she could actually read.

After the service, as the congregation filed out into the churchyard, Klaes fell in with the girl as if by accident. "This is shocking to see," he said, aiming for a bantering tone. "A woman your age with such a large family. And with no husband in sight."

It was a weak joke, but he thought it was a harmless one. He expected the girl to blush a little and to hasten to explain her relationship with the children, which would be a doorway or entry point for discussion of other things related to the life of the village. And he would then be halfway to his goal.

Instead Bosilka put on a vexed expression and turned away.

"Well, well," Klaes pursued. "Doubtless you've suitors enough. Or more than enough. Is this a subterfuge then? To seem a mother hen, with chicks, the better to fright away random cocks?"

Now Bosilka looked at him again, but with no trace of a smile. If anything, she seemed even more angry than before. "Any man who fronts me had better keep his cock well tucked away," she said coldly.

Klaes was not expecting such forthrightness. And he had not even registered his double entendre until the words were out. It occurred to him that the glances the girl had cast his way in the church might not have indicated complaisance but only curiosity.

"They are your employer's children," he said. From his suddenly exposed position, a banal statement of fact seemed like a redoubt.

But Bosilka was neither deflected nor appeased. "Soldiers are the likeliest ones to take away a girl's honour," she said, with a sort of ferocity in her tone now. "Whether she consents or not. And yet they're the likeliest ones to joke about it. Why is that? Does it make them feel better about themselves?"

Beleaguered, Klaes made one last half-hearted sortie. It was a matter of wonder to him how bad he was at this—at simple conversation! It looked so easy when someone like Dietmar did it. "None of my men would violate a helpless woman," he said. "The punishment for that is flogging or summary execution."

Bosilka slowed for a moment, looking at him in astonished silence as if she was struggling to find words robust enough to carry the freight of her feeling. "What you just said didn't even make any sense!" she exclaimed at last. "If none of them ever do it, why do you have a penalty already set aside for it? Just in case? Don't speak to me, Captain. Don't walk with me."

She tugged on the younger children's hands and took them away at a quick march. The older children ran to keep up.

So did Klaes.

"I apologise," he said when he was abreast of Bosilka again. He meant it. The girl's cheeks were flushed, her eyes darting in every direction. There was no doubting the ferment of her emotions, and it filled him with dismay and self-disgust to think that he had been the cause of it. It was as though words were a sort of ordnance, and he had given forth a general volley without gauging range or wind. He was trying now to accomplish the impossible task of recalling a spent shot.

His own experience, of course, was not in artillery but in engineering. What he was most skilled at was undermining an enemy position. Or, as it turned out, his own.

At any rate Bosilka made no answer. She only shook her head and looked away again. But she didn't bolt this time, so Klaes was able to go on talking. Unfortunately, he now had a wider audience. The children were all looking at him with wide eyes and slightly fearful expressions. "You'll have to forgive me, Miss . . . ?"

"Stefanu."

"Miss Stefanu. Or might I call you Bosilka?"

"You don't need to call me anything."

"Army life abrades both a man's manners and his language. He forgets, sometimes, what civil quotidian discourse means."

"I have no idea what it means. But if it's what you're doing to me, I'd like you to stop. Leave me alone, Captain."

"I'm only a lieutenant."

She wrung her hands in exasperation. "Then leave me alone, *Lieutenant!*"

Others were looking now, including the burgomaster, whose expression was darkening into a scowl. Klaes didn't fear the man. His authority was nugatory. But it would be galling to have him complain to the colonel, and to have the colonel apprised, therefore, of how bad a spy Klaes was turning out to be. Outfaced and outmanoeuvred, he had no option but to withdraw.

But he had one shot left, as it were, in his depleted armoury. He had observed Bosilka walking home, and knew the route she would take, along the village's main (almost its only) street to its very end, and then down a narrower track between trees to the cottage half a mile away where she lived with her father, the village carpenter.

He waited for her by a stile which stood conveniently at the midpoint of her journey. He thought he could make it appear as though his being there was a coincidence. It was a place where a man might pause in his walking to scrape the mud from his boots or take a sip or two of schnapps from his *flasquette*. And an offer to help the girl over the stile would be an excellent and almost foolproof way of engaging her in conversation.

Bosilka's irregular working hours meant that Klaes had no way of knowing when she would come. He took a pipe and tobacco from his sabretache and smoked while he waited, a thing he did very seldom. Then he tamped out the knockings on the heel of his boot and waited some more. Men's voices and the rhythmic impacts of an axe floated through the trees at his back.

It was not yet evening, but the day was already beginning to wane. The light was leaking half-heartedly out of the sky, and the wind was getting an edge to it. That thought led Klaes back to the colonel's entirely uncalled-for comment about his sabre. He cursed under his breath, shying away from the vulgar image.

It was true that he was a virgin. But he didn't see this as a character flaw. A private or an officer without a commission had all-too-frequent opportunities to indulge his carnal appetites in tent brothels provided free of charge by a branch of the army's quartermaster corps. Officers above the rank of sergeant were not expected to take part in these demeaning rituals, but if a man chose to have a girl visit him in his quarters, he could be confident that a blind eye would be turned. Klaes had never felt tempted. Women were a slightly fearsome mystery to him, and he was waiting for an occasion when he could meet one, as it were, on his own terms. He was now older than his father had been when he was born, and the opportunity still hadn't arisen.

He stood at last, reluctantly conceding that he was wasting his time. The girl had anticipated him and gone home another way. Or perhaps she had an assignation elsewhere. He already knew that she lacked the modesty and diffidence that became a young woman—or a woman of any age. He was now beginning to wonder if her chastity was not similarly wanting.

It was at this point, as he was poised on the brink of going, that he caught sight of Bosilka walking towards him along the path. She was no longer in her Sunday best, but had changed into a plain smock and shirt. Her light brown hair was bound up into a ferociously tight bun from which the wind had nonetheless contrived to release a few stray wisps.

She saw Klaes a moment after he saw her. Her face had already a solemn aspect, but at sight of him she positively grimaced. He thought she might actually turn back rather than meet him, but she kept up the same pace and only stopped when she came to the stile itself. She said not a word, but only looked at him expectantly—or perhaps suspiciously.

"We're met again, *Panna* Stefanu," Klaes observed.

"*Panna*," the girl echoed. "*Panna* Stefanu. Is that meant to flatter me, Captain?"

Klaes shrugged, all innocence. "Is it flattery to use your own language?"

"It might be, if you got it right. We don't say *Panna* here. We say *Slečna*."

Bohemian, or something like it, not Silesian. Why hadn't he known that? Because this region had a hundred dialects, and wherever two of them met they melted together and made a third. Everyone made shift by using Meissner Deutsch as a lingua franca where it was needed, and that was close enough to Klaes's own Schönbrunner that he needed no translator and could make himself understood without difficulty.

So he had made what seemed like a reasonable assumption and put his foot in the slop bucket yet again.

"I'm sorry," he said, gritting his teeth. "*Slečna* Stefanu."

"Why?" Bosilka demanded.

"I beg your pardon?"

"Why are you sorry? It doesn't matter. Stand out of my way, please. I'd like to get over the stile."

"Allow me to help you."

He held out his hand, and she stepped back from it very quickly. "No."

Klaes persisted. "I promise you, I mean you no insult. I know I offended you earlier, and you thought I was speaking lewdly to you, but I assure you I wasn't. Let me help you, and walk with you until you reach your house."

"Why?" Bosilka asked again. The same wary look was on her face.

Klaes groped for an answer. "For your own safety."

"And what should threaten me?"

It wasn't always like this, Klaes decided. It couldn't be. If all women challenged everything that all men said, without exception, then no conversation would ever have been finished in the history of the world. This was almost as bad as an argument with that horrendous trull, Drozde. And all discussions with her became arguments sooner or later. He would have slapped her with the flat of his sword more than once, except that it would have demeaned him more than it hurt her.

"Wild beasts," he said to the girl. "Footpads. Anything."

"Wild beasts, footpads and anything." Bosilka smiled faintly. "You think you're a long way from Vienna, don't you, Captain?"

"Oh yes. A *very* long way," Klaes said feelingly. Then he parsed his own words and apologised again. "Miss Stefanu, I know that this isn't the edge of the world. All the same, a young woman walking alone—"

"Not a hundred paces from her own house."

"—in the middle of a forest, where if anything untoward befell her, her cries might not be heard."

"Oh, and that sounds like a threat." The smile vanished at once. She folded her arms and glowered at him.

"It was not a threat," Klaes said, exasperated now. "You take everything I say the wrong way."

"Do I?"

"Yes, you do."

"Well, then there's nothing to be done. We should both get about our business and stop wasting each other's time."

She made a move to pass him. On an impulse he reached out and caught her arm. As soon as he touched her, Bosilka screamed and pulled away from him so violently that she almost fell.

She stifled the scream almost at once, though she was still shaking and she struggled to speak, the words catching at first in her throat. "I don't like to be touched. You shouldn't have touched me."

Klaes had no answer to that. It was true, of course, and he might have apologised again. But he felt certain that any apology would be an occasion for further misprisions, so he waited instead for Bosilka to recover herself, dropping his hands to his sides to signal that he would keep his distance.

"I don't like to be touched," she said again, with a movement that might have been either a shrug or a shudder.

"I shouldn't have touched you," Klaes offered earnestly. "It was disrespectful."

Bosilka nodded. This was something, although perhaps not much—an acknowledgement of his words at their own face value. Thus encouraged, Klaes gestured to her to sit on the crosspiece of the stile. "Until your spirits are restored," he suggested. Then, noticing that the crosspiece was muddied, he took out his kerchief to wipe it off. It was something of a performance—ridiculous, really, given that the kerchief was silk and her gown rough homespun—but he carried it off tolerably well. And of course once it was done, it would have been very hard for her not to sit. Klaes stepped well aside to allow her to do it, tucking the ruined kerchief into his belt rather than putting it back in his pocket.

Bosilka arranged her skirts and sat.

"Thank you, Captain," she said, her voice low and still a little tremulous.

"Lieutenant," Klaes said. "Lieutenant Wolfgang Klaes."

"Thank you, Lieutenant Wolfgang Klaes."

"You are very welcome, *Slečna* Stefanu."

"Nobody ever calls me *Slečna* anything. It just sounds stupid."

"Not even the young men who court you?"

The girl looked at him hard, and he immediately wished the words unsaid. "I only meant . . ." he began.

"You meant a compliment, I know. If you don't try to compliment me, we might get along a little better."

Klaes bowed, accepting the point. That made her laugh. "You learned your manners at court," she said.

"I've never been to court."

"No? But you lived in Vienna, surely."

"Most of my life. May I?" He indicated the stump of a tree next to the stile, and then—since she made no objection—sat down. He made a rigmarole of this too, playing up to her view of him as a dandified *Viennois*. She didn't laugh this time, but she did look amused by him. And he was content to be a fool if it caused her to feel comfortable in his company.

"And now here I am." He indicated with both hands the woods around them, the valley, the village sitting just beyond the treeline.

"At the edge of the world," Bosilka said. His own words from just before.

"At the edge of the empire," Klaes amended. "Carrying the archduchess's mandate into the rural fastnesses where its writ is most attenuated."

"What does *fastnesses* mean?"

"Fortresses. Redoubts. Castles."

"Castles? In the forest?"

"The castle *is* the forest," Klaes explained. "It's a figure of speech. It means that this terrain is as hard to take and to hold as though it were fortified with walls and earthworks."

Bosilka looked all around, her expression sceptical. "It doesn't feel that way to us."

"No? Then it's fortunate you have the bravest soldiers in the empire to protect you. The heroes of Banja Luka and Grocka." Determined to keep the tone light, Klaes inflated his voice with comical bombast but maintained a grave face. He did not mention the fact that at both Banja Luka and Grocka, the imperial forces had been beaten to the wide.

"To protect us?" Bosilka said. "Is that what we're meant to think? That you're here for our sake?"

Klaes's surprise was strong enough to throw him out of character. "Yes, of course," he said bluntly. "Why else?"

"I don't know. Because the archduchess thinks we need a watch kept on us, perhaps?" The girl was staring at him with the same hard scrutiny as before. "You're not the first soldiers we've had here, you know. They never seemed very much concerned with our protection. They only told us what to do, and what not to do, and threatened all sorts of things if we disobeyed. And laid a levy on the village for their provisioning. And beat Rupen Taelep for a brace of hare that weren't even poached."

"Well," Klaes said. "I'm assuming these were Silesian militia? We're not like that at all. Imperial troops, wherever they're stationed, operate under the strictest of discipline. We harbour no pirates."

"Of course not."

"Nor no tyrants. Our authority is laid down in terms, and has its limits."

"Limits! My friend Agnese said they—" She stopped mid-sentence and shook her head violently, as though she admonished herself for saying too much.

"Said what?"

"Nothing. It's not important."

"Please," Klaes said. "If you have fears, I want to allay them. You may speak to me frankly, *Slečna* . . . Miss Stefanu. I'll keep your counsel and work my utmost to answer your concerns."

"Thank you," Bosilka said heavily. She stood. "But I don't have time to talk any more. I've chores to do at home."

Damnation! He had had her talking freely and then somehow undone it all again by an incautious word. He wasn't even sure what it was he'd said.

"Then may we talk again?" he asked her. "I've enjoyed this conversation very much."

"I've chores," Bosilka repeated. She set her foot on the stile and made to climb over. Unthinking, Klaes once again offered his hand. She ignored it, but in navigating around it she ascended the stile at an awkward angle, leaning away from him. He could see that she was unbalanced but didn't dare touch her, and as she put her foot down on the further side she slipped and fell, crying out as she tumbled onto the hard ground.

With a muttered exclamation Klaes leaped over the stile. But once he was beside Bosilka again, he was stymied by the requirement not to touch her. He hovered over her, arms half-extended, waiting for her to accept his offered help. She seemed not to see the gesture, but struggled to right herself while keeping both hands clasped to the skirts of her dress to avoid a shaming display. She was flustered and angry but, as far as he could see, unhurt.

It seemed that this fiasco was already as bad as it could be. But there was comfortable room, still, for further complications.

Running footsteps made Klaes look round. Three men were approaching along the narrow path. All were in labourers' clothes, loose shirts and trousers, buttonless waistcoats and flat sandals. One wore a straw hat whose edges were so ragged it looked as though it was returning to a wild state. Another, whose stature was huge and muscular, carried an axe.

"Oh!" Bosilka muttered as they approached—a strangled sound of desperate exasperation. She was on her feet now and brushing dust from her dress.

"What is it?" the big man called out to her. "Silkie, what's he done to you?"

"Nothing," Bosilka said. "Nothing, Kopesz. I'm very well, thank you. I only tripped and hurt myself, is all."

"Tripped?" straw hat repeated. He gave Klaes a narrow-eyed glare. "Tripped and hurt yourself. Say true now, Silkie. You've nothing to fear with us here."

"I feared nothing before you came!" Bosilka exclaimed. "I'm fine, truly. There's nothing wrong with me."

The three men slowed to a halt some few feet away, nonplussed. They'd thought themselves a rescue party and had now been told that they were no such thing. A change seemed to come over them as they considered this. It was an ugly change—a dawning of some deep and guarded emotion that stole over all three of them at slightly differing speeds.

"Well then," the third man said, "what were you and the captain talking about, before you tripped and hurt yourself?"

"I only said good afternoon to the lady," Klaes said, but none of the three were looking at him or seemed to hear him.

"I wasn't talking to him at all," Bosilka said. She looked genuinely appalled at the imputation. "I don't want to talk to him. He was waiting here, and I was about to pass by him."

"Waiting," said straw hat, giving the word the same insinuating emphasis he'd supplied for *tripped*. "What were you waiting for, Captain? Have you got some business with our Silkie?"

Klaes sighed heavily. His patience was as worn as that ludicrous piece of headgear. "Everybody in this district seems incapable of reading imperial insignia," he said. "My rank is lieutenant, and I'd be obliged if you would make the effort to use it. As to my business with this lady, it is mine and not yours. I don't, therefore, feel obliged to discuss it with you."

The big man swished the axe through the air a few times with tight flicks of his muscular wrist. "What if we was to oblige you?" he said.

Klaes was incredulous. "Oblige me?" he demanded. "You'll oblige me by giving me some room. I've nothing to discuss with you."

"No, you've not," straw hat said belligerently. "Nor with Silkie, neither. So that's agreed, then. You can go your ways and not have discussions with anyone."

Klaes considered. He had nothing to gain by disputing with these yokels, and a great deal to lose in terms of personal dignity. He turned his back on them deliberately, returning his attention to Bosilka. "I trust you took no harm, Miss Stefanu," he said.

Bosilka would not look at him, but kept her gaze on the ground. "I'm very well," she repeated. "Thank you, Lieutenant Klaes."

"Bugger off, Lieutenant Klaes," straw hat jeered.

"Before we give you a haircut," the axe-wielder added.

"I'll take my leave of you, then," Klaes said to Bosilka. "And hope that you enjoy what's left of this Sabbath day."

Her face still averted, Bosilka nodded wordlessly.

"Do you know what we do to soldier boys who cut too much of a swagger?" straw hat demanded.

Enough was enough. Klaes turned to face the three men.

"Speak politely to them, I imagine," he said, drawing his sabre, "and then swear at them behind their backs. That's what your kind generally do. Now be off with you, before I flesh this steel in your backside."

He stepped forward, swishing the sword briskly. He had half-expected the men to flee just at the sight of him—a soldier of the empire with his blood up and his weapon bared.

They did not flee but they did back away, at the same time spreading out so that it was harder for Klaes to keep them all in view at once. The big man was holding the axe *en garde*, as though he thought it might block a sabre thrust. The other two were casting about for sticks to use as clubs.

"Oh, stop this!" Bosilka wailed.

"I'll give you one last warning," Klaes told the three. "Leave this place now, and don't look back. If you make this into a fight, I'll have no other option but to treat you as enemies and show you the same quarter I'd show a Prussian."

The men didn't seem particularly awed by this threat. Straw hat bent and snatched up a branch. Klaes kept his sword up, judging distances. He wasn't seriously intending to use lethal force on these louts—they were barely even armed. But a thrust to straw hat's stomach, checked at the last minute, and a blow to the axeman's arm with the flat of his sabre, just enough to make him drop his weapon, should teach them a valuable lesson.

"Stop!" Bosilka cried out again. She sounded close to hysteria, and Klaes wished he could reassure her. None of this was her fault, and he would make that clear when he reported the incident.

Straw hat was advancing, scuffling his feet through the mush of fallen leaves. Klaes tensed, drawing his weapon back across his body to prepare for a horizontal thrust.

He didn't see what it was that hit him. He was not even really conscious of the blow. One moment he was facing his aggressors with—at the very least—a plan of attack and a determination to prosecute it. The next he was stretched full-length on the cold ground, blackness and light jangling inside his head like church bells without sound.

He tried to rise, but his limbs would not obey him. A formless moan rose in his throat. He had lost for the moment the thread that winds between past and future, so he had no idea where or even who he was.

All he felt was a sense of spinning without moving, and a turbulent stirring in his stomach as though he was about to vomit.

"He's still alive," said a man's voice.

"Of course he's still alive!" A woman now, her tone loud and strident. "And you'll leave him that way too, Kopesz Vilken!"

In recognising Bosilka's voice, Klaes recovered the knowledge of his situation. He had to get up or he was lost. His arms moved feebly, without coordination, like the arms of a baby trying to essay its first crawl.

"He'll tell on us," said the man.

"He doesn't know anything. What would he tell?"

"About Petos. About the cellar, and all that stuff."

"Kopesz, we didn't speak about those things! Not a word!"

"Well then. But what will he say about all this, now? He won't like it, will he?"

"You leave me to worry about that. Go. Go, go, go! You've done enough harm already. Now you'll let me right it, or I'll tell Meister Weichorek what you've done! I will! And then you can answer to him!"

The response to this was fervent in tone but low in volume—as though the men were remonstrating with each other or discussing possible strategies in the face of this apparently dire threat.

"We'll go then," one of the men grunted at last. "But you look to him, Silkie. And don't you be seen around him again!" After these contradictory instructions there was silence for a while, after which the male voices resumed at some further distance. They sounded truculent and defiant, but they were receding quickly.

Klaes returned to his unequal struggle against gravity. He still felt that it was incumbent on him to trounce these ruffians and beat them back into the village with the flat of his sword, the way a farmer drives geese with a paddle. But it seemed this project would have to wait.

As gradually as a cloud drifting by, he rolled over onto his back and sat up. When he touched the back of his head, with gingerly care, his fingers came away bloody. He might have stanched the wound with his kerchief, except that he had fouled it in wiping the stile clean for Bosilka—who was now, he saw, watching him from some distance away. Her face was white and her eyes wide.

"I hit you on the head," she blurted. "And I'll take whatever punishment it might be. But nobody else touched you! Only me." She scowled at him in what might have been defiance, but then her face crumpled and she burst into tears, backing away from him until she bumped into a tree. She sank back against the bark, her head in her hands, sobbing and shaking.

"What did you hit me with?" Klaes demanded. "Oh. This." There was a grey rock lying beside him on the grass. He picked it up and examined it. It had a round face and a flat face. The round face bore a dark smear of his blood.

He climbed to his feet. It wasn't easy, but once he was there he began to feel a little more like himself. The promptings of nausea receded, and the throbbing pain in his head became somewhat more bearable.

Bosilka was still leaning against the tree, weeping. "Enough of that," Klaes said. And, when that elicited no reaction, "Miss Stefanu, stop. This is to no purpose."

"Oh—what's—to become—of me?" the girl moaned between her wrenching sobs. "M-my poor father—he—he can't do—without me! He can't!"

"No, I dare say," Klaes said. "But he won't have to. I understand what you did. I don't like it, but I understand it. I'm not angry."

Bosilka quieted, and after a moment or two raised her head to peer at him with one bloodshot eye. Her expression was at once calculating and hopeful, which made Klaes wonder if perhaps she had exaggerated the tears to enforce his pity.

"I only w-wanted to stop you from killing them. Or them from killing you. You were all so angry with each other, and you wouldn't listen when I said stop."

Klaes tossed away the bloodied stone and once more explored the outline of his wound, wincing as he did so. "I promise I'll listen to you next time," he said gloomily.

Bosilka was watching him closely and anxiously. Real tears streaked her cheeks, for all that she might have coaxed them along.

"Will you tell your commander about this?" she asked in a child's half-pleading voice.

"That I was involved in an altercation with three farmers, and then had my brains knocked out by a girl?" Klaes asked. "No, I believe I'll keep that tale to myself."

He went back to the stile and sat down to recover himself a little more before leaving. If he left now, he was sure that he would either stagger or fall over. It was important to him that he did not do either of those things.

Bosilka still watched him at first, but when he did not speak she bent her head, seemingly busied with some part of her attire. To spare her modesty Klaes looked away, which made his head start spinning again. He heard the rending of cloth, but kept his head averted.

"Here," Bosilka said, from much closer than he expected. Her hand came into his line of sight, a ragged strip of cloth clutched between her fingers. She must have torn it from one of the many layers of her skirts.

Klaes hesitated, but only for a moment. He didn't want to go back to Pokoj looking as though he'd just walked off a battlefield. He held the cloth to the back of his head, where there was now a sizeable lump. After a few moments a better idea occurred to him. He wadded the cloth up, opened up his *flasquette* and poured some brandy onto it. With this he began to swab at the wound. The smell of spirits would be less embarrassing than the sight of blood.

"You won't tell?" Bosilka asked him again.

"I've said that I won't. I'm not a man to be foresworn."

She laid her hand, for the briefest of moments, upon his sleeve. This surprised him, considering how badly she had reacted to being touched by him. "It would go hard with them," she said, "if you told. I know it. And I'm thankful for your silence."

Klaes nodded. But this had little to do with gallantry or honour. Even if he had borne a grudge against the three yokels and wished to feed it, he would have died rather than let anyone know about this ridiculous affair.

"My silence," he told Bosilka, "you can rely on."

He considered offering once again to escort her to her father's door, but it would have felt as absurd to him as it no doubt would to her. He gave her good day, climbed once more over the stile and went on his way. And as he walked, he considered the unexpected and indirect success of his stratagem.

Petos and the cellar, and all that stuff. The words of the peasant, Kopesz, spoken while Klaes lay apparently senseless on the forest floor.

These were his starting points. His enterprise was launched. And that more than made up for a buffet on the head.

15

Molebacher's mood grew darker with the season. Over the next few days the big guns were the centre of attention, and Jursitizky and his men held drinking parties every night. The quartermaster was a welcome guest at these gatherings—he could, after all, contribute more than his share of the drink—but the artillerymen had a reputation for heroic over-indulgence, and made it a point of pride not to stop while there was a cask left unbroached. Molebacher began to look sour whenever the call went up for more wine.

Then, too, he seemed to find the guns themselves less enthralling as the days went on. He was used to being master of the feast himself, Drozde supposed. Perhaps he found it galling to be sidelined by lumps of machinery, or perhaps his temper had just turned with the wind, as it so often did. Whatever the reason, the effects were clear enough: the sergeant grew brooding and silent, and increasingly, when Drozde made her entry into the kitchen of a morning, there'd be nothing for her but an empty plate and a curt instruction to go and sniff out her own breakfast.

Drozde had seen him like this before: the seething irritability coming slowly to the boil until it spilled over, burning whoever had the misfortune to be close by at the time. She decided to clear off for a couple of days, just long enough to remind Molebacher of the need to keep up his end of the bargain. If he wasn't inclined to feed her, then she saw no reason why she should grace his bed.

The camp was unusually quiet: there were no drills or manoeuvres on a Sunday, but even the routine turnout and tent inspections seemed not to have happened. Drozde wondered if Sergeant Strumpfel was still snoring. On Sundays the men were usually left to themselves for a good part of the day, to worship or amuse themselves as they saw fit. Some were already playing dice next to their tents or straggling into the woods for a morning's hunting. She found her friends finishing their bread, as dry and unappetising as her own. Ottilie, whose family were Protestants, was minded to go to church, and Libush offered to accompany her. She had no particular beliefs, she said, but she'd made a couple of acquaintances in the town and might meet them there. Drozde had no interest in church. The last time she'd entered one, as she recalled, they'd thrown her out for laughing. But she had no wish to stay in camp at the moment, and readily agreed to walk into the village with the other two.

"You might ask Molebacher to make us some more bread," Libush reproached her as they made their way down the rutted lane. "It's been hard as nails all this week."

Her friends had a flattering belief in Drozde's power over the quartermaster. "He really doesn't listen to me," she told Libush.

"He trusts you to go to the market for him!"

"That's just because he's too lazy to go himself," Drozde said. She had cause to be grateful for Molebacher's laziness: it was the only thing which kept his other vices in check and without it, she suspected, he would be loath to let her move about as freely as she did. "And it's useful for the show," she added. "There's a lot I can pick up at the market here."

"It's certainly bigger than you'd think," Libush agreed. "I came up last week and the place was crowded. I wouldn't have guessed there were that many people in the whole town."

"I don't think there are. Most of them come from over the river."

"That can't be so!" Ottilie cut in. "That's Prussia on the other side. They're the enemy."

The girl was perfectly serious. Drozde suppressed a smile. "The Narutsiners don't see them like that," she said. "They're just neighbours. Some of them have married people from across the river."

"But that's treason," protested Ottilie. "Frydek says it's betraying the empire to have any contact with the enemy, even to talk to them! How could they do that?"

Libush laughed. "Why wouldn't they? I've tumbled with Prussians before now. They're built like any other men."

Ottilie was only eighteen, and had worked in a pie shop before she fell for the charms of Sergeant Frydek. She turned fiery red and looked at her feet. Libush was sorry; she was a soft-hearted woman and hadn't meant to tease the girl. "They're just poor villagers," she said. "I'm sure they're not thinking any disloyalty; they just want to sell their milk and eggs. And it's hard to have near neighbours and never speak to them."

"Tell me, Libush," Drozde cut in, seeing that Ottilie was still embarrassed, "Did I see you with a tortoiseshell comb in your hair? You surely didn't find that in the market here?"

They talked the rest of the way about combs and hairstyles, the immaculately piled curls of Dame Tusimov and how long it must take her each day to maintain them, and from there the various peculiarities of the officers' ladies. The walk passed pleasantly, and Drozde was sorry to leave her companions when they reached the village. The church was already full. She saw them both seated at the back and withdrew hastily before the hymns could begin.

It seemed that the whole town was at church. The deserted square outside and the street beyond looked somehow narrower without the stalls and people of the market. Drozde wandered aimlessly until the drone of singing and sermonising at her back began to irritate her, then struck off into the woodland that bordered the road to the carpenter's workshop. The trees had a bare, starveling look, especially near the road where the branches had been stripped up to head height, she supposed for firewood. But there were still yellow leaves above her, and birdsong, and for now she relished the solitude. It was a while since she'd had much time to herself, she thought. Maybe, when spring came, she would take the puppets and her savings and make her way on her own again.

She was roused from her thoughts by the sound of an axe. *Someone violating the Sabbath!* she thought with a certain amusement, and found herself quickening her pace as she headed deeper into the wood towards the sound.

The woodcutter was working on a tree already felled, splitting it into logs. He was shirtless—a slender man, compact and well-muscled. Drozde watched him with pleasure as she came towards him. He heard her approach and raised a hand in greeting without turning from his work. She was close enough by this time to recognise him: Anton Hanslo, the carpenter's man.

He turned at last with a look of annoyance at the interruption, which changed to astonishment at the sight of Drozde.

"The puppet mistress! What brings you here?"

Drozde greeted him cautiously, but he seemed genuinely pleased to see her, and in no way embarrassed by his half-dressed state. "I took some friends to church," she told him.

His smile widened. "You didn't stay with them?"

"I've got out of the habit of going to church," she retorted. "As have you, it seems."

"Oh, I go most weeks," he said indifferently. "Old Stefanu likes me to be there, and Silkie will scold me for not showing my face today. But it's likely to rain soon. I wanted to get some of this wood into the shed before it starts."

She glanced up. What could be seen of the sky through the leaves was grey and heavy. "That'll be quite a job, working on your own!"

"It's nothing," he said. He gestured to a handcart behind him. "It's not far, once I have the cart loaded, and I've only a few more to cut now." He made to go back to his work, then stopped. "You could help me, if you've nothing better to do."

Drozde was about to tell him tartly to do his own work. But it was true: she did have nothing else to do right now. The girls were in church, and if she returned to Pokoj she'd find most of her other friends with their men. She couldn't even get to her puppets without running into Molebacher. She shrugged. "Why not?"

She stacked logs on the cart while the carpenter chopped. It was tiring work, and the cart held everything he had cut: it would be heavy for him to push. She was wondering whether to offer her help with transporting the logs as well when Hanslo laid down his axe with a low oath.

"I was all set to take you back to the workshop!" he said. "Your wood rounds are ready; you could have taken them now. But Stefanu locks it on a Sunday, I was forgetting, and he'll have the key in his pocket. I'm sorry for it, puppet mistress, especially after your kindness today, but I'll have to make you come out twice."

Drozde laughed. The rain had held off so far, the birds still sang, and she realised that she was enjoying herself. She was suddenly in a better humour than she had been for days. "That'll be no hardship to me," she said. "And my name's Drozde."

She went with him to the shed anyway: he refused any help in pushing the cart, but she felt inclined for the company now. As he bent to his work, Drozde watched with approval the play of muscles under the carpenter's tanned skin. It had been a long time since she'd walked with a well setup man.

"You have an admirer back at the workshop," he told her as they went. He moved the cart swiftly, and his voice was only a little ragged from the effort. "Silkie—Bosilka, I mean, Stefanu's daughter—she's asked me twice now if you'll be bringing any more puppets. Do you remember her, the girl who came in as you left?

Drozde remembered her very well. "She seemed bright," she said. "If she'd been a boy she'd have made her father a good apprentice. And no doubt you'd be out of a job."

Bent over the load as he was, he could not see her face, but perhaps the jibe had sounded more unkind than she'd meant it to. He stopped and looked up at her.

"She has all her father's skill," he agreed. "I should know; I was the one taught her to carve, when she was little and I was still apprentice. And only two, three years ago he had some thought of maybe training her up alongside me. She asked him often enough, and I'd have been glad to have her." He took up the cart handle again. "It was what happened with Agnese put him off."

Drozde waited for him to go on, but he was already heaving the cart into motion again. "What happened?" she asked. "Who's Agnese?"

It was a moment before he answered. "A friend of Silkie's. She was wild; she ran off, that's all. And Stefanu thought that was what came of letting a girl have too many notions of independence. He swore then that he'd see Bosilka settled before he died."

Drozde snorted. She'd heard this sort of tale before. "Settled meaning married, whether she wants it or no?"

His back was still to her, but he nodded. "Though she's shown no interest in young Jakusch Weichorek, nor he in her, as far as I hear.

I don't think she's a mind to marry at all, not yet at least. I dare say Stefanu won't push her." He sounded doubtful and rather unhappy.

"I was wild myself at her age, I suppose," Drozde said. "Wilful, certainly. And I ran off too. It did me no harm in the long run."

"It harmed Agnese," said Hanslo shortly.

He would not say any more. He gave the cart a fierce shove which ran it into a rut, and the conversation lapsed as she helped him to extricate it.

The woodshed was in the next clearing. It was a rough enough shack, but sturdy, with a pitched roof caulked with tar. The wood inside was stacked neatly in various lengths, already filling three-quarters of the available space. Drozde helped the carpenter to carry in the new logs, grateful for something to do to dispel the awkwardness that had fallen between them.

By the time they'd finished a breeze had sprung up and the air had a definite hint of dampness. Drozde flexed her aching arms. Hanslo dusted off his hands and grinned at her, suddenly cheerful again.

"Safe and dry!" he said with satisfaction. "And I've your help to thank for it . . . Drozde. You won't refuse that drink now, will you?"

"Now?" Drozde was taken aback, as much by his sudden change of mood as by the suggestion. "There's an inn here that's open on Sunday?"

Hanslo laughed. "Not that I heard." He reached behind the door of the shed and pulled out a bottle. "But a good craftsman can always make do."

And there was that unguarded smile of his again: guileless as a boy, Drozde thought, as if there were no consequences in the world. But she took the bottle, just for one mouthful. It was brandy, and a finer quality than she'd ever tasted. She allowed herself a second, deeper drink, and smiled at him as she handed it back. Hanslo did not drink at once; he raised the bottle as if in a toast and looked her full in the eyes. It was a look that Drozde knew only too well. She lowered her gaze abruptly and took a step back from him.

"It's good, thank you," she said. "But I have to go now."

Hanslo looked disappointed, but he didn't protest.

"I'll say farewell then," he replied. "I hope we'll see each other again soon, Drozde."

He kissed his hand to her as she walked away.

It was late afternoon by the time Drozde got back to the square, and the service was over. There were a few children chasing each other in the street, and an appetising smell of cooking from the nearest houses which reminded her how little she had eaten today. Libush and Ottilie must be long gone. She set out after them, hoping she could make it back to Pokoj before the rain began. She walked fast, trying to counter a sudden feeling of panic, as if she had narrowly avoided some great threat. But she had liked plenty of men before, had even fallen for one—a boy, in retrospect—in the village where she had grown up. That folly had earned her the worst beating her father ever gave her, but she had learned better since then. She could master her feelings now, or hide them at least. Hanslo was no fool: he'd seen her ring and would understand that another man had a claim on her.

The last stretch of the road before Pokoj had once been wooded on each side, but the trees had long since been cut down to uneven stumps. Drozde slowed as she reached them. On the highest stump, some way back from the path, sat a man, slumped with his head in his hands as if fainting or weeping. He was in uniform. Drozde walked more softly, considering leaving the road to go around behind him— the soldier might not appreciate having his sorrows overlooked. But he made no sound, and as she came closer he tipped forward a little as if he might really fall. Drozde ran to him and took him by the shoulders, and the man jerked upright. It was Lieutenant Klaes. He gave her a slightly bewildered look and tried to stand, but staggered and sat down again heavily.

"Are you all right, Lieutenant?" Drozde asked. She was quite concerned. A strong smell of spirits rose from the man, but it seemed he was suffering from something more than mere drunkenness. Besides, this was Klaes. What could have driven him to get drunk in the first place? She'd never even heard him swear.

The lieutenant was clearly making every effort to recover himself: he took a long breath and produced a ghastly half-smile. Then it seemed that he recognised, belatedly, who he was talking to. His face creased in consternation.

"Thank you, ah, Drozde," he said stiffly. "I'm quite well; only . . ." He winced slightly. "Only engaged in private thought. Please, don't let me trouble you." He waved her on down the road with a feeble hand that fell immediately into his lap again.

Drozde looked at him more narrowly. His hair was tousled, his uniform trousers were scuffed and muddy and there was a great smear of mud on his jacket. He was twisting a rag of some kind in his hands, and she could see blood on it.

"You've been—" She stopped herself. Fighting was common enough among the soldiers, but would surely mean disgrace for an officer. "Hurt," she finished. "I can look at it if you like."

He flinched away from her. "No! I'm well, I said!" This time he succeeded in getting to his feet, although he swayed a little.

"At least wipe the mud from your uniform," Drozde said, no longer troubling to be polite. She pulled the kerchief from round her neck and thrust it at him. "You surely don't want your men to see you like this."

Klaes took the cloth with bad grace and scrubbed at the dried mud, dislodging some of it. "What business did you have in the village anyway?" he asked her with something of truculence in his voice. "You weren't in church, were you?"

Drozde had half a mind to say yes, just to see his face. But he'd probably think she was lying anyway. "Just meeting a friend," she said.

He returned the kerchief with a mere nod for thanks. "Well, don't get too friendly. We won't be here for ever, and they're not the best sort of people."

Drozde made a point of looking him up and down before she replied.

"I've seldom been lucky enough to mix with the best sort."

Klaes saw her meaning well enough and was angry enough to come up with a rejoinder, though he looked sick and pale. "The army keeps you and feeds you," he snapped. "You might show a little gratitude at that, instead of plying your whore's trade at every hovel we pass."

Drozde was taken aback—not at the accusation, which was all of a piece with Klaes's puritanical squeamishness, but at the idea that she owed a debt to August's regiment for the room and board it afforded her. As if she came out better from that bargain than Sergeant Molebacher did! As if the army had no need of women like herself and Alis and Libush, and merely opened its arms to them out of kindness!

"I choose my own friends, Lieutenant," she said levelly. "Eat where I will, drink where I will, and lie where I will. I'm a follower of your army, not its subject, and you don't have any writ to command me. What's more to the point, you don't know the first thing about Narutsin or its people—as far as you're concerned it's just another bit of territory where you can throw your archduchess's weight around." She gave Klaes a withering glare. "What's it to you if I talk to a few people, as one living creature to another? It's a skill you'd do well to learn too, if you want to get anything out of them. But they say you need to start early with such things, if you ever expect to master them. Probably you should stick to the things you already do well. Whatever they are."

Drozde stalked away from him. She could feel him staring after her, but it was too good a speech to spoil by turning to check.

By the time she reached the gates of Pokoj, though, she felt a certain uneasiness. There was no harm in Klaes: for all his self-righteous cavilling, he had a reputation for fairness, and his lack of soldierly vices was a standing joke among the enlisted men. It was widely believed that the colonel himself despised him for it, and Molebacher treated him with near-open contempt. She supposed the man might deserve some sympathy. He was hurt, possibly badly, and had had too much pride to accept her help. Just to be seen by her in that state must have been a bitter humiliation for him.

She loitered near the gates until she saw him come in, walking slowly but upright. He had managed to get the visible mud off his clothes, she saw, and had done something to smooth down his hair, though she could still see the patch of clotted blood at the back of his head. No matter, she told herself. The little prude was safe, and she'd done all she could for him.

She slipped away to the camp, where Libush and Ottilie were waiting for her.

"Where were you?" Libush demanded. "Alis made soup; we've saved you some, though you don't deserve it."

"Guess who we saw in church!" Ottilie told her excitedly. "Skinny little Lieutenant Klaes! He was only three seats in front of us. He joined in all the responses; not like some."

Libush cuffed her good-naturedly.

"He didn't see us, though," the older woman said. "We stayed in our seats after the service and he came right by us without noticing. He was looking at one of the village girls. Mousy little thing, she was, but he seemed properly smitten. Who'd have thought it, eh?"

"So what about you, Drozde?" Alis asked, bringing her a bowl of soup. "You were gone ages. Did you have any adventures?"

"Oh, I just went for a walk in the woods," Drozde said. "Nothing exciting."

16

The wound on Klaes's head took two days to heal; the damage to his pride took considerably longer.

To his intense relief, he had managed to get back to Pokoj and into his own quarters without attracting any more attention. He told his orderly that he had returned from church with a fever, which would keep visitors from his door for a while. Of course, he reflected ruefully, all this was beside the point after his damnable luck in meeting the puppet woman on the road. By now the story of his misadventures would be common currency among the camp followers and the lower ranks, and it was only a matter of time before word spread to the officers. If only he'd sent the harridan away before she'd had a good look at him! Now he had to make up a story to explain not only his wound but the mud she had seen on his clothes. A fall seemed best. It would make him look foolish, but not as foolish as being caught fighting with yokels.

He held a clean kerchief to the cut until he was satisfied that it had stopped bleeding, then brushed his hair over the lump as well as he could by touch. He wished he could borrow Dame Konstanze's looking glass. He stayed in his room till darkness fell. He would have liked to go to bed early, but his presence would be missed at supper, and if the rumours had already started they would only get worse if he hid. With a sigh he checked his reflection in the glass of the window—he looked tolerably neat at least—and went out to face the others.

And found everyone just as before. Pabst, somewhat tipsy already, offered him a drink. Tusimov clearly thought it a huge joke that Klaes had attended church on the Lord's day, and Dietmar treated him with lofty indifference. The boorish quartermaster Molebacher, who was capable of astonishing rudeness, was no more than sullen towards him. But the quartermaster was Drozde's lover! Whom would she have told if not him?

Klaes sat down to supper with a small resurgence of hope. No one seemed to notice his head. Pabst's wife, Dame Margarethe, asked him kindly if he was better: apparently Private Leintz had passed around the story of the fever. Tusimov opined that a man might expect to pick up such things if he insisted on going to church in a bog, and he and Dietmar sniggered. And, those courtesies out of the way, they left him to eat in peace.

The next day, too, none of the men under his command behaved any differently towards him. True, some of the women in the camp giggled and pointed as he passed them, but some of them giggled at everything. The lump on his head gradually subsided. And the next time he saw Drozde she paid him no attention at all. Perhaps he had misjudged the woman. Then the word went around that she would be performing another show on Wednesday night.

All Klaes's uneasiness returned. Maybe that was why she had not yet spread the story: to make more of an impact at her damned performance! He could not stop her. He didn't think he could even avoid the show—it would undoubtedly be worse if everyone knew what she'd said about him but Klaes himself.

The old abbey was packed that evening. It was growing colder, and Drozde seldom performed in bad weather: it might be a long time before the next show. Klaes, full of trepidation, took up his position in the overgrown pear orchard at the back of the audience, concealed between a gnarled tree and a thick stand of thistles. At least, whatever the wretched woman made of his escapade, they would not be able to stare at him.

The performance started, as they always did, with a hideously tuneless fanfare which for some reason was greeted with huge enthusiasm. Klaes did not often attend the shows, but it was impossible to avoid them entirely, and he knew the routine well enough. It opened with the general-puppet, his absurd medals jangling as he instructed the men to keep up their courage in battle by drinking all night: "It's what I've always done, and look at me now!" A pretty girl-puppet came on and the general went into various contortions, trying to hide his alcohol-laden breath, conceal his giant bottle of brandy and flirt with the girl at the same time. The men loved it. Klaes could not help being impressed by the puppeteer's voice, which was thunderously deep as the general and unexpectedly cultivated as the young woman. But he was too tense to pay much attention.

A musical number came next, accompanied by Private Taglitz on his flute: a soldier singing of his love for his girl—who turned out to be the great gun Mathilde. Drozde was plainly using the quartermaster to get her material. Klaes remembered Tusimov's mocking of Dietmar at supper on the day the guns arrived—though Drozde had made the singer of this song Sergeant Jursitizky rather than Dietmar; probably wisely, Klaes thought, seeing the golden curls of Dame Feronika among the little group standing separately at the back of the audience. The gun itself, a framed cloth silhouette adorned with two long-lashed eyes, was lowered from the top of the stage, nearly crushing the singer, and performed a little dance with him which was rapturously applauded.

And then there was a puppet Colonel August, encountering a prancing jackanapes of an officer who was introduced as Lieutenant Klaes. This caused general hilarity, and Klaes's face grew hot, but he took care not to move. The colonel was at first too busy filling his pipe to notice the lieutenant, who indulged in a freakish series of parade manoeuvres to attract his attention. At length August put down the pipe and told the lieutenant he had a job for him: the camp was running out of tobacco, and he had heard that the mayor of Narutsin had a special stash of fine Turkish which he kept hidden somewhere in the village. As the colonel's main contact among the villagers, Klaes was deputed to find the precious treasure and bring it to him.

Klaes was familiar with this piece of gossip. He did not use tobacco himself, but Pabst and Tusimov did, and Dietmar's failure to bring any Turkish leaf back from Opole had caused some tension between the older officers. He could not understand, though, why Drozde had mixed him up in this story. He watched with more bafflement than irritation as his puppet repeatedly bungled the assignment, his searches turning up cinders, a string of sausages and a cowpat. During this last episode he was propositioned by a milkmaid, and walked off with the cowpat only after misunderstanding everything the girl said to him. Klaes repressed a snort: the whole episode, cowpat and all, would not have cost him a tenth of the embarrassment he had suffered from his real-life encounter with Bosilka Stefanu.

Finally the puppet received word that the precious tobacco was stored behind the altar in Narutsin's church. He tried to attend Sunday service there, but found the church so packed that he had to stand outside in the rain. A local man then sold him a packet of Turkish leaf for an inordinate price, and the puppet-Klaes brought it back to Pokoj through a series of misadventures involving storms and falling into ditches. He arrived (Klaes had foreseen this detail) with a fever, but triumphantly holding up the packet, which August inspected and pronounced to be filled with oak leaves. The piece ended with the colonel disconsolately stuffing the leaves into his pipe anyway. The audience laughed delightedly, though without the applause that had greeted the dancing gun. The colonel stalked off and was replaced by a private and two camp followers, who sang a song lamenting the tattered state of their tents and the various difficulties this caused the girls when getting undressed at night.

Klaes barely noticed the next couple of items. He felt light with relief, and at the same time oddly foolish. The woman had said nothing about him that he hadn't been twitted with many times before. And he'd been afraid of her!

He had come out from behind the thicket now: the concealment suddenly struck him as ridiculous. He turned away from the group of officers at the back of the audience and headed towards the edge of the crowd where half a dozen of his men were laughing uproariously. Privates Rasmus and Leintz leaned against each other as if they could hardly stand for mirth. Klaes stood unobtrusively beside them to watch the end of the show.

She was a skilful performer, he had to admit, watching a complicated dance in which a group of villagers pursued a boar through the forest, armed with ladles, spades and giant needles. Klaes's men, still unaware of his presence, guffawed and made raucous comments. The boar was finally caught by Private Standmeier in a big net, and carried off by three soldiers while the villagers ran in the wrong direction. The real Standmeier—who had actually killed no more than a brace of rabbits the week before—whooped and punched the air. Klaes found himself fascinated: how was it possible to move so many puppets at once?

The final act featured a raid on the camp by a dragon, a preposterous beast which always seemed to make an appearance in the shows in some form. It had been lured by the scent of Molebacher's stew, wailed the private who raised the alarm, while the creature loomed above him, slurping alarmingly. The company deployed all their guns against the monster, led by Mathilde, her long lashes fluttering fiercely. At the first sight of the giant cannon the dragon was smitten, and ceased hostilities to sing a song in her praise. The piece ended as the dragon bore Mathilde back to his ice palace, waved off by a heartbroken Jursitizky.

Klaes laughed along with his men and joined in the applause at the end. He nodded pleasantly to the startled Leintz, who hadn't noticed him till that moment, and went with the others to give his *grosch* to the performer.

"If it isn't Klaes!" cried Tusimov, catching sight of him. "We don't often see you here! What happened? Church service not enough excitement for you any more?"

"No indeed," Klaes said gravely. It was probably unwise to say anything more to Tusimov, who would only use it as a fresh excuse to mock him. He walked on, waiting until his back was turned on the older man before he allowed his face to relax into a smile.

"That went well," Alis said to Drozde as she and the others seated themselves in Libush's tent after the show. "I liked what you did with that stupid gun. And it's true about the tents—the wind comes right in. Whenever it blows from the east you might as well be outside."

"They're like sieves," agreed Sarai. "But you don't think Drozde's show will help matters, do you? We'll just have more men coming over to look through the holes."

Libush gave her cockcrow laugh. "Well, that'd help keep the wind off."

Drozde was only half-listening. The takings from the show were a little less than last time's, though that was to be expected with only a couple of weeks between them. But the introduction of Mathilde had been a general success, and once she'd got her supplies from the carpenter, she had some ideas to build on for future performances.

"Girls, I might ask for some needlework from you," she said. "I want to put some of the Narutsiners in the act—the mayor and his wife, and maybe the priest, so I'm making a few outfits. I can pay a *cruitzer* a time, if anyone's interested."

They were: there were few enough ways to earn money when the company was stationed somewhere like Narutsin. Drozde discussed clothing styles with them for a while, arranged to lend them a puppet apiece and promised to go to the market again soon for the materials. She said goodnight then. Molebacher was not cooking this evening, and she'd seen him dicing with some of the other sergeants straight after the show. If she hurried she could return the puppets to their storeroom without meeting him.

Magda was waiting for her in the kitchen, perched on the table where Drozde had sat the day the company arrived. She leaned back and swung her legs, grinning widely at Drozde.

"Did you see me this time?" she demanded.

She had sat on the ground in the very centre, against the legs of the audience in the front row. When Drozde first caught sight of her, the General Schrecklich puppet had almost lost his voice. "Yes, I saw you," she said, sounding as severe as she could. "It isn't polite to make faces at someone while they're performing."

Magda pouted and hung her head for a moment, but she couldn't stop her face creasing with laughter. "It was so funny!" she exclaimed. "When the general dropped his brandy bottle . . . and when the lieutenant pulled out the string of sausages . . . and the dragon . . ." At the thought of the dragon she burst into loud giggles.

"I'm glad you liked it," Drozde told her. She headed down the stairs and hastily stowed the puppets away while the child watched, still giving little snorts of laughter. Drozde considered. She'd have to see Molebacher soon: he'd had time to calm down by now, and if she avoided his bed much longer then his mood would only worsen. Besides, he'd expect her to hand over tonight's takings. But he could wait for another day. "Come on," she said. "Let's go visit your friends."

She was starting to recognise the faces of some of those who gathered to meet her in the ballroom, both the ones who had told their stories and a few who had featured in them. There was the old Jew, Gelbfisc, along with two others in monks' clothing who congratulated her on her performance: Tomas Lauzen, the sometime abbot of

Pokoj, and Grigorjus Hurr, the infirmarian. There was the wild-haired woman, Arinak, who fixed her with a glittering gaze and pronounced, "You tell me about these wooden men, and how you make them play. Soon, yes? I'll like that."

Drozde was conscious that she had left in anger the last time she had visited the ghosts. She received their warm welcome all the more gratefully because she had been afraid—and it was only now that the fear was past that she recognised it at all—that she might have saddened or offended them to the point where they would not want to see her again. Smiling a greeting to them all, she selected one of the room's spindly-legged chairs and sat down—she normally used the floor, but the show had tired her. She found that the ghosts adjusted themselves to her level, sitting comfortably on thin air as if they had imagined themselves chairs of their own. She supposed that this mental act was no odder than the fact that the ghosts wore clothes, or that Arinak had a twist of gold wire hanging from a leather thong around her neck.

There was a sense of ease and relaxation about the gathering, but also some difference that she could not at first identify. Then she realised that no one had yet come forward to tell a tale. "No story tonight?" she asked.

It was Thea who answered, as if the explanation were obvious. "Oh, tonight it would be discourteous. You'll need to sleep soon."

She'd be the judge of that, Drozde thought. Her arms and back were tired to aching, but she wasn't in the least sleepy. Still, it might be pleasant to sit and talk for a change. "Magda told me . . ." she began, and then noticed another oddity. The child was no longer with them. "Where is she?"

"She's there!" said the dark-eyed woman, Thea's friend Cilie. "Playing with her little cat." She gestured towards the balcony, where chairs had been set for musicians long gone. Flicking in and out of vision through the balcony rails, the little girl jumped and twirled in flashes of pink and black. Drozde heard a soft giggle. It was hard for her to see the child clearly, but Cilie and Thea laughed as if appreciating some wonderful game. "Shall I call her?" Cilie said.

"No, no—not if she's enjoying herself." Drozde looked back at the two women. They were smiling indulgently as they watched Magda playing, for all the world like the mothers of Narutsin giving their children a few minutes more to run about the square before their

Sunday lunch. "Tell me," she said. "What do you do all the time— when I'm not here, I mean?"

For a moment they looked at Drozde in confusion.

"When you're not . . ." Cilie repeated, as if the very concept puzzled her.

Then Thea's face cleared. "Oh," she said at last. "Well we talk, of course, and walk in the grounds. And Cilie sings to us sometimes."

"And you read your books," Cilie put in eagerly. "She loves reading," she told Drozde.

How could a ghost read a book?

Her incomprehension must have shown in her face. Thea tried to explain. "I had so many books when I was a child, and loved them so much . . . so it was easy to find my way back to them. Perhaps it's more remembering than reading. But the words are all there."

"Reading belongs to the world of the spirit," said a deep-voiced man who had come up behind Thea. "And with God's will the spirit can transcend all boundaries. The holy books are as clear to me now as they were in life."

It was the old abbot from Gelbfisc's story, Father Ignacio, who had been silenced by the rest of the ghosts when last Drozde heard him speak. And here was another mystery. How did such a man, with a rock-firm belief in God's providence, react to finding himself a lost soul?

It would not be tactful, Drozde thought, to ask him that question. But tact had never been her virtue. "So, Father," she said, "how is it you're here at all? I'd have thought you'd look to be in Paradise by now."

"That, *mene dame*, is because of your ignorance," the old man said in a tone of patient reproof. "Scripture tells us that the Day of Judgement is not now but at the end of time. And till that day the dead sleep . . . all but a few, blessed as we have been blessed to wait out that time in wakefulness, to bear witness every day to God's glory."

"Even Meister Gelbfisc?" Drozde asked him. She heard something like a cough from beside her, and realised that Cilie had smothered a laugh.

The abbot's expression was as clear as any living man's: irritation, self-belief and a touch of weariness. Drozde had the feeling that he had been teased like this before, and had given the same answer many times.

"The Jew is blessed above all of us," he said tightly. "With an eternity in this place, and the good example of the brothers, he may yet overcome his intellectual pride and come one day to stand before the Throne. Who else among us has been given such mercy?"

"Every soul here, Father!" protested Tomas Lauzen. Gelbfisc, beside him, put a hand on the younger man's arm and shook his head, smiling.

They talked to each other like members of a family, Drozde thought: squabbling and teasing and knowing each other's weaknesses, with shared jokes and references that no outsider could understand. And she was no longer an outsider, she realised. Perhaps she never had been. She didn't know yet what she thought about that; she wasn't even sure she knew what it meant. The ghosts of Pokoj were too far removed from the other people she knew, the terms of their offered friendship too alien to any relationship she had formed before. The living always wanted something. Life was hard, and staying afloat yourself meant that you had to push others under as often as not. It was a harsh truth, but one that she had seen in action, and acted upon herself, more times than she cared to recall. You lived however you could, and when you died a shadow lingered on in your place.

But the dead of Pokoj were different. They asked nothing of her but that she bear witness, listening as she asked the company to listen every time she blew a fanfare on her battered trumpet. Whatever her feelings on the matter, she was of their party now, and she found, with a certain surprise, that this knowledge did not frighten her as it would once have done.

She came to herself with a start. She had slipped sideways on the narrow chair, her chin sunk to her chest and one hand dangling. The ghosts had left her, and the room was dark. As she stirred, Magda came out of the shadows and put her small hand on Drozde's.

"I knew you were tired tonight," the child said. "Do you want to go back to your tent now? I'll come with you. I won't talk or anything. I know you had a long day. Did you have fun with everyone? Father Ignacio is funny, isn't he?"

Drozde let the child lead her through the dark. The ghosts were good company, she thought, if you could overlook their strangeness. But she had no map for their world, no rulebook, and sometimes it seemed as if they were equally baffled by hers. There was so much about them that she didn't understand: they spoke in riddles and expected her to know what they meant; they told her everything about their lives, except why they were telling her. Every time she went to the ballroom her mind worked its way back to the questions which had occupied it since she first met them, confusion nagging at her like a knot she couldn't untie.

17

Molebacher's kitchen bore some resemblance to a battlefield. Every orderly under his command was hacking or hauling, or scurrying between the racks and the central table where the quartermaster was hard at work with Gertrude on a flayed carcass. His men had found a richer farmer to plunder, with fields close by the river: the cow they had taken was a big, well-fed beast, and Molebacher was seizing the opportunity to lay in supplies for the winter. Beside him Hulyek sliced strips and gobbets of fat and carried them to the fire, where Muntz tended a seething cauldron that sent out heavy bluish fumes. Fast laid out rack after rack of meat to be salted, while Rattenwend, almost as big as Molebacher himself, hauled a great leg to the drying cupboard. The air was thick with the clang of metal and the fumes of blood, offal and burning grease.

Drozde might have taken the opportunity to enter unobtrusively, but that was not her way. She strode into the midst of the reek and clatter and faced Molebacher across the great table, hands on hips. The pouch with last night's takings dangled from one hand, where he could see it. She did not speak; when Molebacher was in his chopping humour he had no tolerance for conversation. But she twitched her hand so that the coins jingled in the pouch, and quirked her lips in a careful blend of teasing and invitation: *Well? Are you pleased to see me?*

Molebacher glared at her, barely pausing in his bloody work.

"Crawling back, are you?" he growled. "Three days in the wind, and then you barge in here when I'm busy."

Drozde dropped the smile; gave him a level stare.

"I had a show to prepare," she said. "But I can see now's a bad time."

She'd almost reached the door when she heard the throat-clearing that meant Molebacher had more to say. She turned back, slowly.

"I didn't say you could go." His head was still bent over the carcass, the chopper coming down with rhythmic savagery. Drozde stood still. "Now you're here, I dare say there'll be some use for you," Molebacher conceded. He looked up. For an instant his eyes met hers and she thought he might be managed after all. But next moment he seemed to forget her.

"What—the fuck—do you think you're doing?"

He was shouting at Muntz, who had stopped stirring the great cauldron of rendered fat, and was now pulling the whole thing, on its rickety stand, away from the fire. Muntz paled a little.

"It's . . . it's done, Sarge!" he said. "All melted down. We got enough tallow here to fill the barrel and more, once we let it cool a bit."

"And did I say you could stop, you little gobshite?"

"Ah, no, Sarge, but we've got enough right here; barrel's full. We couldn't burn more than this all winter . . ." He tailed off under Molebacher's scowl. The quartermaster turned to roar at another orderly.

"Swivek! Where's that other barrel?"

Swivek vanished into the scullery. Almost at once he re-emerged to summon Standmeier, and the two of them trundled a giant tub into the kitchen, rolling on its side and spattering the floor with brownish drips as it came. The thing stank: even through the kitchen's fumes, Drozde could smell the sickly odour of rot that came from it. The inside seemed to be coated with thick yellow slime, darkening at the bottom to green and black.

Molebacher nodded with apparent satisfaction. "You don't waste good fat in my kitchen," he told Muntz. "Got that? So you melt down the rest of it like a good boy, and we'll get an extra barrel cleaned out for you."

"Ah, Sarge . . ." protested Standmeier, eyeing the tub with horror. Swivek, who had more experience of the sergeant's moods, gave the young private a kick and a surreptitious headshake. But Molebacher did not erupt. He treated Standmeier to a friendly smile.

"But scrubbing things out," he said. "That's more like woman's work, is what you were maybe about to say?"

Standmeier cast a wild glance around him, but his fellow orderlies were all suddenly looking elsewhere. Molebacher grinned wider, showing every tooth. "Right, my boy?"

Standmeier managed a small, terrified nod, and flinched as Molebacher clapped him on the shoulder.

"And by coincidence," the quartermaster said, "we just happen to have one here. A *helpful* girl. Who'll be only too glad to do the job for us—eh, Drozde?"

"You want me to . . ." The incredulous words were out before she could help herself. Drozde did not do this kind of work. Molebacher didn't trust her with heavy lifting, and he'd never given her the filthy jobs: he wanted her sweet for his bed, and he knew she had few clothes. For a moment she thought he was joking. He reached over the steaming carcass to pick up Gertrude and ran his finger down the cleaver's blade, flicking the drops into the great bowl of congealing blood that stood nearby. Then he put down the blade with a clatter and walked to stand over Drozde: three paces, sounding loud in the new silence. He rubbed his red hands together, close to her face.

"You'll do this for me," he said softly. "Won't you, now?"

His face gleamed damply; only his eyes were dry, and blank as two pebbles. All around her Drozde felt the orderlies shifting their feet. He might not do her too much harm while they were watching, she thought. But if he laid her out on the flagstones not one of them would make a move to stop him. Perhaps if she turned and walked away right now he might let her leave; he did have work to do. But he'd come after her, sooner or later.

She shifted her stance, making herself relax, and held his gaze.

"You'll have to get them to take it outside then," she said. "Unless you want that filth all over the floor."

The door to the yard was through the scullery. Molebacher dismissed the men back to their work and stood in the opening to watch her. Drozde discarded the rag he had tossed her, and selected a leafy branch as long as her arm from one of the bushes. Under Molebacher's stony stare she heaved the tub onto its side and began to scour the stinking thing.

"You'll need to do better than that," he told her. "I want it clean."

She tried to ignore him. Breathing shallowly, she gouged out swathes of thick, rancid grease and dumped them on the ground. She worked as slowly as she could bear to. Finally, as she'd hoped, a crash sounded from the kitchen behind Molebacher, and he turned away with a curse. She waited until she heard him inside, roaring abuse at three orderlies together, before she stood up. Quickly, she tied up her hair with her neckerchief and undid the bodice of her dress, tucking it down into her skirt and rolling up the skirt to her knee. Her shift offered precious little protection from the cold wind, but it couldn't be helped. Shuddering, she crawled inside the foul tub and started work in earnest.

It took perhaps an hour. Once, near the start, she had to stop and vomit, but luckily she had not eaten that morning. Molebacher came out a few times to watch. She took care that he saw little more than her feet, and enough of the foul stuff was spattered on the ground around her to stop him approaching too close. He never spoke, and she pretended not to notice him. When all the grease was out, the inside still glistened and stank of rot. As she went to the well for water to sluice it, Private Fast came out into the yard with a bucket. He was the orderly who had made sheep's eyes at her that first day in Pokoj, she remembered. At the sight of her now, he goggled like a fish and ducked back inside without a word.

Maybe Molebacher had noticed his too-quick return. Drozde had hoped to make her escape without seeing any of them, but as she heaved the tub over to let it drain, the quartermaster appeared in the doorway. He gave her a slow, appraising look, head to feet, and smiled. "Is it done?" he said.

Drozde had to swallow before she could speak to him. "Go and see for yourself," she said. "I'm going to wash."

"Yes," Molebacher agreed. "You do that. I'll want you in my bed tonight. Three days without so much as a sniff; it's not right. A man needs more than that!"

He shouted the last words after her. But at least he let her go.

The little stream of the Drench ran close to Pokoj on the north side. A few minutes upstream from the house was a place where the trickle of water widened into a shallow pool overshadowed by trees: that was where the women of the camp did their washing. Drozde hoped that none of them would be there now. She'd had to stop off in the camp to get her other dress and her cloak, and to borrow a shift from Alis, but she'd avoided seeing anyone else so far —or at least seeing anyone close enough to need to answer questions. It was too late in the day for laundry, she told herself, and no one would be bathing in November. Still, she looked all around her before finally stripping off her clothes. The shift and kerchief were past saving: she balled them up and dropped them into the latrine pit they'd dug in the bushes. The dress might be salvaged, she thought, draping it over a willow branch to examine it. But first things first.

Nobody bathed in November. She held her breath and entered the water at a run, wincing as the cold gripped her legs, her thighs, her waist. She had to duck down to get her shoulders under. Kneeling on mud and pebbles, she scrubbed at herself like a soiled sheet, using a stone to scrape off the worst of the grease, then the oil-and-ashes mixture that Alis had given her. Her arms were the worst, and she worked on them until the skin was raw, as if she could wash away the memory with the smell. Then she ducked her head and rubbed the ashes into her hair.

Alis had been full of questions and concern, but Drozde had cut her off before she could say much, offering the briefest possible explanation of the state she was in. It was no way to ask for help, but Alis had run to fetch her a spare shift, as well as the little tub of ashes, and had mercifully held her tongue as Drozde accepted them. She would have to thank her properly later.

She wrapped herself in her winter cloak to get dry, stamping up and down the bank until the shivering subsided. She pulled her clothes on, tied up her wet hair and busied herself with the stained dress. But she could not put those two faces out of her mind: Alis, her eyes widening in shock and horror as she saw her, and Molebacher, with that blank, dispassionate, slaughterer's look. She could not shake off the thought that the dread she had seen in her friend's face mirrored something in her own.

Drozde found she was shivering again. He had stood over her, twisting those big red hands, smiling his sly smile, and he'd threatened her. It wasn't the first time either. *Leave your pretty things lying around and they will get broken, Drozde.* She wondered now how she could ever have thought that the slashed face of her coquette was an accident. And now she'd let him frighten her; she was still letting him. She wrung out the dripping dress savagely, enraged at her own weakness. *He'd make me his drudge, would he?* she thought, *his little dog, to be kept in line by whipping?*

He was so sure that he owned her; she'd seen that in his face this morning. He would come after her if she didn't go to him tonight. He'd batter her, not in a drunken passion, but deliberately, to prove who was master. Her stomach leapt into her throat at the thought, but she summoned the rage again to push it down. She'd go, then; she'd let him think he had control for a little longer. And when she was ready she'd take her money and she'd leave.

She was striding back towards the camp now, the damp clothes heavy in her arms. But she wouldn't stay there, she told herself, to wait on the quartermaster's pleasure. She had her own work and life. If he harmed her puppets she could repair them. She had wood to buy, and somewhere else to be.

Hanslo was at his workbench when she pushed open the door of the carpenter's shop. He jumped up as soon as she appeared, smiling that wide delighted smile.

"I knew you'd come!" he said.

"Of course I've come," Drozde retorted. "I've paid for the wood— had you forgotten?"

His good humour didn't lessen. "I knew you'd come today. It was the weather: the wind all up and down and the clouds never still for a moment. Just like the last time we met. It brought you to mind."

Drozde leaned on the bench and waited for him to get down to business. There was no harm in him, after all; there was nothing but goodwill and honest liking. At this moment the thought was so warming that she almost returned his smile.

With an air of producing a gift, Hanslo reached down a package from the shelf behind him, unrolling it with an expansive gesture to show the wooden cylinders she'd ordered.

"Will they do?" he asked, his voice uncertain. She bent over the little sticks of wood: they were neatly turned and sanded to a smooth finish. "They're perfect," she said. "Thank you. They'll do very well."

Hanslo visibly relaxed. "In that case," he said, "I've something else to show you. If you don't mind seeing it."

"What is it?" she asked guardedly. But he was already opening a small door at the back of the workshop. "This way!" he called. Drozde followed with misgivings.

It had once been a store cupboard, and still had one wall lined with crowded shelves. Along the other wall was a narrow bed. The space in between the two was barely wide enough to take a three-legged stool, which Hanslo gestured to her to sit on while he lifted something down from a high shelf. He had laid it out on a woollen cloth, the different parts touching but not yet connected.

It was a puppet. She was unpainted apart from her face, but finished as expertly as the cylinders—even more so. A puppet's body did not require finishing: male and female characters were distinguished by the clothes they wore. But this little figure had sloping shoulders, small breasts and wide hips, all smoothly sanded. The face, too, was more detailed than necessary, the nose wider and flatter than those of Drozde's coquettes, and the chin a little longer. He'd attached hair already, thick strands of black wool which would make her harder to paint. Drozde picked up the three parts of a little arm and hand. The joints would need some filing, but it was an admirable piece of work for a beginner. She had opened her mouth to say so when she looked again at the face, and realised what it was he had made.

"It's not the best likeness," Hanslo said. "But for a start . . . I hope you like it. I'm not sure how to attach the strings; I was hoping you'd show me."

Drozde was not often speechless. He had made her into a puppet. He'd taken her face without asking, and now he was asking her to finish the job! Despite his protestation, it was a good likeness: did that make the case worse or better?

She found that she was laughing. It was only what she did to others, after all; she'd just never expected that someone would return the favour. "Let's see what string you have," she said.

They went back to the workshop to join and string the puppet. Hanslo had a great ball of fishing twine. It was not as flexible as what Drozde was used to, but thin and strong enough. It fitted with ease through the holes he had bored, which were smooth and perfectly rounded.

"I used a bradawl," Hanslo told her shyly when she complimented him on their neatness and precision. "It's meant for boring screw holes." He crossed to a toolbox on the bench and pulled out a thin blade with a wooden handle. Drozde eyed it admiringly. She had never seen one before: it was wickedly sharp, and she could tell at once that it would work much better than the thin chisel which she employed for the job. Hanslo saw her covetous look, and offered the tiny instrument to her eagerly.

"Take it! I have a hundred of them."

Drozde did so with gratitude, slipping it into the pocket of her dress.

She showed him how to thread his twine through the narrow holes in the puppet's hands, knees and feet, and how to hide the knots. He was a quick learner, but the task was a delicate one and took some time. After a while Hanslo rose and locked up the shop for the day. Drozde thought uneasily of Molebacher. It really would not be wise to leave it too late to visit him. But it was afternoon still, though the light was already fading; she had hours yet.

They talked as they worked, Drozde telling him a little about her travels, and Hanslo recalling his childhood exploits. He had never been more than ten miles from Narutsin, and was fascinated to hear of the streets and palaces she had seen in the cities she had visited, the painted coaches and outlandish fashions. For her part Drozde found the carpenter's stories almost equally strange: he seemed to have spent all his life in a tiny, charmed world, untouched by war or hunger.

"We used to fish in the Drench when I was small," Hanslo told her. "That was before they dammed the river and it dried up. It could be a torrent some years, in the rainy season. And Casparlin and Bobik and me, we used to cross the bridge walking along the railings, like we were acrobats. One time I fell in and was swept away; I would have drowned only my coat got snagged by that big rock at the corner of old Stefan's field. When they got to me, I was stuck fast between the rock and the bank. But they panicked and tried to drag me out anyway. I still have the scar, look."

He pulled down his shirt to show her the pale line along his shoulder blade, glancing at her sidelong as he did so. Drozde was not disconcerted. She had noticed his well-muscled shoulders the last time they met, and had no objection to viewing them again. "It seems to have healed well," she said.

She showed Hanslo how to loop the stiff pieces of twine at their tops. "You should make a crosspiece to take the main strings," she told him, "but you'll work her better if these ones loop over your fingers. Look." His hand was warm in hers. "Then you can do more than one thing with the same hand. That's how you make her bend, or do a dance."

Hanslo was not looking at the puppet but at her. "That wasn't why I made her," he said. "I never meant just to pull your strings, Drozde."

His face was stricken. How could a man of his age be so defenceless?

This time she met his gaze full on. A little voice in the back of her mind hissed at her not to be a fool. Now, of all times! So he wants you, it jeered; so you like him. You'll get yourself into a world of trouble, just for pity?

But it wasn't pity, she knew. She looked at his face, so openly longing, at his brown arms, his hands so sure and careful on the little puppet.

"Put her down," she said, and took him by the shoulders. She pulled him towards her and kissed him on the mouth.

His skin was smoother even than she'd imagined. He was nervous and eager, fumbling with the buttons of his breeches, and mumbled an apology when his narrow bed creaked beneath their weight. But he knew what to do, and his body was compact and trim and beautiful. She reached to clasp the curve of his buttock, and felt him tremble and sigh with pleasure. He was gentle for all his frantic haste: he knew to withdraw and spend outside her, and was quick and attentive to learn how to bring her own rise and fall. Afterwards he drew her to him, murmuring her name with a softness she had never heard in any man's voice. And she let him, knowing that a time like this might not come again.

She lay partly on top of him, relishing the way his body fitted against hers. Their legs were tangled together, and his arms were so tight about her that she could hardly move. She breathed in his scent, which had something in it of resin and something of fresh mushrooms. She had to go, she told herself; it must be almost time for dinner back at the camp. She gave herself another few moments, and another few. She realised that she was struggling to keep her eyes open. She had to go. But the moment was so sweet: warmth and tenderness, and this small space of peace. She'd spent so long looking over her shoulder. She nuzzled her face into the warm hollow of Hanslo's neck. A minute or two more of respite, before she went back to the fight.

She awoke—she didn't know how many hours later—with a muted curse. How long had she been asleep? Too long, certainly: the little room was pitch dark. Molebacher would have missed her by now. Still wrapped in her arms, Hanslo was snoring gently. For all her urgency, Drozde sighed as she disentangled herself and reached for her shift. He stirred sleepily, then pushed himself up, looking at her in alarm.

"You're not going?"

"Yes, I'm going." She smiled at him and reached to stroke his belly. "I'd stay longer if I could, and glad to. But I have things to do, and so have you." She straightened her dress and looked around for any bit of metal that might do as a looking glass—she'd have to pin her hair up somehow before venturing outside. He caught her arm and held on to it. "Stay with me."

"Let go!" Drozde said, irritated.

Hanslo was instantly crestfallen. "But you want to stay," he said, making it half a question. "Weren't you . . . Didn't I please you?"

"You did. You do," she said, trying to keep the softness out of her voice. "But I'm not free. You saw my ring!"

"You're not married," he said with absolute certainty.

"No! But I do have a man at the camp—we all have. We wouldn't be with the soldiers else. Please, Hanslo."

His face had frozen, but he smiled again at the last words. "But you don't love him."

"What does that matter!" He was impossible. She shook her head at him, disengaged his hand and laid it down. "This was . . . I wanted to do this. I've nothing to regret, not if you haven't. But I must go now."

"Will you come again?" he asked, suddenly serious.

She was on the point of saying, *No, of course not*. It had been stupid enough to do this once. But oh, she thought, he was a sweet man. "Yes," she said. "Not at once. But when I can."

His face cleared. "In that case," he said, "you must call me Anton. And kiss me once more before you go."

18

Late in the evening the colonel's adjutant, Bedvar, came to Lieutenant Tusimov's room and knocked. He knocked tentatively at first; Tusimov had retired only half an hour before and doubtless would not like to be disturbed. But it was a matter of character too. The adjutant was a man of a timorous stamp and hated to be placed in situations in which he was obliged to provoke and exasperate men of high rank and uncertain temper. Unfortunately his position required him to do this on a daily basis, so he was not— generally speaking—a happy man.

The first knock yielded no response. To his horror, Bedvar thought he heard the rhythmic creak of bedsprings from the room beyond. He drew back hastily and paced the corridor for a few moments as he weighed the prospect of enraging a lieutenant against that of displeasing a colonel. Eventually, he knocked again. And then again. Each time he stopped and listened, but heard nothing to indicate that he'd succeeded in rousing the lieutenant from his more compelling occupation. So he swallowed his misgivings and continued with increasing volume and quickening tempo until he was finally acknowledged with a profane oath from within.

"I'm sodding well awake, you whoreson. Be quiet!"

Padding footsteps on the other side of the door. Then the rattling of the latch. Tusimov thrust out his head, big and choleric and bewhiskered, and demanded, "What?"

The lieutenant was in a long nightshirt of white cotton, his feet thrust without stockings into his unlaced boots. He clutched in his hand a wad of grey fabric that was probably a flannel nightcap. In the room beyond, Bedvar saw, a candle had been lit. Dame Konstanze was sitting up in bed, blushing furiously and clasping the covers to her chest. She looked anxious, as though she was expecting bad news. But surely she must know that if the Prussians were coming there'd be a general muster with bugles blaring like sheep in a fog, not a polite knock at the door.

"The colonel's compliments, sir," he said to Tusimov. "He wishes to see you in his rooms."

"Now?" Tusimov was both astonished and belligerent. "It won't wait until tomorrow?"

Bedvar didn't know how to answer that. He imagined himself delivering that message. *The lieutenant's compliments, Colonel. He'll see you in the morning.* A muscle clenched somewhere in his gut. He wasn't well equipped by nature even to think those words. He gave a wan, apologetic smile by way of an answer.

Tusimov grunted. "Very well. I'll be up in a moment. I don't suppose he wants to see my bare arse in his rooms!"

No answer to be made there either. Bedvar saluted and withdrew.

A scant few minutes later, Tusimov was trotting along the upper corridor (the one where Drozde had seen the kitten Amelie delivered into the world). He tucked his shirt into his trousers when he was twenty yards away from the colonel's door, fastened his belt at ten yards, and smoothed down his hair as he presented himself, all smiles, to his commander. His rudeness to Bedvar was in direct proportion to his deference to Colonel August.

August gestured Tusimov to a chair and offered him a cordial, which he declined.

"I wanted to talk to you about *morale*," he said impressively. The French word was a new import, replacing the more familiar *auftrieb*. Officers liked it because it carried the hint of a mystery specific to the military (since *auftrieb* still prevailed in civilian life). Tusimov felt that you should generally call a spade a spade. The men were up for it, or else they were in a funk. At the moment, in his opinion, they were neither. The prospect of a Prussian attack was remote enough to be exciting rather than frightening, but nobody had enjoyed the forced march and nobody liked being so far out here in the sticks. So it was an ounce of this and two pecks of that.

Still, August must have his own ideas on that score, and Tusimov wasn't prepared to pin his colours to an opinion until he could see which way the wind was blowing. "*Morale*," he echoed, nodding thoughtfully. "Yes, sir. I think I understand you."

"We just don't know," August went on, "how long this business will drag on. Prussia's like a dog that has only just learned to bark. The only way to shut it up is with a kick or two. But we can't kick until they get past barking and try to bite."

"And do you think they will, sir? Bite, I mean?"

"No. I don't think Frederick's a big enough fool to try his luck against the archduchess."

"He can see her teeth are bigger than his, what?" Tusimov chipped in, warming to August's theme.

August nodded. But the lieutenant felt that his attempt to join in with the metaphor had ended in confusion and embarrassment. Had he just called Maria Theresa a bitch?

"So it's all just talk then," he said, trying to steer his chief onto safer and more prosaic ground, "Frederick's claim that there's a Prussian Silesia that's somehow owed to him?"

"Sabre-rattling," August agreed, pacing to the window and back. "And yet, now that he's said it, he may be compelled to put up some sort of a show at least. He's not yet nine and twenty. A young man, probably with a young man's pride and stubbornness. He may not want to be outfaced and made to look a blowhard. So I'm not ruling out a little adventure on Prussia's part. Most likely he'd pass to the south of us in such a case, and head straight for Wroclaw. Not that he'd get there, of course—one step into the lowlands, he'd find himself in a hornets' nest, and no mistake.

"But still, Tusimov. Still, you see? The men may be out here for months, waiting for an attack that doesn't come. And then again, they may be called at any moment to fortify Lubin or Polcowice, or to relieve them in the event of a siege. I don't want them losing their edge up here, imagining that they're good and settled in winter quarters. That sort of thinking does a man no good at all."

Tusimov nodded again, with more confidence this time. So the colonel's concern was that inactivity would reduce the detachment's readiness and soften its resolve. It wasn't an empty fear.

"Perhaps, sir," he ventured, "a sortie of some kind would be a good idea. To get to know the neighbouring terrain—so that if they *should* have to fight on it, they'll know it better than the enemy does."

The colonel pondered this. "War games?" he hazarded.

"Not war games as such." Tusimov was emphatic. The detachment was a patchwork quilt consisting of survivors from several companies decimated in the Turkish war. In his unit alone there were five languages, any one of which contained a cornucopia of insult words for speakers of the other four. And that was before you even got started on the regional dialects. No, there was no need to encourage them to fight. "I only meant," he said, "that if one of us were to lead a column, for purposes of mapping and reconnaissance, it might be time well spent. The men will feel more confident once they know the ground, and the activity itself—so long as they're not whipped to the double march—will do them good." Another thought occurred to him. "And the villagers will see our strength and our discipline, which would also be no bad thing. They'll know they've got nothing to fear from Prussia while we're here."

"Or nothing to hope, perhaps," said August shrewdly. He winked at Tusimov, who smiled to show that he got the joke. Low church siding with low church, as sometimes was wont to happen. And citizens at the ragged edge of a polity forgetting which side of the bread had the dripping on it. Privately, Tusimov doubted that the good townsfolk of Narutsin had brains enough between them to form a political opinion. But then this was the land that had thrown up Hus and Žižka, so he could easily be wrong there.

"All the more reason to march," he said to August, and August laughed and said that he agreed.

Which meant that Tusimov won his point—and as a reward was given the colonel's maps of the region to take back to his bed with him. He was to choose a route and rouse the men at sun-up for a patrol in the hills to the north of the valley. "Or the south," Colonel August allowed expansively. "Any direction will do, really, so long as your march takes you along the village street. And make sure the men turn out smartly, Tusimov. Make a show of it, eh?"

Tusimov was chagrined. It was all very well being in the colonel's good books, but to rise at dawn while Pabst and Dietmar and that pimple Klaes snored through to *grand réveillé* didn't appeal to him very much at all.

Nonetheless he saluted smartly to show willing, and only then seemed to consider. "Might it be better, sir," he said, "to stagger the manoeuvres a little? Let each of the units take a turn separately? If, as you say, part of the point of the exercise is to make a show, then to be active over a longer period might suit the purpose better."

"Possibly," August said slowly. "Yes, there might be something in that."

"And it might be of more effect to start out later in the day, when the light is better and the villagers are out in the fields. To be a visible presence, sir, if you take my point. It's a matter of . . ." Tusimov groped for a word ". . . of ripeness."

"Ripeness. Well, well." August appeared only half-convinced, but he was nodding as he waved his lieutenant out of his presence. "The details I'll leave to you, Tusimov. But you'll take the vanguard, yes? And draw up a schedule for the others. I'd like all four units, including the gunners, to be involved."

Tusimov knew he'd pushed his luck as far as it would carry. He saluted crisply and made his exit.

In the event, they started out closer to noon than to sun-up. He held his men back after *grand réveillé* and told them they would be on manoeuvres in exactly one hour. "That's twenty minutes for breakfast, twenty for ablutions and twenty for uniforms and packs. So jump to it yeomanly, my lads. Because anyone who rolls up late will be written down for an offence."

But Tusimov was distracted several times in the course of the hour. First by Klaes, who for some benighted reason wanted to know if he had the keys to the house's cellars. Then by the mysterious absence of his greatcoat, which his wife had brushed down and then hung in an empty room to air. And finally by a civilian, who wandered in through the gates just as Tusimov was at last heading for the stable yard where he'd ordered his unit to assemble.

The man was a peasant from the village. He was of middling height but more than middling muscle, and he stood fairly in the centre of the overgrown carriage drive with the uncompromising air of a man who other men were wont to walk around. The look on his face, though, was somewhat bewildered, as if he wasn't quite sure where he'd fetched up, or why. A simpleton, Tusimov decided, but once he accosted the fellow he seemed clear-headed enough—and civil, after his fashion. He gave Tusimov good day, and asked him where he might find Drozde.

"Drozde?" Tusimov repeated blankly. "Drozde the whore?"

The man flushed darkly. "I don't think she'd like to be called so," he said. "Saving your presence."

Tusimov was now bewildered in his turn. He'd meant the term in a literal and descriptive sense, and saw no reason to retreat from it. "The camp follower," he qualified. "Sergeant Molebacher's doxy. That's who you mean, yes? I haven't seen her today. I wouldn't expect to. But in any case you can't be here. This is a military camp, not a marketplace. You can only be here if there's some reason—some military reason—for your presence. Do you understand?"

The man nodded curtly. "As well as the next man," he said.

"Good," Tusimov said, and he pointed to the gate. He had no more time to waste on this. But the man didn't move.

"Can I leave a message for her, then?" he asked.

"A . . . a message?" Tusimov boggled. What did the man take him for? "No, you can't. Off with you now, fellow. Don't try the length of your stride against mine, or I promise you'll be sorry. Here! Here, you!"

This last was not to the peasant but to two privates who he saw walking between the kitchens and the main house. He didn't know either of their names, but he knew them well enough by sight. They were of Molebacher's *meinie*, and they'd do well enough for the present purpose.

"See this man back onto the high road," he said as they approached. And he walked away without wasting another word.

But by then it was five past the hour. Having threatened, very publicly, to put anyone who was tardy on a charge, Tusimov was obliged to walk across the stable yard to his troops, already formed up in columns by the ever-reliable Sergeant Strumpfel, five minutes after the time he'd decreed. It was provoking. It made him look a buffoon, and (which was worse) a hypocrite. And there was no way of getting around it or even referring to it. An officer couldn't justify his actions to his own men. He relied on discipline, not fellow feeling. Damn

Konstanze for not putting his uniform where he could find it. Damn Klaes for blathering at him when he could see bloody well he was in a hurry. And thrice damn that fucking yokel for a fucking fool. If he ever saw the fellow again, he'd lay a horsewhip across his shoulders.

The men stood to attention as the lieutenant walked up, reading his stormy mood in his face. He took the reins of his horse, Dancer, from Strumpfel and mounted smartly into the saddle.

"At the single," he bawled, bringing the old girl around with just a touch of his crop to her right flank, "—march!"

Strumpfel executed an about-face that was much less crisp than the horse's, and led the way through the rear gates onto the rutted road beyond.

Elsewhere, Anton Hanslo was walked to the front gates by Private Fast and Private Standmeier, who felt obliged by the dignity of their calling to give him the occasional push.

"Off with you," they said when they came to the road. "And don't let us catch you round here again, sonny."

Hanslo took this insult with a grave, impassive face. Both men were his junior by the best part of ten years. One looked as though the soft down on his neck and chin had never seen a razor. "I'd like to leave a message," Hanslo said. "For Drozde. Or to see her, if that's possible."

It was no small thing that he'd come here. He didn't share the fear and dislike of the company that was so prevalent in the village, but he knew its cause and was therefore well aware that to be seen here, talking to these soldiers, would earn him the censure of all who knew him. But there was no help for it. Since their last meeting he'd been unable to put Drozde out of his mind. He'd cut his thumb on a chisel and banged his knuckles twice with a framing hammer. He had to see her, or else the accumulation of these minor injuries would make it difficult for him to work.

So he was civil, even though these young lads were somewhat less so. He only asked them if they knew Drozde, and if they'd be prepared to tell her that he was here, so he might walk in the lane awhile in case she was free to join him.

"Are you a sodding idiot?" one of the soldiers demanded in response to this request. "Do you want your arse nailed to a tree?"

"Drozde's not for you," the other man supplied. "She's warming our sergeant's bed, and he's worth ten of your kind."

"And he'll bloody well kill you," the first took up again, "if he sees you sniffing around his cunt."

Hanslo looked from one to the other, digesting this very unwelcome news. "His cunt?" he repeated quietly.

There was a moment's silence. The two men glanced at each other, parsing those words.

"The cunt he's put his mark on," the second man clarified. "Is what I meant."

"Exactly. Now you just bugger off. Or we'll tell the sergeant you're eyeing what's on his plate."

"If you'll tell her I was here, I'll be obliged," Hanslo said again. "For what you tell your sergeant, that's up to you. Certainly I'll not trouble you to give him my regards."

He nodded to them both and walked away, conscious of their hostile gazes on his back as he walked down the road.

At the same moment, and very close by, Drozde was getting ready to return to the kitchen. In the workshop with Hanslo, Molebacher's tyranny had seemed as though it belonged to a different age, distanced from her by a fog of warmth and soft light. But last night, returning as fast as she could along the dark road to Pokoj, every step she had taken brought the memory of his expressionless face, dripping blood and sweat, more vividly before her.

By the time she'd reached his quarters and found him snoring, the idea of lying down beside him had filled her with a wave of disgust, and no small amount of fear. The thought that he might wake before she did, yesterday's rage still in him, and find her vulnerable, was a deeply unpleasant one. When she saw him next, she wanted to be in control. So she had slept in her tent, leaving their inevitable confrontation for the morning.

Now, as she smoothed down her dress and pulled on her boots, she saw a silhouette appear outside. It bent down and put its head to the flap.

"Drozde." It was Alis's voice. "Are you in there? I need to talk to you."

"Alis!" Drozde ushered the woman in with a smile. "Thank you for your help yesterday. I don't know what I would have done if you hadn't been there."

Alis did not appear to have heard her. She sat down, facing Drozde but with her eyes downcast, twisting her hands in her lap. Drozde was just about to ask her what the matter was when she spoke.

"Did he hurt you?" she asked. "Molebacher?"

Drozde started at the suddenness of the question. "Of course not, Alis. He's never even touched me!" It was the truth, but somehow the denial sounded hollow. Alis raised her head, her expression wretched.

"I'm so sorry, Drozde," she said, the words spilling out of her. "There's something that I should have told you about him, long before. Something that he . . . that happened to me when I first knew him."

"What?" Drozde asked. Her voice came out louder and blunter than she had intended. There was a note of panic in Alis's tone that was beginning to scare her, just as the look of horror on her face had done the night before.

"You know that I like to cook," Alis began. "There was a time—it was before you joined us, but you've probably heard about it—when I used to help Molebacher in his kitchen. He never paid me, but he'd turn a blind eye if I wanted to swipe a few loaves or an extra portion of stew, and he needed the help, so it worked out well for both of us. There was nothing more to it than that though. At least not at first.

"One night when I was scrubbing the pans, he came up to me and put his hands around my waist. I pushed him away. I know, I know—" Alis waved her hand as if expecting Drozde to interject. "—I'd no reason to be choosy. But I'd never liked the way he looked at me. His eyes were too blank, like there was nothing behind them. He left me alone after that, and I thought no more about it. But about a week later, he'd set me to frying potato cakes, and the pot of hot oil slipped off the trivet and fell on me."

Here Alis paused, and slowly began rolling down her left stocking.

"It was only my leg was hurt, thank Christ," she said, her voice trembling a little. "I'd never have worked again, else. But it was bad enough."

Her leg, from knee to calf, was a hectic, feverish red. The skin was mottled, with a strange sheen on it as if it had melted and reformed again. Drozde felt her gorge rise at the sight, and tried hard not to recoil from her friend.

"I should have warned you. For a long time I tried to put it from my mind. I told myself I'd just been clumsy, that I must have knocked it somehow. But that trivet had never been unstable before, and the day I was burned it was wobbling around like someone had taken a hammer to it. It was him. I know it was.

"We all of us love you, Drozde, you know that." Alis's voice was barely more than a whisper now. "Please be careful."

There was a long pause after she had finished speaking. For an endless moment Drozde felt almost compelled to silence, as if to speak would be to acknowledge what Alis had said as true, wrenching it into the here-and-now from the fireside tale of violence and vengeance to which it seemed rightfully to belong. But fear would do her no good, she knew, and the longer she sat frozen, the worse Alis would feel. So she collected herself and, with an immense effort, smiled at her friend.

"Don't worry about me, Alis," she said. "If I didn't know a thing or two about handling Molebacher, do you think I'd still be here?"

She wished that she felt as sure as she sounded.

When Drozde entered Molebacher's kitchen some three-quarters of an hour later, she came prepared. After Alis had left her she had sat in her tent a long while, and she had thought. Now was a time, if ever there had been one, where the sergeant would require careful handling. Everything must be planned, and thoroughly. Drozde found that it helped her to quash a rapidly mounting sense of panic if she imagined the interview to come as a puppet show.

First, the fanfare. Drozde picked her moment carefully, waiting until she had seen all the orderlies dispatched on various errands before making her entrance. Molebacher wouldn't tolerate her making a scene with other people watching, and a scene was exactly what she needed right now. Her opening gambit needed to be surprising enough that he would take notice and listen to her without interrupting. Lose the stage, and she lost the battle. Molebacher would be expecting fear and deference, she guessed, so she went for anger instead. She marched into the kitchen, her eyes blazing. She had undone her hair so that it flew out behind her as she walked and swept across her face in tangled curls. The effect was unladylike, wild even, but not unpleasant.

"Where the fuck—" Molebacher began.

She cut him off. "Where do you think?" she growled. "You gave me that stinking work, and then expected me to come creeping back to your bed? I wasn't fit to lie with pigs after what you put me through!"

As she had hoped, Molebacher had no reply to this. He stared at

Drozde, and she could see that he was thrown by her rage. But she couldn't stop yet.

"If you thought I was going to come to you last night, you had another thing coming," she continued, her voice rising. "I had a good mind to never come to your bed again, Molebacher, do you know that? I had a good mind to leave!"

She paused as if to catch her breath, her chest heaving. Molebacher's face remained impassive, but she noticed his eyes following the rise and fall of her breasts. She knew then that he was ready to come around, if she could only offer him a way to do so without losing face. She had to tread carefully here: push Molebacher too hard, even in a direction he was going already, and he would likely thwart you just for spite. She waited. After what seemed like an age, he spoke.

"But here you are," he pointed out. Right on cue.

This was where things got really tricky. Drozde knew the line that she was treading, and it was a dangerous one. She couldn't subdue Molebacher with threats, and if she slipped into deference and apologies then he would almost certainly beat her. He did not respect weakness and would give it no quarter. She held his gaze, allowing the moment to stretch out until the silence hung thick and heavy in the room like a pall of smoke.

"Here I am," she agreed, and her eyes said, *Of course I came back. I couldn't resist you.*

The quartermaster breathed in, and Drozde saw his chest swell, almost imperceptibly, as he took in what she had said, and what her eyes had spoken. For a man like Molebacher, ownership came a poor second to mastery. He would never beat Drozde into submission if she could convince him that her submission was given willingly, pulled from her by a power in him that she could not withstand and did not wish to. In that moment she knew that she had pulled it off, that Molebacher thought he saw, after his long, slow siege of her, a white flag above the battlements. She was torn between self-disgust at the cravenness of the lie and pride at its success. On the whole, she reflected, it was one of her better performances. And then it was over. Molebacher shrugged massively, and returned to chopping vegetables.

"And running your mouth off like a common trull already," he observed, as if nothing more than words had passed between them.

"I've got better things to do than listen to your whining."

"Much better things," Drozde agreed. "If we go next door we'll be undisturbed. We could go and do some of them there."

She led the way, and Molebacher lumbered after. Even then it was hard work, reconciling him, but she had a gift and a will for it.

The face of the carpenter kept drifting to the forefront of her mind as she worked. It did no harm.

19

Klaes knocked on the big solid front door of the burgomaster's house. Then waited a while and knocked again. There was no knocker: he was obliged to rap with the edge of a coin taken from his pocket.

It was Bosilka who answered, which he might have anticipated but had not. He was outfaced for a moment, as she struggled and failed to hide her dismay on seeing him.

"What do *you* want?" she asked.

"I need to speak with your master."

"He's not in."

"Then I'll wait," said Klaes.

A serving maid can't easily bar her master's door, unless to gypsies and mendicants. With extreme reluctance, Bosilka stepped aside and allowed him in. "May I take your coat?" she mumbled, her gaze darting away from his every time their eyes threatened to meet. "Who shall I say is calling?"

"Well . . . me," Klaes said. "Lieutenant Klaes. I've eaten at his table, Miss Stefanu. It's not necessary for me to present a card."

"No. Sorry. I meant . . . what shall I say the matter is?"

"The matter is private." Klaes took off his greatcoat and handed it to her. She held it draped over her two arms, which made her look like Mary cradling the body of Christ in a pietà. Klaes suppressed the irreverent thought.

"Private. Yes. Very well." Bosilka pointed to a door off to her left. "You'd best wait in the closet then. He'll come and get you when he's ready for you. Or I will. Most likely he will. I'm busy with the wash." She turned away, seeming angry and unhappy.

"Miss Stefanu," Klaes said quickly. "Wait."

She stopped. "What?"

"My being here. I won't . . . That is . . . I have no intention of implicating you."

Bosilka gave him a cold look. "I don't know what that means, Lieutenant Klaes. Is it a *quotidian* sort of thing?"

She didn't wait for an answer but strode off, leaving him surprised and chagrined once again at how easily she'd given him the hip and thrown him. A woman like that, he thought sourly, had better not marry. Her husband would kill either her or himself before the year was out.

He went into the closet, a room even narrower than its name suggested. There was a chair with a misericord, a rack hung with the family's winter coats and a great many jars of homemade preserves. A tiny window, made even smaller by the heavy wooden frame on which its shutter hung, allowed some light to dribble down the nearer wall. The overall effect—apart from the preserves—was of an eremite's cell.

Inactivity stretches time and deceives expectation. It felt like a long while that Lieutenant Klaes stood at the window and waited. On the misericord there was a single book. He picked it up and read the title: *Tausch's Gazetteer and Almanac of Country Matters Mostly, MDCCXXXII*.

He set it down again.

He had already decided on the course he was going to take, but he rehearsed the words in his mind several times over while he waited; honing his delivery, anticipating possible objections, making the performance watertight.

The door opened at last, and the burgomaster ushered him out of his confinement with a shooing gesture, like a farmer herding sheep. "This is a fine to-do!" he exclaimed. "Nobody told me you were here,

Corporal Klaes. I only noticed your coat on the table as I came through the hall, and asked whose it was."

"It's no matter," Klaes said. He thought, *I'm amazed she didn't lock me in. Or bid me wait on the roof.*

They went through into the drawing room where the family had received him the day the detachment took up residence at Pokoj. The chairs had been pushed back against the walls, but Weichorek set out two of them directly facing one another as though he expected this to be an interrogation of some sort. "Ease you," he said, gesturing Klaes to sit.

Klaes did so. The burgomaster took up his place opposite, not bothering to sweep the tails of his jacket out from under his descending backside. No wonder they looked like the folds of a sack.

"Now," he said briskly, "what brings you here?"

"A matter of some seriousness," Klaes said, making his tone match the words. "And some delicacy, too. In the normal course of things, it would require me to make a formal report, but I would rather not involve my commander if it is possible for me to deal with it myself."

Weichorek looked concerned—or perhaps he was merely puzzled. "A matter . . ."

"I have heard," Klaes told him, "about Petos."

For some moments the burgomaster did not speak. He merely regarded Klaes with the same air of troubled innocence. Klaes was content to let the silence continue for as long as it would. He had searched the cellar at Pokoj and found nothing incriminating or even interesting there—only the trunk and personal effects of the gypsy woman, Drozde. So he had decided to adopt another strategy, which was to extort information by seeming to possess it. And for that it was necessary to allow the other man to speak as much as possible while he himself said little but implied much.

"Petos," Weichorek repeated at last.

"Yes."

"I see." Weichorek nodded. "And if I may ask, Captain, who was it told you about this?"

Could they not even keep his rank straight in their minds for two minutes? Klaes began to correct the error, but stopped himself. "The source does not matter. Only the facts in the case."

"Ah. It was Bosilka, then."

Klaes started. How in the world had Weichorek jumped to that conclusion? Because he'd been seen talking to the girl? Were rumours so quick, and so current? "I have no remit to give a name," he said, striving to maintain a calm, impassive, card player's face. "But I can tell you that it was not Miss Stefanu."

"Who then?"

"A countryman of yours." Klaes was aware that he should remain silent—let the burgomaster bring words and revelations to him. But he was obliged now to lay a false trail. He didn't want Bosilka to suffer as a result of his subterfuge. "The man was in his cups. He spoke indiscreetly, and though I did not intentionally listen, I was compelled to overhear."

"Ah," the burgomaster said again. "So that's how it was? And where did all this take place, Sergeant? If I'm permitted to ask? I didn't know you men of the company were drinking in town with us. Certainly I've not yet seen you in Kolchek's parlour—that's our posthouse, and our inn, for want of anything better. Though if ten men sit there at the same time, half of them have their legs out of doors." Weichorek laughed uproariously at this image, and Klaes gave a tight smile.

"No," he admitted. "I have not, and the men in my command have not, drunk in the village. The colonel does not approve it." When spoken, these words sounded evasive to Klaes, and pusillanimous. "And I," he added. "I do not approve it either."

"In Stollenbet then. The Sign of the Tartar."

This guessing game could serve for nothing save to erode Klaes's position. "I have said I will not name my informant," he said. "He did not, in any case, mean to speak to me, and I would be sorry if his loose tongue brought him into censure."

"Yes," the burgomaster agreed. "That would be sad." He threw out his arms in a shrug. "Well, this is an awkward thing, Lieutenant, and it somewhat gravels me how to continue."

"I too," Klaes said. "But I thought I would consult with you before I resolved upon how to proceed."

"With me? Why with me?" The man was looking at him shrewdly now, and Klaes had to work hard to keep from looking away—which would be a virtual admission that his candour was only a facade.

"Well," Klaes said, "with your knowledge of the local people and their situation, I felt you might have your own opinion as to what needs to be done."

"Does anything need to be done?"

"Perhaps not. But I should like to hear your thoughts all the same."

The burgomaster sighed, and scratched his head in a pantomime of deep rumination. "My thoughts. Well, of course. Why not? But I don't know yet, my dear Klaes, what it is you've been told."

The shift from his rank to his name was interesting, Klaes thought—and frankly something of a relief. The request for circumstantial detail was less so. "I believe I have most of the facts in my possession," he said.

"Such as?"

Klaes found himself thinking back to that shooing gesture that the burgomaster had used to get him out of the closet and into the drawing room. Now, as then, he felt somewhat like a sheep being penned. "I know about the cellar," he said. And then, taking a further gamble, "The cellar at Pokoj, I mean."

Weichorek grimaced. "That's far from the worst of it," he said. "But I ask again. It was not from Bosilka that you heard all this?"

"No!" Klaes exclaimed. "Why from Bosilka? I have barely said good day to Bosilka. And what is this to her?"

"It concerns her," the burgomaster said, calm in the face of Klaes's slightly over-emphatic denial. "Not closely, perhaps, and not as one might assume, but it concerns her. And some aspects of it . . . well, they touch on her honour, Captain. They do. I feel, to some degree, as if I'm being asked to share confidences that are not my own to dispose of. You see? I'm sure you're a man of discretion, but still . . ."

Her honour? This sounded like a murky business, and Klaes was sorry all over again that Colonel August had obliged him to try to fathom it. It distressed him, too, to discover that Bosilka Stefanu's honour was compromised. He had himself thought unworthy things of her as recently as two days ago, but after their encounter in the forest he had come to have a better opinion of her. It was not that she had brained him with a rock, it was that she had acknowledged the attack afterwards and stood ready to take the consequences. He admired that. And if he now found her to be mixed up in some tawdry scandal, it would force him to withdraw that recently bestowed respect.

"Before I speak any further," Weichorek said, "I need your assurance that what I say will not go beyond this room."

"I can't make that promise, Meister Weichorek," Klaes said scrupulously. "I wish I could, but I cannot. My overriding responsibility is to my commander, Colonel August."

"What, a colonel command a captain?"

"I'm not a captain, I'm a lieutenant. And a colonel commanding a lieutenant—or a captain, for that matter—is the normal order of things. Even if I *were* a *rittmeister*"—he used the Schönbrunner word—"Colonel August would still be three full ranks above me."

Weichorek waved the correction aside with just a touch of asperity. "I'm not trying to make you party to a conspiracy," he said. "Obviously, if you need to report this to your major—"

"My colonel."

"—to your colonel, then you'll do so. But I'd be desirous, in that case, of having your undertaking to omit the names of any third parties who might be hurt by it, do you see? Not to restrain your hand against the guilty, but to protect the innocent."

"That I will vouchsafe to do," Klaes said. "With all my heart."

"Then I'll fill in the gaps for you," Weichorek said, slapping the table. "For the devil thrives on secrets, does he not?"

"Petos—Nymand Ilya Petos, son of Jan Petos and Saska Lubisch, who was Sandra's daughter, from Grünberg, that married Lion Tchalk—"

"I think, if third parties are to be protected," Klaes interjected hastily, "you should be less categorical about names and places."

"—was Bosilka's cousin. He was born in Narutsin, and grew up here. A quiet boy, always, and some said a strange one. But Bosilka pushed him out of a tree one day, when they were both seven years old, and after that the strangeness was more in evidence. It was in the course of a game, not in spite. But then, there it was. If only our motives counted, there'd hardly be any sin at all, would there? After that Petos would be found in the middle of the night, standing stock still in someone's field, or their barn, or even on one occasion in their bedroom.

"There was no harm in the lad, he was just simple. Perhaps it was always there in him, and the falling from a tree had done no more than bring it out. Or perhaps that impact with the impacted soil of Girn Hoyter's orchard had scrambled up his vital spirits past untangling.

"Then there was an incident involving a sheepdog. The dog died, and Petos was accused. He was fourteen years old. He cried a great deal, and said he'd never hurt the dog, which was Otto Bibran's sheepdog, Lightning. But Otto was furious. The dog was the last pup of his old bitch, Phye, and he treasured her more than she was worth. He would take no compensation, he said, but he would have the boy whipped out of town for her death.

"Well, Petos was not whipped—I intervened, poured oil on the waters, brought the various parties to some sort of amity—but he was obliged to leave. The family sent him to Grünberg, where his mother still had kin. Kin on her mother's side. Bledviks. They raised the lad," Weichorek said with a slow shake of his head, "as something between a serving boy and a pet. He slept in the hayloft, not in the house, and they didn't take him to church with them on Sundays. A sorry state of affairs, but what could you do? My cousin's cousin, Molinesz, is town clerk in Grünberg and he knew what was going on, but I had no voice that I could raise there.

"Time passed. In Narutsin, Nymand Petos was all but forgotten. Then something awful and unprecedented happened—a wave of thefts that had the whole village gossiping and pointing fingers. First it was Gelen Stromajik's ladle. Then a silver-gilt hair slide from Dame Dubin's bedroom. And from my house, too, something was taken," Weichorek said. "A dollar—a hard dollar, I mean, not a rix-dollar—that was given to my son Jakusch on his first name day. It was a special pressing, with the face of Jakusch's saint, James the Fisherman, alongside that of the emperor. He prized it highly, and it was a hard loss."

Klaes began to suspect at last where this rambling story was going. "Was Miss Stefanu suspected?" he asked.

"That she was. She was the only one, you see, with a foot in all those three houses. Gelen Stromajik was her father's sister. She was thick as thieves—pardon me, was close friends, I should say—with Dubin's daughter, and always up there helping her collect eggs from the hens and the geese. And of course she worked for us.

"So yes, she was suspected. And then she was accused. And when it was put to her, she admitted it."

"Admitted her guilt!" Klaes exclaimed. He could not help himself.

"Yes. To me. But not to the priest. When she was urged to make confession, she would not do it. She only wept and wondered what would become of her." Weichorek scratched his head again and then passed his hand across his brow. "It grieves me now to think on her distress," he said. "But once she had said it, of course I had to act on it. We have no constable here. I sent to Stollenbet, where there is a parish officer and a gaol. A cell, rather, for it's only the one room in a Martello tower that was once a lookout against the border men. They came and took her, and locked her up. A date was set for her trial."

Klaes tried to reconcile this image with the forthright and even fierce young woman he had met. It made a bad fit. "I find I cannot believe this," he said.

"It troubled me too," the burgomaster admitted. "Especially that detail of her not making confession. I wondered if there was some other side to the affair that was hidden from me. And then, you know, once she'd been taken away and we were all examining our consciences, or counting our spoons as it might be, the most curious thing happened.

"The thefts went on, just as before. One man lost a milking stool, spirited away from his barn between sundown and sunup. Another, a poker from the fireplace."

"These are not precious things," Klaes said.

"No." Weichorek looked grim. "Nor was Dame Stromajik's ladle. I might have thought of that before, but I didn't. I didn't even think of it then, to tell you the truth. I thought only of Bosilka's innocence, and I made up my mind to go to Stollenbet and have the charges against her withdrawn before she came to trial. Only my wife, God bless her, thought that was a sign of undue partiality on my part. To be blunt, she thought I looked on Silkie with an improper affection, and wanted her home again for that reason. And while we argued the point back and forth, with more heat than sense, the snows fell. They fell thick, and they fell deep.

"You would have thought a foot of snow on the ground and a wind you could shave your beard with would deter a thief from going abroad. And so they did, for two nights and three days. But on the third night we were all roused from our beds with great halloos and alarums. Jorg Stefanu came running into town to say that his workshop had been broken into in the night, and two of his hammers were gone.

"A man's tools are sacred things, but I suspect that had little to do with what happened next. One of the village lads, Tilde Shweven's boy, points out that the thief has left his footprints in the snow. And then all the men are fetching up knives and cudgels and torches and talking themselves into a great fervour. They'll catch this rascal and serve him properly for his tricks.

"I tried to calm them. I pointed out that the tracks would keep until dawn, and that daylight would make their enterprise safer and surer, but it would not do. Off they ran into the dark, hunting like hounds but braying like donkeys. And soon enough the trail led them into the woods—and yes, there is someone running before them. They've roused up their quarry. So some yell at him to stop, while others throw their weapons at him as though bread knives and paring knives and chisels and awls were javelins.

"He did not stop, naturally. He must have been afraid they would tear him to pieces. He ran on. Now he was out of sight among the trees, now they caught a glimpse again, and to make the story short they drove him before them all the way to Pokoj. In Pokoj he went to ground, and they lost him for a while. But only for a while. They found him in the first of the cellars, the one with the empty wine racks all along the wall and the broken table in the far corner.

"The room stank of shit and sweat and rotten food, and they could see why. The thief had made himself a nest there behind the broken table, and stuffed it with blankets and curtains from the rooms above. He had evidently lived there for some weeks, in the most impoverished and degraded conditions. Someone—it was Bosilka, of course—had brought him clothes, and a slop bucket, and food. The food was scraps from my table. The bucket he hadn't used. He'd just relieved himself against the walls, choosing a different spot each time.

"I suppose I don't need to tell you that it was the idiot boy, Petos. Only he was an idiot man now.

"He had come back from Stollenbet to be close to his former friend, who he still loved. He had followed her, whenever he could, and watched her from a distance, filled with longing for her. Not a man's longing, I think—just a child's longing to be close to someone who'd loved him. All the things he'd taken were from places where she'd been. Which of course had led to her being accused and sent away. And she knew it was him, and took the guilt on herself in order to spare him.

"They were all there. His odd little trophies, laid out in patterns that presumably meant something to him. But we couldn't ask him by then. Some of those absurd weapons must have hit their mark after all, or else Petos wounded himself by running into trees and falling over rocks in the dark as he was pursued. He was dying, at any rate. From these injuries. From exhaustion. Who knows? From heartbreak, perhaps, since storytellers say a man can die from that. He must have thought Bosilka had abandoned him. That would have cut deep."

Klaes opened his mouth to speak, but Weichorek raised a hand, indicating that he hadn't yet reached his peroration.

"We might have called a crowner to come and sit and answer all our questions. To tell us how he died and most likely to hold one of us, or all of us, to account for it. Perhaps that was the proper thing to do. But I didn't see, Lieutenant, what good it would have served. Nobody had meant to harm him. And it might be argued that the blow that killed him had come fifteen years before, when Bosilka pushed him and he slipped and fell from that tree. Certainly she blames herself for it, and will not be convinced that it was an accident. I brought her home. I told her what had happened. I advised her to forget. But then you and your men arrived in Pokoj, and to some of us here—saving your presence, in their eyes one authority is very much like another— it seemed that you might have come to call them to account for this sad business. So. Forgetting, at the moment, is not easy for her. For anyone."

Weichorek sighed and shook his head again. He waved his hand, inviting Klaes to say what he had been about to say before. But Klaes had been going to ask about Bosilka's imprisonment and how she had been delivered. With that question resolved, he found he had nothing else to say. The whole grotesque affair reflected well on nobody, and yet he was impressed both with Bosilka's courage and with the generosity of her heart. He felt, too, that the burgomaster had probably made the right decision in a difficult situation. He hoped that he could persuade Colonel August to do the same.

He stood. "Well," he said, "I'm answered. And I commend you, Meister Weichorek, for your frankness in this. While I can't promise, I think it unlikely that we'll need to speak any further on the matter." He paused, choosing his next words with care. "And it goes without saying that I'll keep Miss Stefanu's confidence. If I'm obliged to repeat any of what you've told me to my commander, I will take care that her name is not mentioned."

"I'm sure of it, Sergeant Klaes. I know I may rely on your discretion." Weichorek smiled in a way that might or might not be seen as conveying some hidden import. He also stood and offered Klaes his hand. They clasped and shook solemnly, as though they were men of business concluding an agreement.

Then the burgomaster waved Klaes out of the drawing room, gave him good day, apologised for not offering him any refreshment, commended his good wishes to the colonel ("A colonel, you say he is? That's fine, now!") and his wife, commented on the way the weather seemed to be turning and excused himself to attend to other business, in that order and without a pause. Klaes was left blinking in the hallway, bemused at the speed of his dismissal.

He was about to open the door and see himself out when Bosilka emerged from the closet, almost colliding with him in the narrow space.

"Your coat," she said, thrusting it at him.

"Thank you," Klaes said. But he did not immediately take it. "Miss Stefanu, did you purposely omit to mention my arrival to Meister Weichorek?"

The girl bridled, then blushed. "I told him right away that you'd come!" she exclaimed. "Almost right away. Very soon after. I do have other duties, you know. Hirschel is meant to be answering the door today, but he's nowhere to be found. So everybody complains that I'm slow, when I'm up to my elbows in washing."

"I'm not complaining," Klaes assured her. "Only, I'd like you to know that you don't have to be afraid of me. I wish you'd believe that. I'm not trying to work you harm."

Bosilka's mouth set into a tight line. "I believe that, Lieutenant Klaes."

"Thank you. I'm glad of it."

"But the harm may come, whether you work it or not."

Klaes cast about for an adequate reply, but found nothing. He opened the front door instead, intending to depart before she could lambast him any further. He was turning towards Bosilka to take his leave when he noticed that her eyes had widened, a look of horror on her face. And then, as if underscoring her words, he heard shouts and cries from the street behind him, and the dull thud of flesh hitting flesh. Filled with foreboding, he turned and met a scene which gave him some taste of the harm Bosilka had in mind. And he swore in terms which no gentleman should ever use in a lady's hearing.

20

Lieutenant Tusimov's expedition had started off well enough, but it had not ended propitiously. Not at all.

The Glogau valley at this point was very wide and very shallow, its breadth greater than the elevations on either side. At its centre was the Mala Panev, a tributary of the Oder, which at certain times of the year was a considerable torrent. It lay peaceably enough within its banks now, but Lieutenant Tusimov noted how high those banks were. He decided he would make the river the westernmost point of their progress, since in any case it marked the legal boundary between Silesia and Prussia, where they had no business to be. Not, at least, until Frederick Hohenzollern made himself such an irritant to the empire that it became necessary to set his teeth on edge.

Until then they were peacekeepers and guardians, not warriors and angels of vengeance. Desirous though he was of glory, Tusimov was content to let it come to him in its own time. He would scruple to vex the Fates with the overzealous prosecution of his duty, as though he were some questing knight of old.

He marched his unit through the village at a smart pace. He was tempted to order the double march at that point, but when he came to it there was no need. Once they came among the slovenly cottages and the gawking peasantry the men quickened the pace of their own volition, their clomping boots raising spume from the puddles and flecks of mud from the pressed earth. If there had been cobbles, they would have raised sparks.

There were a good few onlookers out on the main street. There were more still, Tusimov was certain, watching from behind sack curtains or through the cracks of doors. The faces that he saw wore a variety of expressions, mostly speculative or solemn. But a few scowled openly, as though the sight of the soldiers so emphatically treading down their thoroughfare were an affront of some kind.

Well, if it was an affront, let them open wide and swallow it down. Tusimov considered that he and his men had more right to walk this street than those who merely lived in its vicinity. They, after all, were the guarantors of its continued existence. Dancer paused as they left the village, raising her tail to drop a sizeable load of manure into the centre of the street. As she trotted on, an old lady in a black dress that swept the ground came running out, sack in hand, to claim the prize. She carried no spade; she just scooped the shit into the sack with her bare hands.

From Narutsin they marched on westward and downward, along cart tracks whose ruts were deep enough for a man to step in up to his knees. It was slow going, but the general mood seemed to be good. And in due course they reached the river, where they paused so the men could refill canteens and eat a little dried meat from their trail rations. More than half of them lit pipes too, and since he hadn't expressly forbidden it, Tusimov was content to let it pass. There was something cheering about the grey clouds of their own making that soon hovered over their heads—a riposte to the larger and darker masses sitting on the peaks all around them.

After a decent interval they moved on, turning north now and keeping the river on their left hand. The ground was sodden and overgrown, the path merely notional in places, and Tusimov began to wish that he had taken a different route. He felt that he had better keep to it now, though. They would march to the head of the valley on this lower elevation, ascend the eastern slope via what was marked on the colonel's maps as a wagon road, and so return to Pokoj along the flank of the mountain called Zielona Góra. The name (Green Hill) promised pleasant views. Better, at least, than their current surroundings, which were quickly becoming a morass.

Morale suffered accordingly, but it was nothing that wouldn't mend as soon as the going got a little easier. Tusimov urged the men onward, staying in the van where they could all see him. After a while, and choosing his moment with care, he dismounted. Better they should see him slip and stumble in the mud than that they should view him as the sort of officer who made demands of them he wasn't prepared to meet himself.

They slogged on like this for another hour. Tusimov kept his eyes peeled for a track that was further removed from the water, but the map showed nothing and nothing offered itself. Eventually he sent out scouts. They came back wet, discouraged and empty-handed.

Another hour brought them to the wagon track. It was nothing of the kind, unless the wagons in question were pulled by goats. Near-vertical in places, it was strewn with rocks that the men in front had to navigate with extreme care in order to avoid bringing them down on the heads of those behind.

Halfway up, the slope became so steep that their progress could no longer be called a march. It was a climb, and not an easy one. Dancer was doing her best, game old girl that she was, to pick her way through the scrub and furze and treacherous scree, but her own weight dragged her down two steps for every three she took, and it was only a matter of time before she fell and broke a leg.

"I'm going down and around," Tusimov told Strumpfel. "I'll meet you on the lee slope."

"Yes sir," Strumpfel said, loosening his grip on a clump of couch grass to essay a clumsy salute. Tusimov led Dancer back down the precipitous incline even more slowly than they had ascended it. The men watched him go, wordless and unhappy.

"Stick to it, lads," he exhorted them as he passed. "Nearly there."

Approached from the other side, the mountain held fewer pitfalls, but whoever had called it Zielona Góra was bloody colour blind. It was grey gravel and grey scrub all the way up to a crown that was bald and gaunt. He actually got there before the men, whose route had taken them around a spur a half-mile to the west and back again to what counted as the summit.

"And there," Tusimov said, when everyone had struggled to the top and could see where he was pointing, "is Prussia. Like a boil on the arse of Europe." The men nearest him laughed despite their exhaustion, but he suspected it was only because they were in his line of sight. There was silence from behind him, which goaded him to further verbal flights. "The abscess of syphilis, no doubt," he suggested, raising his voice. "*Morbus gallicus*, my lads, the French disease. Young Frederick has turned Berlin into a brothel, after all. So who should wonder if he turns his country into a tart's welt?"

This got a cheer, despite the train of ideas being a tenuous one. What Tusimov was thinking was that this was murderous terrain from which to launch an invasion. Unless the Prussian maps were a bloody sight better than his own, a general could wander up and down these sheep runs for days and not find an actual road. And while a company could go two or three abreast at need, an army couldn't. He defied anyone to hold a line of march through this sopping wet cunt of a country.

Tusimov liked glory, and the radiant furniture of military adventure. But he was greatly deficient in physical courage, by means of which glory is usually procured. His beguiling fantasy, in moments of leisure, was a commendation for valour won without any personal risk at all. In the absence of that, he was happy to find himself defending a position that was unlikely to be attacked.

"We'll give those cabbage farmers hell, my boys, just won't we? If they drag their muddy feet across our borders, we'll teach them manners at a bayonet's end and make them clean up their mess before we send them home again, by gravy!"

A murmur of assent rose from around him. Buoyed up by it, Tusimov tugged hard on Dancer's reins to make her rear—a hazardous operation on this tilted tabletop of a landscape, but he knew what a dashing figure he cut when her hooves slashed the air like that. "For Maria, Austria and God!" he cried, and the men huzzahed.

That mood sustained them, for a while at least, as Tusimov led the way back down into the valley. He had abandoned the map by this time, finding that his own eyes served him better, but ironically they betrayed him when they were back on more level ground. Dancer stepped into a rabbit hole, stumbled and pitched onto her side. Fortunately the horse's collapse was gradual enough to enable Tusimov to jump clear.

The leg seemed to be broken—or at least, Dancer was unable to right herself again, but Tusimov felt for the break and couldn't find it. Utterly wretched, he decided to put her out of her pain but was unable to finish her off himself. He deputed Strumpfel, who in turn rapped out an order to one of the privates at the head of the line to load his musket.

Tusimov watched, dismayed, as this was done, but then cried out "Halt there!" as the soldier took aim. "It may be she's just hurt," he explained to Strumpfel. "I'd hate to kill her if there's no need. I'll wait a while and see if she rallies."

"Yes, sir," Strumpfel said. "As you say, sir. Orders for the men, sir? Shall I tell them to fall out?"

No, Tusimov decided, *that wouldn't do.* He'd raised their spirits up on the crown of the mountain. Now they'd see him waiting, passive, unable to move or to command. That would be the image they'd carry away with them, and the thought appalled him. He ordered Strumpfel to take over and lead the men back to Pokoj himself, and once there to have another horse sent out. It might be that Dancer, recovered, would be able to trot but unable to carry his weight. Or it might be that she'd have to be shot and he'd require another mount to bring him home.

Strumpfel relayed these orders to the unit and got them moving again quickly. Some glanced back over their shoulders at their commander diminishing into the distance behind them, shipwrecked on dry land. Most were more concerned by this time about the leaks in their boots or the pains from injuries sustained in that precarious climb. All were muddied, and more than a few bloodied besides. Huzzas notwithstanding, they were not in an ebullient mood.

And Strumpfel was not assertive enough or loud enough to be an effective shepherd of the human species. In truth, he was one of the most complaisant and soft-hearted sergeants ever seen. In the presence of senior officers he could summon a halfway-effective bellow, but the men of the company knew that it was the reverberation of a bran tub rather than the voice of the thunder.

They were therefore rather more relaxed on the return journey than a good line of march required. Those most eager to get back to their billets and take a little solace in hot rum or clean clothes drew ahead of the mass. Those most debilitated by sodden boots and turned ankles fell behind.

It was in this besmirched and enfeebled state that the soldiers of

Lieutenant Tusimov's unit retraced their steps through Narutsin, an hour shy of sunset. The villagers who had watched them with resentful or fearful eyes on their outward leg watched them again now with barely concealed grins as they limped and straggled home.

The bedraggled troopers were well aware of this amusement. They felt it keenly, because the prevalence of dirt in and around the village made up a large part of their perceived superiority to the local population. They had joked about the nourishing meals that could be made from sheep dung, and for what price mud (depending on its purity and consistency) might sell in the regional markets. Now, carrying some of that sheep dung and mud on their own persons, they were obliged to parade themselves for the entertainment of smirking farm boys and dullard prentices. It was hard to bear.

Most quickened their pace, wanting the shame to be over with sooner. But some of the disaffected stragglers at the tail end of the line took a different tack.

"What are you looking at, hayseed?" Private Renke demanded of a man who was leaning on a walking stick outside an open front door (presumably his own). Renke had chosen his target with some nicety. The man was more than twice his age, overweight and dignified. He was probably a pillar of the community, so insulting him meant something.

Possibly Renke expected the man to look away or mutter an apology. Instead he laughed. "I was hoping you could tell me that," he said jocularly. "Something that came up out of the wetlands—fairy or changeling, maybe, for I never saw a woman's son look so wild!"

Renke was incensed. "You a gleaner, grandad?" he demanded.

"Not in November, sonny."

"Well you're going to be gleaning your fucking teeth once I spread them over the street. Look away, you old shite. Seriously, look away or I will break the fucking grain of you."

The old man gave him a look of contempt, shook his head—and dropped his gaze to the ground. Good enough. Renke resumed the march.

He and his comrades—a round half-dozen of them—were the very last of the unit. The rest were not in sight. A number of village men were, though, and some of them appeared now to have condensed into a tight knot in the middle of the street ahead of the soldiers.

Renke was for walking right through them, and devil take the hindmost, but Private Lehmann and Private Schottenberg contrived to lead him off at an angle, avoiding a direct collision.

"Bloody yokels," Renke observed, loudly enough to be heard. "Faces like cracks in a bloody wall."

They walked on.

But one of the village men answered him as he passed by, "Well if I had a face as pretty as yours, I'd keep it indoors on weekdays, swear I would."

It wasn't the words that made Renke stop, it was the burst of laughter that followed them. He turned to face the little knot of men. "Which one of you said that?" he demanded.

"Piss off," one of the villagers replied equably, "you arse-faced lackwit."

Renke took a step forward. Private Lehmann interposed himself hastily. "Nobody here wants a fight," he urged.

"Why'd you join the fucking army then?" one of the village men sneered. "Do you just like dressing up?"

Lehmann threw the first punch, and was put down by the second, his lower lip split wide open and one of his teeth rattling loose in his mouth. By the time he staggered upright again, soldiers and villagers were in a rolling ruck along the street, brawling and battling in the dirt.

Anton Hanslo was on his way back from delivering an oak doorknob to Meister Kolchek at the posthouse when he heard the shrieks and curses from the main street. He ran to the end of the path, rounded the corner and stared open-mouthed at an astonishing sight. It looked at first as though some blow from heaven had struck a dozen men at once with desperate convulsions. Then he realised that they were fighting each other. And some of them were in uniform.

"Jesu!" he gasped.

Women were keening from the sidelines as the men hurled themselves against one another, punching and cursing. In the doorway of the burgomaster's house at the other end of the street, Silkie was staring at the scene. Another soldier, an officer by his uniform, stood beside her. His mouth gaped like a fish, and he seemed rooted to the spot, one hand raised as if to begin a call for order which had frozen on his lips. Then Meister Weichorek himself barged past them and came running towards the disturbance. His wife and son were at his heels, at least at first, but Jakusch's youth and vigour told over the distance. He arrived first.

"Stop them!" the burgomaster yelled. And it may be that this was Jakusch's intention. But at the moment when he reached the skirmish, one of the soldiers was holding Matheus Vavra's face down in the dirt and seemed to be trying to throttle him. Jakusch launched himself at the man and sent him sprawling.

Weichorek was now at the outer fringes of the fight himself, but he stopped dead when he got there, unable to find a place into which to insert his authority. "For the love of God!" he pleaded. "Stop them, somebody! Separate them!"

The anguish in that cry galvanised Hanslo. He sprinted across the street and laid hands on the first man he could reach, a villager, hauling him away from his opponent by main force. Other men were running too, from the houses all around. A few seemed to want to get their own blows in but most, like Hanslo, were trying to stop the fight. If the soldiers took a few more buffets in the process, so did the village men they were battling with.

And now women were intervening too, with greater effect. Two opponents pulled out of each other's reach would try to find each other again as soon as they were released. But where a woman stood in the way, weeping and wringing her hands, they were hindered as they tried to find a way around her—and then as often as not, some sense of themselves and of their surroundings would come back to them and they would lower their hands, abashed.

Like oil stirred into water, the melee gradually separated out again into its two distinct ingredients. All the men were battered and filthy, and all were still furious, but for the moment neither moved against the other. They only stood and panted and eyed each other with defiance and hatred.

In another moment the battle would surely have flared again around some real or imagined insult. But fortunately the officer—a lieutenant—intervened at this point and with a string of shouted orders made the soldiers back away from their former enemies into a tighter group. And Meister Weichorek was in his proper element now. He knew how to handle truculence and block-headedness. It was only violence that baffled him.

"Now by Christ," he said in ringing tones, "I am ashamed to be a *Schliesener*! If this is what we breed, I had rather have been born a Turk!"

He let his gaze sweep one man after another, full of stern reproach. "Aye, you may hang your head, Sivet Ulsner. Jan Puszin. Martek Luse. Is this how you were taught? Piek Lauvener, how would it grieve your mother to see you brawling and biting like a dog in the street?"

"I'm right here, Berthold Weichorek," Dame Lauvener said from behind him. "And I can tell you it grieves me a fair deal!"

Her tone as she said this was so ferocious that her son Piek actually hid from her behind another man. A ripple of laughter ran through the village men, sheepish and in a way relieved. A mother telling off her son put this violent outburst into another perspective. It made them feel like children, whose faults might be pardoned, rather than like men who had broken the civil peace.

Berthold Weichorek was not so sanguine about this, but he knew that sometimes the best way to save your salt is to throw just a little of it in the devil's eye.

"You may be sure, Lieutenant Klaes," he said, turning to the officer by his side, "that all here will be sorry for this day's work. I wasn't appointed burgomaster to see my village descend into chaos and licence. Nor will I stand for it. There will be punishment and shame for all who took part in this disgraceful riot."

He was grimly determined to be as good as his word, knowing that a great deal might depend on it. He sent a boy to fetch the priest, who in the absence of a clerk could be relied on to write down the names of all involved.

Father Kazen, looking very unhappy to be performing in this civic arena, solemnly recorded on the inside back cover of a hymnal the given and the family names of every man who had taken part in the fight. This took a long time, during which the malefactors might easily have slipped away, but they stood by patiently and endured the shame.

The soldiers, meanwhile, fell in behind their officer and limped away with many backward glances and dark threats. They had given as good as they got, but the accounting in such affairs is seldom to the complete satisfaction of anyone concerned.

21

The tail end of Tusimov's unit returned from their manoeuvres in a dishevelled enough state that their arrival at Pokoj provoked a flurry of concerned activity. Wives and doxies ran to their husbands and lovers, exclaiming in dismay over their bloodied faces. Sarai, who acted as an unofficial nurse among the camp followers, hurried to wash their cuts and prepare poultices of arnica for their bruises. Lehmann, Renke and the rest were led to their tents with tender pity.

Once the news of the fight had spread through the camp, however, that pity swiftly turned to laughter.

"The archduchess's finest beaten by a bunch of farmers," Libush chuckled. "What'll they do when the Prussians get here?"

Drozde found that she could not join in the general merriment. Her mind kept drifting to Anton, and each time she thought of him it was with a growing sense of anxiety. None of the accounts of the fight she had heard mentioned the villagers involved by name, but it was generally agreed that a goodly proportion of the young men of Narutsin had taken part. Surely he had more sense than to join in a brawl? But Drozde thought of his naivety, how openly he displayed his feelings, and she was not so sure.

The talk in the camp that night was all of the fight. A cluster of privates sat around a fire, cheering and hooting while some of Tusimov's men recounted again the glorious tale of the pounding they had given those hayseeds down in Narutsin. A short distance away Ottilie and Alis and some of the other girls giggled at how ill the men's account tallied with their torn uniforms and black eyes. Drozde wanted no part of any of it. They might be quartered here until the spring, and a fight had broken out less than a fortnight after they'd arrived! Tensions between the camp and the village had been bad enough before this—now the soldiers probably wouldn't even be able to visit Narutsin on market day without some sort of a scuffle. "What will you make of this in your next show, Drozde?" one of the privates called out to her as she passed by. *I'll show it as the pissing match it was,* Drozde thought, but she made no reply.

She was angry, and somehow her concern over Anton nettled her and made her anger worse. If he had been hurt in the fight then it was his own fault! The camp was not somewhere that she wanted to be right now, she decided, but neither did the thought of walking into the village appeal to her. So she went to see the ghosts, in whose company she could hide from the follies of soldiers and Narutsiners alike.

The ballroom was starting to feel as familiar to Drozde as Molebacher's kitchen, and a good deal more welcoming. The ghosts smiled to see her, but they did not cluster around her as they usually did. Their unaccountable instincts seemed to tell them before she had even arrived that she was in no mood for a lively welcome.

Magda touched Drozde's arm. "The fight is stupid, isn't it? I wish they could all be friends, like us."

Thea smiled sadly. "I wish that too, my love. But some people are only happy when there's a quarrel. Look at my family: all the men ever did was fight." She spoke to Magda, but the look she gave Drozde was full of understanding.

"Let's have a peaceful story tonight," Drozde suggested. She had heard more than enough of violence for one evening.

The ghosts shifted and murmured for a moment, and then a young man stepped forward. Drozde recognised him as the handsome soldier in the unfamiliar uniform, the one who had spoken up after Arinak's tale.

"My story ends in war, as do so many others," he began, "but that is not its subject. It would be a short one else. I was seventeen when I went for a soldier, and nineteen when I died."

I counted my age in summers, because summer was my favourite time. The winters on a farm are desperate bad. You wake up in the dark and work in the dark for hours and hours, pulling at the cows' teats with fingers almost breaking off from cold, your body so numb it's like you're already dead. You have to look at your hands all the time because you can't feel them. The only way to know what they're doing is to squint your eyes and watch them as though they were someone else's.

Then when the sun comes up, it's not any better. It doesn't bring warmth with it, only light to see by. And what you see is just grey on grey, frost and dead grass and weathered wood, everywhere and everywhere, until you feel like you might drown in it.

But in the summer the sky is like a bucket, pouring hotness down on you, and the fields are painted in so many colours you can't count them or name them. It's warm enough to think. And it's warm enough to love.

This was in Janowo, which is in Majki, which is in the east of Prussia. I know that now, because when you go to be a soldier you see things outside what you knew. And that means you learn where the things you knew really stand in the world. But back then it was just Janowo, and not even Janowo really (because when did I ever walk into the village?) but my father's farm three miles outside Janowo. I lived in a tiny world, though of course I didn't know it until later. All worlds are the same size when you live in them.

The young man's voice, never very loud, faltered into silence. The ghosts all around him murmured encouragement.

"What happened then?" Drozde asked him, speaking softly because he was so young and so beautiful and so pale. She was afraid a harsh word might break him.

It's hard for me to say. If I tell you everything directly—well, it makes the story meaningless. Or at least, makes it seem less than it was. And it was everything, to me. It was all I knew of life before I went to war. And when I went to war, I died.

I think I'll tell it as though it was someone else's story—I'll say "he" and "she" and "they." "They did it." Not "I did it." And you'll know, when I come to it, why I chose that way to tell it. Because this is a story about choices, and I'll never know whether the choices that were made were right or wrong. Perhaps you can tell me that when you've listened. When you know all of it.

There was a girl, and there were two boys. The girl was Ermel, Herdein Holz's daughter. The Herdein whose father was from Shnir, and who was crippled in his left leg, and whose wife's name was Müte.

The boys were Kristof and Max. Each was a farmer's son, and each reached his sixteenth year in the same month that Ermel did. Born in the same season, they were.

And fast friends they were too, from that season onward. They grew up together; the three farms was nearest neighbours, and none of the three children was ever seen without the other two coming right after, the way you hear a goose honk and look up to see the whole skein quartering the sky.

They played boisterous games. Stole apples from Alte Hankel's orchard, chased the hens across the green and back again, and fished in streams that was rich men's trout runs, that they would have been whipped if they'd been found there. The girl was no different from the boys in these adventures. They were just three friends that did everything alike.

But you know that tale, I think, and the ending of it, which is always the same. They grew up. And though a little girl is allowed to be a boy sometimes, an older one must look how to be a woman. Ermel went to her mother one morning, bewildered and frightened, to show her a bloodstained nightshift. Forthwith she was taken away from her two best friends, and given skirts to wear instead of breeches. It wasn't proper now for her to be with boys in the way a child might, or else she'd soon enough come by a child of her own. That was what her mother told her. As if those companions of so many years had overnight become enemies that might work her ruin.

She grew up lovely, though. So lovely. Everyone said so. Everyone wanted her. She had blonde hair so fine her mother said you could put it on a spindle and spin it into gold. And her smile would charm a cat out of a tree, her father and uncles swore. They meant nothing by it, only to encourage her to smile again.

This was in Prussia, as I told you. And in Prussia there is a thing called the *cantonal Gesetz*. A village, say, or a number of farms that lie together, is called a canton. And every canton has to supply a soldier for the army, whenever one is asked for. If that soldier dies, the army sends to ask for another, and so on. It means the strength of the army stays the same, even if the mother country is fighting lots of battles. New recruits are always there to draw on.

Where the canton is a village, it usually goes well enough. There's a public ballot, with everyone's names on stones or papers put into a bucket. And everyone can inspect the names, to see they're all there. And a child draws one out, or else a blindfolded man does, or one as can't read even their own name, so it's sure to be fair.

But with farms, it's different. Our canton was five smallholdings. Majki Zagroly, that was Ermel's father's. Soldany, that belonged to Max's family, and Krusze Wielkie, that was Kristof's. The other two, Kownatkie and Nawawies Wielka, was fallen in and no one lived there now.

So that was three families. And out of the three, only two boys of army age to be had. Max's brother, Eberlin Slezak, had gone up last, so that should have meant that Kristof's family, the Neissers, should send the next. But what were they to do? Both the households had ageing fathers, and both were relying on those rising sons to work the fields and tend the cows. Ermel's father was a little younger, but his left leg was halt after a bad fall, as I think I already told you. It was all he could do to tend the holding he had and provide for his family. He had prayed so long for a son he'd worn his voice hoarse with praying, and only a daughter to show for it. A pretty daughter, but what's that when the leaves fall?

So the Neissers were beholden, but they didn't want to admit it. And the Slezaks dug in their heels and said—what was true enough—they'd lost one son already. All amity between the families vanished like smoke up the chimney as they argued it bitterly back and forth, back and forth. And finally they determined that the recruiting officers must sit on it and give a judgment, because neither side would budge.

Only the two boys kept up their friendship, like before, and took some refuge in each other's company from the bitter tears and harsh voices that were given out in both their houses. And more than ever they missed Ermel, that had been their other self, their sister and more than sister when they were all three growing up.

To be honest with you, they did more than miss her. They went to Majki Zagroly some nights when the moon was full and the sky clear, and threw stones at her window. And the three of them ran the woods again as they'd used to do when none of them had a thought of war or womanhood. They stayed together until cockcrow some nights, and crept exhausted home, each to his own back door, taking off their clothes only to put them on again and pretend to be just risen from sleep.

And if you ask me whether either of the boys touched Ermel privily on those near-daylit nights, the way a man touches a woman, I say this. They were children, in their hearts at least. They had no more thought of coupling than they had of death.

But their parents, by this time, had no thought of anything else. The Neissers and the Slezaks had talked and argued and planned and fretted themselves into a fine lather, and the fruit of their labours was alike on both sides: that if their bonny boy paid court to Ermel, and won her hand, then when the recruiting officers came they'd have an easy choice. No one would take a young man whose banns had been read and throw him into a battle line when he should be in a different kind of skirmish altogether, under the blankets of a marriage bed.

So Kunrat Neisser and Dietl Slezak took their sons aside and urged them on to plead suit to young Ermel. If they could lie with her and get her with child, they would do very well. But failing that, her bare word would be enough.

Max and Kristof were dutiful boys, and did what was asked of them much more often than not. The thought of using Ermel in such a way didn't sit well with them, but there were other thoughts that came into their heads too. To be with their friend forever, and live with her, and raise a family with her. That was on the one hand. And on the other, to run in a line of men against a line of other men, and be stopped with musket balls, and have death for a purgative.

When next the boys met, they didn't speak of what they'd been bid to do. It ran too deep for words. They talked of other things instead. Mostly, they talked about their friendship. They swore to be friends forever, as though swearing it would make it so. And then because they knew it wouldn't they cried and fought and walked apart from each other, their hearts too full of that dreadful knowledge to hold anything else. They'd meant to call on Ermel, but they couldn't do it. They couldn't be all together as they used to be, when they had such thoughts bearing down on them.

After that night, it seemed the old trinity they'd had—if it's not sin to call it such—was broken. Some evenings, when the farm work was all done, Max would come to Majki Zagroly and offer to chop wood or cut shingles for Ermel's father. Herdein Holz never spoke on these occasions, but only pointed to the woodshed or the barn or wherever it might be, and went back inside.

And on other nights it would be Kristof who came. He was more skilled with his hands, and had done some smithing with his uncle Janke, so he might fix a bent coulter on the plough or fashion a fine new handle for one of Dame Holz's knives.

The reward for these good deeds was to sit in the kitchen for a half-hour or so with the family. There would be desultory conversation about the weather or the harvest. Ermel would be present, but would not speak to the boy, whichever boy it was. That would have been considered forward. The kitchen was too hot, and in spite of its high ceiling not very large. Strings of onions, heads of cabbage and cured sausages hung from a rack at head height and rocked gently when anyone moved. The floor creaked. The air was heavy with steam from something seething on the stove. And Ermel and whichever boy it was sat and stole shy glances at each other and felt like two-thirds of something that might never be whole again.

That was a bad season, for all of them. It was the end of summer, which in times gone they would have loved to walk in, but now if felt like dead winter and nothing to hope for. The boys were vying to see which of them would live. Even the winner would feel like he had lost.

One night, instead of going to Ermel's house, Max went to Krusze Wielkie instead. Kunrat Neisser opened the door to him and asked him what he wanted. Only to talk to Kristof, he said. To talk for a moment, and then he would go away.

The old man wasn't happy about it, but he went inside and soon Kristof came out. The two boys sat under a plane tree that grew at the edge of the furthest field in the Neisser holding, watching the old man sun bow his head to the earth.

"I thought I might ask Ermel to be trothed to me," Max said. Kristof already knew this, of course. If Max had done as he was told, he would already have had that conversation. But something kept him from it.

"It's a good thought," Kristof muttered, staring at the ground. "I was turning it over in my own mind, somedeal, that I might put that question to her myself." And that was true too, yet here he was with the words still inside him.

It seemed pointless, in the face of this, to say they'd always be friends. Two would stay, and one would go. Max knew from his brother's example that the one who went wouldn't be coming back. In asking for Ermel's hand, he'd be asking her to throw the first handful of dirt onto Kristof's coffin, though the wood for the coffin might not be cut or sanded yet, nor the flowers grown that would deck it.

"I thought I might ask her tonight," he said, and waited.

"Tonight is good," Kristof said. "It's broad Sabbath already, and the recruiting officer's coming on Monday morning. A man shouldn't linger too long."

A man! They were seventeen. What they knew of manhood was all hearsay and hopefulness.

"Well then," said Max. "Come with me, and ask her too."

The two boys looked long at each other without saying anything more. It was surely the only fair way to do it. And yet, in being fair to each other, what would they do to Ermel? How would she live, knowing what she'd done? How would any of them live?

"I'll come," Kristof said. "But I may not speak. I'm not yet fully resolved."

"Well, no more amn't I," Max said. "Not resolved, as such. But only thinking it."

They got up and walked together down the track that led to Majki Zagroly. The sun was lying on the ground now, and the light all around them was like fire coming out of the ground, almost. Red and gold and all good colours you could imagine.

It was too late to pay a formal visit, but they both thought that was probably for the best. They threw stones onto the roof above Ermel's window until she put her head out and saw them. Then they waited until she came down to them.

It was only a half a moon, and the sky none too clear, but there was some light below the horizon yet—as though the ghost of the sun still shone after the sun had died. They walked down the path to the river, and they sat there listening to the voice of the water as the darkness grew upon them.

It seemed like a spell was on them. A word would be enough to break it, so they were careful not to speak. Or only with their eyes, anyway—such talk as you can have that way. And round and round it went. Ermel looking at Kristof, and Kristof at Max, and Max at Ermel.

I know, their eyes said. And *I know that too.* And *What's to be done about it?*

Ermel kissed Max on the mouth. She kissed him long and deep, holding him to her as though he was her lover and her everything.

She did the same to Kristof.

Then she took off her clothes and walked into the water. She swam out into the centre of the river, where she turned onto her back so she could watch the stars through the gaps in the scudding clouds. She only had to kick her legs a little to hold her place against the gentle current.

She knew what must be, but she could not choose for them. She could not even tell them what she knew, beyond what those kisses must surely have told them. For the rest, they must make their own choice.

When she had given them what she thought was long enough, and then a little longer, she swam back to shore. She found them where she had left them in the nest the river grasses made, their limbs entangled, their beautiful bodies shiny with the sweat of love.

She thought for a moment of leaving them there together. But then Kristof opened one eye and beckoned to her, so she elbowed and fussed and slipped herself in between them, and they folded themselves around her. That was how they spent the night, all three of them wrapped together in a knot of friendship like the knots they put on brooches.

The next morning, the recruiting officers, which in truth was only a sergeant and a drummer boy, were met on the road by a handsome young man who saluted them as smartly as if he was already in uniform.

"I thought there was some dispute to settle," the sergeant grunted.

"It was settled," the young man said. "I'm for you."

And he was sworn in there and then, at the turning of the road, with the drummer boy standing witness and nobody but birds to cheer him.

He met his regiment the next day. It was encouraging, at least, to find he was not the youngest. He trained for three months with sword and musket, and he was so quick on his feet they put him in the *Schuetzen*, the light infantry. It was some while, though, before he had to fight. In the first year after he enlisted, Prussia prosecuted no wars. It declared itself ready to fight against Sweden once, but Sweden declined the honour. Apart from that, all was peace and amity.

The boy could not write, and so he sent no letters home. When he came up for leave, he spent it in Berlin. But he thought often of the friends he'd left behind, and wondered if they were happy. He hoped they were. He had done all he could to make it so.

Then the new king came, with warlike thoughts and talk of honour. Prussia would be one, he said, and Prussia would take all her old strength on herself. So that meant joining the divided territories of the motherland, and it meant taking back Silesia, which was Prussia's by a very old treaty. Everyone thought that the unification would come first, but it was Silesia where we were sent.

The young man was a skirmisher in the first battle, here where your river runs, and he fought well. Again and again he fought, through the winter and into the spring. He was at Mollwitz, where three thousand of the enemy died for three hundred of ours; he marched on into Bohemia, and saw host after host break before Prussia's will. He was there when they agreed the ceasefire that nobody, not even he, thought would hold. And then he came back here to Pokoj when the weather turned, to wait out the winter.

And here died, not from the fighting but from the frost and from a desperate flux that wrung his guts out for eleven days, until he finally succumbed to it.

I did ever hate the winter.

The soldier took off his cap and smoothed down his blond hair. Though a little wild and unkempt, it was—Drozde saw—very fine. Perhaps not fine enough to spin into gold, but she could see why a mother would say that. And yes, the smile was charming enough. Drozde wondered, now, how she could ever have thought the soldier a man. But then Ermel jammed the cap back down over her ears, and squared her jaw, and was a man again.

"I gave them two years," she said. "What was I to do? They had only just found each other, and it would have broken my heart to sunder them. Perhaps they ran away together. Or perhaps the recruiters came again, two summers later, like reaper men out of season, and took one of my lovely boys with them to war and woe.

"It is not my story—not that part of it—but I know which ending I prefer."

There was a murmur of sympathy among the other ghosts as Ermel finished speaking.

"Thank you for your story," Drozde said to her, and the others flowed around the soldier, offering their thanks with sorrowful faces, for the tale had been a sad one. Magda reached up to stroke the woman's hair, and Ermel knelt down and removed her cap again so that the child could reach it. The sight of the two of them, Magda's face rapturous even though her hand went through Ermel's head as often as it made contact, touched Drozde in a way that surprised her.

But something about Ermel's story had made her uneasy.

"You said you were from Prussia," she asked the young soldier, "and that you fought in this place and triumphed. How can that be? The soldiers here are forever boasting that Silesia will never fall into Prussian hands. Your conquest must have been a long time ago if no one now remembers it." The young woman hesitated. She seemed suddenly constrained—wary even—and Drozde knew that she had come up again against that invisible barrier, the unspoken promise which bound the ghosts to silence. Ermel spread out her hands in a gesture of helplessness.

"I'm sorry, Drozde. That's one of the things we're not supposed to talk about. But you know, even if I was allowed to tell it I couldn't, not really. It's hard to even think about time very much once you're here."

Drozde knew that she would in all probability get nothing more from Ermel, but still she persisted. "Can you try?" she asked her.

Ermel frowned in concentration, staring beyond Drozde as if trying to sort her memories in her own mind. At length she said, "It was on the day after the comet, I know that. A star with a long tail, over in the northern sky. A beautiful thing, it was, and we only saw it that one night. Our captain said it was a sign of victory, but there were others feared it meant death. For me, I thought of Max and Kristof, looking at it the same time I was, and I hoped they were together, and thinking of me." She resurfaced from her memories and smiled shyly at Drozde. "So that might help you find out a time."

For a moment Drozde was tempted to observe that dying seemed to addle the wits. A star with a tail was all very well, but had none of the ghosts ever come across an almanac? When they did not deliberately evade Drozde's questions, they seemed hopelessly confused by them. Thea had been similarly uncertain about time, she remembered: although the woman could recall the story of her life in minute detail, she had said that it only took three days to get to Pokoj from Leipzig, which was clearly absurd. But Ermel had answered her as well as she could, she told herself. There was no justice in blaming her for the attempt, and for all her uncertainty about times and dates, she and the rest of them understood more than did most spirits.

Their eyes were on her now, waiting for her to ask for another story or to conclude the night's proceedings. So she swallowed her irritation and thanked them all for a pleasant evening, laying her questions and frustrations aside for the time being.

But some hours later, when full night had fallen over the camp and she lay awake while Molebacher snored beside her, she thought of Ermel's story and what it had told her. If the dead girl had spoken true, and her confusion about some aspects of her tale did not call the whole into question, then the Mala Panev was a barrier already breached before, and Pokoj a fortress long since fallen. That knowledge was troubling to her, for all that no one seriously expected war to come. Drozde shivered in the dark, and drew more of the blankets over herself. His cradle rocked by fine brandy, Molebacher neither knew nor cared.

22

When he and Tusimov delivered the unpleasant news to Colonel August in his quarters, Lieutenant Klaes was surprised at his commander's reaction. He was hoping for calm, but feared a great explosion of anger. Instead August nodded with what seemed like a sort of grim satisfaction.

"I knew there would be some such eruption," he said. "A good officer must be a reader of men, Klaes," he said, turning a condescending eye on him. "That was why I set you on to watch these people. I knew they were not all they should be—that there was some deformity in their lives, or their loyalties, or both. If anything, I'm pleased this has come to a head so quickly. We'll deal with it, and then they'll know where they stand with me. They will know it very clearly indeed."

August delivered this speech with considerable relish, and Klaes could see that the news he'd brought had slotted like a polished stone into some mental mosaic the colonel was building. He viewed this with distaste. His own weakness was for suspending judgement rather than rushing towards it. Yet he had enough awareness of that fact to realise that August's way, for a leader of men, was probably more productive of results.

"Tusimov, dismiss," the colonel said. Tusimov saluted with visible relief and left the room. It looked like Klaes was going to have the honour of cleaning up this mess by himself, which was hardly fair, he reflected bitterly, given that his only crime had been to see it take place. But of course, as the only officer present at the time, he was in the unique position of both knowing the details and having the required authority to act on them.

"It's too dark now to pursue this any further tonight," August told him. "Take a squad of ten and go into the village at first light to arrest the ringleaders. You'll know them by sight, I suppose?"

"Of course, sir."

"Bring them here then, and put them under guard. We'll try this matter out and put them to their punishment in the morning. That will be all."

"One last thing, sir," Klaes cut in hurriedly. He had not forgotten his conversation with the burgomaster, and wanted to report it before it got lost in the wake of the day's more dramatic events. "It concerns the other matter you entrusted to me. The question of whether the villagers were trying to conceal something from you. I think I have determined—"

August waved him aside impatiently. "Later, Klaes. If it doesn't bear directly on the issue at hand, then it can wait. Surely you can see that it's of scant importance now that there's been open, demonstrable riot."

Klaes was dismissed before he could say another word, but when he was halfway down the corridor Colonel August came to the door and called him back. "Molebacher," he said.

"I'm sorry, sir?"

"Sergeant Molebacher, Klaes. He's the man you want on a delicate matter like this. They look at his bulk and they're subdued, you see? Beaten before they start. Before they even think of starting. No offence to you, but you don't look much like a bruiser—and your role in this current matter bears that out. Where you stood and looked, Mole would have acted. So take him with you, and tell him to assemble the rest of the detail. Bring along a few of his burly kitchen boys, perhaps. They'll take no nonsense."

The door slammed to, leaving Klaes to digest this insult by himself.

Had he been another kind of man he might have uttered some sort of oath, or at least let his chagrin show on his face. As it was, he turned away with no discernible change in his expression or his movements.

Early the next morning he went to the kitchen, where Sergeant Molebacher was not immediately to be found. Klaes would have been content to leave him in that condition, but unfortunately the most perfunctory of searches turned him up. He was sitting behind the house, close to the open kitchen door, smoking a pipe of tobacco and enjoying the wintry sunlight. His boots were unlaced, the tops pulled as far apart as they'd go, and every second button of his uniform jacket was unfastened—the furthest a man could go towards undoing it without collecting a charge.

Klaes told the sergeant curtly to choose ten men of proven reliability and meet him at the gates. "For what?" Molebacher demanded. "Begging your pardon, sir."

"Special duties," Klaes said. "That's all you need to know." But he could hardly order the man to assemble a detail without telling him what its brief was. "We're going into Narutsin to arrest the villagers who fought with Lieutenant Tusimov's men yesterday. Colonel August seems to think you're the man for the job."

At the colonel's name, Molebacher's whole demeanour changed. He came quickly to his feet, brushing tobacco ash from his sleeves and trousers, and hurried off without even troubling to lace up his boots.

Ten minutes later he appeared at the gates with a ragged column of men behind him. Klaes took one look at them and shook his head. "Not these," he said.

Molebacher bridled. "Begging your pardon, sir, you told me to make my own choices."

"And that was my mistake. Dismiss, you men."

Complaining at the very limit of audibility, Sergeant Molebacher's chosen dispersed. They were not all thugs—or at least not all immediately identifiable as such—but Klaes's knowledge of the faces he did recognise gave him no confidence whatsoever in the rest. He didn't want to start a second street fight while arresting the perpetrators from the first.

He reeled off some names from his own company. Toltz and Schneider. Egger. Haas. Langbrun. Nestroy and Fingerlos. Kuppermann. All good men who could be relied on to do what they were told and not to go beyond that without good reason.

Molebacher went away and returned with a sour face and the new detail. He had added, without being asked, Swivek and Rattenwend—two of those kitchen boys the colonel had mentioned, whose chief virtue seemed to lie in being able to keep pace with their sergeant when he drank and to peel potatoes without cutting off too many of their own fingers.

"At the single," Klaes said, and they set off. He allowed no time for questions to be asked and nobody raised any. Presumably Molebacher had told them what their business was in Narutsin, and they kept their excitement in check.

In the village, everyone they passed—man, woman or child—stopped what they were doing to watch them go by, their faces turning almost imperceptibly like the heads of flowers following the passage of the sun.

At the mayor's house Bosilka answered the door to Klaes's knock. Seeing a column of armed men outside, she stared at them dumbly for a moment—but rallied, ignoring them to favour Klaes with the grimmest of curtsies. "Yes?" she said at last. "Can I help you?"

"My compliments to Meister Weichorek," Klaes said. His voice sounded absurd in his own ears, but there was no escaping these strange formalities—at least, not without descending to something more brutal and uncivilised. "I need to speak with him about yesterday evening's disturbance. I'm happy to attend him. Or it might be he prefers to come and speak to me here. I'll take as little of his time as I can."

"You can wait out here," Bosilka decided, without even consulting her master. She slammed the door, which stayed shut for some minutes. Klaes did not turn, but heard his men stirring restively behind him. The insult had not gone unnoticed, and they'd taken it (no doubt correctly) as a snub aimed at all of them. The men Molebacher had selected first would probably already have been looking for some heads to punch.

The door opened again, and Meister Weichorek stepped out. "Lieutenant Klaes," he said, civilly and with an attempt at a smile. "It's good to see you again. Is there something further I can do to help the regiment settle in?"

"No, sir," Klaes said. "It's not for that I'm come."

"No," Weichorek agreed. "I knew that, really."

"The miscreants from the fight yesterday. Do you know their whereabouts?"

Weichorek shrugged unhappily. "I know the whereabouts of mine. Presumably you know where yours are."

Klaes knew he should not let that pass—not with Sergeant Molebacher and the others all listening at his back. Too late, he wished he'd had them wait back at the mayor's useless gateposts. "This is a serious matter," he said. "Soldiers of the archduchess were assaulted in a public street. It's a miracle nobody was killed."

"Aye," Weichorek agreed. "We've that to be grateful for, at least."

"And now there has to be a reckoning. I'd like the men of Narutsin to line up in the street. You will arrange it. And then I'll pick out from them the faces I recognise from the incident."

"I took their names," Weichorek said.

Klaes stood on his dignity. The man had brought this on himself. "Nonetheless. I would rather put my trust in my own memory than your list. See to it, please."

He turned on his heel and led his men back out onto the street. He knew that Weichorek hadn't moved because the dry wood of the porch would have creaked loud enough to be heard. He wondered with a sort of terror what he would do if the burgomaster simply disregarded the brusque command and went back indoors. This was what happened if you allowed yourself to be provoked. You stepped outside your limits, and placed yourself in positions that you were then forced to defend, however precarious they were.

But Weichorek moved at last. He walked out past them into the street, and began the process of knocking on each door in turn for a brief, urgent conversation with the householder inside.

Klaes was surprised, and outfaced. He'd expected Bosilka to be sent, but clearly Weichorek had decided not to hide behind his servants in delivering this unhappy news. Perversely, that generosity of spirit shamed and angered him. It seemed almost as though the mayor was purposefully scoring a point at his expense.

He turned to Molebacher. "There are more houses than this," he said. "Go around the outskirts of the village. Make sure no one is missed."

Molebacher stared at him for a long, strained moment, then executed a louche and grudging salute. "You heard the lieutenant," he roared, much louder than was necessary in the uneasy stillness of the village. "Let's roust these goat-fuckers from their unsavoury liaisons. Step to it."

The ten soldiers snapped to attention, roused by the magical authority of the sergeant's hectoring voice, and marched away in his wake—leaving Klaes alone in the village street, feeling more foolish and more exposed than ever.

To complete his misery, Bosilka came out of the mayor's house now, her outdoor coat loose on her shoulders, and walked briskly by him.

She spat on the ground as she passed. On the ground, and—just a little—on the toe of Klaes's boot.

Oh, I'll make sure no one's missed, Sergeant Molebacher said to Lieutenant Klaes in the privacy of his own mind. *I'll do everything I'm told to do, and step dainty as a maid, and never say a single word to contradict you. But you'll be sorry you showed me up in front of my own people, you whey-faced bastard. That you will.*

The fringes of the village were an unruly sprawl of fields and barns and dwelling places and middens. There were not, in truth, very many houses, but such as there were, were widely spread and in some cases only to be reached by trudging across muddy pastures or wrestling with wire-latched gates. Molebacher split his detail into four and sent them to the four cardinal points of the compass, taking cold north for himself along with Swivek and Rattenwend.

The first dwelling they came to was a farmhouse. There were two men there, a father and a son, but the father was so old and decrepit Molebacher took it upon himself to tell him to stay put. It seemed vanishingly unlikely that he'd been involved in the brawl. He looked as though a gentle poke in the ribs would send him to meet his maker.

At the second house they found a widow and her extensive brood. There were three sons who all seemed quite likely, but Molebacher was certain from the tension of their bodies and the furtive glances they exchanged that there was more to discover here. He had Swivek and Rattenwend conduct a search, and in due course they dragged in a fourth lad who they'd found hiding under his bed.

"Do you love your old mum?" Molebacher asked this newcomer.

The boy gave him a surly nod.

"Well you go on out and join that line in the main street, then.

Because if I go out there and I don't see your face front and centre, I'm going to give you a brother."

He paused just long enough to be sure the threat had sunk in. Then he gathered Swivek and Rattenwend to him with a jerk of his head and they left.

There was one more house, set deep in the trees. A young woman ran past them as they headed towards it. It was the girl who'd answered the door at the mayor's house, gone to warn her own menfolk, no doubt, about what was happening. Molebacher and his men kept to their own unhurried pace. Let her roust the pigeons if she wanted to; there was nowhere to hide in these clapboard shitholes, and the sergeant was confident of his ability to see through any subterfuge.

The house, when they got to it, turned out to be a carpenter's shop—marked as such by the hammer hung up under the eaves. They ignored the front door and walked around to the rear, where they had seen the girl go. There was a door there which was unlocked. They stepped inside without knocking.

They found themselves in a narrow, cluttered storeroom, just as a man in his fifties entered through another door on the far side of the room. The carpenter, evidently, or else the carpenter's man, for he had an apron on with a square rule protruding from its pocket. The girl who had passed them in the lane lowered at his elbow.

"What's this, then?" the carpenter asked.

"Speak as you're spoken to," Rattenwend countered. The carpenter's tone had been mild enough; it was the girl's scowl that moved Rattenwend to belligerence.

"Are there any other men besides you biding here?" Molebacher demanded. "Say true, now, or it will go hard with you."

"I've my Bible to teach me to speak true," the carpenter said, "without your prompting. Yes, there's one other. Anton Hanslo, my indentured man."

"And where's he?"

"He's cutting wood," the girl said. "Fetch him then," Molebacher ordered.

The girl made a tutting sound of contempt and annoyance. "He could be a mile or more into the woods. Fetch him yourself, if you can find him."

Molebacher considered. There was no reason to believe the girl was lying. But she had gone to some effort to get to the house before them.

It might have been to give this Hanslo the word that he should go to ground.

"Have a look around," he told Swivek and Rattenwend. "Make sure there's no one else here."

"This is my shop!" the carpenter protested. They ignored him, shouldering him aside as they passed. The place had an upper floor—a loft of some kind, reached by a ladder. Swivek climbed up there, and Rattenwend went into the yard, where there was a small outbuilding. Probably a chicken coop, but there was plenty of room for a man to hide in a chicken coop.

Molebacher went into the workshop, which was small and tidy. He cast a quick look around—enough to satisfy himself that there was nobody crouching in a corner or behind the workbench. Then he turned to leave.

But his eye was caught by a shelf on which a group of wooden carvings stood. They were nicely done, and he thought at once of stealing them. The carpenter would keep his mouth shut, if he knew what was good for him, and they'd fetch a pretty penny at some market. Drozde could sell them on for him. Not here in Narutsin, of course, but as soon as they moved on . . .

Drozde.

Perhaps it was only because she was uppermost in his mind that he recognised her so quickly. There she was at the end of the shelf, a puppet like one of the woman's own making, dangling like a prisoner in a gibbet. Except that there was a flirtatious smile on her painted face, and her wooden body was naked, leaning forward from the hip as if to begin a dance.

Molebacher picked up the carving and raised it in his hand to examine it more closely. The man who'd made this thing had spent time with Drozde and paid attention to her. He knew the shape of her body. More, he had caught her look. Her wildness. Not perfectly, but well enough for such a tiny thing. The quirk of the painted mouth, that air of teasing invitation.

He had fucked her.

The knowledge bit into Molebacher's mind like a nail into a beam. He gasped aloud at the dismay that filled him, overwhelmed by its intensity. He stood for a moment on the balls of his feet, uncertain of his balance, the world moving under him.

And in that moment, when it seemed there was nothing in the world but him and that terrible, bodiless pain, he became aware that he wasn't alone. Swivek had entered the room behind him and was looking at him open-mouthed.

Molebacher set the puppet down, but the damage was done. Swivek had seen him holding it, and had seen it unman him. His hand when he let go of the thing was shaking like the hand of a man in a fever. There was even a little moisture in his eyes, though he would have boiled them in their sockets sooner than shed it.

"Where is the carpenter?" he demanded, his voice hoarse. "Bring him in here."

The carpenter was brought, Swivek and Rattenwend flanking him menacingly on either side.

"Did you make this?" Molebacher demanded, pointing at the puppet.

"No." The man folded his arms categorically. "I did not."

"Who did, then?"

"Hanslo, of course. All of these little nonsenses are his."

Not the master, then, but the man. It made no difference really, but Molebacher felt that his humiliation was complete. Strangely, the feeling gave him strength. From the valley of the shadow, all roads lead upwards.

"Find this Hanslo," he told the two privates in almost his own voice. "Make sure he stands with the others."

Swivek and Rattenwend saluted and left. The carpenter remained, staring at Molebacher in bemusement. Clearly, whatever the sergeant's voice might be doing, his face had not yet found an expression that approximated to that of a normal man.

The girl was watching him through the doorway. He wasn't sure whether the look on her face was pity or hatred.

He wasn't sure whether it mattered.

Lieutenant Klaes walked up and down the long row of men three times. His memory was really very good, and he was confident that he could have identified the street brawlers on the first pass. But the second and third allowed him to sift his mind for corroborating evidence— moments of time preserved in this or that mental compartment, yielding themselves now to his inspection. He wanted to be absolutely sure. To be less than sure would be to connive at injustice, either by sparing the guilty or by punishing men who had done nothing. Either outcome would be unacceptable.

When he was sure, he pointed.

"You. And you. You, with the grey hair. And the young man there without a beard. Yes, and you. Step forward, all of you."

The five men did as they were told, and the soldiers took possession of them.

Klaes hesitated. But if justice was partial it was nothing, or worse than nothing.

"And you," he said, pointing to the mayor's son, Jakusch. The boy's face was comically crestfallen. He had been standing half-hidden between two taller men, and clearly thought he'd managed to avoid being seen. But out of all of them he was the one Klaes needed no prompting to remember. He had spent an entire evening staring at the boy across a table—and it had been a long evening.

Meister Weichorek watched the soldiers take his son with a face as impassive as if it had been carved out of stone. His wife, who was standing beside him, gripped his arm tightly. Seeing her stricken face, Klaes felt impelled to speak, but since he had no idea what punishment the colonel had in mind, he did not know what reassurances he could reasonably offer.

"Any more, Lieutenant?" Sergeant Molebacher asked, with a sarcastic inflection.

Klaes hadn't even seen the sergeant return. The man could move quietly, for all his bulk.

"No," he said. "No more. Just these six. Carry on, Sergeant."

They walked out of the village as they'd entered it, with all eyes upon them. And all the way back to Pokoj, Klaes thought about what he might have said to Dame Weichorek to still her disquiet about her son.

Something about military justice being swift, perhaps. It was unlikely that Colonel August meant to draw this out.

But reflecting on the kinds of justice that were swiftest filled Klaes's mind with unpleasant intimations.

23

Drozde wandered restlessly through the house. She had slept badly last night, and woken before dawn, unable to put Ermel's story from her mind. Even now it fretted at the edges of her consciousness. There was something about it that disquieted her. It was not just that it had left her head filled with visions of marching boots and bloodshed. It was its uncanny familiarity, the fact that the young soldier's account of her childhood had been uncomfortably close, in many respects, to Drozde's own. The fighting of which she spoke must surely have taken place a relatively short while ago, perhaps even in living memory, but if that were the case then why was no one in the camp aware of it?

Only the ghosts seemed to know that it had even happened, just as they had known Drozde's name before they met her, and when she would fall asleep, and whether kittens would live or die. Their unaccountable, impossible knowledge disconcerted her more than anything else she had encountered in Pokoj. She was beginning to feel, too, that the things they knew where more than just a fascinating and unnerving mystery, that they were things that she too needed to know with some urgency.

The aftermath of the fight was not helping her sense of unease. Early that morning a rumour had spread through the camp that the colonel had ordered some of the townspeople to be arrested, and that they would be brought back to Pokoj today to be punished for their actions. The news had cast yesterday's incident in a whole new light. Suddenly, the fight had been elevated from a mere scuffle to a serious criminal offence. Whether they thought this turn of events no more than justice or a gross overreaction, no one was laughing any more.

Drozde's wanderings had taken her to the far end of the house, an area the officers mostly avoided as the walls of the outer rooms were mildewed and damp. Good, she thought, and opened a door at random. Some time undisturbed might help her regain her equanimity.

The room had a faint whiff of damp but looked far less damaged than the others she'd seen, perhaps because three of the four walls were hidden behind bookshelves. They were not over-full but neatly stacked, in the manner of a household whose library is intended more for show than use. And clearly, Drozde thought, the house's previous owners had not been over-fond of reading: they had taken almost every stick of furniture with them but left the books behind.

Not that she was going to complain. Drozde knew how to read: Vanek had taught her to keep his accounts when his eyes started failing, and she had helped him jot down new songs and ideas for the shows. At the bottom of her trunk she still kept his tattered chapbooks of old tales: *Aschputtel*, *The Magic Donkey* and the like. She was always happy to find new stories, and the books in this room looked as if no one would ever miss them. She scanned the shelves. Those facing the door were given over to works of theology and moral instruction, in matched bindings that had once been gold-tooled. But round the corner on a bottom shelf was a row of much smaller, shabbier volumes: travel books, ballads and romances. She picked out a few interesting-looking ones. It would be good to have a book to read on the nights when Molebacher didn't require her. She had no lamp, but there were fire pots; she'd read by firelight many times.

A sound behind her made her turn—no, not a sound, a vibration in the air, such as the ghosts made. "Magda?" she called softly. But it was not the little girl. One of the other ghosts, barely visible, was standing at the far end of the room. Something about the figure seemed familiar to her, but it spun around as she turned to face it, and faded from sight, leaving only the sense of its presence.

With a start, she recalled the figure—or figures—that had withdrawn from the ballroom on some of the nights of storytelling. Why would any of the ghosts wish to avoid her? They respected and trusted her—they'd said so many times—and she couldn't see what need ghosts would have to lie.

"Hello?" she said aloud. "You don't need to hide; we're friends, aren't we?"

The ghost did not answer. Drozde started to speak again, and checked herself. Whoever it was, they had gone.

But her solitude was broken. She wrapped the books carefully in her shawl and left the room: she'd go and see to the puppets for a while.

She had expected to find Molebacher hard at work. Instead, Muntz and Standmeier were desultorily peeling potatoes while Hulyek smoked a quick pipe in the open doorway to the yard. Their relaxation told her at once that the quartermaster was away. He had gone to the town, Standmeier told her with careful politeness, to help Lieutenant Klaes with the arrests.

"To help *who*?"

Standmeier laughed. "You're not wrong, miss. I doubt the lieutenant could bring them in on his own. That's why he took the sergeant along, no doubt."

Drozde's unease deepened. She'd thought Klaes had been given the job of talking to the townspeople, trying to win them over. Had the colonel decided to make enemies of them overnight, turning the friendly envoy into an arresting officer, with Molebacher as his enforcer? If any of the accused men showed any resistance, Molebacher would break heads, and nothing the prissy little lieutenant could do would stop him. If August had wanted to provoke a further riot, she thought, he could not have sent two more likely taskmasters.

She suddenly felt the need for some more sensible company. She nodded to the orderlies and went outside to the women's camp.

Libush and Sarai shared her dismay. They had heard about the arrests from Katerina Lehmann, whose husband had been one of the first to join the battle. She was full of indignation at the injuries he had suffered, but even by her account it seemed that he had struck the first blow.

"By Katia's tale, it was just name-calling at first," Sarai said. "Our men parading back and forth past their houses, and some silly lads tried to make fun of them. The lieutenant had no call to take them through the town at all."

"All of them brawling in the street like a pack of puppy dogs," said Libush gloomily. "It's nobody's fault. Or everyone's. Why not just let it pass?"

"I suppose," Sarai said. "Something needs to be done, doesn't it? To restore order." But she didn't sound convinced.

The prisoners were brought in at midday: six of them, ranging in age from a grey-haired man of over fifty to a youth still in his teens. Most of them still had visible bruises; all looked confused and sullen. Lieutenant Klaes, leading the procession, seemed nearly as miserable as his captives. His men, flanking them on both sides, were carefully stolid. Even Sergeant Molebacher, who brought up the rear, seemed less satisfied with his role than Drozde would have expected. She took care to stay out of the quartermaster's line of sight. She was glad there had been no further violence, at least, but the sight of the six wretched men, escorted like criminals by those who had provoked the fight, filled her with anger.

Colonel August received the prisoners with massive dignity, and directed them to be taken to the north side of the house where one of the unoccupied rooms had been turned into a cell. They would be sentenced that same day, he said.

"Sentenced!" Libush muttered. "Was there a trial?"

The mood in the camp was ill-tempered and uneasy. Some of the men spoke of the arrests with vindictive satisfaction, viewing yesterday's fight as an attack on the honour of the company. But the majority, including many who had been there, shared the women's view.

"It's hitting a gnat with a sledgehammer," complained Fingerlos, one of Libush's regular visitors. "What does the colonel think to gain by it? He's just making more trouble down the line."

"There'll be ill feeling from now till we leave," agreed Haas. "And I heard Strumpfel say it was our boys began it."

The prisoners' fate was known less than an hour after their arrival. Alis came to Libush's tent supporting a tearful Ottilie, who had heard the news from sergeant Frydek: there would be a public flogging the next day.

August planned to make an example of his culprits. To this end he had sent a squad of men to extend the makeshift parade ground that had been cleared in the field to the west of the campsite, scything the tall weeds and clearing the molehills so that the whole town could be assembled to see the spectacle. And he had ordered the town's carpenters to assist his own men in building three whipping frames.

The arrival of the giant wooden posts, on a gun carriage pulled by two horses and attended by twelve of Dietmar's men, drew a smaller and more subdued crowd than the one that had met the guns a month before. Drozde refused to join it. But she could not stop herself, later on, from following the sound of hammering into the parade ground.

She felt the breath of Magda's touch on her hand. She had never seen the child outside the house, but somehow her presence here did not surprise her. "This isn't a good thing for you to see," she told her.

The little girl's face was more sombre than she'd ever seen it. "I know what it is," she said. "And I know you have to come here. I just wish you wouldn't, when it makes you so sad."

"My sadness has nothing to do with it," Drozde said, unable to keep the edge from her voice. "It's a monstrous thing they're doing, and a stupid one. And someone I know has let himself be involved with it."

Magda nodded unhappily. "You have to tell him not to. I know that too. But don't be too mean to them, Drozde. They don't know what will happen."

"And you do, I suppose," Drozde retorted. But the little girl had gone.

She nearly ran into Klaes at the edge of the field. Four soldiers were already hoisting the first of the frames into position; a second was being hammered together. The lieutenant was watching with a stricken expression, as if he had not seen this sight a dozen times before—or as if it had only just struck him that the men to be pinioned on the vile things tomorrow would be there through his doing. Well might he feel guilty, the little weasel. But it was not Klaes who concerned her. She had someone else to see here, and for the life of her she did not know what she would say to him.

Anton was there with his master, a greying man who must be the girl Silkie's father. She'd taken a sort of liking to the girl, which might have extended to the father if she had met him first in his workshop. Here and now, she wanted to box his ears, him and his man both. The two of them were planing the surfaces of the tops of the triangle to fit them into a smooth joint, with the same careful craftsmanship that she had seen in Hanslo's work on a table leg.

She had already gone too close to them: both looked up. Without thinking she took Anton's arm and pulled him away. The soldier hammering at the triangle's foot ignored them both. Meister Stefanu began to protest, but something in her expression must have dissuaded him.

"What are you doing?" she demanded. "How can you let them use you like this!"

He tried to back away from her. He looked sheepish, but in no way guilty: he really did not understand. *God preserve us from such innocence!* she thought in despair.

"I'm sorry you think less of me for it," he said. He really was, she could see. "It does grieve me to see my neighbours shamed like this—whipped like naughty schoolchildren. But Meister Weichorek says we're to cooperate with the colonel's orders. And, you know, they were brawling. I pulled Martek off one of your men myself. They would all have spent time in the stocks else, and the mayor doesn't order that lightly."

"No more would he order this, if he knew! Anton, you think this is a beating like a schoolmaster's switch? Look at what you're building! They tie a man to this so he can't move. They flog him with a six-tailed whip till his back is bloody. Some die. Are you going to stand here tomorrow and see your neighbours tormented on an engine of your own making?"

She saw how the words hit him. "They'll do that?"

"Yes, Anton, they will. And you're helping them!"

He shook his head. "No. That can't be. It's just a beating; we've all been beaten in our time. You can't mean . . . It couldn't really kill someone?"

"The loss of blood. Or the wounds fester, afterwards." He was pale now. She'd said all she could. "They keep a surgeon on hand."

Anton was silent for a long time. He glanced over at his master, who had stopped his own work and was watching them with misgiving.

"I'll tell him," he said. "Silkie would never forgive us. But I don't know what we can do."

"There's nothing you can do, not now."

She hadn't meant her voice to sound so cold. He was ashamed, not looking at her. She said, "You didn't know."

One of the soldiers hoisting the frame had seen them talking and pointed them out to his comrade. Another moment and someone would come over to order the men back to work, and shoo off the whore wasting time with them. She turned away. She heard Anton say, "We'll do no more of it, Drozde," and wished she could go back and give him her hand on it—some touch, at least. But one of the soldiers at the frame was Rattenwend, one of Molebacher's orderlies.

She stopped again at the field's edge. Klaes was long gone; if he'd seen her with the carpenters, he would certainly have felt it his duty to send her off himself. She saw Anton in anxious talk with his master. Neither had picked up his tools, and both of them looked over in her direction. Well, she could do no more. It wasn't as if she'd achieved anything. They'd still build the hideous things without him, and use them; she couldn't stop that. But it gave her a small satisfaction that Anton would not finish their work for them.

24

Lieutenant Klaes found himself at a loss. He had set his men to clear the western side of the parade ground, as instructed, but had been given no further orders since then. August had not summoned him to hear the rest of his report. The prisoners had been taken from his custody on arrival and handed over to Tusimov, and he had heard no more of them till the dismaying news, early in the afternoon, that they were to be flogged.

Hearing that, he had returned to his quarters and taken up Spinoza, trying to calm his mind. But he could settle to nothing, and finally found himself wandering back to the parade ground to check on his men's progress. The sound of hammering greeted him as he approached, and he saw, at the far end of the field, the first of the whipping frames being erected: a gaunt triangle of raw wood, taller than a man.

In his present grim mood, he was not in the least surprised to find that Drozde was there. She seemed to be rehearsing a conversation she intended to have with someone in the near future.

At any rate she was both speaking and gesticulating to the empty air. She broke off to stare at him as he passed, though. It was a stare of such soul-shrivelling contempt that he might have taken issue with it if his spirits were not already so low. As it was, he only shrugged. *Your bad opinion of me? Yes, by all means throw it to me as I pass, but forgive me if I don't stop to add it to the list.*

He went to August's rooms in the hope of finding the colonel there and speaking a word to him in private, but Dame Osterhilis was alone there. She directed Klaes to the billiard room. The table was piled deep with the colonel's papers, the maps laid out across the uneven surface so they looked as though they'd been rendered in haut-relief.

Tusimov, Pabst and Dietmar were sitting around the table on folding stools, and August was holding forth to them. That made Klaes the only one of the lieutenants not called to what was obviously a strategic briefing. Unless he had been summoned when he was at the parade ground, and was therefore arriving late.

Either way, overlooked or in dereliction, he must look uniquely foolish. But he did not wish to spare the time either for offence or for apology.

"Colonel," he exclaimed, as the eyes of all four men turned towards him, "I wondered if I might speak with you?"

Colonel August frowned. "Later, Klaes, by all means," he said. "At the moment we're discussing the likeliest routes for a Prussian advance on Wroclaw. If they cross the border at Sagan or Halbau, we might be well placed to come in from the north and cut them off. Sit down, please. I'd value your opinion on this."

You didn't go to much trouble to get it, Klaes thought glumly as he took the offered place at the table. For the next hour he listened with scant patience and less interest as a number of scenarios for a Prussian attack were offered. The Prussian forces would press on directly to Wroclaw. They would burn the border towns and then withdraw. They would take a walled town—Świebodzin perhaps, or Sulechów—and overwinter there, pressing on towards Wroclaw in the spring.

Did anyone here believe there was the remotest likelihood that any of these things would occur, as the year drew to its end and every day brought the snows closer? Only a fool would cross the Beskids now, and risk wintering in a newly conquered city in hostile, unpacified territory. Klaes did not think that Frederick Hohenzollern was a fool.

So he contributed little to the conference, beyond his presence and the occasional shrug or equivocal gesture when a question was canvassed around the group. Despite Colonel August's supposed enthusiasm for his counsel, he was never asked for an opinion and never offered one. He just endured in silence until the colonel rolled up his maps and set them aside.

"Well, well," August said. "Time will tell. Our primary concern, of course, is to guard the pass here at Glogau and to send word to Graf Khevenhüller if any troop movements are seen on the other side of the Oder. But it does no harm to be aware that we're—*in potentia*, of course—part of a larger theatre of war. I think we should continue with our manoeuvres, and make sure we're all thoroughly familiar with the routes to the south. If it comes to it, we want to make our knowledge of the terrain, and our consequent speed of deployment, count in our favour. So I expect all of you to borrow these maps and con them, over the weeks to come. Dietmar, would you like to take first watch, as it were?"

He handed the maps to Dietmar, who took them with a strained show of enthusiasm, then turned to Klaes. "Now, Lieutenant Klaes," he said. "What was it you wanted to talk to me about? I assume it's related to this other business you've been investigating for me. Go on, then. What have you found?"

Klaes was expecting August to dismiss the other lieutenants before the two of them had their converse, so he was caught off guard by this blunt demand. "It's not exactly . . ." he stammered. "Perhaps in private, sir, if I may? This is more in the nature of . . . of . . ."

"In the nature of what?"

Klaes didn't want to say. Not while his brother officers were standing by, their curiosity aroused by his flushed face and his evident inability to finish a sentence.

"I was hoping to discuss . . ." Klaes tried again.

"Yes?"

He swallowed, aware of how thin and querulous his voice sounded when it was up against the colonel's hectoring staccato. "The beatings, sir."

"The what?"

"I mean, sir, the order you've given that the villagers who brawled with Lieutenant Tusimov's men should be flogged."

August's expression became grave. "There is little to be said on that subject, Klaes, whether in private or in public."

Klaes looked around. All eyes were on him, and none of them were friendly. But he saw no way out of this now, so he ploughed on. "If you are determined on this course, sir, then no. Of course not. But I hope that you are yet to be swayed."

"Swayed?" This was Tusimov, bridling as though Klaes had smacked him in the face. "Swayed? My men were set upon. Waylaid in the street, and beaten. What should sway the colonel, when he's responding in the only way he possibly could?"

"That does not entirely accord with what I saw," Klaes said doggedly.

"Doesn't it, by God? Then rub your eyes, Lieutenant Klaes, and see clear. Those men were returning to camp, worn out from a whole day's strenuous military exercises. They assumed, as they had every right to assume, that they would be safe breaking their march in Narutsin. But the villagers saw an opportunity, and took it. They jumped on my soldiers like dogs on a rabbit. Disgraceful exhibition!"

"It sets an unacceptable precedent," August summarised. Klaes realised now that this was the colonel's standard justification for any overreaction to small or imagined transgressions. It was necessary to jump on them hard in case they led on to large or at least real ones.

He tried again. "I'm not defending the villagers' actions, sir," he said, addressing himself only to August now. "I do question, though, whether exemplary punishment is the best way to proceed. You said yourself that you were afraid there might be some instinctive sympathy in this region for Prussian claims and Prussian aspirations. If that's so, surely we need to be wary of doing anything that might further alienate the people here from the empire and make them feel that a change of regime might offer them some tangible benefits."

August was clearly not impressed, and neither were the other lieutenants. Tusimov was still looking affronted, Pabst pained and Dietmar coldly amused. "Follow that logic to its conclusion," the lieutenant of artillery observed, "and we'd shy away from punishing any criminal for fear of driving them on from bad to worse."

"I speak of this particular situation only," Klaes protested. "The practicalities of it. The weighing up of our procedures against our mission—what we desire to achieve. And the punishment of criminal offences, I mean where the offenders are civilians, is hardly in our—"

"Set upon, don't you know?" Tusimov broke in, looking from Dietmar to Pabst and back again. "In the street. Baited like bears. There's no other way of expressing it. A mob, howling around them. An ill-intentioned riot."

"And yet the injuries seem evenly distributed on both sides," Klaes felt obliged to point out.

"They were attacked and they defended themselves, you young idiot," Pabst huffed. "What would you expect?"

Klaes was wading deeper and deeper, into waters where riptides lurked, but he seemed unable to stop himself now. A recklessness had seized him, almost like the impulse towards self-destruction. It was not just the floggings—it was the calling of this meeting while he was away on other business, and the colonel's remark about his sabre, and the assumption of every officer here that he was unworthy because he was untried. Yet what did their experience consist of besides defeats?

"I would expect an officer in charge of a unit to stay with his men," he said crisply. "Or to depute their organisation to a competent subordinate. Not to abandon them, and allow the line of march to break up so badly that these few soldiers were completely out of sight of their comrades." He parsed his own words, turned to the colonel and added a dilatory "sir," but it sounded like a challenge rather than a palliative.

Certainly Tusimov took it as one. He stood, his face flushed and his posture rigid with anger. "I will not be accused in that way, Klaes," he said. "Not by a fellow officer. Not by anyone. You have implied that I am a poor commander. If you don't withdraw that imputation, then you'll answer me in a private arena."

In a duel, he meant. But he could not say that in front of his commanding officer, who would then be obliged to rule against any such proceeding.

Even so, August seemed unhappy with the way this was going. "Lieutenant Klaes, enough!" he said. "We have weighty matters in hand, and this is not—not at all—a subject that should detain us. A few peasants were unruly, and they must be disciplined. Discipline is not an imposition, it is the foundation of good order in all things. If you think this through you'll realise that I have no other option. To let the offence pass would be to advertise weakness and encourage licence. Do not, sir, petition me further. But before we let the matter drop, I believe Lieutenant Tusimov is correct in saying that you have cast a slight on his judgement. You will apologise."

Klaes hesitated. Tusimov was still staring at him, triumphing in his discomfort. Pabst, embarrassed, was pretending to examine the moth-eaten curtains. Dietmar had already turned his back, giving the clear indication that he wished to waste no more of his time on this tale of a tub.

The silence grew beyond its lease.

"Lieutenant Klaes," August said darkly. "I am ordering you to—"

"I apologise, Lieutenant Tusimov," Klaes said, "if anything I've said has offended you. That was not my intention."

"Good," Tusimov grunted. "Perhaps you'll watch your intentions a little closer another time."

"And now, Klaes, having defined everyone else's duties for them, perhaps you can report to me on your own performance." August nodded to Tusimov and Pabst, who saluted and withdrew. Dietmar had left the room on the first word of Klaes's apology, presumably remaining only long enough to have a sense of the outcome—and of which of his two fellow officers had come away humiliated by it.

"You indicated earlier that you had something more to add on this matter of the villagers and their guilty consciences," the colonel said, closing the door before returning to Klaes. He did not sit down, but stood before the lieutenant like a stern and expectant schoolteacher—and certainly Klaes felt that his reddened cheeks must recall those of a chidden pupil. "I checked you then because there were more important things that had to be attended to first. But I will hear you now."

Klaes nodded curtly. "I've determined what took place, sir," he said, "and can assure you that what the villagers have been concealing is of no concern to us." He recounted to August the story he'd heard from Meister Weichorek about the idiot boy, Petos, his thefts and his unfortunate death in the cellars of Pokoj. He was concise but circumstantial. The only detail he left out was Bosilka's involvement, which he honestly judged to be irrelevant.

The colonel heard him out in silence, betraying not the smallest response. When Klaes was done he raised his hands and brought them close together, the tips of his fingers almost but not quite touching as though he held the story between them for closer scrutiny. His head was bowed, his grave face immobile.

"The mayor told you this?" he asked.

"Yes, sir. Eventually. I had to tease it out of him by seeming to know more than I did."

"You had to tease it? Tease it out of him?"

"Yes. By means of a bluff. I told him that I had heard about—"

"Klaes, you're a fool." August spat out the words.

Klaes tailed off into silence. The colonel left him foundering as he searched among the papers on the table. "Know it's here somewhere," he muttered. "Yes. This." He held up a letter, his finger tracing the lines from left to right as he scanned it.

"Nymand Petos," he said at last. "I knew it."

"Petos?" Klaes repeated. "Petos was the idiot who—"

"Nymand Petos was my predecessor, Klaes. He is a captain in a Silesian militia unit, and he was placed in command of this post. A command of a dozen men." August brandished the letter in Klaes's face, much too close for him to be able to read it. "He was based here—right here in Pokoj. He should have been here to receive us when we arrived and to hand over command in good order. That's how these things are meant to be done.

"Instead I was told by that tin-button fool Weichorek that the militia had moved on to another post. Taking, it would seem, every last bloody stick and stitch of their equipment with them, and leaving us only this hovel to camp in as we'd camp out in a bloody field."

Klaes shook his head. He was still trying to process this information. "Meister Weichorek gave me a very circumstantial account, sir. There is no possibility of error."

"No," August agreed. "Every possibility, though, that he lied to you for his own purposes. And to me, through your deputation. If all of this relates to Petos, then I wouldn't be at all surprised to find that Petos is still in the offing somewhere. Probably deserted his post and got the locals to hide him. And then Weichorek gives you this rigmarole of idiot boys! Perhaps he took you for an idiot boy, Klaes, do you think?" This last uttered with a snort, as August threw the letter down and gesticulated at it as though he were trying to raise Nymand Petos's spirit directly out of the offending paper.

"This—now—is starting to make us look foolish," he exclaimed. "I told you, did I not? When we first arrived here, I said that these people were hiding something from us. My instincts are sound. Now we know that what they're hiding bears directly on the archduchess's writ and on our wider business here. Petos! If Petos has gone to ground you must smoke him out, Klaes. He had a duty to carry out here. Then he sees a cloud, thinks it's the smoke from a Prussian gun, and he's off like a hare. It won't do, Klaes. It won't do at all. Smoke him out, damn it. Smoke them all out. These people think they can . . . can bend us like bows, and play us like fiddles. But they can't. Smoke them out, or by God I'll know the reason why."

Klaes had not thought, after making his apology to Lieutenant Tusimov, that he could feel any deeper embarrassment or discomfort. But now he had fallen into a pit so deep he could not even see his previous position. Red-faced, he began to stammer out assurances, but the colonel was disinclined to listen. "Dismiss," he said. "Dismiss, Lieutenant Klaes. Go and get me some answers."

He walked directly towards Klaes, forcing him to retreat to the doorway, but the doorway was filled with the bulk of Sergeant Molebacher, as solid as any door. "If you have a moment, Colonel?" he said, speaking to August through Klaes's intervening body.

"Yes, of course, Mole. Come along in."

The sergeant did, forcing Klaes—who was now caught between them—to step sideways out of his path. Apparently Klaes's dismissal meant that August did not need to acknowledge his presence any more, and Molebacher took his cue from his chief.

"If I'm not disturbing you, sir . . ." Molebacher said in his basso rumble. Faced with the choice between an undignified exit and even more undignified eavesdropping, Klaes exited in haste. He closed the door behind him as he left, which at least allowed him the luxury of shaking his fist at it.

His humiliation was now complete. He had been shamed in front of his fellow officers, dressed down like a green private by his commander, and now slighted in front of a junior. A man without commission, whose uniform was as filthy as a chef's apron. He strode away, his face as dark as his thoughts.

Well, it was something, after all, to touch the bottom of the ocean and know that that was where you were. Unless he were to be court-martialed, he could sink no lower than this. And yet he felt he had done no more and no less than he had been asked to do.

Except in that encounter with the mayor. He should have seen through Weichorek's lies.

And with Bosilka. He might have pressed her harder and forced her to surrender up some clue.

And August might have given him that bloody letter to start with, instead of leaving him to flounder in the dark.

He slowed to a halt, thinking with unaccustomed clarity. In the dark. Yes. That was where he had been, all this time. Asking questions whose very vagueness and superficiality made it clear that it was safe to hide the answers from him. Making a parade of his ignorance and expecting passersby to give him the truth in the same spirit that they would give alms to a beggar.

That had to stop. And stop it would.

Colonel August sat down, and indicated that Molebacher should sit too. But Molebacher had a very sure sense of how the colonel should be handled, and he didn't take up the invitation at once.

He set down a basket on the table, with exaggerated reverence. "Saw these and thought of you, sir," he said, stepping back again. He clapped his hands together in a gesture he'd seen a Frenchman use once in a mess hall in the Low Countries. "*Voilà! Bon appetit*, Colonel, as they say in the Bourbon court."

August unfolded the cloth cover from the basket and inspected the contents. A dozen slices of candied apple lay on a clean linen kerchief. The light from the low sun outside the window struck the lumps of sugar crusted onto the fruit and gave them a tempting lustre.

"Thank you, Mole," August said. "Thank you very much indeed." His eyes were shining. Molebacher knew his commander—and his sweet tooth—very well.

"I hear the French call their king the *bonami*, the well beloved," he said jovially. "Isn't that so, Colonel? But love him or hate him, I doubt he dines on fruit as sweet as these are. A month in the syrup, they were. I was steeping them all through October. And they had your name on them, Colonel, right from the start. Strumpfel offered me three *grosch* for them, or an ounce of snuff, but I'd set them aside for you, and now I deliver them."

"Well, it was a kind thought," the colonel said. And Molebacher sat at last, having prepared the ground for what he had to say. But even now he went about it with indirection, trusting August to give him a suitable opening when the time came. The two men enjoyed a good understanding, based on the privations they'd undergone together, and it was not attenuated by the difference in rank. If anything it was strengthened, because befriending a man who was not even an officer made August feel that his humanity was of the transcendent kind that triumphs over social niceties. Though not at all sentimental himself, Molebacher encouraged and indulged the colonel's sentimentality in this, both (as now) with gifts and with frequent reminders of how the two of them had been forged in the same furnace. He invented stories about occasions when Colonel August had shown him some peculiar favour, and recounted them loudly in the same way that a fisherman might throw out a stickleback in order to catch a pike.

"So," he said now, "Lieutenant Klaes comes on, sir, does he not?" Molebacher had heard the altercation between August and the lieutenant as he lingered outside the door, waiting for an appropriate moment to make his entrance. He was obliged to Klaes for drawing down the lightning, as it were. The colonel was never more expansive than when he had exercised his temper.

August grimaced. "Not as much as I'd hoped, Mole," he said. "To be honest, he hasn't distinguished himself of late."

"No, sir? I'm sorry to hear it."

"I gave him a job to do, and it was simple enough. But not so simple as Klaes himself, it seems. He lets himself be led by the nose."

"Not a good quality in an officer, sir, certainly."

"And he treats these villagers with too much diffidence. Doesn't close with them. Doesn't make them feel him. I wanted him to turn them out with a stick, and he uses a feather."

Quietly and neatly, as the colonel spoke, Sergeant Molebacher took a flask from the pocket of his jacket, unscrewed the lid (which turned itself into a cup) and poured out a generous measure of schnapps. He slid this across the table to August, raising the bottle in a salute.

"Your health, sir."

"Yours. And devil take the bastard at the back!"

August emptied the cup in one, and Molebacher guzzled down a deep draught.

Thus encouraged, August told the sergeant the full story of Lieutenant Klaes's researches, and Molebacher commiserated with his commander about the poor calibre of young officers these days. It was his place, though, to be both respectful and bluffly optimistic. "He only wants the sharp corners rubbing off of him, sir, and you're the man to do it, I dare warrant. You'll shape him, if he only listens to you."

"Perhaps, perhaps."

Molebacher refilled the cup. "It is an issue, though, this business with the villagers. You must feel, sir, that recent events have proved you right. Give these people too much licence and they'll always misuse it."

"Of course they will, Mole."

"I wonder, sir . . ." Molebacher seemed to hesitate, but he was only waiting for permission.

"Yes?"

"There's a matter that's troubling me, sir. A matter of some delicacy—and as you know, I'm not really a delicate man."

August laughed heartily. "You do yourself too little credit."

"No, sir. I'm a happy man with a knife and a frying pan in my two mitts. Or a gun, for that matter, for I'm no coward." He raised his hands, large and reddened, seamed with old wounds, and displayed them to their full effect. "But that's just it. I think with these, sir, not with my head. So I was wondering if you could help me with a little advice."

"Tell me the facts of the matter, Mole." So Molebacher did.

25

The floggings were due to take place the next day, and everyone in the camp was tense, most with apprehension, but a few with excitement. Molebacher, Drozde knew, would be of the latter persuasion. She had seen him at floggings before. He took a kind of grim delight in the spectacle of it, engaging in macabre speculation over who would die, whose wounds would become infected, who was most likely to faint from the blows. Drozde hated it, and she would be damned if she was going to spend any time in his company tonight. She went out to the tents instead, in search of the other women. But Ottilie was with Frydek, and Libush (who had a dozen relationships to service to Drozde's one) was nowhere to be seen.

There were campfires a-plenty, and Drozde would have been welcome at most of them, but where the company of the other women would have been restful, that of the soldiers was likely to be boisterous and tiring. It might be enjoyable, but it was unlikely to distract her from the matters that were pressing on her mind, most of which related in one way or another to Pokoj's invisible household of phantoms.

She needed to see them again, and to put her questions to them. Ermel's story had finally convinced her of that. So she went back into the house, intending to go directly to the ballroom. She found Magda first, sitting in the love seat under the stairs, her ghost kitten curled up against her as she stroked the fur of its neck. The girl jumped up, and the kitten mewled in faint reproof as she tucked it under her arm.

"Shall we go in, milady?" Magda asked. She put on a haughty voice, holding out her crooked elbow to Drozde as though the two of them were old society ladies out for a stroll on the streets of Wroclaw.

Drozde fell in with the game, though it went against her mood more than a little. They walked on together, the woman putting on a gentlemanly swagger while the dead girl held up the train of an imaginary dress. "Tonight we talk on my terms, though," Drozde said, feeling the need to assert herself. "No stories until I say so. And I won't say so until I've had some of my questions answered."

"All right," Magda said quickly. "I promise we'll try. Unless it's something . . . you know. Something we can't talk about because we promised."

"As soon as we come to something you can't talk about, I'm leaving," Drozde said grimly.

The ballroom was already full when they arrived, but the echoes raised by Drozde's boots reverberated as loud and hollow as if she were the only one there. Ghost bodies did not muffle sound, and ghosts packed in together did not breathe or sniff or shuffle. Only when Drozde was right in the midst of them did they raise a murmur of welcome.

"Well," Drozde said, "and good even to you too, all and some."

"Shall I be first?" whispered a tall and stately man at her right shoulder.

"No," Drozde said. "Not tonight. Tonight it's my turn."

Sighs and susurrations arose from all sides—expressions of wonder and excitement. "Drozde's story!" the ghosts exclaimed. "Drozde will tell her story!"

"Not Drozde's story," she corrected them. "Drozde's questions. Afterwards, if you're still hungry for a story I'll tell you one, but first there are things you have to tell me. Otherwise I'll stop coming here and talking to you, and from what Magda said you wouldn't want me to do that."

Profound silence greeted her words, but the faces of the ghosts showed alarm and hurt. They took the threat seriously, and it didn't leave them unmoved.

"There are things we're sworn not to say," Meister Gelbfisc pointed out. "But that's not the worst of it. If the questions are about how we know you, and when we spoke to you before, then our answers will seem like nonsense to you."

"Those are my questions," Drozde said. "And I don't see how the answers will be nonsense unless they're lies."

"But if we try to tell the truth about things you've never known and never heard of, it will seem like lies. Most of what has happened to us since we died has been very different from what we knew in life. But the language we use is still the same. There is no tongue of the dead that we can learn, to speak about the doings of the dead. Perhaps there should be. But until there is, anything we say will be like . . ." He paused, searching for a simile. "It will be like a boot many sizes too big for you, that you put your foot into and try to walk in anyway. And feel with each step both how foolish you must look as you walk and how hard it is to walk at all. And if someone asks you to dance . . ." Gelbfisc shrugged eloquently. "Disaster."

"But I'm not asking you to dance!" Drozde almost yelled. "I'm only asking you to explain something to me. Something that ought to be simple. You welcomed me into this place like a friend. Spoke as if you knew me. Used my given name as easily as if we'd all grown up in the same house."

"We did," Magda said. She was looking at the kitten again, head bent low over it, and the words were almost too low to catch.

"And that," Drozde said, pointing to the child, "is what I need you to explain. How can you know me when I don't know you? How can you tell me that I was here before when—my oath on holy Jesus—I'm certain that I never was?"

The ghosts' response to Drozde's words was curious and somewhat frightening. They *multiplied* . For a few moments as they murmured among themselves their numbers grew and grew, but without anyone either entering or leaving the room. It was as though each of the dead men and women was present many times in different parts of the room. Then they coalesced again, and Meister Gelbfisc turned—not to Drozde but to Magda—with a brisk smile.

"We think she should hear about the torc," he said. "From first to last. And then you could perhaps show her . . ."

"Yes!" Magda set Amelie down so she could clap her hands. There was no sound when her palms met—and the kitten, once out of her grip, attenuated and dissolved into a ribbon of kitten-textured air. But when the girl bent again and touched it, it resumed its former shape and clambered daintily back into her arms.

Gelbfisc turned to Drozde, hands clasped formally over his chest. "This may further provoke you, madam," he said, "but I must take that risk. The best answer we can give to your questions must once again take the form of a story."

Drozde uttered a bitter oath.

"But it is not the story of any one of us," Gelbfisc assured her hastily. "And it's not for ourselves or each other that we tell it. So we'll tell it plain and spare, and then when the story is done we will show you something that may help you to understand how we live."

"And answer my question?" Drozde demanded.

"And in part, within the limits of a solemn promise we all of us made, answer your question."

Drozde breathed hard. "Very well, then," she said. "But if I don't like the answer, I won't come back."

A silence from all around, and then a shrug from Gelbfisc. "Even that," he said, "though it's not phrased as a question, is hard for me to answer. The things we know are sometimes a burden—the things we can't know, a bigger burden still. But that's in the nature of what we are. Step forward, Petra Veliky."

A ghost advanced out of the silent assembly to stand before Drozde. A woman, young and strong, with broad shoulders and an angular face. Her left cheek was pocked, the right one clear, but despite this asymmetry, there was a certain beauty in her dark eyes and her full lips. She was no more than five and twenty, Drozde thought, possibly younger. She wore a peasant's smock, but a sword hung at her waist. Her clothes were like a man's clothes, shirt of sack and leggings and boots of leather.

"I am Petra Veliky," the woman said. "Of Praha."

Petra Hiskil I was too, but my maiden name is the one I choose to go by. I lived a short but a blessed life, because I heard the word of Jan Hus and accepted it into my heart. If all of you could do the same, you would better bear the burdens you sometimes complain of.

Hus taught us that the lowest peasant who lived in virtue would be a great lord in Christ's kingdom—and the lords would be lower than dogs, because they wallowed like pigs in wealth made by the labour of others. And the lowest of the low would be the priests and bishops, because they'd used the word of Christ only to make themselves rich when they should have used it to light the world.

But Hus died, burned by order of the pope because the pope hated the truths he spoke. And Žižka, who was Hus's shield and spear, died too. Then we became Taborites and followed Kanis and Pelhrimov, who burned with a righteous fire. It was a strange time, with many madmen claiming to be prophets and many murderers wearing the robes of saints. The land was afire, the spires and the steeples awash with blood and the dogs dining daily on bishops and barons—but we, we alone, held to the pure word.

All things we shared, and nothing owned. We lived as Adam and Eve had lived in Eden, and as men and women will live again when Christ returns. Unless Hus *was* Christ, which some of us thought. Perhaps Christ comes to every generation, and is killed again and again until his time comes.

Three crusades the church sent against us, and every last one of them left their bones in the fields and forests of Boheme. We did not spare them, but left God to sift their souls for any grain of good. And there were, besides, counts and princelings who attacked us either because they were blind enough to see our freedoms as sin or because their priests told them so and they were too cowardly to think for themselves.

We always gave better than we got. Kanis had a teaching, which was for a hard word give a blow and for a blow give sword and fire. Our neighbours had to learn that we were holy and not to be touched. So we went against them often, and when we did, whether to punish them for raids against us, or to strike first against those who were screwing up their courage to raid, we had a name for what we did: *spanilé jízdy*, the beautiful ride. Most times it would be a mass of us, but sometimes only a few. And once—only once—I rode alone.

It was against another teacher, Domazlic, who called himself Hussite and Adamite and Taborite and many things besides. He was none of those, but he was a great fighter and had hurt us numerous times when our foragers met his—for we did not farm but lived off what the land would give us, and that mainly meant stealing from the farms of others.

Domazlic, as I say, had done us harm, and Kanis had decided that he must be killed. But his camp was too well defended to fall to a raiding party, and we would lose a great many warriors in trying. So he said I should go into Domazlic's camp—he called it a village, but it was only shelters made of woven twigs in the middle of a wood—and pretend to be one of his followers. Then I should entice him to lie with me, and kill him while he slept.

I agreed to do this. I said we shared everything, and that meant our bodies too. Marriage as the church knew it was a sin, not a sacrament. So I thought nothing of using my sex to bring a man low. If anything, I thought it made me more like our mother Eve, who, when she persuaded Adam to eat the apple, surely used more than words.

And Domazlic was a man of strong and promiscuous desires, so the plan worked well. I walked into the camp without challenge, and walked into his bed not more than seven nights after.

When he was exhausted from enjoying me—and I nearly as spent as he!—he fell into a heavy sleep. I had not brought my knife into the tent, because he might have guessed my purpose, so I used his own sword to kill him, driving it downwards into his throat at an angle so that if he woke before he died he wouldn't be able to cry out.

I wept afterwards. It was strange. I hadn't known Domazlic, but his lovemaking had been sweet and fierce and I was sorry that he was dead. I wanted to remember him, so I took from around his neck a torc of gold that he wore. It was a beautiful thing. Probably it came from some great lady's jewel chest, but the metal was thick and solid and it looked as well on a man.

I took it to remember him by, as I said, and it was all I took from the place. I slipped from his tent before the moon was down, and was gone. What his people thought when they found his body I know not and care not. I'd done my work as God willed it and despite the sadness I was mostly at peace.

But nothing went well for me after that—and particularly in my dealings with men I seemed dogged by misfortune. Every man I had an eye to went for some other woman, or used me and then left me, or worked me ill in some other wise. Much woe I had, until I met Prokop Hiskil and swore to him at an altar made of a sword crossed with a sickle, which was how we Hussite women were married.

But Prokop beat me near to death and left me in my blood when we'd been together only seven months. There was a baby inside me and he came premature because of the beating, so small and so sickly I was sure he'd die. I knew then that the torc I'd taken from Domazlic was cursed—which meant that Domazlic had had the powers of the devil and I'd been very right to kill him.

I prayed for guidance, and Hus himself came to me in a dream, with Jesus by his side. He told me to take the torc back to where it belonged and leave it there, and I'd be free of the evil.

Well, I had no idea where Domazlic had been buried, and his followers were no more. They'd disbanded as soon as they found him dead. But I knew where I'd killed him, and I believed I could find the place again.

So I put myself on the road, and I walked for many weeks—back to the valley of Glogau and the woodlands where the *Domazlici* had made their home. I arrived there in the middle of a windswept and blasted night, a night of storms, when only fools and cutthroats walk the roads—but then I was a cutthroat, of course, so that was meet. The *Domazlici* had built a shrine to their dead leader at the edge of the path, and it was still tended. I almost left the torc there, but it felt wrong to do that, as though I was making an offering to Domazlic, which I had no desire to do.

While I hesitated, wondering what I should do for the best, the moon came out of the clouds for a moment and I saw a place close by where the ground had been cleared for building. In fact, the building had begun. Coming closer, I saw foundations dug, stacks of cut stone, ropes and wood for scaffolding, all that was necessary for a job well underway. And from the shape of the foundations, which was a cross, I guessed that this was to be a church.

I buried the torc at the centre of the cross. If it did have the power of the devil in it, the devil would not like his new lodgings much and might have the courtesy to leave me alone in future.

But as I turned to leave, something came down out of the sky and hit me on the shoulder with terrible force. I fell, and it pinned me to the ground as a dog bears down a rat. It was a tree, toppled by the wind. I could not get out from under it and its great weight prevented me from drawing enough breath to fill my lungs.

Before the night was over I was dead. And saw the church built, and the abbey around the church, and the house rise where the abbey fell, and the wheel of time turn as God has decreed. For the Bible tells us that we will wait in our flesh until the Judgement comes, and this thin weave of nothingness I've become is in reality the very subtlest of flesh.

The girl was done with her tale. She stepped back, and Meister Gelbfisc acknowledged her efforts with a nod of thanks.

"Rupit Zelzer," Gelbfisc said. "Will you speak next?"

"I will," said a man at the back of the room. He came forward slowly, with many nervous glances to either side. "Though I wish to state for the record that I don't believe in curses."

"Nor in anything else, neither!" someone exclaimed, but whoever it was they were shushed and scolded with "Drozde!" "Drozde's rules!" and the man was not heckled any further.

He was a strange fellow, Drozde thought. Tall and well built, as far as that went, but with a rheumy eye, a slouching shoulder and a lugubrious air. He wore a suit of indeterminate brown, and his hair where it remained was of the same colour. But the top of his head was bald, like a monk's tonsure.

"Yes," the man said defiantly, though the tremor in his voice undermined the words. "It's true that I despise superstition. And it's true that the faith I had in life I largely lost. So you could say, if you wanted to, that I believe in nothing. I prefer to say that I believe in man. In all men. And in one woman."

He bowed to Drozde, the gesture awkward and uncertain. "Not this woman," he added, "though obviously I have the utmost respect, the utmost gratitude, the very . . . yes, a profound regard. But she is not my religion, and she never was. My religion was Simona Kaiser."

"You're meant to be telling her about the torc!" Magda admonished the man impatiently.

He gave her an austere and contemptuous look. "I know my brief," he said.

My name, as you have already heard, is Rupit Zelzer. I was born in Ostrawa. And my country, Czechoslovakia, was born in the same year I was, the year when the great war ended.

I grew up in what everyone assured me was a new world. The war that was gone—there would never be another like it. So what would the peace be like? Unimaginable! The rebirth of humanity, without need for religiosity or miracle.

My parents were members of a new political faction that valued equality and the rights of the common man, and I became one too. It was not that they indoctrinated me. It was just that I could see, with perfect clarity, what the future would be like and what my part in it must be. I saw the inevitability of progress towards the perfect worker state. I wanted to be one of its midwives.

But there was another war, even darker and more terrible. The world sickened, and that future died before it was even born. There was a monster at our borders, risen to power through disgrace and treachery, and he swallowed my country in two bites. His forces marched through the streets where I had played as a child, and his soldiers took the place of policemen on our corners.

We were captured without a fight because of the cowardice of our allies, but in my heart I was already preparing for yet another war, which would be a war of humanity against the dead weight of profit. And that thought sustained me through the years of darkness when the tyrants ruled us. They killed my parents, and my older brother— the defining tragedy of my life. They would have killed me too, for my political affiliation alone, but friends helped me to go to ground in Praha, and I lived there under false papers for the duration of the war.

When Berlin fell, the wheel turned and my faction came at last to power. Old scores were paid. Many of German and Hungarian descent were killed, and many more fled into exile. This may seem harsh, but you must remember that these were almost all people who had supported the monster's regime without qualm or question when they were under his rule. They drew their ruin down upon themselves.

But if the peace brought us catharsis, it did not bring us stability. There were demagogues and fifth columnists in the national assembly who spoke out against the rule of this new, better order. They had to be purged. And then there were rabble-rousers who said that the purges were evidence that Czechoslovakia was not a democracy. It was a hard time. I wanted nothing but good for all my countrymen, but many of them resisted the gift. It was time—long past time—for social justice, but it seemed that social justice must be administered like medicine to those who would thrive by it, but, like children, feared its taste might be too bitter.

A hard time, yes, but for me it was when hard striving brought sweet success. I rose in the ranks of the new regime, becoming a member of a committee whose remit was the proper management of those assets left behind by our enemies as they fled, or confiscated by the state from dead ones.

As part of this work, I came in the spring of my thirtieth year to the Mander glassworks in Glogau. Here. To this house in which we now stand. The Manders had left the country over a decade before and were rumoured to be living in Argentina. They had left the glassworks in the hands of a manager, a certain Vramt Kaiser, but he had just been arrested on charges of collaboration during the war. The state was de facto owner of the glassworks now, and did not want the asset to be wasted. I was to manage it, with the aid of my secretary Mikhal Tuss until a worker could be trained to take on that role.

The glassworks was not what I was expecting. It was already running on collectivised lines, the workers dividing all tasks between them and taking an equal share of the profits. Unfortunately, while I stoutly approved of this in principle, I was obliged to make the place run profitably in order to justify my presence, so I returned the glassworks to a more conventional form of organisation, placing all the workers on fixed salaries and rationalising the use of their time within defined hours instead of allowing them to come and go as they pleased (which seemed to be the system that was then in place).

Another surprise to me was that the workers were all women. I now know that Anatol Mander had arranged things in this way, seeing the glassworks as a means of allowing women widowed by war or accident some degree of autonomy. An unobjectionable goal, but since my brief was to expand production I immediately recruited a large number of men—war veterans, mostly, and desperate for any kind of work at all. Their ready availability emboldened me to lower the wage I'd only just set by three crowns a week.

At the same time I instituted a rule that there should be no talking on the workshop floor. The women were accustomed to sing while they worked, or on some days to tell each other folk tales. These bloodthirsty narratives always started in very much the same wise. "A man wandered into the woods, and lost his way . . ." Then there would be a fairy or an ogre or a troll and everything would go extremely badly for the poor traveller.

The women were unhappy to lose their songs and their stories. They disapproved of my policies altogether, and some of them complained to me about them. Or rather they did not complain themselves, but deputed a spokeswoman to do so on their behalf. This was one Simona Kaiser, the daughter of the man who had been the manager before me.

And when I looked into her face, I was lost.

I'd never known love before. To be honest, I'd never even thought about it. It seemed something of a regressive idea, a myth to replace the older, failing myths of religion and douse the flames of revolution. Men and women pledging allegiance to each other and making each other the centre of their lives, when they ought to declare their kinship with the wider mass of humanity.

But now I knew that love was real—real enough to cripple me. Simona Kaiser's beauty cut across my life like a shaft of sunlight across a drab landscape, making everything that was murky clear and resplendent.

Many would not have thought her beautiful. She was as big and well-muscled as a shire horse. But her dark eyes blinded me, and her ruddy face superimposed itself on everything I saw. Even the smell of her sweat, which at the end of a shift was acute, caused my head to swim.

Yet it was difficult. Almost impossibly so. I was Simona's superior, and obliged to keep her at a distance. Moreover, she hated me. She argued that all the changes I'd introduced were bad, and that I was ruining the factory. I tried hard to keep my patience and explain my thinking to her, the more so because of my tender feelings, but I could not make her understand the difference between the selfish striving for one's own profit and the joy that was to be had in striving for the betterment of all.

"The betterment of all!" she scoffed. "I see our beloved leaders getting bettered. I don't see it happening to anyone else!"

This was counter-revolutionary talk, and in theory I was obliged to report it. I didn't do so. But neither did I allow myself to weaken on the core issue of the running of the glassworks. Everything I was doing was in the interests of improving production and making it a vital contributor to the new nation's wealth and standing. If I succeeded, the benefits would flow to all.

But production did not improve. Alarmingly, although I had almost doubled the workforce, I had not managed to increase output by even a small fraction. In the first quarter of the year it even fell back slightly. I felt that the secretary, Tuss, was watching me closely and very probably reporting back to my superiors on my achievements. He had no responsibilities at all, of course, and so could afford to be as censorious as he wanted.

I tried to enlist Simona as an ally, promoting her to forewoman and asking her to work with me to improve the glassworks. I was falling further and further behind on my targets, and was almost at my wits' end searching for ways of reporting an increased profit. I could lower wages still further—the economy as a whole was so depressed, I didn't see any likelihood of my workforce leaving en masse—but that would make her hate me even more, and might in any case have a demoralising effect that offset the immediate gain.

If only people could be made to work for love of their fellow man, as I did, then there would be no limit to human progress. But most people are inclined to follow selfish motives, and so they put chains on themselves without even knowing it.

Simona suggested a new furnace, capable of being raised to a higher temperature. I quailed at the thought of such an expense, but I did it to please her. I might have saved the money and spared the effort: she seemed to like me no better for it. Tuss, for his part, pursed his lips and shook his head when he saw the invoices. The cost of the furnace was equal to a whole month's profit.

But in a sense that decision did change everything. It was just that the change was not one I could have foreseen. The workers who came to install the furnace began by taking up the floor in the blowing room and breaking into the existing foundations. Then they took away most of the material they had excavated, intending to return a few days later and set the furnace directly into the new and deeper foundations they intended to lay.

That night, wandering the glassworks alone and disconsolate, I found myself in the blowing room, staring at the deep pit that had been dug there. It seemed a fitting symbol for my emotions at the time. Most of the room was in darkness, but a bright, full moon laid a single bar of light down its left-hand side, and I saw there, picked out by the light, a small object of a different colour to the surrounding dirt—an object that seemed to pick up the light in a startling way.

I descended into the pit and dug out the small, bright thing. I found myself staring in astonishment at the golden torc you have already had described to you. It was still lying where it had been buried by

Petra Veliky seven hundred years or so before.

I knew little about the buying and selling of gold, and still less how to assay its quality. But the solid weight of the torc, and the way its unspoiled brightness could be seen through the crust of dirt upon it, convinced me that it was pure and of enormous value. Probably more than enough to meet the cost of the furnace and allow me to show a profit on the quarter.

But I found myself thinking of another use to which it could be put, and once the idea had come to me I couldn't push it away again. I hid the torc under a pile of boxes in a corner of the room, and the next day I approached Simona, with great trepidation, to ask her for a meeting.

"You're meeting me now," she pointed out, in a tone that was not encouraging.

"Yes," I said. "Of course. I meant, though, outside of working hours."

Simona stared at me as if I were speaking Greek. "What hours?" she demanded. "What for? What do you mean?"

I meant that we should talk that night, I told her. And no, I was not trying to debauch or compromise her. It could still be here at the glassworks. All I wanted was a little privacy, to ask her something that was of a slightly delicate nature. And to make her—I stumbled over the word—a gift.

Simona agreed at last, but without enthusiasm. And having agreed she avoided me for the rest of the day, as though she had to fortify herself for the coming interview by fasting from my company.

The day seemed like a month to me. I had told Simona to return at ten in the evening, two hours after the glassworks closed its gates. It seemed a safe enough margin, but Tuss worked on until after nine, and finally I had to send him away by telling him I needed to lock the gates.

I retrieved the torc, took it to my office and waited impatiently there for Simona to return. At a quarter past ten I was still waiting. But finally I heard her footsteps—the only sound in the empty building—coming towards me along the main corridor. I surged to my feet and ran to meet her halfway.

When she saw me coming she stopped, and even backed away a little. I realised that I must look somewhat wild, and remembered that she still had no idea why I had asked her to come.

I began to explain, but it was as though my words fell over

themselves as they left my mouth. I was reduced in moments to a stammering wreck.

But the one thing that came out clearly was that I cared for her. And I saw her surprise as she realised that; then her perplexity as she considered what it meant. Though she did not speak, her face softened. I think it had not occurred to her until then that I might have human feelings, still less that I might have them for her.

Encouraged, and daring to hope for a happy outcome, I held out the torc. After a moment's hesitation, Simona took it from my hands. "What's this?" she demanded.

"An antique," I said. "Of enormous value. It's for you. Well, for us."

Simona blinked. "What?"

"I thought that we could sell it. There are black market dealers in the taverns on Pohranicni who would give us a huge sum. Obviously we would have to break it down into smaller pieces and sell a little at a time. We could use the furnace here to melt it, and pour it into thimbles to make nuggets. You see?"

"No," Simona said, bluntly. "I don't see."

I tried to put my plan into simpler words. "If we sell the gold, it will fetch enough money for us to live like kings. We could go to England or France or Spain and have a life together. A good life, in which you'd never have to work with your hands again."

Simona had been staring at me all this time, and her expression had changed again into something I found very hard to read. "Isn't working with your hands meant to be a good thing for a communist?" she asked me.

"It's . . . Yes, of course!" I stammered. "Of course it is. But here in the republic, with me a servant of the state and you a worker under me, it would be difficult for us to be together. With the money we got from selling this—"

She waved me silent. "You wish to escape from your life here?" she said.

And though it was not that simple at all, I nodded.

Simona returned the nod. "Yes," she said. "Very well. I understand now. But you should try the necklace on first, Herr Manager. I think it would look good on you."

She put one hand on my shoulder and spun me round, pushing me hard up against the wall of the corridor. For a woman, she was incredibly strong. With her other hand she slipped the torc around my neck and pulled it tight against my throat.

I struggled, but I was not strong enough to break Simona's grip. Pushing with one hand on the back of my head, and pulling back with the other so that the torc bit hard into my windpipe, she succeeded in strangling me.

Secretary Tuss found my body the next morning. He contacted the governors of the region and told them I was dead. It was a nine days' wonder. Every man and woman at the glassworks was questioned at length. Simona kept her nerve admirably, and said like everyone else that the last she'd seen of me was at eight o'clock when the shift ended.

Nobody was ever charged, and nothing came of it. There were far greater tragedies at that time, and far greater scandals. The death of one minor official wasn't going to make the world stop spinning.

There was, though, plenty of gossip about it on the shop floor. One woman said she thought I'd been murdered by enemies of the regime. Another was of the opinion that the regime itself had done away with me in one of its internal purges.

"What do you think happened to the manager, Simona?" the next woman along the bench asked her.

Simona chewed the question over for a little while.

"I think he wandered into the woods and lost his way," she said at last. "That can happen to anyone."

There was a thoughtful silence after Zelzer had finished his tale, but there was no applause. The story had been told to illustrate a point, Drozde realised (though she was far from clear what the point was), and that changed the occasion and the required etiquette.

"It was the torc," the woman Petra said. "It was cursed, as I said."

"It was not the torc," Zelzer replied. He sighed deeply. "I had shown Simona that I was a man, and she was prepared—for a moment, at least—to see me in that light. But then I showed her that I was a greedy hypocrite, prepared to give up all that I believed for a life of ease."

"It was cruel," said a little bearded man who might have been one of the monks from the old abbey.

"No." Zelzer shook his head firmly. "It was not cruel at all, but kind and compassionate. She killed me to save me from my own weakness. I have taken it as a sign that she did have some feelings for me after all." His gaze had been downcast, but now he raised his head and looked around him defiantly. "I think my story has a happy ending."

Magda tugged at Drozde's sleeve, and Drozde felt the movement. Startled, she looked down.

"Now I have to show you something," the little girl said. "Come on."

They went back along the dark corridors and left the house again by the back door. There was an iron shoe-scraper on the top step that Drozde hadn't noticed before. She wouldn't have noticed it now, except that Magda pointed to it and told her to bring it. Unwilling to argue (her voice might be heard where Magda's would not), she did as she was bidden.

The moon was down now and the night was dark, but Magda was, if anything, more clearly visible than before and it was easy for Drozde to follow her.

In the ruins of the abbey Magda walked back and forth for a little while until she found a spot next to a mossy stone whose sharply angled sides made it clear that it had once been part of a wall.

"Here," she said at last. "Dig. The shoe-scraper is like a little spade, only it's wider and blunter and hasn't got a proper handle."

Drozde was far from keen. "What if someone sees? They'll think I've lost my senses!" she protested.

The dead girl scowled at her, hands on hips. "You asked the question!" she said. "And then you said, 'If you don't tell me I'll go away, ner, ner, ner.' Well, we're *trying* to tell you, Drozde. But you've got to help!" She held up her phantom hands and waved them, head cocked sarcastically. "Or do you expect me to do it?"

Drozde dug.

It took half an hour, and the narrow hole she made was excavated to a depth of two feet before she found what was buried there. With a trembling hand she drew it out.

It was too dark to see clearly, but she traced its outline with her fingers. A curve of hard, cold metal, as thick as her thumb, which did not quite close into a loop but terminated in two irregular bosses that were twice the thickness of the rest.

"My God!" she whispered. The words seemed forced out of her, and after them nothing else would come.

"Simona Kaiser puts it back where Mr. Zelzer found it," Magda said. "Then a builder digs it up again when they start to turn the old abandoned factory into a hotel. But that's not until my time. Well, almost. Almost my time. In my time it's sitting in a glass case in the little museum we've got, with some of the pictures from the gallery upstairs and some relics from the abbey. And there's a card that tells how it was found and that it's probably a thousand years old but nobody knows who made it or what it was doing there.

"Do you understand, Drozde? This is your lifetime we're in right now, because you're still alive. And you lived a long time *after* Petra buried the torc—so long that the church they built on top of it has all fallen down again—but a long time *before* Mr. Zelzer finds it under the floor of the factory. Before Simona Kaiser kills him and then puts it back where he found it because she doesn't want to be rich but only to keep her job and do the work she's happy doing."

"I . . ." Drozde tried to speak. She felt as though the world was spinning under her feet and she might fall headlong. But the sickening spin she felt, the sense of movement, was not fast at all; it was something that played out over centuries, and if she once lost her footing she was afraid she might never stop falling. "Magda! Tell me, when were you born?"

"Two days after the millennium. January the second, 2001."

"No! Tell me the truth!"

"That is the truth, Drozde." The little girl's tone was reproachful. "I wouldn't tell a lie to you, because I love you."

"Dying is not so very different from being born," said another voice. It was Gelbfisc. He stepped into view, walking unhurriedly through the remaining wall of the ruin to stand at Drozde's side. He looked at her with something of concern in his face. Unless it was pity. "Do you believe, madam, that the soul is eternal?"

"I . . . I hadn't thought about it very much," Drozde said.

The Jew shrugged. "Not many of us ever do," he said. "And when we do, we mostly miss the point. If the soul is eternal, where does it live before it enters into us?"

"I have no idea."

"Why, in eternity, of course. And when we die, where does it go back to? Eternity again. That's still where it belongs. But before birth the soul had no name, no memories, no sense of itself. All things were as one to it. After death . . ." Gelbfisc spread his arms. "Why, after death, the soul is the man, the woman, the child it was when it lived. All that's left of us. Like the lizard of Afric in the story, it has taken the colour of its surroundings.

"That's what we are, madam. Poor, unhoused creatures, delivered out of time in a second birth that was more painful than the first. Lost in a maze, although the maze has no walls. And though we seem to be tethered to the *place* of our death, we are free to roam when it comes to the time before and the time after. Only imagine! There *is* no before and after for us. In eternity nothing comes first and nothing comes later. It all happens at once. And so the time when we walked the world alive, in our flesh, is like a single room in a house that has a thousand million rooms. When we find it we are happy to see it again, or else appalled. Were the walls really that colour? The space so narrow? But most of our time we spend elsewhere."

Drozde shuddered and hugged herself, overwhelmed. Magda stroked her hair and whispered reassurances she didn't even hear. "Horrible!" she whispered. "Horrible!"

"Yes, horrible. That's the word. And the horror enters into us, and breaks us, like a robber's crowbar wedged into the jamb of a door. We lose ourselves slowly, become grey shadows and fading echoes. You've seen ghosts that are like that, I think? Ghosts who have lost what I can only call the *self* of themselves. The *haecceitas*, the thisness. Ghosts that become only words or gestures, or less than that, a slight prickling of the skin as you walk into a room."

Drozde nodded without speaking. All the ghosts she'd met before Pokoj had been of that kind.

"But then someone came," Gelbfisc said, "and taught us a new trick."

"Stories!" Magda spoke the word as though it were the answer to a riddle. As though she was saying, *It's so simple. Don't you feel like a goose that you didn't guess it?*

"When we tell ourselves, we become stronger and more certain in ourselves," Gelbfisc said. "It is, almost, a kind of magic. But where magicians are supposed to charm spirits into a circle, we charm our own spirits back into ourselves. We keep ourselves close. We do not fade. The one who came—it was as though she lit a fire for every one of us, and so long as we keep the fire tended we can be warm and safe there for as long as we want to. And because that is such a very great gift, because it saved us from the cold and the dark, we honour the one who gave it."

"I didn't!" Drozde shook her head violently. "I would know if I'd . . ."

"You would, yes. But for us, no before and after. She always comes. We always honour her. We like to be close to her, because of the strength she gives us. And if in our thoughtless chattering we've brought her any pain or unhappiness, we beg her pardon. Truly we do."

"Yes," Magda said contritely. "We're sorry, Drozde. But you said you had to know, so we told you. Please don't be sad. None of it is as sad as you think it's going to be, even when the horrible old colonel—"

"Enough," Gelbfisc said, but he said it very gently. "No more for now, child. Give her some peace."

"When the colonel does what?" Drozde demanded. But the ghosts were already fading, Magda with a smile and a wave as though—underneath the terrible weight of these revelations—everything that had happened was still part of a game, and the only thing they'd forgotten was to tell their new friend the rules.

26

Considering his earlier errors, and determined not to repeat them, Klaes went back to first principles.

The only substantial pointer to what it was the villagers were trying to conceal—and it was clear now, if it hadn't been before, that they were trying to conceal something—was the words spoken by the yokel Kopesz when Klaes was lying on the ground and presumed to be stunned.

About Petos. About the cellar, and all that stuff.

That had given him two directions to investigate, and he had been remiss in both. First of all, he had taken Bosilka's threat to tell Meister Weichorek to mean that it was to the burgomaster that this secret belonged. And he had taken his lack of knowledge to the mayor and tried to bluff the secret out of him, with predictable results. He had no desire to repeat that experiment any time soon, although he promised himself that when he got to the bottom of this he would pull Weichorek's beard hard enough to hurt.

But he had also assumed that the tiny room behind the kitchen where the gypsy had made her nest was the only cellar that the mansion boasted. He knew now that this could not be the case. Weichorek had described much more extensive cellars, complete with wine racks and broken furniture. Perhaps if he were to seek them out, he would find something in them that would either answer his questions or point him in a new direction.

So he descended the main staircase to the mansion's wide entrance hall and began to search the rooms on the ground floor. Most of these were still empty, apart from Molebacher's kitchen and the adjacent apartments that he was using as storage space.

Klaes began there, at the rear of the house, and made a slow, methodical clockwise circuit, through the sodden, mildewed wilderness of the east and north extensions, then back into the habitable part of the house via a vast echoing ballroom. His skin prickled unpleasantly here, but most likely it was only the chill.

Nowhere did he find what he was looking for: a door or trap with a staircase behind it, leading down into the mansion's underground levels. Was this another lie of Weichorek's? Was Drozde's rancid hideaway, after all, the only cellar Pokoj possessed? It seemed highly unlikely now that he thought about it. A house whose living space was this large would surely have needed storage on a similar scale. And yet it seemed there was nothing.

Klaes completed his circuit at Molebacher's kitchen again. This was the most likely place for a cellar door. The mansion would have needed a spring house or icehouse, or something of that kind, and such accommodations were typically below ground. He walked round all the walls of the kitchen itself—the quartermaster sergeant was evidently still closeted with Colonel August—but nothing presented itself to his eye. The only stairs were those that led down to the room the gypsy had claimed.

He turned his attention to the floor. No trapdoors could be seen, and there were no coverings beneath which one might have lain hidden.

He was about to begin a second circuit of the walls when it occurred to him that there was another telling mystery in all of this. When they had first come here, a few short weeks before, they had found a house open to the elements and obviously deserted. If there had been a militia detachment here, what rooms had they occupied? Why had they left nothing behind of themselves, not even the rubbish from their meals or the shit from their latrines?

Perhaps the colonel was right, Klaes thought, and Petos had deserted. But then, what had happened to the rest of his detachment? Surely they had not gone with him: a dozen militiamen to turn into ghosts, all at once, and leave no shadow or footprint? It was hard to credit.

But what if one were to start from the opposing premise? If they had been here, then the signs of their presence would be here still. It was just that he hadn't seen them.

He walked the rooms again, looking this time not for doors but for evidence of human habitation—by a large group of men, and in the recent past. He found none.

He went back up onto the upper floor and did the same. He could not, of course, go into the other officers' quarters, but then he had been largely responsible for supervising their installation and so he felt reasonably sure that memory would suffice here.

Nowhere in the house could he find any relicts of Petos or his militiamen. No lost items of clothing, no personal belongings forgotten in the haste of a sudden departure. No apple cores, nutshells or cheese rinds from hasty barracks meals. No scuffs or scrapes left by pallet beds pushed up against walls or boots dragged across floors. Above all, no indication that anyone had ever tried to make this bleak and decaying place more homely or comfortable to the tiniest degree, except in the rooms that August's officers had taken over. If they had ever been here, the militia had taken away with them every last atomy of their goods and of their detritus.

Klaes leaned against the window frame in one of the rooms that overlooked the ruined abbey, gazing out through the shattered window. It was here, in the extensive grounds to the front and the southern flank of the house, that the enlisted men had set up their tents. And the camp followers, of course, had gone where the enlisted men had gone, just as surely as water runs downhill. There were a great many tents, but they were most thickly clustered close to the mansion, like children clinging to their mother's skirts. Behind them and to the west was where the carpenters from the village were building the whipping frames for the next day's flogging. The sound of their hammers came to Klaes on the crisp, cold air.

On the east side Pokoj directly adjoined the road.

What of the rear of the house, though? The stable yard was all he had seen, because the back door opened straight off it. He went there now and found a gate that took him past the well into a narrow kitchen garden bordered on all sides by walls of moss-covered stone. Another gate on the further side, closed with a bolt, led to an orchard with about a dozen trees. Some were obviously dead, bracket fungus spilling like intestines from their split, dried-out bark. A wicker basket lay under one, as though someone picking fruit had been called away or distracted in some long-ago summer, and had never returned to finish the task. Couch grass grew up through the basket's broken weave.

Klaes walked on through the orchard, keeping the rear wall of the house on his left until he came to the corner. All was ruin and neglect here. The coulter of a plough, half-buried in the ground, almost tripped him. It was as though unimproved nature was triumphing over the men and women of the house, now dead, who had tried to tame and teach her.

He went back to the garden. This must once have been a well ordered kingdom of herbs and vegetables. Stone flags marked it out into three separate beds of roughly equal size, except that a heap of dry straw at the bottom of the middle bed left a smaller cultivable area. Nothing was being cultivated here now in any case: left to themselves for many years, all the beds were dense tangles of weeds. Some of the brambles had stems almost as thick as Klaes's wrist.

He was still looking for discarded waste from the meals Petos and his men might have eaten here. That was why his gaze was on the ground, and why he saw what he would otherwise have missed. The grass and weeds had been cut away around the mound of straw. It hadn't been dumped on top of the weeds: it had been set down in a cleared space between them.

Where had the straw come from in the first place, in a kitchen garden? It had most likely been brought in from the stable yard, but why would anyone do that? To start a compost heap? But the work had been done recently—too recently for the days when this garden was still fruitful and might have derived some benefit from composting.

Gingerly, because it was a little damp and musty, Klaes cleared away the straw. Underneath it was bare soil raised into a low, untidy mound. Someone had dug here and then heaped up the straw to hide the fact.

Klaes went to find a spade. There were no sappers with the detachment, but Sergeant Strumpfel kept six shovels for the digging of latrines. He found them leaning in a row against the walls of the stables and took the nearest.

There had been no serious frost yet, so the earth was soft enough. Klaes took off his coat, folded it carefully and set it on the ledge of a ground floor window. Then he rolled back his sleeves and set to work.

After some minutes' digging, he struck something soft. He squatted down in the hole he'd made and scooped away the soil with his hands, revealing what looked at first like the fabric of a sack. A little further excavation, however, showed that this was not the case. Sacks have no buttons.

Klaes went and closed the gate that led to the stable yard. There was no bolt here, so he propped it shut with a stone. Then he returned to his work.

Ten minutes later he had dug all the way around the outline of the buried thing. It was six feet long, two broad, and had an army greatcoat draped over it. The greatcoat had been grey once, but now it was harlequined blue and white with mould and lustrous with the spoor of worms and snails. On its shoulders were the eagle and diamond lozenge that marked a captain's rank.

By this time, of course, Klaes knew what it was that he had found. The foetid smell that was rising from the ground was as good in that respect as any gravestone. So he was not surprised at all when he peeled back the collar of the greatcoat and found himself staring into the sunken eye sockets of a corpse. He only winced as the stench intensified, billowing up like the dead man's last pent breath.

"Captain Nymand Petos, I think," he murmured, covering his mouth and nose with his cupped hand. "Pleased to make your acquaintance, sir." But that was just a sort of graveyard humour, spoken in bravado to push against the quiet horror of the moment.

He was not pleased at all. Not when he thought of what this would bring.

If it were not for the floggings . . . But he had ample evidence now that Colonel August would react in an extreme and intemperate way to the news of Petos's death. And Klaes did not really know, yet, what his death portended. It was even hard, at this remove, to determine what had caused it. There were rents in the front of the greatcoat that seemed to suggest violence. But perhaps the captain merely kept his coat in poor repair, or perhaps Klaes had torn it himself by thrusting in the blade of the shovel as he was digging. The dead man's shirt had already rotted off his back and most of the flesh beneath had fallen away, so there were no clues there. The side of the skull was squashed in and misshapen, but was that from a blow or from being thrown into the hole?

He resolved that he would not act, or inform anyone of what he had found, until he had some answers to these questions. To do so, in the current climate of mistrust and resentment between Narutsin and the camp, would be to inflame emotions already roused and tender. He emphatically did not want to bring more fuel to the colonel's fire.

So he would wait until the floggings were done, and then he would approach Bosilka again. He had trusted Meister Weichorek once, and would not do so a second time, but he believed he could explain to the girl what was at stake. She was intelligent enough and brave enough to tell him the truth, and once he knew the truth he would decide what needed to be done.

Until then he would keep his counsel.

He straightened, picked up the shovel and set to work to hide all over again what he had just uncovered.

Sergeant Molebacher returned to his kitchen, his mind distracted and his emotions agitated. His interview with Colonel August had had a favourable outcome, but he was still in a sort of suspended state, and would remain so until another interview—with Drozde—had taken place.

It was time to start the preparations for dinner, and he hadn't even decided what the menu was to be. He had beets and hogweed, so he could make a proper borscht, and there were chickens for the main course if he could think of something suitable to do with them. He needed either carrots or potatoes, or possibly swedes. And flour for a *staka*.

He went into the larger of his two food stores to see what was there. Empty space, for the most part. Normally he could perform miracles even with empty space—and normally he would be calling up some of his little demons now, his light-fingered skirmishers, to go about among the fields and gardens and take a secret tithe from the farmers of Narutsin. But he had been thrown off balance by his discovery in the village. He could not face the privates he normally bullied and hectored so easily, knowing that they had seen him broken, for however short a time. Now he was running to catch up with himself, and a fat man running is an undignified sight.

As he was rummaging among the shelves, hoping to find some vegetables that had escaped his attention, he chanced to glance through the window. It looked out onto a walled space that might once have been a garden. It was a wilderness now, and offered nothing of any use to anyone except a dumping ground for scraps.

But there was Lieutenant Klaes in his shirtsleeves, squatting on the ground at the far end of the enclosed space. What was Snotwipe doing out there? Taking a shit? No, he was looking into a hole in the ground, with a mound of earth beside him and a shovel lying at his feet.

And now he was standing, and shovelling the soil back into the hole. Sergeant Molebacher put his face closer to the fly-specked pane. He could see the troubled expression on Klaes's face, the furtive glances he cast over his shoulder as he worked. He looked towards the house once or twice too, but Molebacher remained perfectly still and let the lieutenant's gaze sweep right past him. He must surely be invisible in the darkened room, the contours of his face lost in the window's filthy constellations.

Klaes put all the earth back in the hole, and then heaped straw over the place where it had been. It was an extraordinary thing for an officer to do. Molebacher couldn't think of anything the lieutenant might have to hide that would justify such a laborious procedure. Even if he'd killed a man in a fight, say (as if Klaes would ever have the balls to do a thing like that!), it would be easier to leave the body by the side of a road than to bring it home with him and give it a decent burial.

So there was something here, and it piqued the sergeant's curiosity even in his present preoccupied state. He had not yet repaid Klaes for shaming him in front of his men, and Molebacher did not easily forget those sorts of debt. Besides, the colonel didn't like Klaes, so anything that put him in a bad light would bring the added benefit of pleasing August and assisting Molebacher in his ongoing programme of ingratiation.

There were other things to see to first. There was dinner to prepare for the officers, which would need to be served up promptly. And the floggings were set for the next morning: it was important that he was present for that entertainment.

But he would keep an eye on Lieutenant Snotwipe, he decided. And he would find out, as soon as was convenient, what was buried in that hole.

27

On the morning of the twelfth of November, the able-bodied men of the town of Narutsin were drummed out of their beds at sunrise and escorted to the parade ground outside the temporary barracks at the mansion of Pokoj, to witness the punishment of their townsmen for the crimes of riot, public disorder and mutiny against the legitimate orders of a military representative of Her Imperial Highness, Maria Theresa.

The charge sheet had been drawn up by Lieutenant Klaes, on August's dictation, but it was read out that morning, loudly and with relish despite some stumbling over the longer words, by Lieutenant Tusimov. Klaes himself was in disgrace, placed at the very end of the row of officers and given no active part in the proceedings. He much preferred it that way. He had made clear his objection to this day's work, and could not now withdraw it even if he'd wished to. And damaging as the show of insubordination might well be to his career, he could not persuade himself that he was in the wrong. Because of his neat hand, or perhaps simply to humble him further, he had been tasked with recording the offence and its sentencing in every sorry particular, and the job had given him ample time for self-reproach—but his chief regret was that he had ever reported the affair in the first place. He doubted whether Colonel August had the authority he claimed to punish the townspeople. He was far from sure that mutiny was even an offence among civilians. And now, watching the little parade of convicted men led out to receive their punishment, he wished himself a thousand miles from Pokoj.

A soldier facing the lash would be allowed to keep his shirt on until the last minute, when he was accorded the respect of being allowed to remove it himself. The Narutsiners, knowing nothing of military protocol, had been forcibly stripped before leaving their makeshift prison. They shivered in the chilly morning air. From where he stood, just to the left of the whipping frames and at a right angle to the crowd, Klaes could see that Jakusch Weichorek was struggling to hold back tears. The prisoners' fellow townsmen stood in ragged rows in the centre of the parade field, flanked on each side by soldiers.

As the condemned men were led towards them they let out a collective groan, which splintered into mutterings. A woman's voice called out, "Shame! Shame on you!" and the sergeant nearest her hammered his pike on the ground with a cry for silence. Klaes was momentarily stunned: there were women present! But of course there were, he reminded himself. Over at the edge of the field, where Lorenz the surgeon sat with his stretchers and his buckets of water, a small group of the camp followers had come to watch. Harpies, he thought bitterly. But their faces were as pale and distracted as those of the villagers, and Sarai had brought her bag of remedies.

The whipping frames looked even uglier in the low, pale sunlight, the crude triangles now staked in place by extra beams which propped them up like parodies of an artist's easels. Only two had been properly joined; the third, erected in haste last night as the light began to fade, had its three beams crossed at the top like a giant bonfire, and lashed together with stout ropes. Word had it that the carpenter and his assistant had abandoned the work, leaving unskilled men to finish the job. August had only noticed the dereliction at sunrise: he had scowled, Private Leintz reported, till his eyebrows met in the middle, but seeing that it was too late to remedy, had said nothing. Perhaps by now the colonel had declared that this too was a punishable offence— Klaes would not have been surprised.

The prisoners were halted in front of the frames. Seeing them above him Jakusch let out an involuntary cry, which was answered by a hiss of shock and outrage from the crowd. Klaes steeled himself. Anything he said, any plea he might make for the boy, would do no good. But to his amazement the stolid Lieutenant Pabst was moved to protest.

"Colonel, that one's only a lad! He can't be more than fifteen. Do you not think, sir, that in this instance—"

"He is seventeen, and a man," August said. His eyes never left the group of prisoners. "Return to your place, Lieutenant."

The old man saluted and did as he was told.

The boy would be sixteen in December, Klaes recalled. He had broken bread with the family not a month ago, and had thought the son was forward for his age. In the front rank of the Narutsiners Meister Weichorek stood, utterly motionless. For the first time Klaes saw that Dame Weichorek was beside him. She was dry-eyed and held herself as still as her husband.

Lieutenant Tusimov was to oversee the floggings. He barked an order, and three drummers stepped forward: Edek, Renke and Heinrich, beefy men who had done this work before. Others were waiting to take over from them when they tired. Cunel, the corporal in charge of the equipment stores, carried out the whips, each in its separate bag. Tusimov waited until each was in place; then, swelled with his own importance, he placed himself before the prisoners and barked out a name.

"Jan Puszin, bootmaker. That you did, two days since, maliciously insult and feloniously strike an officer of the empire, and did inflict on said officer bleeding and contusions." Edek and Renke took hold of the unfortunate man, one by each arm. Renke could hardly restrain his smile, and Klaes suddenly noticed the bruises on the private's face. "Fifty lashes," Tusimov intoned.

Klaes bit back an exclamation. A general gasp rose around him, and some of his own men began to murmur in protest. Fifty lashes was an extreme penalty even for a serving soldier, but the town magistrates' courts imposed an absolute limit of thirty, kept down by custom to twenty-nine, so fearful were they of exceeding that number by mistake. Puszin cried out and began to struggle, but the two privates held him fast. They hustled him to the nearest of the frames and tied his hands above his head; splayed his legs to fasten an ankle to each upright.

Tusimov was already calling out the next name as they worked. Choltitz and Heinrich grasped the arms of Sivet Ulsner, who seemed paralysed with terror, and carried him to the next triangle, his feet not quite touching the ground. The last to be taken was Jakusch Weichorek, who was condemned to only thirty lashes, "on account of his youth," Tusimov said piously. The boy began to shake as Renke and Edek came for him. Dame Weichorek gave a single harsh sob but then fell silent, grasping her husband's arm. Tusimov gave the order to begin, and the three drummers took up their whips. The lieutenant, feeling every eye upon him, waited a moment longer as if, Klaes felt, he expected a drum roll to accompany him. Finally, with an almost audible breath, he began the count, and the men struck in unison.

Klaes had attended several floggings, and had hardened himself to them. It did not do for an officer to turn faint when an offender was disciplined, no matter how distasteful he found the spectacle. But this was beyond anything he had experienced before. Soldiers were schooled to watch their comrades' punishments in silence, but the townspeople had had no such training. As the first blows fell, the cries of the afflicted men were mingled with shouts from their neighbours.

"Courage, man!"

"Give them no cries!"

"How do you say that, blockhead? It's not you they're beating!"

This last was from a woman, and the cries and wails of the women grew louder as the floggings continued. For all their shouts for silence and banging of their pikes, the sergeants could not shush them now.

"Shame, shame!"

"He's just a boy! You're killing him!"

"SEVEN!" Tusimov roared, and Edek, perhaps startled, lashed Jakusch so violently that the frame rattled. The boy screamed, and blood began to seep from several of the welts on his back all together. The surgeon stepped forward, raising a hand, and all the whippings stopped while he inspected the damage.

The intervention did what the sergeants' orders could not: a silence fell, broken by the boy's sobs and the intermittent groans of the other two sufferers. One of the men still awaiting punishment had fallen to the ground: a medical orderly was reviving him with a bucket of water, while the other two had been allowed to sit. They had both been fitted with leg irons, Klaes saw, though neither seemed in any state to flee. One, a stocky grey-haired man, was muttering obscenities with all the fervour of prayer. The other seemed to be praying in good earnest, his head lowered and his lips moving in silence.

Lorenz gave a cursory glance at the backs of the two older men and stepped back, motioning to Tusimov to continue. A deep groan arose from the crowd. Tusimov nodded in turn to the lashers, took up his stance and swelled his chest again.

"Eight!"

Klaes thought that Edek tried to hold back for the next strokes, as if ashamed that he had done his victim so much damage all at once. It made no difference. The boy shrieked and writhed at every impact, and the watchers cried out with him. Dame Weichorek, white to the lips, had let go of her husband's arm and stood without touching him, twisting her hands together. She had not joined in the wails and imprecations of the other women but fixed her gaze immovably on her son's bleeding back, as if willing him strength or insensibility.

At the nineteenth stroke Jakusch fell silent. Lorenz inspected him and shook his head.

"He's fainted, sir. You must lay off."

"Get some water," Tusimov said impatiently. "That'll revive him."

Dame Weichorek made a small sound in her throat and moved forward, but Sergeant Kluzak stepped smartly in front of her, and her husband held her back. The surgeon gestured to an orderly, who ran forward with a bucket. The boy twitched once as the cold water hit him, then hung from his bonds as limp as before. His breeches were soaked red; the cuts on his back, revealed by the washing, began to ooze afresh.

"Sorry, sir," the surgeon said. He addressed August. "I can't answer for his safety."

"Cut him down," the colonel ordered. His face was impassive: Klaes could not tell if the man felt relief or reluctance. Tusimov, on the other hand, was nearly dancing with frustration.

There was a pause in the proceedings while Jakusch was released from his bonds. Klaes saw with approval that Edek did not let the boy drop, but held him over his shoulder while two of the camp followers ran up to free his feet. The surgeon and the two women laid the boy face down on a stretcher and carried him to the far side of the parade ground, out of sight of the watching crowd. One of the women was Drozde, her face set in a furious scowl.

Dame Weichorek craned after her son until he was out of sight, but

August's orders had been clear: the citizens of Narutsin were to watch the punishments through to the end, and the sergeants would not allow her to go to him.

Tusimov ordered the lashers to be replaced and the whips to be cleaned before continuing: the sight of the clotted blood and tissue being washed from the long strips of leather caused one Narutsiner to vomit noisily, forcing a further delay. And when the floggings resumed, Ulsner fainted after another six lashes. Tusimov left him hanging on the frame, still dripping blood and water, while Choltitz continued to flog the unfortunate Puszin, to the accompaniment of growing unrest from the crowd. The surgeon released Puszin after thirty-six strokes, to Tusimov's obvious dissatisfaction.

But the mood of the townspeople was changing. Jakusch's suffering had drawn sobs and cries from the women, but there were no sobs now, and no one called out as the two men were cut down. Instead they murmured to each other. A few had bent down: Klaes guessed they were scanning the ground for stones or anything else that might be thrown. He cast a quick glance at his fellow lieutenants, but Pabst merely looked sick and weary, and Dietmar was eyeing the men still marked for punishment, as if estimating how long they might last. August, though, had noticed. He gestured to the sergeants guarding the prisoners and summoned one over to him: Molebacher. August spoke a few quiet words to the quartermaster, who nodded self-importantly and went off at a trot. Klaes watched as he made the rounds of the pike-bearing sergeants and directed them into a line between the townspeople and the whipping triangles, weapons menacingly at the ready as the remaining three men were charged and taken to the frames.

The pikemen served their purpose: if any of the townsmen had gathered stones, they remained unthrown. The last of the victims to be taken—the burly grey-haired man, indicted as Matheus Vavra, innkeeper—struggled and yelled as he was dragged away, and almost succeeded in knocking down his captors. Klaes held his breath. But the man was subdued and tied up, fighting to the last, and his neighbours still looked on, their anger not quite reckless enough to overcome their caution.

Klaes tried not to focus as the whippings began again. He was sick to his soul of all of it: the overreaction, the needless cruelty and the gross mismanagement of people who could have been their allies. They had tied the innkeeper to the botched frame, the one held together with ropes, and his struggles as Heinrich laid into him made the structure itself creak and groan. The mutterings of the watching crowd were turning to angry cries once more. Klaes glanced at August, expecting a general order to restore discipline—and saw the colonel in conversation with Sergeant Molebacher again. Deep in conversation. August had turned away from the floggings and was staring intently into the crowd at something indicated by the quartermaster. Klaes looked where Molebacher was pointing and saw two of the men who had put up the whipping frames: the master carpenter and his assistant. The colonel watched them for a moment and nodded to Molebacher, his expression grim.

More needless finger-pointing, Klaes thought in disgust. August had intended this day as a demonstration of the awful might of the empire, and the penalty for crossing it. If the people of Narutsin were less cowed than he had expected, that was hardly the fault of the carpenters.

As if to prove him wrong, the botched whipping frame began to sway, and one of its arms slid downwards, pulling the other two with it. The innkeeper screamed and kept on screaming. The surgeon came up at a run.

"Get him down! You want his back to break?"

Lorenz's yell was almost lost amid the howling of the Narutsiners. Vavra continued to roar with pain as he was taken down. Lorenz examined him briskly and announced that his shoulder was dislocated.

The floggings were suspended. As the innkeeper was carried off on a stretcher, his tormentor and both the others dropped their whips and ran to hold up the frame, which was threatening to collapse altogether. Tusimov stood in the midst of the shambles as if thunderstruck.

Colonel August did not wait for his lieutenant to recover himself. He snapped an order to Dietmar: in the mounting chaos, Klaes could not hear what he said, but Dietmar promptly left the field, taking Pabst with him. Then, to the shouts and catcalls of the townspeople and the appalled silence of his own men, the colonel strode out to face the crowd.

Klaes found himself admiring the man's courage even as he wondered at his foolhardiness. But a moment later, like a clap of thunder, a cannon sounded, so close at hand that the smoke and the acrid smell of it came over the field at the same time. There was a shocked silence, and into that silence August spoke.

"Cut both those men down, Lieutenant. Their punishment is suspended." Tusimov opened his mouth to protest. August silenced him with a gesture. "That frame is unsafe. Lieutenant Klaes, have it secured. Men of Narutsin, these neighbours of yours have received their sentence and will be released. But I must require your presence here for a while longer."

A many-voiced sigh rose from the people before him. It was over. Klaes saw the fists unclench, the shoulders slump throughout the crowd, and felt a wave of relief of his own as he ran to follow his orders. He sent his six strongest men to help hold up the posts, and dispatched Janek, who was fast, to fetch more rope. After a moment's thought he also pulled out young Leintz, who had never attended a flogging before and was pale and shaking, and sent him off at a more leisurely pace for tent pegs and a couple of mallets.

The colonel seemed to be delivering a lecture: on a citizen's duty to his homeland, the importance of discipline and the responsibility of every man to stand up and be counted. Klaes suspected that no one was listening, but it did not matter. He applied himself to the problem of the unstable frame, which it soon became clear was damaged beyond repair, no longer even securely attached to its base. With huge relief, he instructed his men to pull the monstrosity down. Neither of the other lieutenants had yet returned to his place, and the colonel was still haranguing the townspeople. Klaes took the opportunity to check on the state of the flogged men. Their treatment, and in particular that of Jakusch, had disturbed him more than he cared to admit.

The boy would likely recover, Sarai assured him, though of course he would be scarred. Of the others, Puszin, who had received the most strokes, was in a bad way, but the rest, she thought, were in no present danger. The old man's shoulder had been reset, and he was already sitting up and cursing. There was nothing else Klaes could do here. He looked around him at the camp followers nursing other women's sons and husbands, and felt somehow ashamed.

He was on his way back to his post when the chaos returned.

The broken frame was down, he saw with satisfaction, and the men had begun to dismantle it. But next to them now were two artillerymen, wheeling a six-pounder on its carriage. Another cannon was already in place on the far side of the frames, facing the

Narutsiners. And behind the townspeople a file of Pabst's men was moving into position, bearing what must surely be every remaining pike in the store. Klaes stopped, aghast, as Dietmar strode past him to August's side and spoke a few words in the colonel's ear.

"Now we are ready," August said. A ripple of unease ran through his audience: those at the front had already seen the arrival of the cannons. And suddenly the colonel's manner had changed. He eyed the men and women before him with the cold fury he usually reserved for soldiers convicted of cowardice.

"Your neighbours have been released, their punishments reduced out of consideration for their injuries," he said. "As long as no ringleader was identified, all were condemned to suffer the same. But the investigations of my men have uncovered the instigator of this attack—and moreover it has been found that this was not the last outrage he intended to perpetrate. This man thought, no doubt, to show himself a tearing young blade by flouting the edict of his archduchess and heaping scorn upon his motherland. He will learn today of the consequences which follow such actions." August's voice rose to a roar. "Bring out Anton Hanslo, the carpenter."

There was a moment of stunned silence. Then many voices spoke at once. Among them all, the carpenter's assistant stood stricken and unbelieving. He made no move at all until two of the soldiers laid hands on him; then he cried out and struggled as he was dragged before the monstrous frames.

"What have I done?" he cried. "What am I meant to have done?"

August himself read out the charge, raising his voice over the man's protests.

"That you did, on the eighth of November, maliciously and with seditious intent incite riot and rebellion among your fellow citizens, to the destruction of good order and the great injury of loyal upholders of the empire—"

"I never did such a thing! Who's accusing me?"

"You were overheard in the very act, by a man in whom I place absolute trust," August said with finality. "Your sentence is one hundred lashes."

At this there was uproar among the watchers. A shrill voice rose above the chaos: Drozde.

"It's not true! I know this man. He's done work for you. He never spoke harm to anyone!"

No one heeded her. The colonel did not even look in the woman's direction. Molebacher, who was holding one of Hanslo's arms, shot her a brief glance; Klaes could have sworn the quartermaster was smiling. He bent down and said something low in the prisoner's ear, which seemed to strike the man even through his terror and confusion: he twisted to look at Molebacher, his face still whiter than before.

Up until this point the carpenter had been mostly obscured from Klaes's view by the men who held him. The motion allowed Klaes a clear glimpse of his face for the first time, and he started violently as he realised that he had seen him before. He broke from the line of officers and strode forward to where Colonel August stood.

"Sir." Klaes had to yell to make himself heard over the shouts of the crowd. "I saw the fight, and this man was not involved. He even intervened to separate the two sides."

August fixed him with an icy stare. "To your place, Klaes," he said. The malice in his tone brooked no argument. The crowd's yelling had intensified. Suddenly a man burst out of it, ducking beneath the arm of the corporal who moved to bar his way, and took hold of Molebacher. It was the old carpenter, who had been standing beside Hanslo.

"Leave him be, for God's sake!" he shouted. "Don't you hear? He's a good lad. He's no conspirator. Not a man here'll say otherwise."

The corporal he had eluded reached him and hauled him back so violently that he stumbled. The soldier pushed the old man to the ground and had drawn back his foot for a kick when Klaes intervened.

"That will do," he snapped. And when the corporal did not retreat at once, Klaes roared at the man with a fury he had not known was in him.

"I said leave him! Now!"

He helped the carpenter to his feet and led him back to the edge of the crowd of watchers. Behind them, Hanslo shouted and struggled as he was tied to the frame. Klaes felt the old man beside him shaking as Molebacher took up the whip.

There were regulations to govern flogging, as with all aspects of army life: it was meant to hurt but not to maim. Molebacher ignored the rule. Hanslo's screams sounded above the noise of the crowd. The quartermaster struck savagely and relentlessly, as tireless as a man threshing grain. By twenty strokes the young man's back was masked with blood; by twenty-five his cries had grown faint. When they stopped altogether Tusimov called for the surgeon with his bucket of water.

Hanslo twitched and groaned as the water hit him, and Molebacher stepped forward once more, shaking his head when Heinrich offered to relieve him. But after half a dozen strokes Lorenz intervened again.

"He's losing too much blood," the surgeon said. "Any more and I won't answer for him."

Before Tusimov could reply, Molebacher addressed the lieutenant himself.

"Begging your pardon, sir, but this man's done treachery, and he's not had half his sentence yet. We need to make an example of him!"

Tusimov hesitated. And Molebacher, taking that for consent, rushed at his victim and rained blows on him, no longer waiting for the lieutenant's count.

"Stop him!" the surgeon shouted, his voice thin against the tumult. Klaes, barely aware of what he was doing, had already run forward again, followed by the carpenter and a dozen other men from the crowd. He and Tusimov together pulled the quartermaster away and Tusimov held him, while Molebacher glared at Klaes like a demon.

Hanslo was no longer moving. Edek and Heinrich cut him down, then stood by uncertainly as the orderlies and camp followers laid him face down on a stretcher. Drozde was one of the helpers again. Her companion, a big red-armed woman, gave the soldiers an evil stare, but the gypsy never looked up from the stretcher, where the blood welling from the man's back showed there was still some life in him.

August stepped forward into the sudden silence. The other lieutenants, even Tusimov, had returned to their places behind the colonel, and Klaes knew he should join them. But the old carpenter, who had shuddered in sympathy with each blow inflicted on his assistant, sagged forward as the young man was carried away, and Klaes was now obliged to hold him by the arm to prevent him falling.

The colonel looked a little rattled, Klaes thought: his demonstration had not gone as planned. But his voice was as strong as ever as he addressed the crowd.

"All the prisoners will be released to their friends once they can walk. Be warned that the same punishment awaits anyone who is found to have shielded these men from justice, and anyone who foments discord in the future, of any kind whatsoever."

He raised an arm, and the artillerymen accompanying the two cannons each saluted and raised his gun's muzzle to point directly into the crowd. The men with pikes already surrounded them on all sides. August was as good as the puppet woman at setting up a piece of theatre, Klaes thought, though he had nothing but contempt for his audience. He swept them with a final, baleful stare and gave his last order in a tone of weary disgust.

"Now go back to your homes. And if you care for your own peace and safety, stay there."

He turned on his heel and left, followed by the three older lieutenants. The pikemen and the cannons stayed where they were, in a menacing ring around the townspeople. Klaes stayed too: the colonel had not looked at him nor summoned him, and he was glad of the excuse to avoid his fellow officers' company for a little longer.

Drozde was running for bandages when she found her way blocked by Molebacher. Dark spatters still marked his clothes. She took an instinctive step backwards: just now the thought of touching him was unbearable.

"Didn't see you back there," he said. There was something strange in his expression. His eyes were glazed, whether from exhaustion or fury Drozde could not tell, and his jaw worked as though he were trying to swallow something too large for him. But his tone was one of heavy joviality. "Entertainment's over; I need you in the kitchen."

It took a moment before she could trust herself to speak clearly. "Go fuck yourself."

Molebacher was so dumbfounded it might have been comical at another time. He opened his mouth to protest, but Drozde interrupted him. All her rage and horror went into the shout.

"And get used to it! Because you won't be fucking me any more!"

Some of the women were heading their way, carrying cloths and basins. Drozde ran towards them, leaving Molebacher standing behind her, and she did not look back.

They had cleaned Hanslo's back as best they could, but his beautiful skin was welted and clotted with blood. Sarai had shown Drozde what salve to use, and she spread it on his wounds with more gentleness than she had ever shown in lovemaking. Sometimes he would wince and moan at the contact; she welcomed it as a sign of life, but each time she raised her hand and would not touch him again till he had quieted. Some of the wounds still bled; the surgeon had warned them to leave those alone, only putting on fresh dressings as the old ones were soaked through. The pile of bloodied bandages lay beside her now, uncollected. Libush had seen the way Drozde looked at the hurt man. She had withdrawn without asking any questions, and kept the others away too.

There was no caress Drozde could give that would not hurt him further, but when she had tended him all she could, she took hold of his hand and crouched on the ground beside him so she could see his face. After an age he gave a deep groan and his eyelids flickered. She had hoped he would be glad to see her, but all she could read in his expression was fear and pain.

"No one will hurt you any more," she told him. But he was not calmed. He spoke to her without breath to form the words. She laid her head down by his to catch the whisper.

"Drozde . . . that man . . ."

His eyes flickered beyond her, back to the parade ground. "The man who beat you," she said.

His eyes stilled, looked into hers again. "Yes, I know him."

His lips moved again, but no sound came out. There was nothing she could do to hold on to him.

"He thought I was his, the sack of shit," she said. "Trust me, he won't lay a finger on me, not ever again. I'm done with him." Her voice was too loud, and not quite steady, but she had to tell him before he fainted again. "Only get well, Anton. Get better, and I'll come to you whenever you like."

He heard her. No one in such pain could smile, but his face relaxed and he moved his head in a sort of nod. Then his eyes closed again, as though the lids were too heavy to support.

She pressed his hand, and thought she could feel an answering pressure. But his eyes never opened, and she would not wake him to feel more pain. After a while the surgeon came by: he looked again at Anton's wounds, held a feather to his lips and shook his head.

She stayed with him for some time longer. His hand was still warm in hers, and from this angle he was unscarred, as beautiful as ever. When his chest and face grew cold she went to fetch the others, to tell them there was a body to lay out.

28

Having done their damage, the whipping frames could be dismantled. Klaes, with the carpenter still leaning heavily on his arm, could not oversee the work himself, but he had to be doing something. He called over Sergeant Frydek and tasked him with taking down the remaining two structures. The sergeant received the order with what looked like relief, and in a very few minutes had assembled two teams of men, some of them noticeably pale and gulping, to begin removing the traces of their commander's display of justice.

The townspeople paid them no attention. Many seemed stunned; some of the women had begun keening. A number of the men were still watching the departing backs of August and his lieutenants with angry looks that quickly became angry words and gestures. Jursitizky, in charge of the larger cannon, had his men raise the muzzle to point directly at the troublemakers, but the threat was not enough to still their resentment: a furious buzz of protest broke out, and a stone flew past Klaes's head and landed near one of the cannons.

Dame Weichorek wheeled in an instant and

seized the thrower by an ear. "As God is my witness, Pieter Hessel, you make another move and my husband will have you in the stocks! All of you! Put your stones down and go home!"

She glared at the young man until he let the second stone fall and turned away. In twos and threes, the Narutsiners began to leave. Klaes watched with sudden admiration: grieving and distraught as she was, the woman had authority. On an impulse, he went over to her and her husband. Beside him, the carpenter had regained his feet, though the old man was still shaking.

"Meister Weichorek; madam," he said. "Your son is recovering. I'll conduct you to him, if you wish."

She started as he addressed her, then gave him a look of freezing scorn.

"You are kind to offer, Lieutenant. But I can find my own way."

Weichorek, in silence, took the arm of the carpenter, and the three of them left him without a backward glance.

Drozde walked through the camp in a zigzag line, veering away from every solid object that came into her path. She had no idea where she was going, or why. Voices were ringing in her head. Each seemed hard-edged and angular, glancing off the other voices around it until her brain was full of sounds that lay over and across one another, jammed solid to block all thought.

And yet the thoughts found their way through, soundless, in blood-red dribbles.

"Drozde. Are you well?" A hand came down on her shoulder, and in pulling away from it she got half-turned around. It was Taglitz. He took a step back, hurriedly, hands raised to show he meant no harm. "It was a brutal sight for a woman to see," he said. "I was just worried for you, that was all."

"Worried?" Drozde repeated.

"That you might be sick, or something. From the blood. Or that your emotions might get the better of you. If you want to sit down, my tent . . . it's right here. Only a step away. And I've beer, to refresh you."

"You saw me in disputation with Sergeant Molebacher," Drozde translated, "and you thought it might be time to go to market."

Taglitz didn't blush at being so quickly found out, but he looked sheepish. "If you want to go with another man, Drozde, you'll have your pick. Of course you will. I know a pottle of beer won't buy you.

But sit with me anyway, until you feel a little better. I'll lift your spirits one way or another, or chuck my flute in the stream."

"Fuck off, Tag," Drozde growled. "And take your flute with you. Touch me and I'll gnaw your hand off."

She walked away from him, but Taglitz was not put off. He gave a strained laugh and continued to walk along beside her. "I'm only a private," he said. "Is that it? Or that I'm fond of my drink? For I can mend, if it's that. Only let me show you. I can be a sober man and a good one when I put my shoulder to it."

"Be as sober as a judge," Drozde invited him. "But your bench is somewhere else." She headed for the house. The enlisted men knew they could not enter there—and unlike her, they took that prohibition seriously. Now, of course, without Molebacher's patronage, she was as likely to be whipped out of doors as they were. Even with those images fresh in her mind, the men's backs like ploughed fields rucked and ruined, she didn't care. She'd do damage to anyone who tried it.

Taglitz fell back at last, his steps slowing. "Only tell me what I have to do," he shouted at her back. "I care for you, woman. Tell me how to have you."

She stopped and turned. "You want me?" she demanded.

Tag threw out his arms as though to summon her into his embrace. "Yes!"

"Then kill Sergeant Molebacher."

The soldier's eyes went wide with shock at this heresy. "Kill—? I can't do that!" he yelped.

"Why not?"

Tag looked comically puzzled. So many reasons. Which would he choose?

"He's too big for me."

"Then get some friends to join you in the enterprise. I'll fuck you all."

She left him standing there, still calling after her. He wouldn't do it, she knew. He might carry a musket, but he would never kill a brother soldier. He probably couldn't kill at all without the smell of blood and cordite on the wind and the holy terror of a Prussian battle line, or a French or a Dutch or a Russian or a Turkish one, rushing down on him. He had cheered on the floggings, but that was something a man did because the men around him were doing it—which in the end was why men like Taglitz did anything. He could strike out in a quarrel when his blood was up, but he would never kill for his own advantage. And if he ever did go after Molebacher, he'd break on him like water on a rock. There was not enough harm in Taglitz to help her.

She went down to her cellar room, and closed the door. She thought it would be some comfort to be among her puppets, and it was, but it was a foolish place to have come, after all. It would be the first place Molebacher would search for her, if he searched at all.

She looked for a bolt, and there was a stout one, but it was on the outside of the door. The builders of the house had never envisaged somebody wanting to lock the cellar from the inside.

She gripped the edge of the cupboard and pulled it away from the wall, leaning back to apply her full weight to the task. It was of solid wood and moved slowly, with a great deal of scraping and creaking and catching on the edges of the tiles, but gradually she was able to drag it across the room, an inch or two on this side and then an inch or two on that, until it blocked the door.

She finished her work none too soon. She heard the rattle of the door handle, and a dull report as the door hit the back of the wardrobe.

"Drozde?" It was Molebacher's voice, breathless and angry. She didn't bother to answer him. It was obvious that she was there, and beyond that she had nothing to say.

"Come out of that, you stupid bitch. I want to talk to you." The cupboard creaked as he set his weight to it. Drozde leaned hard against its back and dug her heels in. It slid a few inches, then held. Molebacher was much stronger than her, but he wasn't able to push directly against the cupboard. All he could do was throw his weight against the door, which touched the cupboard at a shallow angle. She could hold him for a while.

"Are you mad?" Molebacher snarled. He kept his voice low, presumably because he was wary of being overheard and bringing onlookers to this dispute. She understood him, and it filled her with a sort of bleak disgust that she had known him so well and judged him so poorly. He always settled his scores.

He stopped to get his breath back. Quickly Drozde looked around her. Some old timber in the corner of the room caught her gaze. She snatched up a baulk of wood, threw it aside as being too short, grabbed another. She wedged it against the door of the cupboard and jammed the other end between two flagstones.

Once that bulwark was in place, she picked out another, stouter and longer. She could hear Molebacher grunting with effort as he pushed at the door again. The wedge she'd set in place began to bend, but before it could break Drozde slid the long plank between the cupboard and the further wall of the room. It was a tight fit, leaving only an inch or two of play at either end.

She kicked away the wedge and the cupboard slid again at once, but not very far. It hit the plank, drove it into the opposite wall, and then stopped dead. As soon as Drozde could feel that it was held firm, she let go of it. Nothing would move the cupboard now.

Molebacher was cursing at her from its other side. There were scratching sounds as he slid his hand around the partly opened door to explore what was blocking it. Drozde took her first makeshift wedge, which was now surplus to requirements, walked around the flank of the cupboard and peered into the crack between its front face and the door. It was dark, but she could just about see Molebacher's fingers wriggling about in there.

She swung the plank into the narrow gap and felt a solid impact. Molebacher wailed in anguish and the fingers withdrew.

But he hadn't gone away. "You dirty little whore!" he whispered into the gap. "I'll fucking starve you out. You're mine. Do you hear me? You fuck me, and no one else."

Drozde put her own mouth to the gap. "I was never yours, Eustach," she said. She used his given name with deliberate malice, knowing that he hated it. And she spoke much louder than him: if he wanted to keep their falling out quiet, that was reason enough for indiscretion.

"What? What did you say?"

"I was never yours. You were just a man I befriended for a while, because good food's not cheap and I was hungry. I'm fine now. You can go your ways."

Molebacher made no answer, but the cupboard creaked and groaned like a ship in a gale as he threw his weight against it. The plank held.

"Don't hurt yourself," Drozde warned him. "You're not a young man, Eustach. You must learn to take things easy."

She waited for another assault on the cupboard, but it didn't come. For a while there was nothing to be heard apart from Molebacher's ragged breathing. Then that ceased, too. Either he'd withdrawn himself or he wanted her to think that he had. She knew better than to put her head out and see. In his present mood, Molebacher would tear it from her shoulders.

She sat down on her trunk, alone at last with her feelings. Apart from misery, she found she did not know what they were. She had hardly known Anton. His death was terrible, but he had never belonged to her in the way that Sergeant Molebacher thought Drozde belonged to him. What did his death mean? Nothing. Barely anything. Except that the quartermaster set more store than she did on the exclusivity of their relationship, even though he knew she'd been a whore before and would be a whore again after.

But misery without meaning was enough, right then, to fill her. She put her face in her hands and began to sob.

That was how Magda found her. The little girl put her arm, lighter than gossamer, around her friend's shoulder and embraced her, issuing urgent pleas into the spaces left by Drozde's in-breaths.

"Don't. Please don't. Don't be unhappy. We love you. Everybody here loves you. It's all right. Nothing can hurt you. Everything is fine. I'm here. I'll stay with you. You can have Amelie. She's the best. The best kitten. You can stroke her whenever you want."

Eventually this constant stream of reassurance made Drozde laugh in spite of herself. The offerings were so slight, set against the torrent of her unhappiness, that they were ridiculous.

"I'm fine," she told the girl, rubbing her eyes with the heels of her hands. "I'm all right, Magda. You can stop now."

Magda drew back to appraise her with earnest eyes. "You're still unhappy," she said. "Tell me what the matter is."

"It's . . ." How to tell a child about death? But then, this was a dead child. Presumably she knew more about the subject than Drozde did. "A friend of mine was hurt. Very badly. He died of his hurts, and I couldn't help him."

"Anton," Magda said.

"What?" Drozde raised her bleary eyes and stared at the ghost-child. "What did you say? What do you know about Hanslo?"

"Everything," Magda said simply. "You always say anything less than that isn't enough."

"That again!" Drozde shivered, and shook her head. "Go away, Magda. Please. I don't have time for this foolishness right now."

The girl threw her head back and laughed. "That's what you always say when you don't really understand something and you don't want to ask about it!"

Drozde stood. "That's enough," she said. "If you want to make yourself useful, go outside and see if Molebacher is still waiting for me out there."

She pointed to the cupboard. "All right," Magda said at once, and walked through it.

She was not gone for long. "Yes, he's still there," she said. "He's sitting on a folding chair at the top of the stairs. Off to the side a bit, so you wouldn't see him until you got to the very top and stepped out. He's all by himself. And there's a pan on top of the stove that's all boiled over and gone dry. I think it had soup in it. Red soup, like with beetroots or something."

"Borscht."

"Yes. That. He should take it off the fire, because the pan will be ruined."

And the officers will be waiting for their dinner and wondering what the world is coming to, Drozde thought. Molebacher would need to watch himself. He tended his camaraderie with Colonel August the way a gardener tends a fruit tree, and for the same reason—to increase the yield. But if Drozde knew one thing well it was the minds of men, and she could count on her fingers the number of missed meals a friendship like that would survive.

Still, that was not for her to worry about. Molebacher's fortunes were not hers any more.

"Thanks," she said to Magda. "We'll let him wait a while, shall we? Perhaps he'll fall asleep."

It would take more than that, though. The noise she'd make when she moved the cupboard away from the door would surely wake him, even if he were in his cups. And she had brought nothing with her to eat or to drink, so she was poorly placed to stand a siege.

These troubling thoughts must have shown on her face. The ghost girl stroked her cheek, wide eyes beseeching her to be of stouter heart. "Shall I tell you a story?" she asked.

Drozde shook her head emphatically. "No more stories. This isn't the time."

"It might be, if you knew what story I meant."

Drozde pretended not to hear. She stood and walked around a

little, to ward off the chill. She'd never lingered in the little room for more than a few minutes before, so she hadn't noticed how cold it was down here. A freezing draught was blowing in from somewhere—from under the door, perhaps. She folded up the canvas that made up the wings and backstage of her puppet theatre when she performed, and wrapped it around her shoulders.

It became clear to her that she wasn't going anywhere. Not for a long while. Not until Molebacher had given up on his vigil or been called away to other duties. The man was tenacious and wily. If anyone would watch a mousehole better than a cat, it was he.

She turned to glance at Magda, sitting cross-legged on the floor and watching her in silence.

"Go on then," she said. "Tell me a story."

Magda brightened at once. "I will," she said, clapping her hands. "I'll tell you your favourite. How would that be?"

"Which is my favourite?"

"'The Man Who Stole the Moon.'"

"All right. Tell me that."

Magda patted the tiles beside her. "Then come and sit by me!"

"It's too cold down there," Drozde said. "I'll sit on the trunk."

She set herself down, rearranging the canvas so it went under her as well as around her. It would do well enough. It kept off at least some of the chill, and protected her from being scratched by the nail-heads that stood proud of the trunk's lid.

"But you're too high for me up there," Magda complained. She wriggled her skinny body a little, and somehow swam in the air as a fish swims in water, raising herself to a position about level with Drozde's chest. Drozde was inured to the girl's strangeness by now, but this made her shiver a little in spite of herself.

Magda seated herself on the empty air as though it were a cushion and turned to Drozde.

"I tell it like Ermel told hers," she said. "Like it happened to someone else, because that's how it feels to me now. I was Madigan then, and now I'm Magda. And when I was alive, Mr. Stupendo was my favourite of all, but I hadn't met you then, and it all changed so much after you came that nothing was the same any more. Are you sitting comfortably?"

"No."

"Drozde, say yes!"

"Yes."

"Then I'll begin."

Madigan loved Pokoj from the moment she arrived. For one thing, it was old. It had been an abbey in the Middle Ages, her guidebook said, and after that it had been a lot of other things too: an army barracks and a glass factory and a big house, and finally the Pokoj Heritage Site and Hotel, where Madigan was now staying. Madigan liked old things: they seemed more permanent to her than everything else, as if all the time they had been around already was useful preparation that would help them to last out all the time to come.

As soon as they had driven up the long gravel driveway and parked the car, Madigan climbed out and pressed her hands up against the building's weathered stone walls. They felt cold against her skin. Madigan thought that they were full of secrets, and imagined underground passages and hidden rooms, like in the pyramids in Egypt, which were older even than Pokoj. She thought about how the hotel had been there before cars and planes and toaster ovens, and how it would still be there when everyone was gone, and the thought made her feel peaceful, like its name.

In the huge reception hall, Madigan clattered slowly up and down the stairs, pretending that she was a great lady and everything in Pokoj belonged to her. But then she got tired, so she sat down on the bottom step to listen to her mom talking to the receptionist while she collected their keys. "We're not staying long," she was saying. "Madigan has an appointment at the clinic in Stollenbet, so we're only here while we sort a few last details out." She smiled and leaned across the counter, like she was telling a secret. "It's the best in the world for her condition." And the receptionist frowned and nodded, and before they got into the lift she gave Madigan a lollipop.

When they got to the room, Madigan's parents started doing lots of things straight away. Her dad heaved the cases onto the bed, throwing clothes everywhere as he looked for his paperwork, and her mom snatched up the phone.

"I'm going to call the consulate again, Nick," she said, jabbing at the buttons on the keypad.

"Okay." Madigan's dad glanced at his watch. "It's not quite five yet;

you should get through. Shall I email the clinic?"

"Wouldn't you like to play a game first?" Madigan cut in quickly. "I brought the frog one, and the one where you have to rhyme all the words." She had to describe the games instead of giving them their proper names because mom and dad never knew what they were called. Her dad smiled at her and gave her a hug, but he shook his head.

"Sorry, sweetheart, we can't play today."

Madigan wailed in dismay. "But you always say that! I have the frog one, dad, that's your favourite!"

She ran to get it out of her bag and show him, but it made no difference. "There'll be plenty of time for that soon," mom said, stroking her hair. "Right now, we have to focus on getting you well."

After that there was really nothing for Madigan to do. She was too tired to go and explore, and there was no one to play with in the room. So she counted the little swirls on the patterned carpet for a while, and then she imagined an adventure for herself where Pokoj got attacked by goblins and she had to save everyone, and then she fell asleep.

When she woke up it was dinner time, and all the phone calls and the emails were done for the evening. She and her parents went down to dinner together. The restaurant in the hotel was called The Old Ballroom, because that was what it had been, once, back when Pokoj was still a house rather than a Heritage Site and Hotel.

When he saw the sign on the door, Madigan's father grinned at her. "A ballroom? Well, in that case . . ." He swung her off the ground and waltzed her inside, and her mom put on a silly voice and said, "Announcing Lord Nicholas of Pittsburgh, and his daughter, the lovely Madigan!" Madigan laughed and laughed. She laughed so hard that she started to cough, and her chest felt like a tunnel of jagged rocks that caught and scraped at the air as she sucked it in. When her dad put her down, she stumbled and almost fell over. The waltzing had made her dizzy, and the room was covered with dark blotches all running together, which hadn't been there before.

"Dad," she mumbled, "I think that thing's happening again," and he was beside her at once, kneeling down with one arm around her and a bottle of water in his hand. "Oh Mads, Mads, I'm sorry," he murmured. "Are you out of breath, sweetie?"

Madigan nodded, so he picked her up again very carefully, and carried her to their table. She lay in his arms and tried to take deep, slow breaths until she could see the room properly. After a while the jaggedness in her chest calmed down enough for her to sit up and look around her. The restaurant was very posh: there were some people playing violins and cellos up on a stage at the back, and waiters in black suits wandering around carrying silver plates with lids on. Whatever was underneath smelled delicious, but Madigan wasn't sure that she could eat much right now. So she just had the bread and butter that was already on the table, in a basket with a white ribbon on the front. Her parents talked quietly as they ate, and Madigan knew that they were talking about her, and worrying that the thing with the black blotches might happen again.

But by the time the dessert menus arrived they had cheered up, and she felt much better again too. As their plates were cleared, Madigan's mom stretched her arms and looked around the table. "Now," she asked, "who wants ice cream?" She meant Madigan, of course. But Madigan frowned at her.

"I'm not allowed," she pointed out.

"Why are you not allowed?" Her mom said it like it was a game Madigan was playing, but it wasn't. She frowned harder.

"It's against the rules. I had a cake at the service station before, you know that!" The rule was that she was only allowed to eat one dessert a day. Her parents were very strict about it, most of the time. But now her mom was smiling, and pointing to something behind Madigan's head. She turned with a sort of twisting feeling in her stomach to see another black-suited waiter, carrying a large glass bowl. They had ordered her some without telling her. Her dad was laughing as if it was a wonderful surprise, but Madigan felt her face getting hot, like someone was filling her up with water from a kettle. She shoved the bowl away from her, hard, glaring at them both.

"I don't want it. It's against the rules."

Her mom was still smiling at her, but her smile had gone wrong somehow. When she smiled like that Madigan always knew that really she was sad, but trying to pretend that she wasn't.

"Mads, sweetheart," she said, "the rules don't matter. You can have as much ice cream as you want."

"But I don't want! I don't want any!" The buzz of conversation in the restaurant got suddenly quieter, and Madigan realised that she had been shouting. She felt like everyone was staring at her. She was breathing too quickly again, and her mom had an expression on her face like she had broken something that she didn't know how to fix. Madigan wanted to tell her she was sorry, only she couldn't now because the hot water inside her was trying to spill out from her eyes, and she had to screw up her face to stop it from escaping.

And then she felt something brush against her cheek, and she looked up to see a man standing by their table. He was wearing a long cloak, dark blue with silver stars on it, and a top hat to match. His eyes when he looked at Madigan were deep green and brown, like the reflection on a pond in the middle of summer.

"You don't want any?" the man repeated gravely. "Well this won't do at all then, will it?"

He pulled a large cloth from his pocket—it looked like the sky, Madigan thought, all black silk and silver sparkles—and shook it out like a toreador's cape so that it covered the ice cream on the table.

"Now then . . ." The man looked at her, one eyebrow arched in a question.

"Madigan," Madigan supplied.

"Madigan; a pleasure to meet you!" He took off his top hat with a flourish and bowed to her. "Allow me to rid you of this inconvenient ice cream."

In spite of her shame and the tears still seeping from her eyes, Madigan giggled.

The man flexed his shoulders and stretched his arms as if he was preparing for a race. His hands darted back and forth in front of Madigan's face, fingers wiggling over the covered ice cream as he said the magic words. Abruptly one of his hands held a fork from the table, which he handed to Madigan's father.

"A drum roll, if you please, sir."

The man paused, and looked into Madigan's eyes again. Then he pulled off the cloth. The ice cream was gone. Madigan stared at the empty space on the table, her eyes wide. Then she looked at her parents. Her dad was clapping, her mom laughing in delight. She had her proper smile again, the sadness vanished along with the ice cream. Madigan had never seen anything so incredible in her entire life.

That was how she first met Mr. Stupendo.

He stayed in the restaurant after that, sometimes at other tables and sometimes at Madigan's, but never so far away that she lost sight of him. Every now and then he would glance over at her and smile, or raise one eyebrow as he had before. She watched him all the way through her parents eating dessert, and when they were done she pretended that she wanted a hot chocolate, just so she could watch him for a little longer. She sipped it as slowly as she could: by the time she was finished, they were almost the only people left. Mr. Stupendo came back over then, and Madigan's mom shook his hand.

"Thank you so much for your wonderful trick earlier," she said. "It really cheered Mads up."

"You're the best magician in the world!" Madigan burst out. Mr. Stupendo grinned at her.

Madigan's parents chatted with Mr. Stupendo while the waiters tidied up for the night and put the chairs upside down on the tables. He told them about how he was staying at Pokoj for a few months while he worked in the restaurant and in the pub in Puppendorf, the nearby village. He was mostly doing magic, he said, but also some child-minding for the hotel. Madigan gazed at his cloak and his hat and his beautiful smile, and eventually she gathered up enough courage to ask him if he would do more tricks for her while she stayed at the hotel.

"I accept the commission," he told her solemnly. "And I will place myself entirely at your disposal."

"Thanks so much," Madigan's mother said. "We've got a lot on at the moment, and she gets so bored when she's on her own."

"So long as she doesn't get to be a nuisance," her father said.

Then Madigan's mother started explaining about the clinic, and about all the phone calls and the emails. "We're not staying here for long, only while we sort the details out." Madigan watched her fingers dance and drum on the table as she spoke, like she was saying magic words.

Next morning, Madigan went to see Mr. Stupendo as soon as she woke up. He lived at the very top of Pokoj, in the attic: the lady at the desk had told her where. The hotel had a lift which would take you to the first and second floors, but it didn't go all the way up there, so Madigan had to climb the last flight of stairs herself. It made her so tired and breathless that she was afraid the blotches might happen again, but by stopping after every few steps and sitting down to have a rest she managed at last to make it to the top.

When she knocked on the door and Mr. Stupendo opened it, he seemed surprised to see her. He didn't have his top hat on, but he ducked back behind the door and then reappeared wearing it, just so that he could doff it again as he bowed to her. Madigan laughed.

"Good morning, Mr. Stupendo," she said in her best polite voice. "I hope I'm not disturbing you."

"Not at all, Madigan," he replied, equally seriously. "If you'll give me just a moment or two, I'll be with you presently."

He didn't invite her in, but he didn't close the door. While he gathered his things, Madigan stood in the doorway and looked past him into his room. It was small: just a narrow bed, a wardrobe and a sink with a crack in it squashed together against peeling white walls. His suitcase took up most of the space on the floor. Madigan thought that a magician as good as Mr. Stupendo must be able to stay in a nicer room than this. But maybe he had booked into Pokoj at the last minute, and this was the only one left. As he went over to the wardrobe to get his cloak Madigan saw his face reflected in the mirror on the inside of the door. For a moment he looked as tired as she had felt when she climbed the steps, and so sad that she wanted to run to him and hug him. But she didn't, because she knew that she wasn't supposed to have seen the sadness, just like she wasn't supposed to notice when her mom's smile went wrong. Mr. Stupendo's expression smoothed out into a smile as he turned to face her, and he held out a hand towards the corridor.

"Let's go and explore," he said, shutting the door behind him.

They couldn't explore very fast because Madigan was still tired out from the steps, but Mr. Stupendo didn't seem to mind. Every time she needed to stop and rest, he pointed out something interesting that they had just passed. He knew so much about everything! When she paused for breath halfway down the corridor outside his room, he showed her a square patch in the carpet just next to where she stood.

"Touch it," he said.

Madigan did, and felt how the floor underneath was a little lower within the square than to either side of it, and wobbled slightly when she trod on it.

"When Pokoj was a mansion, that used to be a trapdoor," Mr. Stupendo told her. "This whole floor was used to store things like sheets and pillows, and there were doors like this all over it which the servants could use whenever they needed to make the beds in the rooms upstairs. They're all sealed now, but once upon a time you could use them to get into almost every room on the second floor."

"Secret passages," Madigan breathed in awe.

"Exactly."

They carried on chatting as they walked down the stairs, about magic tricks and goblins, and how cool it would be if the trapdoors still opened and they could use them to sneak into people's rooms and spy on them. Mr. Stupendo took Madigan to the hotel museum on the ground floor, which had vases and bowls from the glass factory and a gold hoop which was found in the ground when the builders came to turn it into a hotel. There were paintings from when Pokoj was a mansion, and a wooden cat from the same time which Madigan looked at for ages. It was a beautiful kitty, even though the carpenter hadn't finished it.

They made up stories about all the things they saw. Mr. Stupendo said that the gold hoop, which was almost as big as Madigan's head, was a giant's earring. That made them both laugh. After they left the museum, they went and sat outside on the terrace and chatted some more. Madigan told Mr. Stupendo about her school back home, and all the places she'd been since she got sick. And eventually, because he was her friend, she told him about the lump in her chest, which was growing and growing and sometimes made it hard for her to breathe and to run around like other people.

"That's why mom wanted me to have extra dessert after dinner," she admitted, "and why she says that I can stay up past my bedtime." She looked at Mr. Stupendo carefully. She was a little worried now that she had told him about the lump, because a lot of the time people who knew about it went strange on her. They looked at her differently, like they might catch it if they stood too close, or like she was made of glass now, and they couldn't touch her any more. But Mr. Stupendo held her gaze, and his expression didn't change.

"And what do you think?" he asked her.

"I think that rules are rules," Madigan said firmly.

"Then I think so too. And I am at your service to dispose of unwanted desserts whenever the need arises."

It was almost midday now, and Madigan knew that she would need to go back to her parents for lunch soon. So she thanked Mr. Stupendo for a lovely morning and told him that she was going back to her room now. When she tried to stand up, though, she realised that she couldn't. Her legs had gone like legs in a dream: she could feel them under her, but however hard she tried she couldn't make them move more than an inch. Not being able to stand made Madigan cry a bit, not because it hurt, but because she was scared that she would be stuck like this for ever. But Mr. Stupendo sat by her and spoke to her in a soothing voice, telling her that it had been a busy morning and she had walked a long way, and that everything would be fine once she had had a good rest. Then he carried her back into the hotel and up in the lift, right to the door of her room. It felt nice being carried, and the rocking motion of his steps lulled and calmed her so that she soon fell asleep.

When she woke up, she was in her own bed, with her mother sitting beside her and Mr. Stupendo hovering just inside the door. He looked worried, but when he saw that her eyes had opened his face relaxed.

"I think we'd better stick to less strenuous activities in the future," he said.

Madigan tried to raise herself up a little on her pillow so that she could see him properly, but she was still too weak, and she flopped back down onto the bed.

"Will you stay and talk to me?" she asked him. "Mom, please let him!"

"He's got work to do, Mads," her mother said. "He's already given up a lot of time to be with you. Let him go and do his work now."

"I've nothing to do until the restaurant opens," Mr. Stupendo said. "I can stay a little longer. That is, if it's not . . ."

"It's fine," Madigan's mother said. "If you're sure. Thank you."

"Please. It's nothing. Madigan, what would you like to talk about?"

"I'd like a story," Madigan replied eagerly.

That afternoon, while Madigan drifted in and out of consciousness and her mother came and went in the background, Mr. Stupendo told her the story of how he stole the moon. It was for a magic show, he said, a really big one. Ten thousand people came from all over the world to a huge round circus tent in a park just to see it. There were lots of magicians at the show, who did all sorts of things. One swallowed fire, and another knew how to escape from a locked chest with his hands tied behind him, and another could tell you your name just by looking at you. But Mr. Stupendo was the star. He was the last person to perform, and when he walked onto the stage everyone in the audience went quiet. He bowed to them. Then he drew back a curtain at the back of the stage and there was the moon, stuck firmly in the sky like a sequin on black paper.

"No one thought it possible," Mr. Stupendo told Madigan. "The moon is as much a part of the landscape as the earth or the sea. How could one man shift it from its place? But I told them that the moon was a coin dropped from the pocket of God. It might fill our night sky with its light, but it is no more than loose change to the heavens, destined to glitter for a time and then to be gathered up again into that vast celestial pocket. You won't miss it; it was never yours in the first place."

He drew the curtain again as he finished his speech, and passed his hands across it once and twice and three times, drawing his fingers together as though to pluck the moon out of the sky. On the third time, he swept the curtain back once more and the sky was empty.

Everyone was too astonished even to clap. Mr. Stupendo had done it! Normally, magicians could only pretend to make big things disappear. They used trick photography, or the studio audience was really in on it all along and only pretending to be surprised. But no one could guess how Mr. Stupendo had stolen the moon, and when they asked him he only raised an eyebrow and smiled in reply.

As Madigan listened to the story, pictures chased each other through her mind almost too quickly to follow: the audience sitting in shocked silence, the full moon hanging in the sky like an apple on a tree, and Mr. Stupendo himself, his cloak and hat sparkling in the lights of the stage.

"You stole it?" she asked him after he had finished speaking. "Right out of the sky?"

"Right out of the sky."

"And then you got really famous, and everyone said you were the best magician of all?"

Mr. Stupendo looked at her and laughed. The laugh sounded a bit like a cough and a bit like a sigh, and not as if he thought that Madigan had said something funny at all.

"Something like that," he replied.

Madigan must have slept then, because the next time she woke up Mr. Stupendo had gone to his shift at the restaurant, and it was dark outside. Her mom was sitting by her bed now, and she stroked Madigan's hand with hers and sang to her, just like she had used to when she was very little.

In Madigan's dream that night, Mr. Stupendo towered as tall as the clouds and strode past trees the size of matchsticks. He pulled the night from his pocket, a cloth of black silk and silver stars, and shook it across the air until the stars glittered. And then he reached up into the sky that he had made, took the moon between finger and thumb, and offered it to Madigan like a silver coin.

It was taking Madigan's parents a long time to sort out the last few details at the clinic. They stayed at Pokoj for a whole week, and then they paid for another week after that. The longer they stayed, it seemed to Madigan, the more time they spent on the phone, or writing emails, or leafing through important looking folders full of paperwork. She had given up asking them if they wanted to play with her.

Madigan had good days and bad days. Sometimes she visited the museum or played in the grounds, and sometimes she was too tired even to get out of bed. However she was feeling, though, she always spent as much time as she could with Mr. Stupendo. When she was having a bad day he would visit her in her room to talk and tell stories, and sometimes he brought her fresh cherries from the market in Puppendorf, because they were her favourite. And on the days when she felt better he would walk with her, or she would sit in the restaurant and watch him do magic tricks for the guests.

Almost every time she saw him Madigan asked him when he was going to steal the moon again. She couldn't stop picturing it all in her head: the moon shining up from the palm of Mr. Stupendo's hand, the black sky vast and empty without it. She badly wanted to see him do it, but whenever she asked him he said no. His excuses were different each time, but the answer stayed the same.

"It's broad daylight now," he would say. "Let's not get ahead of ourselves." Or, "Too much fog tonight—I can't steal it if I can't see it."

He always raised one eyebrow at her as he spoke, because he knew it made her laugh. But he started talking about something else as soon as he could, and sometimes he would just say, "Later, Madigan," in a worn-out voice, like she was annoying him. Madigan began to worry that he wasn't allowed to steal the moon for some reason, or maybe he didn't remember how any more.

The night of her tenth day in Pokoj, Madigan could not sleep. Her chest was hurting more than usual, and she tossed and turned, trying to make herself comfortable. When she did finally drift off, it was only to wake again a few hours later, stiff and sore from lying in a funny position. She pushed herself up onto her pillows and glanced out of the window to see if it was morning yet. The moon stared back at her, round and full, casting its light across her bed in a wide beam.

Madigan could hear her parents' sleepy breathing from the bed next to hers, so she put on her shoes and dressing gown over her pyjamas and slipped out of the room. The stairs to the attic were hard work, but she didn't mind because they looked so beautiful, the moonlight making them shine like they had just been given a new coat of silvery paint. Mr. Stupendo could have no excuses tonight, she thought. This time, he would have to steal the moon.

When he opened his door, Mr. Stupendo did not look like Mr. Stupendo at all. He was wearing his pyjamas, and his eyes were all red round the edges from tiredness. In the room behind him Madigan could see a photo album open on the bed, lit up by the yellow light of the bedside lamp.

"Madigan," he said, rubbing his eyes. "It's two in the morning. What are you doing here?"

"Look outside," Madigan said.

"What?"

"Look!" She pulled him over to the window and pointed to the moon. "Go on," she said eagerly. "Steal it. Like you did before."

"Go back to bed. I'll do it some other time."

"No, now," Madigan insisted. She knew that if she didn't make him do it straight away then he would just come up with more excuses, and she would never get to see it. Mr. Stupendo looked at her for a long moment. Then he sat down heavily on the bed.

"I can't," he said.

"Why not?"

"Jesus," he muttered. "I just can't, Okay? I never could in the first place."

Madigan frowned at him in confusion. "But you said you did," she pointed out.

"Well I lied!" Mr. Stupendo snapped. "It was a trick, Madigan, just a trick. The audience and the stage were on a platform, and when I drew the curtain I pressed a button that made the platform go round, just until the moon was out of sight, and so slowly that no one could tell that it had moved at all. I didn't steal the moon; I moved the world around it. And that kind of trick takes a lot of money, and a lot of people who believe in you enough to give it to you."

He propped his elbows on his knees, resting his chin in his cupped hands so that he was staring at the floor. When he spoke again, the anger in his voice had gone, and he sounded tired and sad. "I don't have either of those things any more. So I can't ever do the trick again. Do you see now?"

Madigan did see. Mr. Stupendo had told her the truth about stealing the moon, even though he hadn't wanted to because the story was better. She looked at him sitting all hunched over on the bed. He had gone quiet, as if he expected that Madigan would leave now that he had snapped at her. She sat down beside him, leaned over, and kissed him on the cheek.

"I still think you're the best magician in the world, Mr. Stupendo," she told him. "And it was nice of you to be honest with me, so I think that I should be honest with you too. There isn't a clinic. Well, there is, but I'm not going there. Mom and dad took me last week, but when they saw how ill I was the doctors there said I couldn't stay. I don't think I was supposed to hear, but I did, and they said that there was no point, that it was too late to do anything now. So mom and dad have been lying too," Madigan explained. "They've really been trying to get the people at the clinic to change their minds this whole time."

She looked at Mr. Stupendo levelly, just as he had looked at her that first night in the restaurant, when he had pulled away the cloth and revealed nothing but empty space underneath. "Mom and dad still think that they can make the lump in my chest disappear, like you made the moon disappear in your story. But they can't," she said. "I'm going to die, Mr. Stupendo. They just don't know it yet."

Mr. Stupendo's face was so white and so shocked that it was as if Madigan was already dead and it was her ghost sitting there on the bed talking to him.

"Madigan . . ." he began. And then again, after a pause, "Madigan. I . . ."

He stared at her, and his expression was the strangest thing. He was looking at her, Madigan thought, but through her too, like he was trying to see past her to all the years that she might have lived but now would not.

"It's nice to be able to tell the truth to someone," Madigan said. "My parents always want to pretend everything is fine, so I have to as well, and that's much worse."

She realised with a sudden wave of sadness that once she left Pokoj the pretending would carry on, and she would not have Mr. Stupendo any more to tell her stories and play with her, and to listen to her when she told him things that her mom and dad wouldn't understand. Her lips went wobbly at the thought, and she had to look away from him quickly and stare at the floor so that he wouldn't see the tears if they came.

"We'll probably go away soon," she said, her voice shaking. "They'll find me another clinic, and that will mean more flights, and pills, and injections, over and over, until I'm all used up and I can't have any more. I don't know where I'll be when I die." Madigan risked a glance at Mr. Stupendo, and started to sob.

He put his arms around her then, and she buried her face in his chest.

"Where would you like to be?" he asked her quietly

"Here," Madigan said. "I like it here. It's old, and there's a museum and a big garden. And you're here, and I love you best of all."

"Then here is where you'll stay," he said, and when Madigan looked up at him he was Mr. Stupendo again, the Mr. Stupendo who stole the moon. He smiled at her, and though the smile was a sad one Madigan found that it reminded her of his grin from that first day, the day when he made her ice cream disappear. He looked now, as he had then, like he was about to perform the best trick in the world, something so wonderful that Madigan would hardly be able to believe it.

He did so the very next morning when he visited Madigan's parents. He talked to them for most of the day, and when he left, although the moon was still hanging firmly in the sky, Madigan was allowed to stay at Pokoj for good.

Mr. Stupendo's best trick turned out not to be a trick at all.

"I never found out what he said to them, to make them understand," Magda said thoughtfully. "But when he came out my mom was crying, really crying. She'd never done that before, not even when she found out I was sick. She just cried and cried, and hugged me, and told me that she was sorry.

"After that, mom and dad never mentioned the clinic in Stollenbet any more, and they started playing games with me again. They spoke to the manager of the hotel and explained everything, and after that they hired me my own nurse to look after me. I stayed in Pokoj until I died, and Mr. Stupendo stayed too, right until the end. He left a few days afterwards; he was going to give up magic and become a teacher, he said.

"I know that he always felt a little bit bad, because he couldn't save me. But really he did, though he didn't know it. He moved everything around me, just so that I could stay put. I wish I could tell him how important that was, because if he hadn't then I would have died somewhere else, and if that had happened then I never would have met you."

Magda had climbed into Drozde's lap by this point, and Drozde realised that her arms had encircled the little girl while she spoke. Somehow she had become more solid, more tangible. Drozde could almost imagine that she felt Magda pressed up against her skin, her phantom breath brushing her cheek. She held Magda cradled against her chest, and now the dead girl returned Drozde's embrace, her touch as light and insubstantial as the hollow bones of a bird. They sat like that in quiet for a while.

"Did you like it?" Madigan asked her at last.

"Yes, Magda. I liked it very much."

"I knew you would. It's because you and Mr. Stupendo are just alike." Magda beamed at Drozde. "You're both funny and kind, and you look after me, and you tell the best stories. But you're most the same because when it's important enough, you know how to tell the truth as well. You make people see."

Drozde barely heard these words. She was drifting into sleep, exhausted by the events of the day and lulled by the strangely comforting embrace of the dead girl, who seemed to love her so much for so little reason.

Her dreams were like fever dreams, a cage of repeated images and sensations from which she couldn't free herself. She woke at last, freezing, her own sweat slick and icy on her skin. Magda's face was close to hers, watching.

"I didn't wake you," she said. "You seemed so tired."

"Thank you, Magda," Drozde mumbled. "That was kind of you. Now do me another favour, please. Go and see if Molebacher is still there."

He was, Magda reported. Sitting exactly where he'd been before, with the same expression on his face. It was as though he'd turned into a statue of himself.

"What time is it?" Drozde asked.

"I don't know."

"Well is it day or is it night?"

"I don't know. I see day and night all at the same time now. We all do. You said—"

"Oh, I said!"

"—that there are only two things you miss when you're dead. Times and places."

"Do I ever say anything that makes sense, Magda?"

"That *does* make sense. All the different times sort of become the same time, and all the places . . . well, there aren't any. There's only here. But the times turn into places, so when we walk it gets to be something that happened before or after."

This made no sense at all, but Drozde raised no further argument. The story of Magda's death lingered in her mind and tangled itself with the other death she'd witnessed that day until there seemed to be nothing left in the world but mourning.

And Molebacher.

29

Lieutenant Klaes was the last man to leave the flogging ground. No one sent for him: he supposed that he might be in disgrace with the colonel, but could not summon the will to go and find out. He stayed while the villagers left with their wounded on improvised stretchers, moaning and gasping. He was still there when the old carpenter returned with two other men to carry back the last stretcher, shrouded and silent. He spoke to none of them, only overseeing the removal of the hideous frames. When those were down, he ordered Frydek and his men to take the wood away and burn it on the waste ground behind the kitchen. And then he was left to himself.

He had attended floggings before, keeping his composure by detaching his conscious thoughts from the images he was seeing and the sounds he was hearing so that they became abstract patterns whose meaning he was not obliged to interpret. But this time he could not hide in that self-made refuge. The suffering of the six men was too monstrous and too unjust, and his own complicity too great. He could not undo the wrong; all that remained was to bear witness. Now even that duty was past, and he could not think what he was to do.

He found himself walking out through the gates of Pokoj, between two sentries who let the surprise show on their faces as they looked at his. Was he pale? Flushed? Or was it his mere expression that made them stare at him? He had no idea.

He did not know, either, where he was walking to. He took the road to Narutsin at first, but quickly veered off it. If he set foot in the village now he would probably be mobbed and beaten. It was not to be imagined that the villagers would contain themselves in patience after this. How could they, with the blood of their kin and their neighbours soaking into the earth at the mansion house?

He walked aimless through the woods, chancing across paths he didn't take, tearing his jacket and trousers on thick brambles. To have no direction, no destination, freed him at least from thinking about what he would do when he stopped.

But he did stop at last, in the middle of some forlorn and denuded timberland. A fallen tree blocked his path. Someone had begun to lop off the branches and to pile them up beside the trunk, ready to be carried away or loaded into a cart. But there was no cart, and no sign of the woodcutter except for his axe left leaning against the tree trunk and a coil of rope dumped on the ground.

In a patch of dappled shadow close by the stump of the felled tree, Klaes threw up the contents of his stomach and, it seemed to him, a great deal else besides. When he was finished he stayed where he was, looking blankly down at the vomit and at the spatter patterns on his boots.

Some time later—a little time or a long time, he could not be sure—he picked up the axe and put it to use, chopping through the remaining branches of the tree to leave the trunk clean and clear. When he began to sweat, which was soon enough, he took off his jacket and then his shirt and worked on.

A strong thirst grew on him. His mouth was sour from the sickness he had voided, and now it was painfully dry too. But there was no water near, so far as he knew. He was several miles from the river. The forest was probably criss-crossed by many small brooks and streams, but a man could wander for ever without finding them unless he knew his way. So he ignored his discomfort and worked on, through what was left of the morning and late into the afternoon. When he finally cast the axe aside, the sun was low in the sky and the light reddening.

The sweat on his arms and torso turned chill and slick as soon as he was no longer working. He slipped his shirt back on with some difficulty over his drenched limbs. He picked up his jacket too, but did not put it on.

He sat down on the trunk of the felled tree and pondered. The hard physical exercise had removed the blockage in his thoughts, as he had hoped it might. He was able at last to reflect on what had happened and on his part in it.

He had not precipitated this catastrophe. He had advised Colonel August against the floggings, and on good grounds. True, he had not foreseen how far things might go awry, and certainly he had taken no account of the bizarre friendship between the colonel and the quartermaster sergeant, Molebacher. But he had stood out against this madness while it was still fomenting.

On the other hand, he had allowed himself to be drawn into August's strange agenda of control and pre-emptive mistrust and to feed it with his efforts. He had pursued the girl, Bosilka Stefanu, and used her very much as Colonel August had used him. He was far from guiltless in this, and he had dragged others into his complicity.

All of this stood very clear in Klaes's thoughts. What was not clear to him was what would come next. He had been until recently an ambitious junior officer looking forward to war because war allowed quicker advancement. But they were never really his own ambitions. They were his father's, learned parrot-fashion the way all good children learn their lessons.

Only now he had learned a different lesson, and it threw everything else into doubt.

In a kind of desperation, trying to salvage something from his life to date, he remonstrated with himself. *You're a fool.* He shaped the words with his lips, and it was even possible that he spoke them aloud. *A fool twice over. First that you thought you could go to war and keep from injuring people. And now again, if you think you can do better anywhere else.*

Surely the villagers he'd just seen mourning their damaged and their dead were killers too. They had murdered Captain Petos or hidden and nurtured his murderers, and still hid and nurtured them. Though the floggings were insane as a punishment for brawling in the street, they were more than just as retribution for murder.

It would seem, by this logic, that everything hinged on Petos's death. Or rather, not everything, but at least the viability of Klaes's position and his ability to rest easy with the decisions he'd made.

He needed the truth. The colonel's vague suspicions had faded into irrelevance now, but Klaes had to know whether they were built on rock or sand. If the villagers were guilty, what exactly were they guilty of? Had they murdered Petos because he'd caught them out in an illegal enterprise? Had it been some set-to, like the fight that had occasioned the floggings—a sign, in other words, that these people were generally ungoverned and out of control? If it was, and if they were, then it might be possible to live with everything that had happened and still feel oneself a man.

In other words, the investigation which Klaes had undertaken with so much reluctance had suddenly become a matter of personal urgency.

He climbed to his feet and began to retrace his steps through the forest. And it was now that his policy of walking entirely at random revealed its defects. He was completely lost. As long as the sun was still above the horizon he could follow it due westwards, which he thought ought to take him to the road. But sunset was coming quickly, and once it was dark he would find it hard to stay on the right line. He might wander for hours and make no progress—or fall over a tree root and break his skull on a rock.

He quickened his pace and was surprised to find, as the last dribbles of sunlight bled from between the trees, the ground falling away under his feet into a great declivity. Then he realised that he must have reached the Drench. It ran between Pokoj and the village and Klaes could therefore use it to find his way back. He could walk along the bottom of the defile and then, when he came to the bridge, climb up again onto the road.

Better still, a thin stream ran along its bottom, disappearing from time to time between rocks or under pebble beds, but always emerging again, and widening in places into pools a few feet across. Klaes knelt at one of these to drink and splash his face. The water was freezing but wonderfully refreshing to his parched palate.

He thought about washing his soiled uniform, but a long march in soaking wet clothes was more than he could contemplate—and if he missed his way, the cold might kill him.

As it was, the walk took less time than he expected. Even at night the bridge was impossible to miss, its wooden pilings the only straight lines in the wild landscape. Klaes climbed the west bank and found himself at once on the road, the moonlight picking it out as a pale ribbon stitched into the fabric of the dark.

From there the way was easy. Easy, too, to gain entry to the grounds of Pokoj without being seen—he just walked in through one of the gaps in the tumbledown walls rather than through the gates. The sentries would have let him pass in any case, but he had no desire at that moment to be challenged and made to explain himself.

He walked through the tents, steering away from the fires that were still lit and the men who still sat and talked in the dark. There were many of these, and the conversations Klaes overheard as he passed were being conducted in hushed murmurs, with no laughter and no song. Perhaps he was not the only one who had found the morning's entertainment hard to swallow.

As he was physically walking back along his former path, he had been doing much the same thing in his mind—thinking back through the chain of words and actions that he had followed since the colonel first ordered him to enquire into the villagers' supposed secrets.

That trail had led him at last to Nymand Petos's dishonoured corpse, but the corpse was only another cul-de-sac. It could not explain itself, or the reasons for its being where it was. For those answers Klaes had to revisit the cellar and search it again. Though it had seemed empty, it was the other half of the mystery and must surely contain some clue. Or if not, then it must point to something beyond itself that he had missed.

Late though it was, lights were still burning in the upstairs windows of the house. The officers seemed to be having no more restful a night than the enlisted soldiery. Perhaps they were keeping vigil for the man who had been killed, though Klaes thought that unlikely.

He went to his own quarters first. From under the colonel's door as he passed he heard Dame August's voice. Her tone seemed oddly formal, almost as though she were addressing a gathering. Klaes paused and listened despite himself, wondering if for some reason the lady had been allowed to speak at some forensic examination of the day's events.

But he was disappointed: she was only reading from the Bible, and her text was a dry one. "Many have undertaken," she intoned, "to draw up an account of the things that have been fulfilled among us, just as they were handed down to us by those who from the first were eyewitnesses and servants of the word." The opening words of one of the Gospels, and whichever it was, it did not seem to be very much to the purpose. Unless she was drawing some sort of a parallel between the carpenter who had died today and that other carpenter.

At the bottom of a trunk in his room Klaes found some candles. He took them with him back down to the kitchen, bringing his tinderbox too in case there was no fire in the kitchen grate to light a candle by.

The fire was dead, but the ashes were still red so it must have gone out not long before. A heavy, bitter smell of burned food hung in the air. Was the ash warm enough to light a wick by? It was worth trying, at least, since striking sparks off a steel in the dark and getting his damp charcloth to burn would be a laborious business.

Klaes knelt by the grate and held the candle into the centre of the glowing ash until the wick kindled slowly into flame. Then he made his way, holding the candle aloft, into the corner of the room where—to the best of his recollection—he would find the stairs down to the cellar.

The stairs were where he expected to find them, but there was something else that he did not expect. Sitting close by on a joint stool, wide awake in the near-dark, was Sergeant Molebacher. The candlelight seemed to assemble him in stages, from silhouette to huge and shapeless mass to finished man. It was a chilling sight to Klaes, like something congealing from his own conscience.

"Molebacher," he said.

Molebacher raised a hand. Klaes thought at first that he was saluting, but he was only shielding his eyes against the light.

"Lieutenant Klaes," he returned. "You were missed, sir. After the floggings. The colonel was calling for you."

"Was he?" Klaes asked grimly. "Be that as it may, Sergeant, I believe you should stand to attention when an officer enters the room."

Molebacher slid off the stool and came upright, without haste. The salute he offered was the thinnest sliver away from actual mockery. "Sir."

"What are you doing here?" Klaes demanded.

"I must have nodded off," the sergeant said. "It's not unheard of, at night. You should try it yourself, sir."

There was a definite tension underlying the insolence, an eagerness.

Molebacher was not averse to a fight, even though he was speaking to a superior. He seemed to be inviting Klaes to try to discipline him.

Klaes chose not to. He would dearly have liked to relieve his feelings by laying into the corpulent quartermaster, but he felt detached at that moment from the chain of command and uncertain of the authority he would be calling on. Nonetheless, he did not wish to spend a second longer than he had to in the man's company.

"Dismiss," he snapped.

"Please you, sir? This is my kitchen, sir. Perhaps it should be me as dismisses you."

Klaes felt anger flare inside him, erecting the hairs on his neck and making the breath catch in his throat. He welcomed it like a friend, but did his best to keep his voice from rising to a shout.

"Dismiss, Sergeant," he said again. "By God, you cur, if you're still in my sight when I set this candle down, I'll beat you out of the room with the flat of my fucking sword!"

He tilted the candle to let the wax drip down onto the end of the nearest table. There was no point in putting it down if it would not stand. He would be reduced to swiping at the sergeant in the dark, as if they were playing a game of blind man's buff.

Molebacher held his ground a second longer, but only until Klaes succeeded in planting the candle upright in the hot wax and drew his blade. Then the sergeant took a step back, bringing him into contact with the wall.

"You can't beat me." he objected. "I'm no bondsman, I'm a fellow officer. And we're both under the colonel's authority!"

"Then by all means, plead your case to the colonel," Klaes said, swishing the sword. Molebacher retreated to the doorway, where he stopped and stared at Klaes. Then, as the lieutenant strode towards him, he turned with deliberate slowness and moved off into the darkness of the corridor.

Klaes retrieved his candle and descended the stairs.

The door at the bottom opened only a few inches before it hit something that blocked it. Klaes pushed it, tentatively at first and then with his shoulder to the wood, but he could not make it move any further.

He slid his hand through the gap to try to discover what was causing the blockage. Then a second later he pulled it back again with a curse. Someone had struck at him from inside the room, catching him a stinging blow across the back of his hand.

"I sleep lightly, Eustach," a voice said, seemingly from right beside him.

Klaes rubbed the injured hand with the fingers of the other. He knew that voice. "Drozde," he muttered bitterly. Of course it would be her, if only because there was nobody he would be less pleased to see.

"Who's there? Klaes?"

"Yes, Klaes. What are you doing locked in the cellar? Did Molebacher do this to you?"

"I did it to myself."

"And now you're fending off all comers? It's possibly a little late in life, madam, to start repelling unseemly advances. You've made yourself a name and a living by inviting them."

Even through the wood of the door and the mass of whatever was blocking it he heard Drozde sigh. "You can't help yourself, can you, Klaes? You have to squeal at everyone else's sins because you haven't blood or courage enough to sin on your own behalf. You're like the old lady at the back of the church, fishing for gossip around the confessionals. 'Isn't it awful? And can you speak a little louder?'"

Klaes was about to utter some fierce rebuke, but the woman's insult struck close enough to his shame to wake it again. He swallowed the tart words unspoken, and cast about for better ones.

"Would it be possible for you to let me in?" he asked at last, with as much courtesy as he could muster.

"Why?" Drozde sounded suspicious, as well she might. But it was the cellar he wanted access to, not her person, and he hastened to assure her of this.

"Are you alone out there?" she demanded next.

"Well, yes, I am. I am alone. But I promise you, I won't seek to take any advantage of your—"

"I mean, has Molebacher gone?"

"Yes. I sent him away."

There was a brief interval of silence, followed by sounds of great effort and concerted movement from within, bumps and bangs and the groaning of wood. "All right," Drozde said at last. "Try it now."

Klaes pushed the door again. It opened halfway, allowing him to slip through into the cellar. In the light of his own candle and another that was already lit inside the room, he was able to see what had caused the blockage. Someone—he supposed Drozde herself as there was nobody else in the room—had dragged the tall cupboard from its place against the further wall and turned it into a barricade.

Drozde still stood with her hands gripping the side of the massive piece of furniture, breathing hard. Klaes stared at her in bewilderment.

"Are you all right?" he asked her. "Did the sergeant offer you violence?"

Drozde laughed—a single hollow bark. "The sergeant offered me the sergeant. I said no thank you."

Klaes nodded. In the light of what had happened at the floggings, he could understand the need to bolster that refusal with a physical barrier of some kind. "Are you hurt?" he asked her.

"No." But she hesitated, as though that was a more difficult question than it appeared. "He didn't hit me. I wouldn't let him get close enough for that. I couldn't let him touch me after what he did to Hanslo."

"Hanslo? That was the carpenter?"

A nod. The woman's face worked, moved from within by strong emotions, and she shook a little. Klaes had never seen her cry—he had always thought her much too hardened and brazen for that—but she looked as though some wild and watery grief were about to escape from her. And it seemed to him that she would not want him to see it.

"Things have gotten out of hand," he said, deliberately putting on some of that old-maid prudishness again. "This whole business has been handled deplorably, with no thought to the wider concerns of our mission here."

The ploy worked, pulling Drozde back from misery to her former irritation with him. "Our mission!" she echoed. "You're an ass, Klaes. Nobody but you is even thinking about the bloody Prussians, though—what? What are you staring at?"

What Klaes was staring at was the wall. There was a door there that he had not seen before: a wooden door bearing a bolt as long as Klaes's forearm. He pointed stupidly.

"The cupboard!" he exclaimed.

"What?"

"The cupboard was in front of that door. It had been moved there to hide it. But you moved it away again!"

He turned to her, unable to keep the excitement from his face or from his voice. "I've been looking for this place," he said. "And you've found it for me. I owe you a debt, madam."

"Klaes, nobody calls me madam, or thinks madam when they see me. If you want to say thank you, give me my name."

"Drozde. Thank you. For your assistance." He gave her an uncertain smile, and then—because formality died hard with him—bowed from the waist. "I'm obliged to you."

"You're far from the first."

The crude joke made Klaes blush like a schoolboy.

Drozde looked on while Klaes drew the bolt.

Magda stood beside her and watched too, seeming both scandalised and excited. "What's he doing?" she demanded. "Why is he down here? Is he your friend now?"

Drozde turned to the girl and put a finger athwart her lips, urging her to be quiet. There would be time for explanations. Right now she wanted Klaes to be done with whatever it was that he needed to do down here so she could leave with him. He had said that he'd sent Molebacher on his way, but it was hard to imagine the stolid and monumental sergeant blown away like thistledown by the weightless, mannerly lieutenant. When she went back up into the kitchen she would walk behind Klaes and set her feet in his bootprints. His presence might deter Molebacher from active hostilities, but there was no way his bare word would do it.

Klaes swore a maidenly oath. The bolt was drawn back but the door still didn't open when he pulled on it.

"Do you want me to help?" Drozde asked.

"It's locked," Klaes told her acerbically. He tapped the lockplate, a square of black iron right at the top of the door. "I'll try to force it— you should probably stand back."

"The key is under the floorboard there," Magda said. "That's where the men always put it after they're finished."

Drozde was careful not to answer her, and she didn't trouble to explain the matter to Klaes. She just went to where Magda was pointing, levered up the loose board and took out the key. She handed it to Klaes, who stared at it in dumbstruck astonishment.

"The board was standing proud," Drozde lied. "I thought something might be hidden there."

The lieutenant tried the key in the lock. It turned freely.

Beyond was a well of pure dark that their candles could not fathom. The two of them shared a momentary glance containing one part of triumph to two of presentiment. Klaes led the way down a short flight of wooden steps into a passage with a dirt floor. Drozde took up the candle from the lid of her trunk and followed, with Magda chattering at her side. "Nobody likes it down here. We hardly ever come. Mostly it's underground, until they dig it out. And then parts of it are underground again later, when they do the rebuilding and put in the spa and the gym. It's not a very nice place to be, most of the time."

"No, it's not," Drozde agreed, keeping her voice low. The narrow corridor stank of dampness, dust and rot—a potent brew of odours that made her feel somewhat lightheaded. Spiderwebs draped the walls and bellied down from the beamed ceiling like bunting at a wedding breakfast. The bones of mice crunched under her boots.

They passed two rooms, really no more than widenings of the passage. Both were mostly empty, though in the first a broken table and some empty wine racks had been propped against the far wall. Drozde's attention, however, was fixed on something else. There was a ghost down here. It was not like most of the other ghosts of Pokoj, but like the phantoms she had encountered elsewhere, or the one on the floor of the kitchen upstairs—a stain on the curdled air, leached of colour and all but shapeless. It had a face, though, or at least the suggestion of one, and a mouth that opened and closed like the mouth of a fish. Its hands moved ceaselessly in a combing motion across its unfinished features. It emitted a low, broken sound like the thrumming of a jaw harp.

Drozde stole a questioning glance at Magda, but Magda didn't notice because she was scowling at Klaes. She seemed to resent the man's intrusion into a moment that she and Drozde had been sharing.

They came to a cross corridor leading off to left and right. Klaes stopped and knelt down, playing the candle flame over the packed earth. To one side it was clear, to the other scuffed and rutted with the passage of many feet and many heavy objects dragged or pushed. That was the way they took.

In a larger room at the end of the passage they found their way blocked and their questions answered. From floor to ceiling, this wider space was filled with barrels. And the barrels, as Lieutenant Klaes soon ascertained by staving one in with his boot, were filled with brandy.

His face veered between emotions, but disapproval won the field. "Smuggling!" he exclaimed. "This is what the mayor wanted to keep hidden from us—and this is why he lied to me about Petos!"

"Petos," whispered a second voice, so faint that Drozde almost mistook it for an echo. She turned her head to find the ghost—the washed-out, vestigial ghost they had passed in the corridor—floating close to her shoulder. It pressed its hands together as though it was imploring her. She recoiled in instinctive disgust.

"What's wrong?" Klaes asked her. "Are you all right?"

"I'm very well," Drozde muttered. "I only stumbled."

"Petos," the ghost murmured again. And then another word that might have been *nigh*. Or *nine*. Or *mine*.

"But why then was Petos killed?" Klaes asked now, seemingly of the empty air. "Did he catch them in the act? But if so, and if they murdered him to ensure his silence, what became of his command? There was only the one body buried in these grounds."

"Nymand," the ghost whimpered.

"Isn't his voice horrible!" Magda said, her lips pursed with distaste. "Nobody likes him. That's why he's down here all by himself."

"One body?" Drozde echoed. The smell of the spilled liquor had now joined the other smells freighting the air. She had not eaten or drunk since early that morning. It was hard to keep the voices she was hearing apart in her mind.

"In the kitchen garden," Klaes said. "I found a corpse buried."

"That's where they put him," Magda agreed. "In the end. After they were finished with him."

"Nymand," the ghost moaned, its restless hands swatting feebly at the air.

"Who is Nymand?" Drozde asked. "Was that his name?"

She knew at once that it was the wrong thing to say. She had responded to the wrong voice. Klaes turned to stare at her, the pupils of his eyes huge in the dim light of the candle.

"What did you say?" he demanded.

Drozde shook her head. "Nothing."

"Yes. You asked me who Nymand was. But I didn't call him Nymand, only Petos. Where have you heard that name?"

His expression was suspicious, belligerent. Drozde's temper flared at the sight of it. She was done with subterfuge, and with fitting herself into the interstices of other people's narrow sensibilities. She was done with this place too, she realised suddenly. She couldn't stay at Pokoj, or with the company, after what had happened here. She had reached a crossroads, and must turn to right or left because the way that led straight on held nothing she could bear. "Here," she snapped. "I heard it here, Klaes."

"From who?"

She pointed at the shrivelled and ruined little thing that bobbed in the air beside her. "From him. Your dead man, whatever his name is. He's here with us. Do you not see him? No, most likely you don't. But he's here, nonetheless. Shall I say hello for you? Ask him what he wants you to do with his mortal remains?"

Klaes stared where she was pointing. He stared long and hard, and his face grew troubled.

"No," he said. "That's . . . I don't know what that is. The light from our candles, making shadows."

There was nothing to cast a shadow, but Drozde did not say this. She was astonished that Klaes had seen anything at all. "Believe what you like," she told him. "Nymand Petos—was that his name?—stands before you. What you found in the garden, buried among the beets and turnips, was only a part of him. This is the other part."

"His ghost?" Klaes tried for a contemptuous laugh, but the pitch of it was off by half a note. "You tell me you can see his ghost?"

"And others," Drozde said. "Why not? You think your eyesight's so good you miss nothing? There are a thousand things you don't see."

"While you . . ."

"Nine hundred and ninety-nine," Drozde said. "I'm exactly like you, with just this one thing more."

"You're not a bit like him!" Magda exclaimed. Drozde could not keep herself from laughing at the girl's scandalised tone, but she shook her head. "Not now, Magda. Let us talk."

Klaes looked where she looked. "Another one?" he demanded. His sarcasm was more successful this time, but only by a little.

"Pay no mind to her. It's Petos you came here for, I think?"

Klaes was like a man struggling in the toils of a dream and striving to awake. "But you never saw Petos," he said. "How would you even know him?"

"He answers to his name."

The lieutenant brought up his hands as though he cupped something, but dropped them again, shaking his head. "No. These things can't be," he said. And then, with deep reluctance, "Ask him how he died."

"He wants to know how you died," Drozde told the pathetic little spectre, hooking a thumb in Klaes's direction. "If you want someone to get the blame for it, he's the man to tell."

"Nymand," the ghost whined in its stick-thin voice. "Nymand Petos."

"Is that all you can say?" Drozde demanded impatiently.

"Yes," Magda confirmed. "You won't get any more out of him."

"Why not?" Drozde asked. "Why is he different? Why is there so much . . . less of him than there is of you?"

"He doesn't tell the stories. We wouldn't let him be with us, or talk to us, and he lost himself."

"So quickly? He can't have been dead long."

"It's like you lose money out of a pocket with a hole in it, you said. One coin falls out, and then another, and you don't even hear them fall. But you can start the day rich and finish it poor. And all times—"

"Turn into the same time. I know. But Magda, are you really saying that the stories make this much difference? The difference between staying yourself and turning into . . ." she pointed with a thrust of her chin ". . . that?"

"They do," Magda said. "They help us. They build us from the inside, like we're adding more stones to a crumbly wall."

"Did I say that?"

Magda giggled. "Yes!"

Klaes was following her side of the conversation, his expression veering between unease and bafflement. "Well?" he asked. "What's the man's story? If you can talk to him, get me an answer."

"He can't answer," Drozde said. She shrugged irritably. She would have preferred to have something solid to push into the face of Klaes's scepticism, but it didn't really matter. What mattered was getting out of this place, past the threatening ramparts of Sergeant Molebacher and into the wide world. She'd be sorry to say goodbye to Magda, but there was only so much she could endure.

"Of course he can't," Klaes agreed.

"But Agnese can," Magda piped up. "It's her story too."

"Who is Agnese?" Drozde asked her.

"Enough!" Klaes cried, exasperated. "Enough with this! Who are you talking to? There are no ghosts here, madam, and no . . ." He faltered into silence in the middle of his complaint, his face going through a range of confused emotions. "Agnese . . ." he said, with a much less certain emphasis. "Agnese was a friend of Bosilka Stefanu's. She came to a bad end, Miss Stefanu said. Is she . . . ?" It was clear that it took him some effort to get the words out. "Is she here too?"

"Is she?" Drozde asked Magda.

The girl shook her head. "She never comes here. Not where *he* is." She glared at the dark smudge of air that was Nymand Petos. "She hates him worst out of everyone."

"But she is one of the ghosts of the house?" Drozde persisted.

"Yes. Of course she is. You've seen her lots of times."

"I don't know everyone's names yet." Drozde turned to Klaes. "If you come with me," she told him, "I think I can get you some answers for your questions."

"Come with you where?" Klaes asked suspiciously.

"Not far. Here in the house."

The lieutenant hesitated for a moment, his mixed emotions visible on his face. To say yes meant accepting that Drozde's version of what was happening here—ghosts included—had some merit in it. But whether he knew it or not, he'd crossed that line when he pressed her to interrogate Petos's phantom on his behalf. Drozde waited him out, confident of what the outcome would be.

"All right," Klaes said at last. "I'll try anything at this point. But it doesn't mean I believe you."

"Of course not," Drozde agreed, throwing his own sarcasm back at him. She led the way back to the steps and up into her cellar room. How would she retrieve her trunk, she suddenly wondered. It was too heavy for her to carry it alone. "Can I bring my things?" she asked Klaes.

"Your things?"

She pointed to the trunk. "My puppets. And my theatre."

"I don't understand. Why do you need them?"

She couldn't say. Not with Magda at her side, hearing every word. "I don't," she admitted. "I was just afraid that Molebacher might damage them to spite me."

"He'll answer to me if he does," Klaes promised her. He threw out his arm in a sweep, gallantly allowing her to ascend the kitchen stairs before him. Stifling her misgivings, she did so.

Molebacher was exactly where she had thought he would be, watching the mouse hole again from his vantage point beside the door. He slid down off his stool and took a step towards her, his lips curled back to show his uneven teeth—but then stopped in his tracks when Lieutenant Klaes appeared at her elbow.

"I believe I dismissed you, Sergeant," Klaes said grimly. His hand was on the hilt of his sword. Molebacher stared at it and said nothing.

"Lead on, madam," Klaes said to Drozde. And she did. But she couldn't resist taking a morsel of revenge. She turned to the nearer wall, where Molebacher's tools hung gleaming on their hooks. There was Gertrude in pride of place at the head of the procession, her square blade so well polished that the candle flame danced within it like a winking eye.

Drozde spat, and her aim was true. Her spit landed at the nexus of blade and handle and began to trickle down.

Insolent, unhurried, she turned her back on the white-faced sergeant and walked out of the room. But the skin of her back prickled, and she expected at any moment to feel the bite of Gertrude's sullied steel between her shoulder blades.

30

For the first time, Drozde opened the door of the ballroom to find no one waiting for her. Empty, the room seemed larger than she remembered it; her voice and Klaes's echoed off the peeling walls. The lieutenant seemed nervous, peering into the minstrels' alcove as if some danger might be lurking there, but he came into the room docilely enough, and sat down on the spindly chair that Drozde found for him.

"Now what?" Drozde asked Magda, who had not left her side. Klaes started and turned to look attentively in the child's direction, peering as if he might make out who Drozde was addressing if only he looked hard enough.

"She'll come now," the child said. "I called her, and she likes this room. Here she is. Hello, Agnese!"

There was a girl with her, appearing suddenly as if from a fold in the air. She was so vivid that for a moment Drozde could not see her as a ghost, and wondered where she had been hiding. She was dressed demurely in a high-necked grey dress, but her yellow hair escaped in tendrils from both sides of her cap, and her mouth quirked as if about to break into a laugh. She did not immediately acknowledge Drozde, but stood in front of the oblivious Klaes, peering into his face as if assuring herself that he could not see her. After a moment she nodded, turned to Drozde and made a little bob, the curtsy of a girl who had not been trained to deference.

"Magda says I should tell you my story, Drozde," she began. "And I'd like that very, very much. Of course I would! But telling you and telling—" she flicked a glance at Klaes "—other people aren't the same thing at all. You're from the same time I am, aren't you? Silkie is alive where you are now, and Bobik; even Birgitta. I don't want to give them any trouble."

"We won't make trouble," Drozde assured her. "The lieutenant found out about the smuggling, but he isn't going to tell his commander. He just wants to know what happened."

The girl looked at Klaes narrowly. "If you say he won't then I'll take your word for it, Drozde," she said, "but I don't think knowing this will help him very much. I'll tell you anyway, though, since you ask me to, and you can pass it on if you see fit. Only make sure no harm comes of it, if you can—there's been too many wicked things done already by men in those colours."

She must have seen the heartfelt assent in Drozde's face. "Well then," she said, and began her story.

Bobik always said, and so did my aunt, that I should not have gone for a maid at the big house, that I was mad to ever go there. And since the place has done for me in the long run, they were right, weren't they? But if you knew me like Silkie did, you wouldn't have said that I was mad.

When we were all younger, me and my friends used to talk about what we'd do when we were grown. Jana said she'd make fine dresses, and wear the best ones herself and sell the rest. Bosilka, she's my best friend, said she'd be a master-carpenter like her dad; she was always funny. And most of the others, it was get a rich husband, a man with a hundred sheep, and have a silver necklace and eat meat every day. But not me. I wanted to go to the city. If a traveller came through when I was serving at the inn, I'd hang around at the table and listen to the talk. Sometimes he'd tell of Praha, or Brno, and it made me want to see them so much. Marble palaces, and theatres with gold and velvet on the walls. And whole rooms full of beautiful pictures, and ladies hung with diamonds just strolling through them. I wanted to be one of those ladies. If I had to marry a rich man to do it, well then. But it was the pictures I wanted, and the diamonds, not the man.

So when the militia moved into the big house and called for a maid, why wouldn't I go? It was the grandest place for miles around—the only grand place really, for all it was falling down. We broke in there once, Silkie and me, when we were little, and it had marble statues and everything. It would be hard work, I knew that: there were rats and spiders everywhere, and the velvet curtains all rotten. But rotten or not, it was still a palace, with pictures, one or two, in golden frames that would shine if you only polished them. And they were paying a lot more than I could make pouring beer with my auntie and Risha.

Bobik wasn't too happy about it. We were walking out: he wanted to call it courting, but I could do very well without that. He was a fine enough young man, Bobik, tall and straight and a hard worker, and his cousin Matheus kept the inn and was the richest man in town but only the mayor. But I didn't have a mind for marriage then, so I wouldn't say yes and I wouldn't say no. A lot of people didn't like me going, now I think of it. There was more than one old biddy who said I was going the same way as my mama, who left the village when I was a baby. My auntie wouldn't hear that, of course, though she was the one who called me mad. But Bosilka, who was always sweet, she kissed me and wished me luck. And Matheus was keen for me to go, because of the brandy he smuggled. He'd been keeping it in the cellar at the big house, you see, and when the militia turned up like that without warning, he didn't have time to move it. I'd never seen him that worried before. He asked me to keep an eye open, see if anyone had been down there, and if not, I was to push something in front of the door to the storeroom, to keep it hidden until he could find a way to get inside the house himself.

Only when I got there, the militia had already found it out. The captain, Nymand Petos—God rot him!—he greeted me at the door, all smiles. I didn't know then, of course, what he was like; he was fat and he smelled of tobacco, but he seemed well-behaved. He called me "my dear." And I was hardly inside the door when he asked me if anyone I knew was storing anything there.

Well, of course I made big eyes and asked him what he meant. He smiled some more, and said no matter. Then he told me to bring a broom when I came the next day.

There were twenty men staying in the house, twenty of them and Petos. Two were corporals, Stannaert and Skutch, but it was Petos kept them all in order. And he had to: some of them were pigs, with wandering hands far worse than what you'd find at the inn. It was a real problem in the early days, when I couldn't tell them apart; later on I knew which ones to avoid.

My first problem was telling Matheus they knew about the brandy. Well, not all of them, as it turned out, just Skutch, who'd found the room, and Stannaert. And Petos, of course. I never knew how Matheus sorted it out with him. There was some kind of meeting between all of them, and then the boys were bringing the casks to the house again as if nothing had happened, only now they had a military guard. Bobik came with them sometimes. The first time I saw him there I waved, and made to run over and kiss him, but he scowled and wouldn't look at me. After that, when I knew he was coming, I went and stayed in the back kitchen with old Birgitta. He was still nice enough when he saw me in town, Bobik. It was only in the house that he wouldn't give me the time of day. Of an evening we'd meet up sometimes and he was his old sweet self. That's how I found out about the new brandy. But he made me promise not to tell anyone, and I never have until now.

Inside of a month they were dropping off more barrels than ever before. Bobik told me one night that the new stuff was coming up the river, all the way from France, he said. And Petos was running it all. He had Lukas the carter going every which way, a new load each day in a different direction. He left all the men's training to Stannaert while he went off with the cart. In the evenings they'd all get drunk, and one night I heard him bragging that he had more money than the mayor. He said he was selling the Prussians their own brandy back to them.

I remember that night because that was the first time I let Petos touch me. I wasn't meant to be there at all; I was supposed to go home when it got dark, and it was Birgitta's job to serve them their wine of an evening. But she was old. So they'd offer me an extra *grosch* to do it instead, and sometimes I did. By that time it was mostly just greedy looks and crude talk: if one of them tried to put a hand on me I'd step away sharp and give him a glare; Petos too. Only that night he got to talking of what he'd do with his money. When his tour of duty was up, he said, he was off to Praha to open an inn of his own: a properly fancy place, in the centre of town among the theatres. He'd serve only lords and ladies, he said, and he talked about the rare stuff he'd give them to drink, and the music and dancing they'd have. He could talk fine, like a gentleman—it made you believe him. And then he said he'd need a pretty girl there to pour the wine for all those gentry, and he looked at me and smiled.

So the next time he went to put his hand on my knee, I let him, and I smiled back. I asked him what it was like in Praha, and he told me. And you know, he had a nice voice, for all he was fat. I thought maybe I could come to like him. I didn't let him do anything more that night, but I drank his wine and I got home late and uncertain on my feet. And in my mind, too.

When I came to the house next day he was different with me. All "sweetheart" and "flower," and giving me little pats and prods like I was a prize horse he'd just bought and he was checking on the bargain. And smiling at me out of the corner of his mouth as if we shared a secret. He'd come in while I was doing the sweeping and stand too close, looking at me with that little smile, and say, "You wouldn't need to sweep floors in Praha."

I let him take liberties. I did. It's something I would undo if I could. He'd put his hands all over me, and his mouth too. I would take his big knobbly cock in my hand and hold on to it while he pushed and grunted, and clean up the mess afterwards. But I wouldn't let him have me, although he often tried. He said it was no more than I'd done before, which was true, though I denied it—I wouldn't talk of Bobik to him. But it wouldn't have been right: Bobik was different. Petos said he'd expect more than that from me if we were to go to Praha. I said, you take me there, and we'll see.

I don't know if I'd have gone with him. I don't even know if he truly meant to take me; maybe all the talk of Praha was just invention. First he was happy enough to have me listen to his stories and let him put his hands on me when he told them. Did I say he could speak like a gentleman, or like an actor on the stage? I used to shut my eyes and pretend I was already there. But after a while he would ask all the time for things I wouldn't give, and then he began to like my company less. He'd get angry with me for small things; he'd box my ears for not hanging up his coat the right way, and shout at me if his soup was cold, though that was Birgitta's doing and not mine. When I broke a glass once, he came at me with a strap. And when he'd paw at me he took to pinching and tweaking; biting too, when he was in the worst mood. He never touched my face. Rich though he was, he knew there might be trouble if I came home with a black eye. But some days my breasts and arms were bruised black and blue, and I could not make free with Bobik till the marks faded.

And one day, I'd gone in the kitchen to get some fruit for him, and Birgitta grabbed hold of my arm. When I shook her off, for it was sore, she had my sleeve up till she saw the marks there, and then she shook me and cried at me for all the world like my auntie would have done. She said I was not to stay here; I should leave right away and not come back. She even threatened to go to my aunt. Well, I talked her out of that. I had more than a florin saved up by then, and how would I make that much money back at the inn? And besides, I still believed that Petos might take me to Praha, even if I had to run away from him when I got there. I'd need money for that too. I told Birgitta that I would stay away from Petos, and not go alone to his room any more. I let her take him his fruit; he shouted at her but he didn't hit her. None of those men could cook.

I got to thinking. And that Sunday, when I saw Bosilka as usual after church, she could see something was wrong and she asked me straight out. She knew a bit about Petos, but I never told her he hit me, though I knew she suspected. And when I finally told her (though not all of it) she took on worse than Birgitta. "He'll never take you to Praha," she said. "You're fooling yourself." She said a man who'd treat me like that wasn't worth staying with.

Well, Bosilka was funny, like I said. She had some strange ideas. She'd ask the priest about God and the mayor about the laws, like it was important to her. But for all that, she had her head screwed on. She told me Bobik would wed me in a heartbeat, and if it was money I wanted, everyone knew that Matheus would leave him the inn one of these days. I said Bobik would never want me if he knew what I'd done with Petos, and she said he already knew it, most of it, or suspected at least. It would make no difference, she said, and maybe she was right at that.

I went back to the house. I served Petos his supper that night, and stood by while he crammed meat into his mouth till the juice ran down his chin, and dropped the bones on the floor without caring where they landed. I'd seen him do those things before, of course, but that night . . . Then he took hold of my backside, and smiled and called me his little whore. He was drunk and happy—he laughed when he said it, as though he'd made a joke. As I walked home I started to think what would happen if he did take me to the city. It would be a long journey there, just him and me together. And then when we got there I wouldn't know anyone: who knew what kind of work I'd be able to find? A florin wouldn't feed and house me forever. It might be weeks before I could get away from him, or months. I thought, *I can't stay with him that long*. And Praha suddenly felt a long way away.

The next day, when the boys came with the casks, Bobik was with them. I hadn't seen him for a week because of the bruises, but this time I didn't hide in the back kitchen. I waited till he came to the cellar steps, and when he put down the barrel to open the door, I went up to him and took his hand, and kissed him. He kissed me right back, I can tell you. I smiled at him and was going to tell him I was leaving the great house, that I'd take him if he still wanted me. But that moment Skutch trotted up with a barrel of his own, and Bobik had to drop my hand and go on downstairs. And when he came back up Skutch was still with him and he couldn't do more than throw me a smile. So I lost my chance.

Birgitta had seen the whole thing, and she was glad. She asked me, would I leave now, and I said yes. If I wanted my last week's pay I'd have to stay till Saturday. But that meant Petos again. It used to be Stannaert—he still paid Birgitta and the boys—but since the Praha business came up Petos had taken to paying me himself. He'd hold the money out of my reach and laugh, and make me give him a kiss before I could have it, things like that. I thought about it and decided it wasn't worth it; I'd rather see the back of him now. Birgitta said, "Just go, then. I'll tell him for you." But I'd got it into my head to tell Petos myself. It wasn't to pay him out, or anything. I think I just wanted it to be certain.

He was in the old billiard room, which he'd made into his office. I think your officer here took over the same one. He'd got a mouldy old armchair in front of the fire; he was sitting in it when I told him, with a glass of brandy at his side. I remember he sat very still. And then he smiled—only it wasn't quite a smile, just his mouth stretched, and he said, "Come here."

I didn't care to. I shook my head and said I'd go now. And he jumped up and ran at me. He got me by the arm and then by the neck, and started to batter me. I caught up the brandy glass and hit him with it; the glass broke and cut him, and he stepped back from me with blood on his cheek and the fire flaming up blue behind him where the brandy had gone. I said he'd better not come any closer. He might be richer than the mayor, I said, but if he harmed me then my friends and neighbours would harm him worse. And he smiled that not-smile again, the blood running down his face, and said he owned my neighbours. He owned everything in this shithole town, he said, and he'd take what was his by rights, starting with me.

I was scared. I still had the broken glass and I made to attack him with it, but he could see I was shaking. I screamed at him to leave me be, and then there was a banging on the door, and a man outside asking was everything in order? It was a private, one of the pigs with the wandering hands; I forget his name. He was stupid: he had the door open before Petos could finish ordering him to go away, and I almost got through it. But he wouldn't let me past. And then Petos shouted at him to hold me, and that he'd caught me stealing. I slashed at both of them and yelled, but they got the glass away from me, and one of them put his fat hand over my mouth. I bit him—they were both bleeding—but I couldn't get away; I couldn't.

They dragged me up the stairs and locked me in Petos's room. I remember the pig private looked startled when Petos told him where to put me, but he wasn't quite stupid enough to ask questions. They threw me in the corner, and Petos sent the private away and stood over me, his face dark red and streaked on one side where I'd cut him. I thought he was going to batter me again, but he put his hand up to his face and stepped back. He called me whore, and this time he didn't mean it as a jest. He said I'd stay there till I gave him what he wanted, till I'd beg him to take me, and he took his knife from the table and stroked it while he spoke. I don't recall all the things he said; I didn't answer. After a while he went out and turned the key behind him, and I heard him going down the passage calling for water. He took the knife with him.

As soon as he'd gone I went to the door, but it was stuck fast; I couldn't move it. I got the window open and screamed from it till I was hoarse, but no one came. Bobik was long gone by then, and Birgitta was deaf, though she'd never admit it. And then I heard him coming back, his heavy feet outside, and he was shouting what he'd do to me if I didn't shut my mouth. There was nothing I could find to hit him with, and I wasn't about to be beaten again if I could help it. I got my head and shoulders out of the window, and caught the sides of the sash to pull myself through. As he opened the door I had one foot on the sill. If I could have got a proper purchase and let myself drop, maybe I'd have managed; I think I could still have run. But he came at me with his fat hands grabbing and his face all twisted up like a demon. I started away from him, the sill broke beneath me and I fell.

From there on it's hard for me to remember things in the right time. The falling was the worst—I won't recall that for fear it takes me back there. It was my head I hit first, or else my arm. There was a crack like breaking a big bit of kindling, and then for a while I was just glad the falling had stopped. I think I was already dead when Petos reached me. He shook me up and down and I didn't feel it: I think I was mostly watching from outside by then. He was shouting, and maybe crying. I'd shut my eyes tight while I was falling and it was still hard to see.

He dragged me round the side of the house and into the cellar. The men were all elsewhere or had got out of his way, though I heard Birgitta clattering pans in the kitchen next door. He put me over his shoulder to get down the steps, and laid me out on the floor while he moved the casks out of the way and dug a grave beneath them. I got a look at myself while he did that. Oh, I looked bad. One of my eyes was swollen so badly it looked like it could never open, and my mouth all torn and bloody, and that side of my face crushed in on itself like an eggshell. I prayed Bobik wouldn't have to see me like that.

He put me in the ground and covered me up—it gave me a shudder when I saw the earth covering my face. While he was moving the casks on top of me Birgitta came to the door and asked what he was doing there. He shouted at her to be gone and shouldered her out of the way to get up the steps. But I saw her looking at the marks on his face, and wondering. I followed them up the stairs, but neither of them saw me.

He told Stannaert that I had stolen money from him and run away, knowing that Stannaert would spread it around the men. He went into his room and locked the door. But Birgitta went straight down to the cellar. She moved those casks, though they were heavy, and she found the grave. She never heard me shouting at her to leave well alone, for I feared it would give her an apoplexy if she found me. She scratched at the earth floor until she saw my foot sticking up. And then she stopped very still, and she covered my foot up again, and she prayed for a long while. She spoke to me, not looking where I was but at the grave. She said she was sorry she hadn't saved me—she should have done more—but the murdering bastard butcher would suffer for it. And she got her things from the kitchen and left without a word to anyone. I left the cellar too; I don't go back to that spot now.

So I heard what happened then by listening to other people. Matheus sent word to Petos that one of his casks was bad and a customer wanted his money back. And when Petos went down to check the consignment he found Matheus and Bobik waiting for him, and four or five others. They made him dig me up, and then they killed him. He cried, and swore he hadn't meant to murder me, but what difference did that make? I was just as dead, and my poor Bobik had seen me in that state, for all my prayers. So they beat Petos with their fists, and stabbed him through and through with their knives. And then, seeing that he was still alive, if only a little, Matheus broached one of the casks, and two of the others stopped Petos from struggling while Bobik pushed his head down into it and held him there till he drowned. It wasn't a nice way to go. But then again, neither was the falling.

They left Petos where he had left me till they could make a deeper grave for him behind the house. And they carried me upstairs, and told Stannaert and Skutch that their captain had done murder, and had deserted when it was found out. Matheus told them that they had a choice: they could leave the house and the town, them and their men. Or they could be taken up as confederates for killing me and hiding me from justice. By morning all of them had gone.

They put me in the churchyard with a fine stone over me; Matheus paid for it. I visit it sometimes when Silkie's there, or Birgitta or my aunt; they tell me the news. Bobik goes there too, for a while: after my cousin Marisha gets him he visits less often. And that's my story.

The girl gave another half-curtsy as she finished, looking sombre and, for a moment or two, actually older, as if she had lived to make use of the experience she had gained so hard. Then she smiled, and was carefree and mischievous once again.

"It was good to tell you," she said. "Magda was right. But he—the schoolmaster—he can't hear a thing, can he? You'll have to tell him again."

Drozde had to bite back a laugh at her description of Klaes. Dead or not, Agnese was a sharp observer: there *was* something schoolteacherly about the lieutenant's earnest look and his slightly stooped posture when he spoke to her, as if leaning forward to listen to a slow child. But she nodded seriously, and turned to Klaes. He had been peering intently in Agnese's direction as if he could see something there—a movement in the air; some colour or shadow.

"She's finished telling," Drozde told him. "Petos was the captain of the militia here; he found out about the smuggling and took it over, with his men's help. All that brandy was his. And he killed Agnese." She told him only the bare details of the girl's flirtation with the captain, her life in the house and her death; they weren't his concern. And she gave him no more names. "An old woman who worked in the kitchen discovered Agnese's body and told her friends. They killed Petos in revenge and persuaded his men to desert. That's the full story, Lieutenant. Does it answer your questions?"

Lieutenant Klaes found that it did. Though he was tempted to doubt his own sanity by this time, he didn't doubt the story he'd just been told. Which meant, of course, that he was accepting as fact Drozde's claim that she could talk to the dead. Indeed, he had felt their presence—had seemed to be on the brink of seeing them himself, a vast and silent audience to the dead girl's voiceless discourse. The flummery of mountebanks was now his science.

"The names," he said. "Please."

"Which names?"

"The villagers who were involved in the smuggling. If I can bring them here for Colonel August to question them, he'll have to accept that the rest of the villagers are innocent of any wrongdoing—that it was only this ring, this cabal, and that their crime was smuggling."

Drozde turned to the air, and listened to it for a goodly while. When she was done, she looked to Klaes again. "She won't give you the names. She wants to know how stupid you think she is. For every name she gives, a man will be hurt. And she's right, Klaes. You were there! You saw what they did to those men. To that *boy*! You should be ashamed even to ask!"

"That's not . . ." Klaes began, but there was no way to untangle this. He deplored the colonel's actions, but he could not simply wish him away or remove his power over these people. The only way to curb his worst excesses was to give him the truth and show him how small a thing he was pursuing.

But he could do that without the names. If the colonel were to see the barrels in the cellars, he would understand at last the reason for the villagers' secrecy and for Petos's death. He would order a full investigation, and some men would be arrested. But then it would be over.

Klaes made a gesture, waving aside his own objections even as he was making them. "It doesn't matter," he said. "My thanks to the lady, and to you. You've given me the answers I needed, and from here I can do what's needful by myself."

He was about to leave, but Drozde caught him by the arm. "What's needful?" she said. "What does that mean, Klaes? You wouldn't take any of this to August, would you? Knowing what he'll do with it?"

"I have to. It's a matter of—"

"It's a matter of your conscience against men's lives!"

"No! Of choosing the path that leads to the least bloodshed."

The gypsy shook her head, as though she were trying to explain to a madman why the sun is hot. "That's not in your power to choose," she said. "Good God! Look what he did when you told him about the fight! Did you think then that you were avoiding bloodshed?"

Klaes's rejoinder died in his throat. The truth was that he had not thought very much about consequences when he made his report—he had only done his duty as he saw it and then stepped back, as a soldier does. But see what terrible things it had led to! Drozde was right, he realised with a growing dismay. He had no power over what became of his words after they left his mouth—and he could not be at all sure that the colonel would restrict his response to the avenues a reasonable man would use.

Not realising that he was already convinced, Drozde continued to hector him. "Isn't there enough blood on your hands already? Are you so very determined to go looking for more?"

He tried to pacify her. "Madam. Drozde. Your argument is a strong one."

"Then listen to it, you idiot, and don't seek to make this sorry situation even worse!"

"I promise you, I won't."

She slowed in the middle of her tirade, the wind squarely gone from her sails. "You won't?"

"No. I'll keep your . . . your friend's confidence, and say nothing of what we found."

He bowed formally to her, and took his leave. But as he approached the door of the room it was occluded by a familiar figure. It was Sergeant Molebacher, his hateful bulk filling the space.

Klaes drew his sword at once and advanced. There seemed to be no shaking the man, but he had been provoked beyond patience and he was determined to try what the flat of a sword would do.

"Here, sir," Molebacher said. "And by'r'lady, I think he means to kill me!"

The sergeant stepped hastily aside, allowing a small troop of soldiers to walk by him into the room. August followed after, glaring at Klaes like a devil in a pantomime.

"Colonel." Klaes acknowledged his commander with a smart salute.

"Take his weapons," August said. "And bind his hands."

So bizarre and inexplicable were these words to Klaes that for a moment he thought they were addressed to him—that he was being ordered to disarm and arrest the sergeant. Only for a moment, though. Then his sword was snatched from his grasp and strong hands seized his arms. He felt his wrists dragged together and a rough cord of some kind wrapped around them.

"Colonel August!" he protested. "What . . . what does this mean? Why are you doing this?" He looked around, thinking that Drozde might intervene, but Drozde was nowhere to be seen. Apart from himself and the other soldiers, the ballroom was empty.

"What does it mean?" The colonel threw his words back at him with grim distaste. "It means you're exposed for what you are, Lieutenant. I was deceived in you, but you were the worse deceived. Imagining that Sergeant Molebacher here would join you in such an enterprise!"

"I've done nothing!" Klaes protested. But the words sounded weak even to him, mined from within by the promise he'd just made to Drozde. He *had* conspired—in the interests of peace. But surely August could not have heard that. "I don't understand you."

The colonel strode up to him, visibly shaking with indignation. "What, nothing? So you didn't find the body? Petos's body? And then hide it again?"

"I—I—yes." Klaes was too astonished to deny it. "Buried it again, yes. But not to hide it. I only wanted to wait until I had more information to present to you."

"Very good," August said, nodding in mock approval to Molebacher. The sergeant rolled his eyes. "More information, yes. Of course. And then when you found the barrels in the cellar, what was your reason for silence then? Was your investigation still not concluded?"

Klaes gasped aloud—which could only sound like an admission of guilt. It had been less than an hour before! Molebacher must have gone down the stairs as soon as they departed the kitchen, and found everything just as they'd left it. And then he must have gone directly to the colonel. But still, Klaes was uncertain what he was being accused of. "I would certainly have told you," he said. But the lieutenant was a fastidious man, and therefore hesitated before laying any further weight on top of such a blatant falsehood.

August shook his head in utter contempt. "You would have told me? But it was Molebacher you went to next—to ask for his help in selling on all that brandy, on behalf of those who left it there."

"No! Sir, I did not!"

"To sell contraband," the colonel insisted, "and then to apply the profits to—say it, Mole. It sticks in my teeth."

"Weapons, sir." Molebacher delivered the word almost negligently. He had advanced into the room and was casting his gaze into its shadowed corners. Clearly he had expected Drozde to be here, too, and was surprised by her absence.

"Weapons?" Klaes's tone hovered between horror and exasperation.

"For Narutsin." Sergeant Molebacher spat on the floor.

"For Narutsin." August looked to the soldiers who were holding Klaes, as though he were pleading a case in court and they were the jury. "I swear before God, Klaes, I never mistook you for a proper soldier, but it hurts me to find out you're a traitor."

"But this is nonsense!" Klaes yelled—and was silenced by a ringing slap from the colonel.

August's face was thrust belligerently into Klaes's own. "Even if there were no evidence," he hissed. "If it were only your word against Mole's, and no weight else on either side, a single word from him would outweigh all the simpering speeches you ever made. But we have the corpse. We have the brandy. And we have you, Klaes. We have you. For just so long as it takes to read out a charge and hang you by the neck. Take him away."

These last words to the soldiers, who half-dragged and half-carried Klaes out of the room.

Looking wildly back over his shoulder, Klaes saw Sergeant Molebacher's face—stern and solemn like the face of a preacher, but with a gleam in his eye that spoke louder than any words could have done. *Shame me in front of my men? Beat me out of my own kitchen? Keep my doxy from me? Well I've the last laugh on you.*

To all of these events, Drozde was a silent witness. She could not help it.

As soon as Molebacher stood aside and August's soldiers marched into the room, she felt a hand slip into hers. And then another, on the other side. And then more and more, laid on her arms, her shoulders, her sides and hips.

A gentle but insistent tugging from all these ghostly presences took her from her place and yet at the same time left her standing exactly where she was. A sort of curtain fell across her face, compounded of time and distance, tasting of dry dust at the back of the throat.

When Molebacher walked right in front of her and looked through her, she knew that she could not be seen. When he spat, his spittle hit the wooden tiles right at her feet.

The ghosts had saved her by drawing her a little way into their own place—which was this place, and yet was not this place at all.

She looked down at Magda, standing at her right hand, and nodded her thanks. The girl smiled and planted an immaterial kiss on her wrist, as though to reassure her in the face of this new calamity.

Then she looked to her left to thank the other ghost who was there. She expected to see Agnese, but it was not Agnese.

It was herself.

Drozde was looking into her own face.

The ghost-Drozde wore an urgent frown, and raised a finger to her pursed lips, advising silence. But Drozde could not have uttered a sound if she had tried.

In an instant, every riddle was solved and every question answered. Of course the ghosts of Pokoj knew her well. She had been here—and would be here—for all eternity.

She was going to die here and join them.

She let go of their hands and ran blindly, endlessly, through the terrible stillness.

31

Colonel August retired into his war room—the billiard room, of course, but its current function caused him to think of it as such—and took counsel. With himself alone, of course, because there was nobody besides himself whom he trusted with so momentous a problem as this.

He had kicked over an ant hill, and in the crumbling soil beneath it an abyss had opened. The people of Narutsin, who he had thought minor malefactors in need of a stern lesson, were in fact enemies of the empire on an entirely different order of magnitude. Something needed to be done, and it needed to be drastic.

Perhaps, in this, he was blinded by the intemperance of the violence already past, and sought to justify it by reference to this wider crisis only now uncovered—as though his conscience could wash itself clean of blood in a bigger bath of the stuff. And perhaps that disposed him to be more trusting than he might otherwise have been of Sergeant Molebacher's account, which if questioned closely might not have seemed safe to bear the weight he was now placing on it. Or it might have been his old devil, the borderlands, come back to fleer at him again.

For whatever reason, he felt as though the whole world was pressing on his head, and the only way he might avoid being crushed to the ground was by issuing some decisive command that would relieve the pressure all at once. But the logic of these thought processes led him to a place that daunted his spirits.

The villagers of Narutsin had conspired with Prussians, initially in a financial escapade. Smuggling. A hanging offence, but normally one would only expect to hang those who were caught red-handed with smuggled goods in their possession.

Then they had committed murder. Of a militiaman (or more than that, for what might have been the fate of the dozen men in Petos's command?). But still, this could be a matter of personal jealousies or resentments.

Then they had suborned one of his own officers.

There was a mental exercise the colonel's old commander, General Polyer, had once recommended to him. Should you find yourself in doubt as to the legitimacy of a decision you intended to make, Polyer said, you performed a substitution: if x were not x, but y, how would this seem?

August tried this now. If the village of Narutsin were not a village at all but an enemy garrison, and they had done the things that had now been uncovered—only those things, nothing else—would he feel justified in launching an attack on them?

The answer was beyond argument. Of course he would.

The way seemed clear. And yet August hesitated. He saw himself, as it were at one remove, ordering a full-scale military action against a civilian population whom he had been sent here to protect. And the yawning gap between those two points of view gave him pause.

If he accepted that the village of Narutsin was, in effect, an enemy garrison, then he had to move against it. But how would it be seen by others far removed from this place and this moment of crisis? He did not wish to do this thing on his own authority, and then to be told—magisterially and arbitrarily—that he had exceeded his remit.

Or to put it another way, he was (on the whole) content, or at least, as it might be, prepared in good conscience, to carry out a massacre if it had already been blessed by those who otherwise might hold him to account for it.

So he called for his adjutant, Bedvar, and told him to bring him a new quill, and some sand for blotting. Ink and paper he already had. As Bedvar scurried to assemble this equipment, the colonel composed in his mind the letter he would send. It would be to the general, obviously, and it would lay out all the heads and particulars of what he had uncovered here. Some elements he would simplify—for example, that he had trusted Klaes and deputed him to investigate, only to discover later that he was himself compromised. The account was easier to understand if Sergeant Molebacher had been the investigator, keeping Klaes under close observation on August's instructions and in the process uncovering the network of traitors and infiltrators at Narutsin.

Bedvar brought the quill, already cut and squared. August thanked him and sent him away to make a chicory-root infusion to be brought to him in the billiard room forthwith (he abhorred the Muslim drink, coffee, which had made such inroads into polite society in recent years). He sat down to write, the letter's structure already mostly clear in his head.

All the same, it was a tasking and aggravating business to write it. August had thought the matter through and his conscience had given him a cautious *nihil obstat*. But it seemed there was some level below his conscience that still retained some reservations. At all events he was agitated, and kept spoiling this word or that with a wrong stroke of the pen. Terse though the missive was, it cost him a great deal of effort.

Another aggravation awaited him when he was finished. He had no sealing wax, and none was to be found on a quick search of his rooms. This was hardly a message that could travel open, but neither could he traipse up and down the house looking for a stick of wax like Diogenes with his lantern.

"Here," he said, handing the letter and his seal ring to Bedvar. "Close this under my seal, Bedvar, and give it to Lieutenant Tusimov. He's a good rider, I know, and speed is of the essence."

"But . . ." the adjutant objected. "Colonel, Lieutenant Tusimov's horse—Dancer—she had to be shot. On the day of the fight, she—"

"Don't trouble me with trifles, Bedvar, for God's sake. Let him ride my Thunderer. Tell him the letter is to go to Oskander barracks. He's to put it into General Sachener's hands, or his man's hands. And he must on no account relinquish it to anyone else along the way. You understand me?"

"Yes sir." Bedvar saluted and withdrew.

But despite his incurious and essentially submissive nature, the adjutant would have been less than human if he hadn't felt the temptation to glance at the letter's contents—and the more so since the colonel hadn't expressly forbidden him to do so. He'd only said that it was important to be quick. So provided Bedvar did not slacken his pace, it seemed to him to be acceptable to unfold the sheet and let his gaze wander over the words that were written on it.

At first he took in very little of the sense. He wasn't the quickest of readers, and the colonel's hand was ornate in the extreme, the curlicues sometimes extending to mask the letters above and below them. But some phrases stood out.

engaged in treasonous

vipers in the bosom of empire

extirpate this threat with the utmost

And by degrees, these islands of meaning joined to declare themselves an archipelago. At which point, Bedvar forgot about the need for haste and stopped on the stairs to read the message in its entirety, his lower jaw detaching itself by increments from its partner until he looked like a man submitting despite inner doubts to having a tooth pulled.

In a highly discomposed frame of mind, he completed his descent. At the bottom of the stairs he chanced upon Sergeant Strumpfel polishing his boots in the hall. When asked, Strumpfel was sure he knew where he could lay his hands on a stick of red sealing wax, whole or very nearly so. But that would not do for Bedvar, who had to unburden himself of the choice gossip that had fallen so unexpectedly into his lap.

"But listen," Bedvar murmured, detaining Strumpfel with a hand on his shoulder. "Listen here, Strumpfel. It's the colonel."

"The curtain?" Strumpfel had served for many years in an artillery company, and consequently his hearing was greatly impaired.

"Colonel August," Bedvar said, raising his voice.

"Well what about him, Nicol? Has he found fault with you?"

"No, it's not that. You won't guess it, Strumpfel. He's going to attack the village. Knock it flat, he says. Because they're a nest of vipers and they've got to be extirpated."

Strumpfel raised his eyebrows. "I should have thought they were all but extirpated this morning. But then what's the letter about?"

Bedvar looked at the letter as though he'd forgotten it was in his hand. "It's for the general. General Sachener, at Oskander. Colonel August wants his permission to use the guns."

"What, even that big one? Mathilde?"

"He just says the guns. Can you imagine? Those field pieces, on wooden houses? They'll go down like a hand of cards." He laughed, but then checked himself. It would be a show, certainly, but it was an astonishing prospect to send an army, even a small one, cannons and muskets and drums and all, against a village street. "I'm not sure I see the sense of it," he finished in a minor key.

"No, but presumably Colonel August has got his reasons," Strumpfel opined. "Otherwise he wouldn't be doing it. You just do as you're told, old man. Keep your shirt tucked in and your gear all trim. You know what else happened tonight, don't you?"

And the two men moved off towards the rear of the house, Strumpfel recounting as they went the "Lay of the Downfall of Lieutenant Klaes" with suitable gestures and accompaniments.

Drozde waited until their footsteps had faded into silence before she came out from under the stairs.

"I don't like those men," Magda said, appearing from the shadows beside her. "They're stupid. And the one with the big moustache has teeth that are all black and horrible."

Drozde found no answer to this. She had sat down in the shadowy recess under the stairs to think about this matter of her death—which had solidified as she pondered it from an abstract notion to a solid thing. She was wondering whether it might be possible to continue avoiding it if she left right now and ran until she could run no more—until Pokoj was no longer even visible at her back.

In other words she was thinking, as Meister Gelbfisc had invited her to do the night before in the abbey ruins, about time and distance.

Now, in the light of what she'd just heard, she considered the same conundrum from a very different point of view. The march from Wroclaw had taken the column five days. But then they had walked at the pace of heavily laden men and even more heavily laden wagons. They had surely never gone more than fifteen miles in a day. The colonel's horse could do fifteen miles in little more than an hour on a good road.

But there were no good roads before Lüben.

Tusimov would not leave until morning. But it was conceivable that he would make the entire journey to Wroclaw and back on the same day.

What could she do in a day? How could she stop this thing from happening, and still get clear herself so as not to become the phantom that had held her hand in the darkened ballroom?

The only thing she could think of was to murder Colonel August.

32

They took Klaes to the room where the villagers had been held. It was high up and towards the back of the house, but not at the very back. It had been chosen because it faced no outside wall, and therefore had no windows.

Sergeant Molebacher, shining in the colonel's favour, presided over Klaes's incarceration. But he made a great deal, first, of inspecting the walls and floor for soundness. "This is a desperate man," he told Private Standmeier. "If he were to get loose, it would be a bad day for all of us. You watch him close, Private. Watch him close and careful."

"I will, Sarge," Standmeier promised. "He'll not get past us."

Molebacher turned to Klaes and smirked. "Then I give you goodnight, Lieutenant," he said. "And trust your lodgings are to your satisfaction, sir, you being a man of delicate breeding."

"Sergeant," Klaes said. "This will rebound on you and it will destroy you. Whatever you think you've achieved, you're a fool and your wretched lies will come to nothing."

Molebacher only laughed, though his big hands

balled into fists and his shoulders tensed. "Do you think so, sir? Well, I don't have the benefit of your education, but it seems to me as it's you that's come to nothing. Not that that was so very long a journey from where you were, so to speak. The wonder wasn't that you fell so hard, it was that you had anywhere to fall from. If you'll take my advice, sir, then rather than getting on your high horse with me, you'll look to yourself. Look to your soul, Lieutenant, and think on your mistake."

"My mistake?" Klaes's tone was mild—he wasn't troubled by the sergeant's barbs since he had come to broadly similar conclusions.

"You got in my way," Molebacher said simply. "You made an enemy of me, sir—and whatever your rank and whatever your birth, that was a reckless thing to do."

"Yes," Klaes said. "I see that. But still, here we are, and we have to make the best of it."

"Not for very long," Molebacher said. And they left him in the dark.

There was an interim time, a hiatus. Drozde felt she could not move until the moon had gone down, the last of the cooking fires had been doused, the last of the soldiers had staggered off to sleep.

She had gone back to the camp to procure a bayonet, which was an easy enough thing to find and would probably be better suited to the task at hand than a pocket knife. Then she retired to her own tent to wait out the time until she judged it safe to proceed.

She did not sleep, but she did dream.

A procession of images moved past her waking eyes as she lay in her tent, on a mattress of damp ticking. Her sister Semilie first, sitting beside her in a summer meadow with a half-finished daisy chain in her busy hands. The memory was so vivid that Drozde could hear the words the two of them said to each other. "You won't ever go away, will you, Darozh?" "No, Sem, I'll never go away." Because at five years old Semilie prattled every last word that was spoken to her back to her dada, and if dada knew what was in Drozde's heart he'd break her legs. Better to speak that easy lie, and take the chance of breaking Sem's little heart.

Her mother next. At a table, in a room without a candle, lit only by a waning fire. Working a spinning wheel while Drozde fed her flax. The old woman did no weaving any more. Arthritis had taken the strength and dexterity from her hands, which had once been so cunning they could make a zigzag pattern on a backstrap loom just by shifting her weight against the rope and forcing the shuttle back on its own base. But now spinning was all she could do. She sold the thread at market, wrapped on spindles made from branches Drozde cut and trimmed and sanded smooth. Other women wove it.

And finally the dead girl, Agnese, whose fate might so easily have been Drozde's own. Her thoughtless, animated face as she talked about her dreams of this man or that man raising her up from poverty and giving her the things she had told herself she needed. That was life, in small—her own life, or anyone's, not just Agnese's. You spent it grubbing desperately for the physical things that would prolong it. For food mainly, and then if you were lucky enough to be fed, for shelter. And all the time in between you spent dreaming of places you couldn't go and things you could never have. You used it up trying to fit yourself into the spaces that would work, instead of unfolding yourself into the space that was yours and then seeing where that took you.

The space that was hers seemed very small now, and contracting quickly. But there was time, still, to set her shoulder against the crushing weight of these events and push. She had to believe that, or else lie here and let all that was left of her life become a whispered tale in a ruined house.

When the horn sounded for the change of watch she got up, put her dress on again over her shift, slid her sturdy, calloused feet into her boots and went to kill the colonel.

Most of the men were still awake, talking in their tents before sleep, but there was no singing. Only a murmur of conversations in which the individual words were lost, blending into a tonic note of unease and querulous question.

Nobody called out to her or seemed to notice her passing, but Drozde pressed the steel of the bayonet flat against her thigh as she walked, her shoulders squared. She would look, she hoped, as though she were only holding her skirts down against the wind. The shadows would hide everything else.

The black bulk of the house rose before her, occluding half the sky. Its outline was clear: an area of solid darkness surrounded on all sides by an area where the dark was punctured by a milky scatter of stars.

A hundred feet from the front door Drozde slowed to a halt. She was looking up and to the left, at a patch of sky over the abbey ruins. Something red hung there. Brighter than most of the stars, and bigger, with a spreading tail. It did not move from its place, but looked as though it was frozen in the midst of violent, rushing progress. A shooting star that had paused for breath.

Drozde mouthed a word, naming what she saw. She had known the word before, and she knew in principle what it meant.

Comet.

There were all sorts of stories about them—mostly about how they portended some form of disaster, or spoke up about murder by hanging over the houses of the guilty. To Drozde, though she was no sceptic, the realm of stars seemed too far removed from the world they lit for any such conversation to be possible. But unless she was very much mistaken, this was an omen of disaster that could not be denied.

She picked up her skirts and ran on into the house. She must have dropped the bayonet, but she had no memory of hearing it fall. Her half-formed plans had fallen along with it.

In the ballroom, her arrival prompted a condensation of ghosts. She walked through them heedless of their edges and boundaries, until she found the one she was looking for. Ermel. The woman who had passed herself off as a soldier to save the boys she loved from being parted.

"Is it now?" she demanded, without preamble. "Is it tonight?"

The woman seemed confused. She looked at the spirits around her, as though hoping for a cue, before turning back to Drozde with a shrug of apology. "Is what?" she asked. "I'm sorry, Drozde. I don't understand."

"You said you rode over the border on the night after the night the comet came," Drozde said, gesturing impatiently. "I see a comet in the sky tonight, but is it the same one? Is tomorrow the last day before the war begins? Is that the day you came, or—or will come, or keep on coming, or however this works for you? Is it now, Ermel, or is it some other time? Tell me!"

The woman stood with her arms at her sides and her lips half parted. Her face showed a great eagerness to answer Drozde's question, but no words came. She only shook her head, to indicate that she could not help.

"Will somebody answer me!" Drozde cried. Her voice sounded indecently loud in the big, empty room; in the big, empty night.

"It's now," Magda said.

Drozde looked down at her in astonishment. She hadn't imagined that Magda understood any of this, and certainly she hadn't intended to discuss such serious matters with a child. But the solemn, sorrowing look in the girl's face gave her pause. "You know this?" she demanded. "You know it to be true?"

"Of course I do," Magda said indignantly. "This is how it always happens. I come here all the time, because of Amelie and because of you, and it's never any different. You come with the soldiers, you meet Anton, you have your big fight with fatface and then you die. And it's because of the war, so that's how I remember there's a war. Because of you dying in it."

Drozde stared, wide-eyed.

"It all happens tomorrow," Magda summed up. "The soldier who went off on the big white horse comes back on a different horse, and then it all happens."

"But what?" Drozde demanded. "What happens then? Tell me everything, Magda!"

"No." The voice that cut in was cold and stern. And although she'd never heard it—never *really* heard it, as she did then—she knew it with a terrible intimacy. She turned, although she wanted very much not to, and found herself staring into her own eyes.

"She's told you as much as she can," ghost-Drozde said. "And more than she was meant to. Go away, now, and do what you must."

"I . . ." Living Drozde floundered for words, outraged at this brusque dismissal. "I don't want you here. I don't want to look at you. I need to talk to *them*."

"But they talk mostly to me," ghost-Drozde pointed out, taking in her spectral flock with a fling of her hand. "They only know you for a handful of days; I'm with them forever. The things that you were told are the things that I was told, and I was told too much."

"But what is too much?" This was the father abbot, Ignacio. And though his tone was mild he stared at Drozde—at living Drozde—with a fixed intensity.

"Good question," Drozde's ghost acknowledged. "You know it's too much when you find you can't move from your place any more. Too much is the lantern that blinds the rabbit, so he stands in place and lets you bash his brains out. Or the candle flame the moth flies around until its wings burn."

"You've been around me too long," Ignacio said with a sigh. "You use my rhetoric now. She needed to be told the time was short."

"And now she knows," ghost-Drozde said. "So now she should bugger off and get working."

"Don't fight," Magda pleaded desperately. "Please don't fight. I can't bear it. I love you both so much. This little bit where you're alive is my favourite favourite out of everything, but it spoils it if you fight."

She looked from each of the Drozdes to the other, holding that same expression of earnest pleading. After a few strained moments, the ghost-Drozde reached out to ruffle Magda's hair—and some ruffling took place, although the palm of the woman's hand slid past and through the crown of the girl's head. "You're right," she said. "And I'm done. Unlike you, Magda, I hate this time. I only come here because it needs such delicate managing. It exhausts me, and I'm always glad when it's over."

"But when it's over, you're dead," the child mourned.

Drozde couldn't help herself. She turned and fled.

A time followed—probably not a particularly long time—when she sat in the kitchen garden beside the dry well, rocking backwards and forwards, her arms folded around her body as though she was trying to hug herself close.

Then by degrees she came back into her right mind, and knew what had to be done. Or at least she had the rough idea of it. The hammer was about to fall. August's soldiers would sweep over Narutsin, would level it to the ground. And the Prussians were coming too. From what Ermel had said, nothing would stand against them.

How to keep the village safe, when the whole world was bent to destroy it? The magician in Magda's story had hidden something that was too big to hide simply by making his audience look the wrong way.

And all the other stories she'd been told . . . was there a single one of them that hadn't been about lies and tricks and treacheries? Arinak tricking the demon. Gelbfisc tricking Father Ignacio. Thea tricking Eckert. Ermel tricking the recruiting sergeant. Petra Veliky tricking her way into the bed of the man she meant to kill.

To steal the moon was a rare thing if you could do it. To put it back in place again afterwards rarer still. But really, when you put on a performance, people mostly saw what you told them to see.

At last, when she had as much of it in her mind as her mind would hold, she rose up and went, out of the house and out of the gates. The roads were not safe at night, any fool knew that, but at least there were roads and she knew the direction. By starlight she walked the three miles to Narutsin, shuffling her feet like a baby's feet to keep from falling.

Before dawn, even, she heard the hoofbeats behind her. She stepped off the path into the dark of the trees and watched Lieutenant Tusimov ride by. Only after he was gone did it occur to her that she might have set a trap for him on the road. Tripped him and broken his neck, and hidden the body in the trees. But the colonel's horse would have wandered back to Pokoj, unless she killed that too, and another messenger would have been sent.

And it would not have served in any case. The war was about to break, the way a storm breaks. Tusimov's death couldn't hold off that greater calamity, or turn it from its course.

The three miles seemed more like thirty, but as the sun rose above the trees she came into the main street.

She waited there while the village woke. A man came out of his door into the street, saw her and went back inside. His wife came next, two children peering from behind her skirts. Then the door was closed again. Elsewhere curtains twitched. Shutters parted by a hair's breadth and then closed again as though they were breathing.

It was a woman who came out to her, at last. A big woman, her fists swinging at her sides. Her face was like a piece of scraped hide and her shawl shifted as she strode like the sail of a yawl in a high wind. She stopped only when her face was right up against Drozde's face, their eyes implacably locked.

"This is no place for you, bitch," the woman said, in a voice of flint.

"I came to talk to—" Drozde began.

The woman swung her fist and Drozde went down. It was a solid punch, delivered to the side of her head. Lights danced behind her eyes, and insects whined in her ears.

Drozde could fight like a man when she had to. Had indeed fought against men, hand to hand, when no better options were available. What she had never done, before now, was to submit passively to a beating. Her instinct, when her head stopped ringing, was to get back up on her feet, thresh this hulking harridan back into her own front parlour and then hitch up her skirts and piss on her. But she collected herself slowly, carefully, and stood again. Her attacker was no longer alone. Others were coming in a slow trickle from the houses on both sides, lining up beside her.

"I came—"

The second punch was delivered left-handed, so it didn't hurt so much. It still knocked Drozde to the ground, but this time she was quicker to rise again.

"I need to talk to the mayor," she said, her voice slurred because her lower lip was split and already starting to swell.

The woman flexed her right hand, which was presumably still hurting from the first punch. But the next blow came from beside Drozde, and she didn't see who delivered it.

That one really hurt.

Drozde was able to sit up after a moment or two, but not at first to stand. While she was still trying, the small crowd that had been forming around her became a larger one. If they all took it into their heads to join in, she probably wouldn't get out of this alive. But now there was a flurry from off to one side. The ranks of the crowd parted for a moment. Then hands were under her arms, lifting her. The woman who had hit her first had her right hand raised again, ready to take another turn, but she lowered it uncertainly.

"This must stop," Dame Weichorek said. Bosilka Stefanu said nothing, but the two women stood to either side of Drozde like a military escort, defying the crowd.

"She's a whore," the raw-faced woman said. "A soldier's bedroll. I wouldn't spit on 'un!" Although having delivered that verdict, she did spit, into the dirt at Drozde's feet.

"When my son was taken down bloody off that engine," Dame Weichorek said, "it was whores who tended him and washed his wounds. This whore included. You will not touch her again, Denina Luce. Not unless you want to fight with me, too."

"And with me," Bosilka said.

"You!" The woman sneered. "You're not but a girl. A smack would blow you away!"

Bosilka held up her hand. She held a chisel with a wicked, narrow blade. "You'd have to land the smack, though," she pointed out mildly.

"There'll be no smacking, and no carving," Meister Weichorek said. He arrived in the middle of the throng, red in the face and huffing, still trying to tie up the string at the neck of his shirt. "Are we animals? Are we turned into animals? Stand away, and give her some room."

"We should send a message to those bastards," a man said, from the foremost row. "Send her back to them all cut, like a—"

Weichorek whipped his head round and stared into the man's face, unblinking. Though he said nothing, his face was the face of a man whose next word, whose next action, could be anything. The crowd backed off a pace, and with averted gaze or hands clasped in front of them as though they were standing in church, variously signified their acceptance of the burgomaster's authority.

Weichorek turned to Drozde. He was trembling with the effort of self-control. "I'm sorry, madam," he said, "that you were subjected to this. It shames us all. What can I—what can any of us—do for you?"

Drozde wiped her bloody mouth. "You can listen to me, Meister Burgomaster, if you don't mind. I've got something to tell you that's very important. Important to all of you."

They walked to the burgomaster's house, with the crowd first parting for them and then drifting along behind them. Dame Weichorek shut the door on them decisively, and then asked Bosilka to make a tisane while she brought cloths and cold water to bathe Drozde's swollen face. Meister Weichorek himself stood solemnly by while these things were done. And once Bosilka had returned, Drozde told all three of them what she had to tell. It wasn't easy, with her cut lip swollen and stinging and the taste of her own blood in her mouth, but she slogged on to the end.

They were by turns terrified and astonished. Meister Weichorek's first question was how Drozde could know about the Prussians' attack. "You said you overheard what your colonel was planning, and that I can understand. But you never said about the other part. Presumably you weren't able to eavesdrop on a Prussian cavalry column?"

"Do you believe in witches?" Drozde asked baldly. She saw no use in walking around this problem.

Dame Weichorek did, emphatically. Her great-aunt had been one, she said, and had been able to heal people's ailments with a laying-on of hands. "I wish she were here now," Bosilka observed glumly, unable to take her eyes off Drozde's damaged face.

"Well, then," Drozde said. "I'm a witch too, and my skill isn't healing but knowing. Now I know this, and I know something's got to be done about it. The colonel's only waiting to hear word from Wroclaw, and then he means to come here and make of Narutsin a great pile of kindling and broken stone. Now, to the Prussians, saving your presence, Narutsin is nothing. But it's the enemy's nothing, the archduchess's nothing, and they won't be chary of you. We must avert these harms or lessen them, and I know a way to do it."

She explained her plan. The two women and the one man stared at her as if she was insane.

But then Bosilka laughed and clapped her hands.

"Oh, if only it might work!" she cried. "If something so wonderful and silly and . . . and *clever* could carry!"

"But it's a terrible risk," Weichorek muttered, scratching his chin. "If we packed up our things now and left the village, we might avoid all this and let them kill each other."

"Aye, but old women and children don't march as fast as soldiers," Bosilka pointed out.

"And then there's Jakusch!" Dame Weichorek exclaimed. "And Martek. And Piek. And Jan. They can't even stand after that whipping."

"Mayhap we could hide them somewhere," the burgomaster said, but he said it without conviction.

"And then to leave our livelihoods behind, Berthold! Everything we own. Everything we know. What kind of life would we have, if we ran away?"

"So we stand." Weichorek nodded. "All right. And then what?"

"Then the world moves around you," Drozde said, "and you watch as your enemies trip and go sprawling."

They talked on well into the morning. There were many more questions, and much dissension and debate, but by the time Drozde rose to leave they had filled in most of the vexing details that would— that might—bring Drozde's grand design to fruition. Banks of cloud were rolling in from the west as she left the Weichoreks' house, their dark bulk covering the sun. When she was halfway across the yard, she heard someone calling her name and turned to see Bosilka running towards her. She held something out to Drozde in both hands, like a child.

"My father found it when he was going through his things," Bosilka said. There was a tremor in her voice, but she gazed at Drozde levelly. "I think—it's yours, surely. Meant for you, I mean. Meant for you to have."

It was the puppet-Drozde. Her wooden limbs slack and dangling, she smiled up from Bosilka's palms. Anton had seen something in that smile, Drozde thought, and it had been his ruin. It occurred to her with sudden and overwhelming force that even if her plan worked, and everyone in Narutsin was saved, he would still be dead, and her smile the cause of it. She knew, really, that that was nonsense.

Molebacher had killed Hanslo, not her. But for the barest moment, his death seemed to blot out everything that she had ever done, and all the things she had still to do.

She accepted the puppet from Bosilka with a nod of thanks, not trusting herself to speak. And she turned her thoughts back to the living, because the dead were beyond her help.

33

Strangely, though he was helpless and awaiting execution, the time did not hang so heavy on Klaes's hands as it had when he was waiting in Meister Weichorek's closet. In some ways, indeed, he felt that he had come to the *end* of time. The unrelieved darkness in the windowless room cut him adrift from the cycle of night and day so that he floated almost like a child *in utero*, and the hopelessness of his position gave him a curious kind of peace. With nothing to be done, there was nothing that could touch him. He was only sorry that he had done more harm than good here, and that the determination to put things right had come at the very moment when the ability to do anything, for good or ill, was taken from him.

He found himself recalling a conversation he'd had with his father not long before he left for the military school in Villach. The unbending old man had shaken his hand—God forbid they should ever share anything so warm as an embrace—but then had leaned in close to stare at him with an altogether unexpected intensity. "I will tell you, Wolfgang, the secret to success in the army."

But you were never there, Klaes had thought but entirely failed to say. "The secret?" he had said instead, noncommittally.

"It is the same as in all other endeavours. Do what you are told to do, but make sure always that what you have been told to do is known. Deference to authority shields you, but authority will always try to shield itself by sending its own guilt down the line to those who can't refuse it. You must ensure that you are never in a position where another man's blame becomes attached to you."

And Klaes had thanked the old man gravely, while privately thinking that he would rather choose a responsible and morally upright superior than mould himself to the foibles of a corrupt one. Since he had no knowledge of hierarchical systems, he had naively assumed that this choice would lie within his power.

But here he was at length, the recipient of guilt that had come not down the line but up. It was true, of course, that Sergeant Molebacher could hardly have done what he had without the complaisance of the colonel, but in any event Klaes blamed himself far more than either of them for the situation in which he now languished. His father had been right on the substantive point. Klaes had trusted his fortunes to a set of formal and defined duties and relationships, and hidden his own conscience in the heel of his boot like a gold dollar too precious to be taken out except in the direst emergency.

Now that emergency had arrived, and when he tipped out his boot he had found it empty. He had been robbed in his sleep. Nothing remained to him but the clothes he stood up in and the reputation of a traitor.

Contemplating this, he sat with his back to the wall in the bare room and stared at the bare wall opposite, unaware of the passage of the hours or of the passage of thoughts across the cloudless sky of his numbed mind.

It was Private Toltz who delivered him back into time. The door was unlocked from outside and thrown open, and a man stepped in holding a trencher. Blinking against the light, Klaes was able to make out the private's outline and infer the rest. "Breakfast, Lieutenant," Toltz said, with an approximation of good cheer. It must be morning then.

"Thank you, Toltz," Klaes said as the trencher was set down before him. It bore a heel of bread, a slender slice of cheese and a pear. No water, though. "Could I be given something to drink?"

Toltz gave his forehead a ringing slap. "Empty!" he exclaimed. "Sorry, sir. I wasn't thinking. I'll get Schneider to bring you a pottle of beer and one of water, once I go back down."

A soldier on duty at the door—one of Tusimov's, still sporting bruises from the fight in the village—looked on with wary truculence, but he didn't stop Toltz from kneeling to transfer the food from the trencher into Klaes's open hands. "And is there anything else you'll be needing, sir?" he whispered. "I think the colonel's looking to hang you and I don't like it much. There's not many like it, come to that."

Klaes was almost too astonished at this show of support to be grateful. "Thank you, Toltz," he said. "I'm well enough, in truth. The beer will be very welcome. But . . . you could do me one favour, though it's a great deal to ask."

"What's that, sir?"

"You could tell the men that I didn't do what I'm accused of. I found the barrels, but I didn't try to sell them. I would have told the colonel, only Sergeant Molebacher told him first."

"Most of the men know Molebacher and his ways, sir, so that won't come as a surprise. But I'll tell them. I promise it."

"And tell them the villagers are innocent of any conspiracy," Klaes murmured urgently. "They were smuggling, that's all. They have no thought to aid the Prussians."

But this was a step too far for Toltz, who looked doubtful and perturbed. Klaes commanded a certain affection from the men of his command, he knew, but it was not unmixed with contempt. Certainly he was not respected for his judgement. "I don't see as that can be true, sir," the private protested. "They're all saying as how there were weapons down in that cellar, too—laid in against a bad day, as it were. And what else would farmers need muskets and rifles for? It's not for killing crows."

"There were no muskets or rifles."

"Well, but the colonel's said we've got to go up against them. He's not going to send us up against nothing, is he? That doesn't make any sense."

"The colonel is . . . he is mistaken. Or else he's deceived."

"That's enough whispering," the guard said from the doorway. "The lieutenant's fed. Off with you now."

"He still needs a drink," Toltz said, but he stood and backed away from Klaes, clearly none too eager to share any further confidences.

"He can drink my piss!"

"Whip it out then," Toltz said equably. "He's thirsty now."

The guard opened his mouth to issue a rejoinder, but when one didn't come he shut it again.

"Thought not," Toltz said. "Too shy to let the other lads see what you've got, eh? Sorry, sir. Looks like it will have to be water."

He walked out and the guard slammed the door to. Klaes could hear him flinging a stream of belated invective at Toltz as the private descended the stairs again.

Klaes's thoughts and emotions were now in the greatest turmoil. It seemed impossible that Colonel August would contemplate what Toltz was suggesting—an actual attack on Narutsin, as though the village represented a military objective in its own right. But he had sounded so certain.

And Schneider, when he came, was no less so. A messenger had been sent to the general at the barracks outside Wroclaw. The messenger was Tusimov himself, underlining the urgency of the message. Colonel August was only awaiting permission before the politically sensitive move of ordering his men to fire on a civilian population. Assuming that permission was given, and there was no reason to doubt that it would be, the villagers of Narutsin would be treated as hostile forces.

All Hell was going to be unleashed on them, in supposed retaliation for the slaughter of Captain Petos and his garrison. That imaginary massacre justified anything and everything.

Klaes's earlier resignation vanished. A great deal of Klaes, already loosened by recent events, vanished with it. He felt exactly as Molebacher had described him a few hours earlier—as though he had been erased, reduced to an absence—and now was faced with the choice either of rebuilding himself or of surrendering to death.

He chose to build—and found that there was some compensation, at least, for the loss of his freedom, his commission, his reputation and his dignity. He had no obligations now, to any man. He could, and would, follow his conscience wherever it led him. Something had to be done to stop this madness in its tracks. So he had to escape, and then to take decisive action.

Unfortunately, the first half of this proposition was fraught with difficulty. There were two men at the door, and they were armed. Perhaps it would be possible to trick them into entering the room and then seize the key and lock them in. If he were to feign illness . . . But nobody would fall for a ruse so trite and transparent.

He could set fire to the room. That would serve two purposes, obliging the guards to come in and extinguish the blaze and at the same time filling the room with smoke so that Klaes's planned ambush would be the less likely to be seen and countered. But unless the men responded quickly, he would burn alive or be overcome by the smoke. And they might just as easily run away as attempt to tackle the blaze themselves. It was too uncertain a prospect. And in any case, he discovered as he searched his pockets that his tinderbox had been taken away from him along with his sword.

If only there were a window for him to lower himself from. But there was no window, and of course no other door. He made a hundred circuits of the walls, his fingers trailing against the clammy plaster, but apart from the locked door through which he had entered it was unbroken.

When his thoughts had chased themselves around in circles for a very long time, he came back at last to his first, reckless plan. He would have to induce the guards to unlock the door, and then when it was open try his chances.

He hammered on the panels and called out, several times. He explained through the thickness of the door that he was faint and nauseous and needed physic. When that failed to elicit a response, he resorted to a great many variations on "Hey!" and "Hoy!" Nothing but silence answered him. He did not even know for sure that the guards were still there. Perhaps they had been stood down and had taken the key with them.

Klaes slumped at the base of the wall again and at length he fell into a fitful slumber.

In his dreams, someone called his name repeatedly. Sometimes the tone was accusing—an indictment that he couldn't answer. Then again it was a plea, the desperate cry of someone lost and helpless begging for his aid. Back and forth it went, and Klaes moaned at each repetition as at a blow.

Until he woke.

"Finally!" Drozde exclaimed. He looked around, dazed, and couldn't see her. The room was dark, of course. And yet it was not so dark as before. The air was suffused with a directionless golden glow, faint but pervasive. With the confusion of sleep still on him, Klaes wondered if perhaps the glow was Drozde. If the gypsy woman had died, and her soul had somehow . . .

"Up here, you idiot!"

Klaes tilted his head back and stared. Directly above him, let into the ceiling of the room, there was a trapdoor. It had been opened from above and now hung down, low enough so that if he stood he might touch it with his outstretched hand.

Drozde's head and shoulders were framed in the gap. She was holding a candle, the source of the seemingly magical radiance, and its light limned her face like a sketch in chalk and charcoal.

"I'm at something of a disadvantage," Klaes told her dryly. "I'd like to invite you in, but I'm not sure how you'd get out again." He didn't want her to know that he had thought her a supernatural being. It was too ridiculous, and he was sure he cut a ridiculous enough figure already.

"Are you mad?" Drozde hissed. "I'm not coming down there. I might let you up, though, if you promise to help me."

"To help you with what, exactly?" Klaes got to his feet so that he could speak more softly. If there were still guards posted outside, he didn't want his voice to reach their ears.

"Something terrible is about to happen," Drozde said. "I want to get people out of the way of it."

"You mean the colonel attacking the village? It's true then?"

"That's only a part of it. There's more."

"Tell me."

"Later. Are you going to help?"

There were any number of grounds on which Klaes might have demurred—the fact that this woman was dictating terms to him; the fact that she was proposing he should mutiny against his commanding officer; the fact that if three hundred men with guns and limbers took it upon themselves to wipe out a few farmers and burn their houses down, there wasn't a great deal he and she could do to stop them. But he didn't hesitate.

"Yes."

"And you promise to do as you're told, and not ask stupid questions that I don't have time to answer?"

"That's insultingly phrased, but yes."

"And what about your men, Klaes? Will they do what you tell them to do?"

"Some of them, I hope. Not all. And not if I ask them to mutiny. There's nothing I could say that would induce them to betray their company and their country."

"No. But there might be something I can say, if you bring them to where I can speak to them."

"I doubt it," Klaes said. "And it won't be easy for me right now to bring anybody anywhere. But if you have a plan I'll hear you out."

"You'll hear me out?" Drozde's echo of his tone was mocking.

"Yes."

"That's good of you. Hold out your hands."

"What?"

"Your hands. Hold them out in front of you, as though you're rocking a baby."

Klaes did as he was told. A dark, moving mass dropped into his arms. He almost cried out before he realised that it was a coil of rope.

"Try not to make too much noise," Drozde told him. "And when you get up here, put your feet on the beams. In between is just lath and plaster. You'll go right through and we'll have to start all over again."

34

The vast roof space of Pokoj was like the upper level of a barn—but a barn at the end of March when the last bolts of hay have been fed to the starveling cattle below and the emptiness foretells either spring or ruin. Klaes wondered as he shuffled along behind Drozde which of the two things was presaged here.

He also began to consider with increasing seriousness Drozde's claim to possess some sense or faculty lacking in the common run of humanity. In the near-dark of the roof space, where the candle cast more shadow than light, she walked with as much brisk confidence as if she were striding through a sunlit meadow.

She took him all the way to the north end of the house. At first, seeing a bright light up ahead of them, Klaes thought that someone—perhaps Drozde herself—had lit a lantern there. He realised when he was closer that this was not the case. There was no roof at all to this end of the mansion: it had collapsed long before, leaving the house below open to the elements.

It was the light of the moon he saw. The realisation brought Klaes to a dead halt.

"Night has fallen," he said. "A whole day has passed. A day, Drozde! Are we not—"

"Tusimov's not back yet," Drozde muttered, gesturing with down-thrust hands to tell him to speak more softly. "And no orders have been given to the men. I know that because they're all still here. But time runs hard against us, yes, and though I've not been idle there's a lot still to do. Too much, unless you help."

"I've said I will."

"You and your company."

"And that I can't promise."

She pointed to another trap, which must be the one through which she'd climbed up. There was no rope here. She indicated in dumb show that he should sit at the edge of the trap and slide himself down. He did so very slowly, fearful both of breaking his leg in falling and of making enough noise to bring the sentries down on the two of them.

But there was a solid surface not far below him. Klaes was able to lower himself onto it, duck down so that his head was clear of the trap, and then take stock of his surroundings. Drozde had stood a chair on top of a table, and though it creaked and moved under his weight it did not collapse. He descended to the floor, where the gypsy woman joined him.

He searched for some form of words to thank her for her rescue. It was no easy thing, since what she had helped him to do was—in effect—to desert, to void his oath to army, country and empire, and place himself outside their collective aegis. Though he had already come to that decision, he had not come to the reality of it until now, and it tied his mind and tongue into a knot. But Drozde spoke first, saving him from his stammering attempts to say what could hardly be said.

"I want you to collect your men somewhere away from the house," she told him. "I only need a handful for what has to be done, but any who stay here are likely to die, so bring them all. Let them all make their choice."

"What do you mean?" Klaes demanded. "How will they die?"

"You'll find out when they do." Drozde's tone was curt, her expression one of furious thought. "The ruins—where the abbey was. It's easy to get to, but far enough from Pokoj that they won't be seen. Bring them, Klaes."

But he needed to know why. He had wanted to help the villagers, and now found himself enmeshed in a bigger plan whose edges he couldn't see. "What should threaten the company?" he demanded. "What do you know, Drozde, and how does it bear on the colonel's plans? Tell me, or I'll not assist you."

Drozde thrust her face up close to his. "Yes," she said, her voice low and fierce. "You will. Or else you'll have all their deaths on your conscience, Lieutenant, and your conscience doesn't seem like it could take the strain. Do as you're bloody well told. But do it carefully. I want only men who'll take orders from you."

"That will depend on the orders," Klaes protested, but he felt the initiative slipping away from him. The truth was that he had no idea how to forestall August's monstrous plan on his own. He had been planning—insofar as he had planned anything—to run or ride into Narutsin and raise the alarm. But what good would that do? The villagers would be more likely to give him a public hanging than an audience. And if they listened, and if they believed, what could they do? It was not to be imagined that they would consent to flee en masse from their homes and their livelihoods, or that they would get more than a league or two if they did.

Drozde was looking at him with exasperated impatience, as though she expected him to say more but had no high hopes of its usefulness. "I'll need to tell them *something*," Klaes pointed out, more humbly. "To make them come, despite what they've been told about me and about the villagers."

"Don't mention the villagers. Don't say a word about Narutsin."

"But then . . ."

"Tell them it's a puppet show. A performance."

Klaes gave a ragged laugh. Despair and wonder filled him. "A puppet show! They're meant to absent themselves from their posts and their commanders to see you go through your usual antics!"

"Tell them that it's free, and that it will be the best one ever. Tell them . . ." She hesitated, her mouth working as she tried out the words. "Tell them the colonel doesn't want them to see it. That it's been forbidden."

"What? Why would I tell them that? Then they certainly won't come!"

"I know my audience, Klaes. Tell them. And for good measure, tell them there'll be brandy to drink."

Klaes blinked, taken aback. "Will there?"

"There will if you bring it. I want them reckless and defiant, prepared to take their lives in their hands, because that's what I'll be asking them to do."

"And you'd fuddle them with drink to make them—"

"To save them. And everyone. This is going to be a night of blood in any case, but if some are washed away in it that we could have saved, then may the devil fuck the both of us."

"You've a foul tongue, woman," Klaes remonstrated, pained as always by the coarseness of Drozde's spirit. And yet his own scruples had often amounted to no more than straining at gnats while gorging on camels. "I'll do it," he said quickly, before she could answer him. "That is, I'll do what I can. I've no idea how many will follow me, but those who will come I'll bring."

Drozde nodded tersely. "In half an hour," she said. "In the ruins. I need to collect my puppets and my theatre and make ready."

"I'll probably need longer than that," Klaes said.

"How long, then?"

"An hour? The men will take some persuading, I'd imagine."

"All right. But no longer than that. Everything has to be finished long before morning."

She turned from him and hurried away. Left alone, Klaes welcomed for a moment or two the mantle of silence and stillness that the house laid on him as he stood there. There was so much to do, and the outcomes were so uncertain, there was a comfort to be had in being lost in the penumbrous maze of the great house.

But he was not truly lost. Following the same route that Drozde had taken he found the stairs easily enough and descended back into the world.

It was safe to assume that in this atmosphere of intrigue and excitement there would be sentries on the doors of the house, so he climbed out through a ground floor window. It was easy enough after that to head for the encampment, though he skirted around the tents at a distance for some time before he heard a voice he recognised and homed in on that.

It was Gulyas, of his own command. The brawny Hungarian was sitting with two or three others close to the limits of the tent village, whittling with a pocket knife at the boiled bone of a sheep or goat. He made these strange trophies into pipes, carved with intricate scrimshaw designs, and sold them to unwary locals with stories about how he'd found them in the hills of Norway while he was on a wholly fictitious campaign there. The few coppers he made from these fraudulent transactions scarcely offset the long hours he put into the work. It seemed to Klaes that Gulyas regarded the successful lie as a part of the reward.

He was now faced with the problem of how to attract Gulyas's attention. He would have preferred just to wait until the man walked off into the dark to relieve himself, but there was no time for that. Crouched down in the weeds and long grass near the curving wall that bounded the estate, he picked up a pine cone and threw it so that it landed close to Gulyas's feet.

The big man stared at it, puzzled, as though its arrival was a profound mystery. Only after a long interval did he turn to look off into the dark. Klaes waved and beckoned to him, but he wasn't at all certain that he was visible.

Gulyas looked at the other men nearby, but they were busy warming themselves by the fire and none of them had seen the pine cone land. Then he looked back at Klaes, and Klaes gestured even more frantically.

Gulyas stood, muttered something that Klaes couldn't hear, and walked away from the tents towards him. He stopped at ten paces' distance, fists raised before him.

"Who's there?" he demanded. "Is that you, Lidmila?"

"No," Klaes said. "It's Lieutenant Klaes."

Gulyas uttered an oath and came a few steps closer. "Lieutenant?" he blurted. "But . . . they locked you away. For treason, Mole said. Helping the enemy."

"Do you think I'm a traitor, Gulyas?"

There was a pause while the big man thought—something which always seemed to require more of a run-up for him than for most people. "No," he said. "I don't."

"Thank you!" Klaes exclaimed fervently. "Thank you, Gulyas!"

"I mean, well—your pardon, Lieutenant, but some of the men call you the little schoolmarm. It's hard to imagine you breaking a rule. You're almost the last man in the world I'd think that of!"

Klaes thanked Gulyas again, with feelings more mixed but still with gratitude predominating. Gulyas asked about the guns and barrels that had been found in the cellars of the house, and Klaes said he'd explain very soon how all of that had come to pass. But first he wanted Gulyas to spread the word about Drozde's show—a most special and unique performance, without the colonel's sanction or that of Tusimov, Pabst and Dietmar and therefore to be restricted to the soldiers in Klaes's own command.

"Tonight, in the ruins," he said, pointing. "Now, in fact. Go tell them, Gulyas. It will be the most outrageous and scandalous thing that Drozde has ever portrayed. Songs and stories that would have the officers and their wives in an uproar. And brandy to drink, and no money to pay. All free. You'll never forgive yourself if you miss this."

Gulyas seemed both enthusiastic and confused. It sounded like a good thing, but now? As late as it was, with the sun already set and most men settled down for the night? Private Melin had promised to bring over a jug of cider and one of—

"Now! Yes! You can sit and drink any night, Gulyas, but this—this will only come once!"

It wasn't easy, but finally by dint of much repetition and elaboration, Klaes was able to communicate some sense of excitement and urgency to the stolid private. Gulyas lumbered away at last to tell his comrades about the planned entertainment.

Klaes pondered the question of the brandy, but only briefly. It was clear there was no way he could lead a raid on the cellar, even if Sergeant Molebacher had been so foolish as to leave it unguarded. Drozde would have to do the best she could without that particular stage property.

After leaving Klaes, Drozde went directly to the main staircase of the house. She snuffed her candle before descending, fearful that a sentry might see its light from a distance and come to investigate. She took off her boots, too, to make less noise, but carried them with her in her hand. If she once put them down in the lightless maze of Pokoj it would be an epic endeavour to find them again.

She walked softly through the empty rooms to the heart of Molebacher's empire, her heart in her mouth as she approached the open door of the kitchen. No lights were lit in the room beyond the doorway, despite the darkness outside, but that meant nothing. The embers of a cooking fire lit earlier in the day in the big hearth still glowed a dull red like rust: ample light for an ambush.

Despite the sense of urgency that plucked at her mind, Drozde waited on the threshold for what seemed like an age. No sound came to her ears, but she knew how quiet the sergeant could be in his dangerous moods, and she placed no trust in the silence. Only when her eyes adjusted to the dim radiance and confirmed that the room was empty did she finally step over the threshold, and even then she took the time to look behind the door and in every corner.

She closed and bolted the kitchen door, then lit her candle again by the fire. There was no help for it: she had no tinderbox with her, and she couldn't do what she needed to do—finding and choosing her puppets and assembling the component parts of her theatre—in the dark.

Boots in one hand, candle in the other, she crossed to the cellar stairs on the opposite side of the room and listened again. Nothing stirred or breathed in the blackness of the stairwell. At her left elbow, the sergeant's stool, on which he had waited so patiently until Klaes came to deliver her, stood empty.

She tiptoed down the stairs, her guts twisting like snakes. Nothing frighted Drozde by day, but she found the thought of walking into a trap in the dark, underground, intensely uncongenial. She waited again at the foot of the stairs, straining her ears to hear a sound in the room beyond.

But she had no choice, in the end. She needed her puppets and her theatre, and she needed all the time she had. Finally she stepped inside, almost tripping on something heavy and angular lying on the floor. The room looked very different now from how she had left it. The cupboard she'd used as a barricade had been toppled and broken, lying almost in two vertical halves on the floor. Someone had thrown her trunk into a corner and that had taken damage too, its side staved in and its lid hanging askew. Some bolts of fabric that she used to decorate the front of the theatre had spilled onto the floor, red and orange and yellow like a nursery frieze of a bonfire. The further door that she and Klaes had opened had been closed again, and the loose timber piled up in front of it. It could still be opened, presumably, but it would take a deal of time and make a deal of noise.

Drozde closed the door behind her as quietly as she could. She paused again momentarily. Nothing seemed to be moving in the house, either close at hand or far away. She hoped fervently that Klaes had not miscarried. She hoped that she could evade or hold off her impending death long enough to finish this.

She hauled her trunk back into the centre of the room, knelt before it and rummaged through its contents. Normally she handled her puppets with obsessive care, both because she loved them and because their upkeep was essential to her livelihood, but now she was reckless, taking out puppets and props and drapes by double handfuls. Those she needed went into one pile, the rest into another. Then when she was done she heaped everything she'd chosen into a blanket and tied its ends to make a bundle.

She put her boots back on at this point, since the candle and the bundle would fill her two hands.

Back up the stairs she went, placing each foot with care to keep from raising echoes. And across the kitchen, past the remnants of the fire, skirting on her left the beached-whale bulk of Molebacher's butcher's block.

Which unfolded itself, as if its dead wood were rebelling against its hard usage, and reared before her, higher than her head.

Sergeant Molebacher had been kneeling behind the block, waiting for her to come. The dull light from the fire turned him into a creature of red clay like the golem the Jews of Praha made. He flexed his bare arms, then folded them across his chest.

"Sit down," he told her.

Drozde swallowed hard, her mouth suddenly dry. Was this the time, she wondered, and was this the way of it? The way she was to die? Strangled by Molebacher because he felt his exclusive right to her body merited such a vigorous defence? The absurdity made her despair, but it also made her angry. She sorted the anger from the wretchedness and dread like a gleaner sorting grain from chaff.

"I don't have time to talk to you now, Molebacher," she said. "I'll come back later, if you like. If you think there's unfinished business between us. But I have things I must do first."

"Unfinished business?" the sergeant mouthed the words as though their taste disgusted him. "Well I do think that, as it happens. But what's between us is more than business, it seems to me, and I'm of a mind to settle it now."

Drozde took a step back from him. She was thinking about how far it was to the door, and whether she could win that race from a standing start. She was almost sure she could, but she'd have to get the bolt undone and the sergeant wouldn't be more than a yard or two behind her.

"I was going to burn your little dolls," Molebacher went on, "but

I could see that wouldn't be enough to put you in your place. So everything's as you left it, more or less. I haven't harmed a thing." He grinned down at her, daring her to contradict him.

"Except for Hanslo," Drozde finished. She knew it was dangerous to name him, but she couldn't forbear.

Molebacher nodded slowly. "Yes. And I'll do the same again, to anyone else you take it into your head to fuck. Do you understand, Drozde?"

Drozde realised with a sudden shock that he still thought that she was his, that the memory of Hanslo's death would wash from her mind as the rancid tallow had from her skin, leaving her as ready for him as she had been before. The murder had been no more to him than a just reproof, like depriving a child of its poppet when it screamed and howled. She realised, too, how easy it would be to let him think that he was right. She could lie to him, as she had lied so many times before.

"I do understand," she said, bowing her head as though in contrition. "I can see that I'm much to blame, Molebacher."

"Good." Molebacher grunted. "That's—"

"I should have gutted you in your sleep last summer in barracks," she went on, meeting his gaze again. "I could have spared myself and the world your filthy weight and kept a good man alive."

With a roar like a wounded bull, Sergeant Molebacher swung one huge fist in a punch that would have taken Drozde's head from her shoulders. But on the word "weight" she'd turned and run, heading for the cellar steps. She felt the wind of the blow, but nothing more.

Molebacher had no intention of letting her reach the stairs. Forgetting in the heat of the moment that they led nowhere, he launched himself headlong after her.

Drozde covered half the distance, and a little more. She knew she wasn't going to cover it all. With the open doorway looming ahead of her she dropped abruptly to her knees and bowed low to the ground, backside raised like a dog submitting to its master. In Katowice they called it the *huscil pus*, the goose-tail kiss, and it was considered a legitimate move even in a fair fight.

Molebacher ran right into her, tripped over her, and fell full-length on the flags with a jarring impact. His skull, making contact with the stone, emitted a sound like a muffled gong. The manoeuvre hurt Drozde too, but she'd had her arse kicked many times and considered the bargain more than fair.

She scrambled to her feet. Molebacher was twitching like a man in the grip of a nightmare. He seemed unable to rise. She turned and fled for the main door, but she lost her way in the dark and found herself groping at cold tiles fouled and furred with ancient grease. She didn't even know, in her panicked urgency, whether she needed to go left or right.

A clack of steel on stone sounded from behind her before she made that decision. She turned to see Molebacher striding towards her with the great cleaver, Gertrude, in his hand. A smear of blood hung like a skewed veil over his forehead, and his teeth were bared.

Drozde groped in the pocket of her dress, found nothing there but an end of candle.

Molebacher brought the cleaver down, and she jumped aside. He turned, quick as a cat and struck out again. This time the blade whickered past right in front of her face.

In the corner of her pocket her fingers closed on something hard and familiar.

Molebacher swung Gertrude a third time, and Drozde stood her ground as the steel sliced into her. She thrust with the tiny bradawl as if it were a sword. Its blade was barely two inches long, but Hanslo had kept it filed to a wicked point so that it would bite deep into dense heartwood. Now it bit deep into Molebacher.

He staggered back, dropping the cleaver to clasp the wooden handle of the bradawl where it protruded from his chest. It was doubtful that she'd reached his heart: the sergeant's body was well armoured with fat and muscle. But the shock and the sting of the wound made him reel.

Drozde snatched up Gertrude and stepped forward, swinging wildly and without aim. Pain had stripped Molebacher of all his swagger and solidity, and he cowered and backed before her. Again and again, Gertrude's razor edge dipped into his fat and sinew.

Then he fell—exactly across the place where the kitchen ghost lay in its vague puddle of darkness. And his gesture as he vainly covered his head with his hand was the ghost's gesture, which she had seen so often. Which meant, she realised as she hewed at him, that the kitchen ghost was Molebacher himself, present here before his death just as she was, and Magda was. But unlike them, kept in the dark and the cold and allowed to render down to this moment of pain and terror. If she had not been so intent on her labours, she might have wondered more at that. The sergeant was so very hard to kill!

Drozde had never thought very much about what butchers did. Certainly she had never thought of them as heroes. But murdering Mole was an odyssey, and when she was done she was as weary as if she'd wandered ten years on the face of a hateful sea.

35

Too restless even to contemplate sleep, Colonel August sat long after midnight in his war room answering correspondence and bringing his journal up to date.

"I feel now as if my coming here was providential," he wrote in the journal.

> If war is coming, it is these all too porous borderlands that will feel it first. And much of a war's future course can be foretold in those initial engagements; the swing of the foeman's steel, the volley of his guns, the extent to which the people of the margins recoil—and then respond!
>
> I have found, by meticulous probing, a weak point. And it is not weak by reason of fear or ignorance. It is wilfully weak, weak by its own wickedness. Narutsin is a place that has forgotten all vows of fealty and all ties of civilisation. In time of peace it could be chastised and reclaimed, but this is not a time of peace and there is no leisure for debate.

An example must be made, and it must be so clear that none misunderstand.

August set down his pen. He had more to say on this subject, and a pressing need to say it: he found himself troubled, still, at the implications of what he had decided. Posterity deserved a full explanation of his thought processes. How else would it forgive him? And without the sense of that forgiveness, trickling backwards through time from some unimaginable future of ease and plenty, how would he be strong enough now to do what must be done?

But his eyes were tired and his mind was running on erratic courses. He could swear he had just heard, from the kitchen immediately below him, the clash of arms. As though Pokoj had become a battlefield! Or perhaps it was merely haunted by the ghosts of battles fought there in former times.

On any other night he would have shrugged off the presentiment and laughed at himself. Tonight he found himself unable to do so. He needed to know that there was an innocent explanation for those sounds, so he took the lantern from his desk and went to see what was happening.

The door of Molebacher's kitchen was wide open, but the room seemed at first to be entirely empty. When the colonel ventured inside, however, he saw by the light of his lantern a figure standing by the butcher's block. The light was not good—it was only firelight from red embers and the diffuse radiance of his lantern—but even with no more than a silhouette to go by, August could see that it was not the sergeant himself but his doxy, the gypsy woman who performed the puppet shows.

"You," he said. "Woman. Was Sergeant Molebacher here just now? I thought I heard a sound, from upstairs. An altercation."

The camp follower laughed—a strident, unlovely sound. "There was, sir, an exchange of words," she said. "For look, my dear Mole was killing a capon just now, to braise it with onions and marjoram for your lunch tomorrow. But when his steel took off the bird's head, see how it painted me!"

The woman gestured towards her face. August did not understand what she meant until, raising the lantern a little higher, he saw the streak of dark blood across her cheek and forehead. It was a startling and disgusting sight, and the colonel recoiled a little from it in spite of himself. "So he's gone now," she went on, "to fetch a wet kerchief to wipe me with, for I'd be shamed to be seen out like this. And—he took his candle with him, which is why you find me here darkling, sir."

"Mole is a good man," August said inanely. He could think of nothing that was more to the purpose.

"A very good man," the doxy agreed. "Bound for heaven, I'm sure, be it late or soon, for what does he lack of virtue?" And she laughed again, somewhat louder. August wondered if she might not be a little crazed in her wits. He had never noticed it before, but there was something amiss in both her face and her voice. But her story explained the clang of steel he'd heard, and he saw besides that Molebacher had left one of his butcher knives—a large and fearsome one—lying on the block, which, like the woman's face, was streaked and smeared with blood.

"Well," the colonel said. "Commend me to him when he returns."

"I will, sir."

He was about to leave, but a happy thought struck him. "And have him broach one of those barrels of brandy," he said. "Let the men have two glasses each, those who are yet awake, to drink the archduchess's health."

"I'll tell him so, sir. Depend on it."

"Thank you." August nodded—the most he could bring himself to do by way of courtesy—and took his leave quickly.

Drozde waited until he was gone, and then until the light of the lantern faded, before sinking to her knees.

She had seen the colonel coming down the stairs as she was about to leave the kitchen, having already unbolted the door. There was no way she could get past him without being seen, and then she had realised with a thrill of horror that he was heading straight towards her.

She might have fastened the bolt again, but would the colonel not wonder who was inside at such an hour? If he had business with Molebacher he would knock and stay until someone answered. She'd be trapped all over again.

So she ducked back inside and ran across the room to the butcher's block. The light from the fire would pick her out there, and if luck was with her the colonel would glance immediately in her direction—overlooking the hacked and mountainous corpse lying in its own blood off to his left.

The whole while she had talked with him, Drozde had felt her own blood seeping from the rent Gertrude had opened in her side. She had not even dared yet to explore the depth and extent of it, but she knew from the lightness in her head and the weakness in her legs that it was no flesh wound.

The blood ran down her legs and into her boots. A faint spattering sound told her that it had also soaked her shift and was dripping onto the flagstones in front of her feet. If August shifted his lantern and happened to see it she would have to kill him too, and she kept her hand close to the handle of the cleaver in case that should happen.

At a certain point in the conversation, when he said that Molebacher was a good man, it occurred to her that she could kill him anyway. August's death might at the very least mean a delay in the execution of his orders. But she could not be sure that she would be able to do it. In her present state, she could not even be sure of standing upright once she had let go her hold on the butcher's block. So she held to her first course and waited him out.

It was as hard, in its way, as the murder had been.

Now, kneeling in a pool of her own blood, Drozde turned her attention belatedly to her injury. She needed to stop the bleeding, but the wound's location made that very hard to do. She took one of the lengths of cloth she'd brought to deck out the theatre and bound it around her chest as tightly as she could, without much effect. Blood welled from under it and quickly drenched it through.

She was starting to feel cold. She drew closer to the fire, but felt almost no warmth from it. It did, however, give her an idea. She took the cleaver, Gertrude, and laid it flat across the flames.

Then when the steel was hot enough, and starting to glow red along its edge, she applied it to her wound.

36

Klaes loitered nervously in the pools of shadow beneath the ruined abbey's crumbling walls, waiting for Drozde. *Where on earth could the woman be?* he wondered impatiently. The hour they'd agreed had come and gone, and a knot of Klaes's men had gathered at the far end of the ruins. They were beginning to look at Klaes expectantly.

It was not a bad turnout, he thought, surveying them all. Gulyas had come, with most of his friends, as had Toltz and Schneider. Most of his unit were there, but there were still a fair few faces missing from the crowd. He trusted that most of those who hadn't turned up would keep the knowledge of the show to themselves for a while, but it was only a matter of time until the rumour spread throughout the camp, and not much time at that. They must act quickly, he knew, and Drozde was still nowhere to be seen.

After what seemed like an age he saw her, hurrying towards him from the direction of the kitchen gardens. But something was badly wrong. She was staggering as she walked, and the bundle which she had slung over her back had bowed her almost to the ground. Klaes ran to help her with her burden, but Drozde waved him away and set it on the ground. As he drew nearer, he saw with a jolt of shock the blood that saturated her clothes and streaked her face.

"What happened?" he asked her. "Are you all right?"

"Molebacher. And I'm well enough."

Klaes would have questioned her further, but the men were growing restless now, so he hurried to help Drozde set up. There would be time later, he hoped, to examine this fresh mystery, and to tend to her wounds.

Drozde had mounted so many of these performances since she joined Colonel August's company that the preparations had become instinctive behaviours, scarcely examined as she enacted them. She only realised this when she found herself down on one knee with the wooden uprights of her tent in her hands. She paused in what she was doing. Tonight would be different in every respect, and there was no point in pretending that it wasn't. In fact, it was better to mark the difference from the start.

Klaes, who was shaking out the canvas with a view to draping it over the wooden frame, was slow to understand that the agenda had changed. He stood waiting for Drozde to slot the uprights together.

Instead she threw them down again, and indicated that he should do the same with the canvas. "I'll do without a backstage tonight," she said.

"But then what will make your proscenium arch stand up?" Klaes objected.

"I'll do without that too. I just need my puppets."

Klaes stood aside to let her get at the pile of figures on the spread blanket. But he jumped forward again immediately as Drozde, in leaning over them, almost fell. His hands as he caught her scraped across her burned skin. The sudden pain shook her like a dog and she came close to fainting, but she still pushed back indignantly against Klaes's grip. It was never a good thing to seem weak, even if you were dying. If people thought you were weak, they'd take liberties. "I'm fine," she told Klaes between gritted teeth.

"Woman, you're as pale as your shift."

"You shouldn't be looking at my shift, Lieutenant." And anyway, it wasn't true. There was so much blood on her, both her own and

Molebacher's, that she was dressed in crimson.

She shrugged out of Klaes's arms and rummaged among the puppets for her starting lineup. General Schrecklich, of course, and all the other soldiers she could lay her hands on. She had none in Prussian uniforms, unfortunately—but then, until she'd met the girl, Ermel, she'd not known what a Prussian uniform even looked like. Her little Austrian army would have to do.

A few villagers, who would also double as Pokoj's ghosts, a coquette to play the part of Agnese, and for herself . . . She reached into the pocket of her dress and brought out the puppet Anton had made. She tilted and dipped the crosspiece and the little figure bowed and danced.

Somehow the touch of it made her feel stronger. When she stood, some of the dizziness had gone from her head and the stiffness from her side. The pain was as intense as before, but that was no bad thing: it would keep her awake and alert. She needed to be both.

She turned to face her silent audience. They were watching these proceedings with troubled faces, their gaze flicking between her and their commander. She nodded to Klaes, indicating that she was ready to begin.

"Pay attention," Klaes said. And he had sense enough to say no more, since he had no idea what was to follow.

On an impulse, Drozde gave him the battered trumpet. She'd done enough to say, "this is different." Now she needed to remind them of why they gave her their coppers each month. Why she was one of them.

Klaes took the instrument, and after only a moment's hesitation blew the softest fanfare ever sounded. Nobody applauded or catcalled, but there was a shift in the way they stood or sat—an aura of attentiveness that spread like a wave from front to back of the huddled group.

Drozde spread her arms. In her right hand she held three soldiers, their crosspieces hooked into a single control bar so that they could do little more than go forward in lockstep. They bobbed from right to left, rigidly erect. Marching. Held in her left hand, her own puppet walked along behind the soldiers, bottom thrust out and hips rolling to suggest a wanton's "look at me" gait. The faintest ripple of laughter went through the assembled men. It was a promising sign, even though this was going to be anything but a comedy. It meant she had them with her, at least at the outset.

"What's that great house?" she had one of the soldiers say. "That's Pokoj," another replied.

And as they marched on, the Drozde puppet detached herself from the column to come forward, facing the audience directly. Her back and her head tilted to suggest her staring, hushed and wide-eyed, at something vast that rose before her.

"Pokoj," Drozde repeated. "I wonder what I'll find there."

It was the damnedest thing, Klaes thought as he watched. How the gypsy could create a scene in your mind without even the benefit of a painted backdrop, a few trees made out of distressed green ribbons, or Private Taglitz's flute.

There was a level, still, on which he could not keep himself from despising her. A woman who had sold her body's favours to one man after another without ever putting her affections into play. A hard and shameless whore who danced across the surface of the world, who shimmered like fool's gold, who played for survival and would pitch any man into the mire when she needed to and never think about him after.

But he had an inkling that night of what else she was, or might be, and of how small a part of her he apprehended.

For he was sucked into the story as everyone else was, and lived its wonders. He went with Drozde into Pokoj. He met the ghosts, and heard their stories. He spoke with the Prussian soldier, and learned of the invasion that was to come. Sooner, or later? When would it be? Drozde asked the man-woman with trembling voice.

"When the comet stands over the roof of the house and points to the Hunter's hound."

And like every man there, Klaes found himself looking over his left shoulder. He quailed inwardly at the sight of that vivid red streak in the western sky, left behind like the scourings of the fallen sun and leering back at him now over Pokoj's roof beam.

Drozde gave herself profligately to the performance. Whatever strength she had left, she spent it like a drunken lord at a gaming table, who throws gold coins in all directions as if to defy the fates and deny the very possibility that he could ever lose.

But she *was* losing. Though the soldiers thrilled at the strange story, it was not enough. For the first time in her life Drozde felt that she was like the men who had paid to use her in the past. Or perhaps she was their opposite. She had bought these men's emotions, but not their action. She had filled them with the things she needed them to feel, but still they were weighted down with custom and obedience and a sense of how things should be. When the performance was over, they would go back to being men who followed a bugle and did what Colonel August told them to do.

But then, gradually and piecemeal, something changed.

Drozde felt it before she saw it. As when Klaes had sounded the fanfare, the men shifted to a new level of attentiveness. They had been absorbed in the puppets' tale to the point where their breath was stilled. They still were, but now they were also looking past Drozde into the darkness, their eyes and mouths opening wider, their bodies half-rising involuntarily as though Lieutenant Klaes had called them to attention.

She should not look. Not in the middle of her story, with the hardest part still to come. She forced herself to continue—out of the past into the future. The soldiers in her left hand now, and General Schrecklich high-stepping onto the imagined stage from the right. "Step lively, you men. We've got to teach these treacherous peasants a lesson, what?"

The soldiers huzzahed and marched off towards Narutsin, which without a stage or a backdrop was as notional as Pokoj was. That didn't trouble her. The audience always did most of the work in turning a few splashes of paint and a twist of lace into a location. She was more worried about the Prussians, but if anything the fact that they could not be seen or heard—that the soldiers fell to invisible enemies, their own volleys seemingly useless—added to the power of the final massacre.

When all of the soldiers were dead, she let the puppets fall one by one to the grass like leaves in autumn, and dusted off her hands.

The men said nothing. They did not applaud. They didn't even move.

Finally Drozde risked a glance over her shoulder, and saw at once what it was that had subdued them. The ghosts of Pokoj had come to see the play. All those she'd seen before in the house she recognised at once. But there were newcomers too, and it took her a moment or two to realise who they were. Private Edek. Private Schottenberg.

Private Fast. Private Renke. Private Standmeier. Sergeant Strumpfel. Lieutenants Pabst and Tusimov and Dietmar.

The ghosts of those who were about to die, in a battle they didn't yet dream of.

Drozde wondered for a moment how they came to be there. Surely they hadn't died in Pokoj's grounds, and from all she knew they couldn't wander far from the place where they had fallen. The place where they were yet to fall. Her question was answered when she saw among the ranks of the ghosts her own hard stare, her own face looking back at her out of the dark as though out of a mirror.

Ghost-Drozde had brought them. Had thrown her own intangible shoulder against the wheel where her living self pushed and heaved, and helped it turn.

"That's all of it," Drozde said, dismayed at the tremor in her voice. "And it's all true. If you go against the village tomorrow, you'll die. All of you. The Prussians will sweep over you like a wave, and there won't be anything you can do about it. But if you help me, and do what your lieutenant tells you to do, there's a way to come out of this alive. It means desertion, and if the army ever finds you again they'll hang you for it. So this is goodbye to everything you were. Either you die tomorrow or you start again, like newborn babes. It's up to you."

A heavy silence met her words. The presence of those voiceless witnesses cowed the watching soldiery, so that even the bravest and the most contentious seemed lost for words.

"Where can we go?" Private Schneider protested at last. "We're known, Drozde! We'd have to go a fair long way to be somewhere where our names didn't follow us."

Drozde nodded. "I'm not saying it's going to be easy. But there is a way. A way of covering that distance in a single step—more or less. You can't do it on your own, but I know some people who will help you. So long as you help them first."

"But why can't we tell the colonel?" someone else asked. "He'd know what to do."

"He wouldn't believe you!" Drozde exclaimed. "What you're seeing, now, and what you've heard—that sways you. But I can't raise the dead to speak to Colonel August. And he'll never believe a word I say to him. He already locked Lieutenant Klaes in a cell for even daring to say Narutsin should be spared."

She groped for words. Her wound was aching, her head both light and hot. She felt as though she were burning like a candle. Klaes stepped forward and rescued her at the point where she thought she must fall down, and lose this contest.

"A show of hands," he said. "Who's with us? Be honest. No one will suffer for standing by his oath and his regiment. They'll only die with the rest when their time comes. But those who stand with us will live to see this out. They won't be soldiers any more, but they'll live to be old and to have sons and to tell them how they fared at Pokoj when Pokoj fell."

The first hand up was Private Toltz's. The second was Schneider's. After that it became harder to count. Finally all hands were raised. Some more reluctantly than others, to be sure, and Drozde suspected that some would default later and steal away when they were not observed. That was their choice. She only hoped that no word would reach August's ears until they were well gone. After that he could do as he liked.

She sat down, with some difficulty, on the remains of one of the abbey's walls. Klaes was issuing orders, quickly and efficiently, to small groups of men—choosing those he knew and trusted best. Things were happening, and for now they could happen without her.

A figure hovered beside her, and she tilted her head to find that she was staring into her own eyes. "I remember this," ghost-Drozde said. "It was almost the worst time. Almost the hardest thing to bear."

"What was the hardest?" Drozde asked.

The dead eyes bored into hers, but no answer came. *When he died*, she thought. *When I had to watch him die. That was the hardest thing.* Her own death, when it came, would be nothing next to that.

The soldier standing guard duty at the stables, where Lieutenant Dietmar had deposited the barrels of powder for the guns, was Corporal Cunel. He was Austrian, but only just, since the small town where he had been born stood squarely on the border with Poland and had been ceded by the Polish-Lithuanian Commonwealth in a bloodless negotiation three years after his birth. As a result, he faced a certain amount of teasing from his comrades on the delicate matter of his nationality. He was mocked for other things too, including his monumental flatulence and his habit of stealing small trinkets from other men's tents. He had few friends in the company and knew it.

So he did not think even for a moment that the half-dozen men bearing down on him out of the silent night were come there to lighten his vigil with drink or a wad of tobacco. He raised his rifle at once and told them to stand off.

Then he felt the tip of Klaes's sword under his left ear, pressing against the fleshy dimple there in a disconcertingly intimate way. "Stand down, Corporal," Klaes ordered him. And Cunel stood down without a murmur.

Gagged and bound, he watched in amazement as the men levered open the stable door, which had been nailed shut in lieu of a reliable lock or bolt, and took away three large barrels of gunpowder. So the colonel had been right! Klaes was a traitor, in the pay of Prussia, and he'd suborned these other men. No doubt the powder was to blow up the loyal officers as they lay in their beds. But in that case why had they not killed Cunel himself? Were they hoping to convert him to the cause?

If so, it must be fairly low down on their agenda. They took four horses out of the stables, one at a time, whispering to them and gentling them as they led them away out of the gates and down the road. Then they took a cart, which they pushed by main strength out through the same gates. More men joined them there and towed the cart down the road. Clearly they didn't mean to harness the horses until they were far enough away from Pokoj not to be heard or interrupted.

And finally, seemingly as an afterthought, two men lifted Cunel up and took him into the powder store, where they set him down with his back to a keg.

"You won't be here long," Klaes promised the terrified man. "They'll be needing guns and powder both on the morrow, Cunel. Just you rest quiet here, and wait until they come."

And as it fell out, Lieutenant Klaes was right. Tusimov came back with the dawn, bringing a letter from Wroclaw. As Magda had predicted, he rode a different horse. Thunderer had died under him a mile from the Oskander barracks, and a new mount—a grey gelding of sixteen hands—had been provided for his return.

He went directly to the colonel, who broke open the dispatch and read it at once.

It was terse and clear, amounting to no more than three words—though it might be argued that much meaning lay in the absence of any qualifiers or palliatives, the implied invitation to Colonel August to use his own discretion absolutely in the interpretation of said orders.

Take the village, the letter said. The details did not matter.

37

When the general muster sounded, the men of Colonel August's command were slow to respond.

It was not that they were tired—although many of them were, having stayed up late hammering out in bare words the intricacies of their consciences. It was the nature of the orders they were about to receive, which had seeped through the company gradually and organically from Strumpfel and Bedvar. Once Tusimov was seen to depart at the gallop in the direction of Wroclaw, and once opinions began to be advanced on all sides about the nature of his mission, neither of the two had been able to hold his tongue for longer than it takes to fill a tankard.

Then they had seen Tusimov return, and bustle into the house with a great show of urgency and self-importance. So it was clear what answer he'd got at Oskander, and therefore what business they were now engaged in.

Not everyone was against it, by any means. Some of those in Tusimov's company who'd already (as it were) seen active service in Narutsin were quite keen to go back there and wipe out the insult through the skilful application of an artillery bombardment and a slow advance with bayonets. And some who'd only heard about the fight now felt swollen up with a sense of vicarious injury and indignation, which feelings they would now be able to lance.

But by far the majority of the men were sombre in their manner. They were veterans of the Turkish campaign, and knew what fighting in a town or village was like even when the enemy were not civilians but merely lodged among them. They had had their share of bloodlettings, and now here they were again on the cusp of another. It made for sober reflection, even for those who were most skilled in the prosecution of such business.

But the colonel when he came out to them understood their mood and addressed it. He reminded them not just of the attack on Tusimov's men but of events now uncovered which made that skirmish seem a trifle. A garrison of militiamen, he told them in solemn tones, had most likely been slaughtered under the roof where they now slept. Murdered by the smiling, welcoming locals they'd been sent to protect. That was the truth of Narutsin, he said. And by way of evidence he had the long-suffering Bedvar walk along the ranks holding aloft Nymand Petos's paletot coat, now disinterred for a second time. The rust-brown spatters and the rents in its fabric had a mesmerising power. No one could doubt the violence of the militia captain's end. And August invited them to imagine themselves in Petos's place. Carrying out their duty, guarding a desolate border so that farmers and herders could sleep safely in their beds, only to have those same men tear them and mash them while they slept, no doubt with blunt spades and rusty sickles.

A murmur of discontent and rage went through the ranks. Petos's coat was a poignant witness—as eloquent as Caesar's cloak held up by Marcus Antonius.

Warming to his theme, August reminded the men that the foul corruption of Narutsin had even spread to infect one of his own officers—the villainous Lieutenant Klaes, who even now—

There was a pause. August scanned the rows of men in front of him more closely. "Are we missing Klaes's unit?" he demanded. "We seem to be almost eighty men down on the muster."

It transpired that Lieutenant Dietmar had taken charge of bringing the men to parade rest, and had deputed two of his surly, moustachioed gunnery sergeants as sheepdogs, but they had failed to find more than a handful of Klaes's men. These few, when questioned, emitted contradictory noises about another, earlier muster. Called by whom, exactly? They were not clear on that point. By an officer? Certainly. But they could not say for sure who that might have been. A comrade had said that he'd been told someone else had heard the order being given.

"Ridiculous!" August fulminated. "Utterly absurd! And where is Dietmar now?"

Enter Dietmar, furious and unhappy. If the colonel would give him leave—

"Out with it, man!" August snapped. "Where are they?"

Dietmar had not understood that he was being questioned. "I have no idea, sir," he proclaimed. "That's not what I wish to report. The powder store, sir. It's been broken into! We found Cunel trussed up in a corner, but we can't get any sense out of him!"

The colonel went at once to the matter of moment. "How much was taken? Can we still mount a bombardment?"

"Oh yes, sir. Of course, sir. We had forty barrels, and only three of them are gone. I'll hang Cunel from a tree and beat the bottom of his feet with a split switch, but . . . but the attack's not compromised, sir. Not at all!"

"Then move the men out!" August said in a grinding voice. He felt that more than enough time had been wasted on this—and that the effort he'd spent in building up the men's belligerence and readiness was in danger of being undone.

"Yes sir!" Dietmar said, saluting smartly. "And the guns . . . ?"

"Will move with the vanguard, Dietmar. The guns are going to announce us."

"Even Mathilde?" Dietmar wanted to be sure. This was, after all, a gun capable of punching a hole through foot-thick stonework, whereas Narutsin was primarily made out of clapboard and shingle.

"Especially Mathilde."

Dietmar relayed the orders, and the guns—already limbered, despite his private doubts—were drawn into position on the house's driveway. Putting them in the van would slow the march, but the lieutenant felt that this might be an inauspicious time to make that observation.

As if to underscore his misgivings, two huge reports sounded— far away, but still loud and deep. An enemy bombardment? But there was no enemy, and nothing besides themselves that was worth bombarding. And after that double blast the morning air was still. Clearly it was the stolen gunpowder they were hearing, but it was much less apparent what it had been deployed against.

Dietmar gave the signal to Strumpfel, who barked the fall-in and the about-face, silencing the murmured speculations of the men. Then he called a single march. The double was impossible if they were not to outstrip the limbers and leave the guns behind.

The men marched out through the gates in moderately good order. Dietmar stayed with the guns after that, which meant that he rode at the head of the column. Colonel August and Lieutenant Pabst rode at the rear, while Tusimov marched along at the midpoint of the column. Alone among the officers he had elected not to ride, because the hard gallop to Wroclaw and back had left his back and lower limbs in such pain that it was hard for him to sit a saddle.

In any event, to make the march on foot was hardly a hardship. They would cover the three miles to the village in less than an hour, even keeping pace with the guns.

In fact, their journey was to be shorter than that and more full of incident. Only a mile out of Pokoj, they heard a third percussion from the north and west. For a moment it seemed to Dietmar that he might have been wrong—that this might after all be the report of an enemy gun. Nor was he alone in that thought. The men tensed and slowed, forgetting for a moment the order of march as they waited for a ball to explode near them. But no ball arrived.

If that was the stolen powder, Dietmar muttered to his sergeant, Jursitizky, then it was all used up now and they could rest easy. But what had it blown up?

They moved on warily. A few minutes later they rounded a corner and saw the Drench up ahead of them. Strewn across the road in jagged, broken shards were a few of the beams that had made up the bridge—now, clearly, all that was left of it. For a moment, the soldiers thought that this was what they had just heard. Dietmar, for one, knew that it wasn't. The explosion had seemed to him to come from much further away, and even if he were mistaken in that there would still be some smoke and debris in the air if a barrel of gunpowder had been sent up in this spot so recently.

Curious, he rode up to the deep channel and reined in his horse at its very edge. The rest of the bridge lay in the channel of the Drench below him, broken and mangled. Each of its stanchions had been laboriously sawn through at either end, until finally it had lost enough support to fall into the channel and be broken.

Hours of work for many men. A waste of time, if the ones who'd done this were also those who'd stolen the gunpowder.

Then a sound from above and to his right made him turn and gasp in horror.

A second before he died, he realised what the gunpowder had been for.

Below Zielona Góra, perhaps seven hours before and in the dead of night, Klaes and his men had arrived to join the men and women of Narutsin at the stone breakwater that held in the Mala Panev at the easternmost point of her great meander. The villagers had been hammering at the stone with pickaxes throughout the day—ever since Drozde's visit—and had made considerable inroads into it, but there was still much to be done.

"Set the powder, sir?" Private Toltz asked Klaes.

Reluctantly, Klaes shook his head. Though it might accomplish the business in a single stroke, they could not afford the risk. They had only the three barrels. If they used them and failed, they might never dismantle the breakwater in time.

Instead he told his men to join the villagers and teach them some of the rudiments of military engineering. A good sapper worked from the bottom of a structure to undermine it, multiplying the effects of his efforts, whereas the villagers had been attacking the breakwater from the top down. He also picked his point of entry, using the natural grain of the stone and any fault lines already visible.

It remained to be seen, of course, whether the villagers would be content to take instruction. For a moment after the soldiers arrived, the Narutsiners clutched their picks and hoes and mattocks at the *qui vive*, drawn up in a ragged line as though they were preparing to attack.

Then Klaes held up in his left hand a wooden puppet, as Drozde had told him to do, and Mayor Weichorek stood his people down with a curt injunction not to be bloody fools. These were the reinforcements Drozde had promised, and they would make the work go easier.

But as soon as they went to it, the soldiers tentatively demonstrating the right way of working and the villagers quickly adapting to it,

Weichorek sidled over to Klaes and clamped a heavy hand on his shoulder.

"Where is she?" he demanded.

"She was hurt," Klaes muttered. "A wound to her left side. Under her heart. She couldn't walk, so I left her behind."

"And who did you leave with her?" This was not Weichorek but Bosilka, who had come along in Weichorek's wake like a dory behind a battleship. Except that she seemed much more warlike than him and showed more ready for combat.

"Nobody," Klaes said. "It was not like that, Miss Stefanu. She said she'd hide herself away, until the house was empty."

"And what if she's found before the house is empty? Or what if her wound opens again, and she falls into a swoon? Do you ever stop to think, Captain Klaes, before you start throwing out orders to those around you?"

"Lieutenant!" Klaes cried. "Lieutenant Klaes! For the love of God, woman, will you dandle me up and down all the ranks of the bloody army like a dress-up doll?"

Bosilka was not to be put off. "Take me where she is," she commanded. "If she's hurt, she may need tending."

"When we're done here," Klaes said, and since it was one life against so many hundreds of lives, Bosilka let it go after only a moment's pause. But he was conscious of her watching him as she worked at his side, swinging a pickaxe with no great skill but ferocious energy.

They worked as the night paled and the sky grew luminous, so deeply absorbed that this slow kindling seemed to be a conflagration rising around them. Whenever they remembered to look it was closer to dawn, and the hour drew closer when their work would either be crowned or else be wasted.

Klaes looked at their labours and called a halt at last. He pulled Toltz and Schneider and four others from the work line and told them to bring up the barrels. As they placed them, ten strides apart, he had Meister Weichorek take his people way back down the slope of the hill, where there was a steep bank and a slightly overhanging rock wall that would offer them some shelter. He instructed his own people to withdraw too.

They had exactly three fuses, and one auger. Toltz drilled the holes, slowly and painstakingly, and Schneider placed the fuses. When all was ready, the fuses were lit with wooden spills, simultaneously, and the soldiers ran quickly down the hill into covert.

They were none too soon. The explosion sounded at their backs as soon as they were behind the bank. Three heartbeats later, rocks that had been hurled high into the air began to fall all around them—but Klaes had chosen their position well and nobody was hit.

But when they finally ventured out to inspect the results of their work, they were dismayed. One of the barrels had failed to ignite. Amazingly, the force of the other two barrels exploding had propelled it down the hill along with all the rest of the debris, without either breaching it or sparking it. Perhaps as a result, the breakwater—though it was cracked from top to bottom—had not fallen. Water spilled through in a leisurely trickle, winding its way down the hillside prettily but ineffectually. It would not do.

"We have to begin again," Weichorek said.

"We can't!" Bosilka exclaimed, waving her arms in exasperation. "Look at the sky! Drozde said we should be done before cockcrow, and the cocks must have crowed an hour ago!"

"We've one barrel left, sir," Private Toltz offered. "But no way of setting it off," Klaes said.

"Might it be done with a musket ball?" Master Weichorek asked. "Fired from the bottom of the slope?"

"Aye, if this were a story told to sots in an alehouse," Klaes said glumly. "No, there's nothing else for it. We'll work with picks for as long as we . . ." But he stopped, because he had chanced to look down at his feet. His days in the engineer corps came back to him, suddenly, and he thought of another, more outrageous proceeding they might try. "Private Toltz and Private Schneider," he said, "put the barrel back in place."

"Yes sir."

"And lever off the lid of it." The two men hastened to their work, while Klaes went down on his knees in the grass.

Under the astonished gaze of the villagers and soldiers, he began to pick flowers. They watched him for a little while, bewildered and uneasy. Then Meister Weichorek enquired of him—meaning no disrespect, and asking only to obtain a fuller understanding of the situation—whether he had gone mad.

"Not a bit of it," Klaes muttered. And he held up, with something of triumph, a fistful of feathery green stalks.

"That's dill," Bosilka said. "You can cook with it."

"Yes," Klaes agreed tersely. "You can also blow things to high heaven with it."

He walked back up the slope toward the barrel, but stopped and turned when he realised that he was being followed. "This will not be safe," he said. "You should take cover."

"What will you do?" Bosilka demanded. "How will dill help you?"

Klaes held the plants up for her to see. "It will help because it has hollow stems," he said. "When black powder is used in mining and quarrying, the men seldom bother to cut a proper fuse. They pour a little of the powder into a tube made of paper, or into the stem of a reed, and light the end of it. The tube, or the stem, works in the same way a fuse does. The problem is that the powder in the tube tends to spark, and also it burns at an uneven rate. You have to apply the fire and then run, as quickly as you can. There's no telling how long after that the explosion will come."

"Then that's madness!" Bosilka exclaimed in horror. "You might just as well sit on the barrel and strike sparks from a flint until it goes up under you!"

"Perhaps we'll try that next," Klaes said, in a ghastly attempt at humour. Nobody laughed, or even smiled. "I really would get back under cover," he added, more soberly.

They all ran pell-mell to do so. Bosilka cast a wild glance backwards over her shoulder at him, but Klaes was at a loss to guess what that might portend.

He walked the rest of the way up the slope, to where Toltz and Schneider had already broken open the barrel. Scooping up a handful of the powder, the lieutenant held his closed fist over the plant stems and let it trickle into them. Most of it missed, of course, but he repeated the procedure again and again, hoping that at least some of the grains would lodge down inside far enough to be efficacious. You didn't need a continuous trail of powder, but the grains had to be close enough so that one would spark the next, all the way to the far end where the last grains would ignite the barrel. Dry reeds would have been far better than green stems, but green stems were what he had.

When Toltz saw what the lieutenant was doing, he shook his head. "That's a fool's trick, sir, if you don't mind me saying so."

"I've been playing fool's tricks for much of my life," Klaes said. He replaced the lid on the barrel and stood his cluster of stems upright in the touch hole like a posy. "Go on, Toltz. Schneider. Give me that spill there. I'll wait until you're at the bottom of the hill before I set it to the fuse."

"That there is not a bloody fuse!" Toltz opined. Klaes made no reply, but he raised his eyebrows meaningfully with the spill only an inch or two from his homemade substitute. The two privates retreated at the double march, or possibly a little faster.

Klaes watched them down the hill and out of sight. Then he touched the flame to the stems and took to his heels. He hadn't gone ten feet when the air barked like the mouths of Cerberus and a great exhalation lifted him off his feet.

The heat of the explosion set his jacket and trousers on fire.

But the waters of the Mala Panev, roaring through the shattered stone, put him out again only a second later.

And four miles downstream, and a few minutes after that, Lieutenant Dietmar, staring into the declivity of the Drench, looked up and to the right as the sound of rushing water reached his ears far too late to be of any use to him.

Swollen by the winter rains, the Mala Panev was a torrent. It was finding its ancient course again, and Dietmar most unfortunately had placed himself full in its way. The wall of water took him and his horse both, pitched them over the edge into the gulley and rolled them over and over. The horse struggled and thrashed and managed to find its feet again. Dietmar, lying face down, did not, and was carried away out of sight in the space of a few seconds. His neck had been broken in the fall.

To the soldiers watching, it was as though the hand of God had struck him down. Some would later say that they had seen a woman's face in the spray, but since rivers do not have faces their testimony can be discounted.

There was too much water for the Drench to hold. It filled the channel in seconds and spread out to either side of it in a broad, frothing apron. Colonel August bared his teeth and snarled at the sight of it. Coming up from the rear to ascertain why the column had stopped, he had not seen Lieutenant Dietmar's death, but he took in at once the broken bridge and the turbulent floodwater and knew it for what it was. Sabotage, well planned and carefully executed. He had been right—of course he had!—not to underestimate this enemy. *Delenda erat Carthago!* The village must be excised from the map, and the spot where it had stood cauterised to prevent reinfection.

However, that had just been made a great deal more problematic. Without the bridge, it was certainly not possible to get the guns and their limbers to the far side of the water, and from here there was no clear line of sight to Narutsin. The steeple of the church, though, was visible over the tops of the trees. Would it be possible to mount a bombardment using that as a ranging mark? Mathilde's reach was a great deal more than a mile, after all, and Narutsin could not be more than a mile away. Dietmar would know.

August turned to Sergeant Strumpfel, who was standing at the head of the column staring dazedly into the water. "Strumpfel," he snapped, "bring Lieutenant Dietmar here."

Strumpfel pointed down into the Drench. "But Colonel," he said, "Lieutenant Dietmar is in there. I—I think he's dead."

The colonel came close to repeating the word with a questioning inflection, in which case he would have sounded like a querulous old woman overtaken by events. He held himself back from it, despite the shock and dismay he felt. Dietmar had been his strong right arm, but all that meant was that he would have to complete this venture one-handed.

Lieutenant Tusimov approached him running, and Pabst came up at a fast trot a moment later. August explained to them both what the detachment would do next.

The power of the flood had abated as soon as its front began to widen, and was abating still. Though it was still strong, it was certainly not strong enough now to pull a man off his feet or to topple a horse and rider. True, at the centre there was a deeper stretch—corresponding to the location of the Drench—which would need to be negotiated with more care. But even here the water would not exceed four or five feet in depth. The soldiers would wade, holding their muskets over their heads, and reform in good order on the further side of the river.

"What about the cannons, sir?" Tusimov asked anxiously.

"Put them under a light guard," August said, "and leave them here." But even as he said it a better idea came to him. "Sergeant Jursitizky. Is he here? Bring him to me."

Sergeant Jursitizky presented himself. "Bring Mathilde around and unlimber her," the colonel told him. "I want you to take the range of the village from that steeple—do you see?—and launch a few balls in that direction. Vary the declination a little to increase your chances of hitting something. I want that place in pieces when we march on it."

"Sir," Jursitizky said with a smart salute. And he went to work.

A few minutes later, with the sun now climbing free of the horizon and full daylight coming quickly upon them, Mathilde spoke. She spoke most harshly. A cheer rose from the men when they saw her muzzle belch smoke and thunder. Fire seemed a suitable answer to the flood that had laid itself across their path. A second shot followed, and then a third. August signalled to Jursitizky to stand down, and then to Tusimov to resume the march.

Tusimov was a veteran and a man of sense, but these manoeuvres resembled no military strategy he had ever heard of. Consequently, although on another occasion he might have sent a small squad across to the other side of the river first, to make a beachhead before the body of the company crossed, it did not occur to him to give such an order. Instead he transformed the column into as wide a line of march as he could manage, had them draw up at the edge of the water, and then at his signal wade in.

The men had not anticipated how cold the water would be. There was much muttered cursing and complaint, quickly suppressed by the sergeants. "It's bath night, you stout lads!" Strumpfel bellowed. "Don't forget to wash behind your ears!" and the witticism was passed on down the line. Someone asked for soap, and someone else said they should boil another kettle.

They were only up to their knees, at first. Then they reached the mid-point, and the ground fell away beneath their feet as they descended into the Drench. The water rose to their thighs, their waists, the middle of their chests. Men yelped involuntarily as the chill bit into them, or swore aloud as their feet slid on the sloping bank. But at the same time, they took it for a good sign. If the deep channel marked the middle of the newly remade river, they were already halfway across.

The footing in the Drench was treacherous, and with most of their bodies submerged the current pushed at the soldiers more insistently. Few of them could swim. But Strumpfel's joke still rang in their ears, making it hard for any of them to acknowledge the danger they were in.

And then they were climbing up the further slope, exposing shoulders, chests, bellies to the cold air. And then they were on the level, trudging knee-deep towards dry land. Their uniforms hung on them like lead cerements, heavy and stiff, but the worst was over.

"The cleanest band of little angels as ever was seen!" Strumpfel cried gaily, to cheers and catcalls.

They were the last words he spoke.

A line of infantry in good order could resist a cavalry charge. It wasn't even rare for them to do so. Certain factors were known to make it more likely. If the cavalry made a direct charge and the infantrymen had time to get off two or three good volleys of musket fire, making gaps in the opposing ranks. If the terrain was broken, so that the riders were randomly slowed and did not arrive all at once. If the infantry line was partially masked by skirmishers or buttressed by flanking fire from one side or both. All of these things would blunt the terrible impact and diffuse the demoralising effect of being cut down from above by fighters moving too quickly to counter.

Colonel August's detachment had none of these advantages. Horsemen were suddenly upon them, among them, without announcement. They were light cavalry, hussars, mostly armed with sabres specifically designed for fighting from the saddle. But there were some uhlans too, with their lances at the drop: a broad, sweeping line of tapering spears longer than a man's body. Had they been on the road their horses' hooves on the gravel would have raised dust and noise. But they came out of the trees, silent until the first of them reached the water and raised a thunderous splash, and by then they were engaged.

And the colonel's men, it should further be observed, were *not* in good order. They were in no order at all. Trudging out of the Drench into the shallows, testing the ground ahead one step at a time, each man kept his own pace at a speed where duty and dexterity reached equilibrium with discomfort and timidity. The line of march had become a sparse and broken and largely notional thing.

And the Prussian Braunschweigers threshed them like wheat.

Ermel had tried to describe this engagement to Drozde, and had succeeded thus far:

> It was the strangest battle I ever fought, and the saddest. And it was the first, of course, so even if it hadn't been strange and sad it would probably still have seemed so to me.

We came to what was meant to be the border, but nothing was as it was meant to be. There should have been a milestone on the road indicating that we were seven leagues from Estingen. It was not there. There should have been a stand of oak trees called the Mile Reach, the southernmost point of the Hunzerwald. But there were none. And to name the biggest thing last, there should have been the Mala Panev, the river that marks the border at that point and for ten miles on either hand.

But the river was gone. There was a bridge, indeed, where our captain's map said a bridge should be—but it was a bridge over nothing! There was only a field of mud there under the coping, with puddles and meres all about, as though the river had shrunk in the heat of a long summer. But this was dead December, so we knew that couldn't be.

So we rode on, worried that we had somehow lost our way, until we came at length to a village. And this village was yet another impossible thing, because our maps said there was nothing now between us and the border except fields and woodland.

A few people—old people, mostly, and some children—came out to cheer us and throw flowers in our path. They seemed to be expecting us.

What is this place? our captain asked.

This is Puppendorf, they said. A strange name, since in Schönbrunner Deutsch it would mean a town full of dolls or puppets.

And where is the border? the captain asked.

They pointed. *Over there, very close. You'll know when you come to the river. But be careful. There are Austrian soldiers. A whole garrison of them, coming here to fight you.*

We didn't know until then that the Austrians had intelligence of us. This was meant to be a surprise attack, after all. So our officers said we must find and engage this enemy, and not leave them intact at our backs.

Finding them was not hard. At that moment they began a bombardment—as far as we could tell, a single piece of heavy ordnance aimed precisely in our direction.

The balls fell first long and then short, but it could not be long before they found our range. And as if to make that clear, the church steeple exploded into fragments as it took a direct hit.

Orders were given and we went on at the double march. We had not gone more than a mile before our scouts came on the Austrians, and the circumstances could not have been more in our favour. They were fording a river which appeared to have burst its banks, and every man jack of them was in the water. We went quickly from marching column into battle array—without a single spoken command being given, for we were hidden from the Austrians only by a hundred strides of sparse forest. All was done by gesture, and at the last by the swishing in the air of the captain's sword.

We came out of the trees and engaged.

Oh dear God, we hit them like a hammer. I was not part of the cavalry charge, but the *Schuetzen* are the fastest and best of the infantry, and we were there to finish what our hussars and Natzmeruhlans began.

Chiefly that meant chasing down the stragglers, because the Austrians had mounted no defence at all. They had broken as soon as we hit them, and run in every direction. An officer was standing in the middle of the river, shouting orders at them, trying to bring them into a square, but even those who heard him were sodden and frozen and moving too slowly to be of any use. And then he was hit by a musket ball and went down in the deep water. If the shot did not kill him then the river did.

It made me sad to see those soldiers fall. There was no courage in it, on either side, and no skill. Those who ran towards us ended up on the lances of our Tartars or ran full tilt into our musket fire. They could not even load before they were cut down. Those who tried to regain the further bank turned their broad backs to us and gave us even easier targets.

After ten minutes of fighting, I saw not a single enemy who was still alive. I saw precious few who were dead, for that matter: the river took them away. And since the

Mala Panev feeds the Oder and the Oder runs through Wroclaw, perhaps their arrival there a day or two later served as King Frederick's declaration of war.

38

Late though it was, Libush was still awake. She'd contracted to meet Fingerlos earlier that evening, and the private was at her tent when Haas came to disturb them with news that Drozde was staging an impromptu and most unofficial puppet show for the sole benefit of Lieutenant Klaes's men.

So naturally, Libush attended too.

She'd heard rumours of Drozde's strange powers; her friend never talked of them, but she'd never denied them either. Libush watched the show with increasing alarm, but not with disbelief. There, after all, was the miraculous star in the sky above them, a sign of upheavals in the world below. If Drozde said the Prussians would attack the next day, and she had a plan to save their lives, Libush was inclined to trust her. And when she saw Lieutenant Klaes himself among the audience, she had no doubt at all.

When the show ended and the men clustered around Drozde to be sent on some mysterious assignment, Libush went back to the camp to spread the word on her own account. And when, an hour later, Drozde came to her tent, Libush was waiting for her.

Drozde stood in the opening with a most uncharacteristic air of hesitation. Libush, bursting with nervousness and curiosity, jumped up and pulled her inside.

"I was at the show, Drozde, so I know what you have to tell me. I've told some of the others; if you've a plan to save us, we'll help any way we can."

She gestured to her to sit on the bedroll. Drozde was slow to move, and sat down gingerly, as if it pained her. Libush saw with shock that there were tears in her eyes. She embraced her friend, and felt her wince.

"You're hurt. Let me see."

"No!" Drozde held her back as she rose to fetch the candle. "There'll be time for that later, Libush. Didn't you say you wanted to help?"

Libush nodded. "Whatever's needed," she said, though something in Drozde's look now was scaring her.

"Here's how it is, then. The Prussians come in the morning, early, after a night ride that will go down in history. They find our men as they're getting ready to attack Narutsin. They kill all of them. Everyone that's there."

Libush waited dumbly until Drozde went on.

"If the women shut themselves in the house, they'll be taken prisoner. The Prussians won't harm them; I think they'll let them be ransomed in a few months. That's what Dame Osterhilis and the officers' wives do. You could stay with them. You'll be safe if you do, as long as you stay in the house. Or you could leave."

"Leave? And go where? How do we escape an army?"

"You don't, not exactly." Drozde leaned forward. Her face was white, and streaked with what Libush thought was blood. What had the girl been doing?

"You go to Narutsin, Libush. And then we make Narutsin vanish."

Libush stared at her.

But Drozde was serious. "What's the boundary between us and Prussia?" she pursued.

"The . . . ? The river, of course. The Mala Panev."

"We're moving it. That is, we're trying to. Tomorrow, when the soldiers have left, take Alis, take anyone who'll go with you, and get to the village. Be careful when you cross the Drench. Listen out for three explosions, and when they come, stay well clear of the channel. That's where the river will go.

"If our plan works, by tomorrow night Narutsin will no longer exist. It'll be a Prussian village on the far side of the Mala Panev. Puppendorf. And the mayor and his wife will make you welcome there. I've seen to it."

Libush gaped, then laughed. For a moment she was delighted with the plan. Then she remembered how many men would die by this same account, and was serious again.

"Alis will come with us for sure, and Sarai. Ute and Lidmila and Kirsten, probably. I don't know about Ottilie; she'll want to stay with her sergeant."

"He won't be a sergeant after tomorrow!" Drozde's voice was strained. "And if he's still alive, her best chance of seeing him again is in the village. Tell her that."

Libush nodded. "Well, Alis and I are packed already. I'll go round the others at first light tomorrow. Did you want some help moving your puppets?"

Drozde did not answer at once. Libush had never seen her so pale. "I'd be grateful for it," she said at last. "Wait until the soldiers have gone; no one will stop you then. But you'll need a strong stomach."

Libush was not given to hysterics. She took in the sight of Molebacher's body with no more than a sharp intake of breath, and asked no questions, for which Drozde was grateful. By daylight he was a spectacle as much pathetic as fearful. Drozde had crammed him into the meat closet, only just managing to shut the door on him: a temporary measure, but enough to avoid raising the alarm when the orderlies came in for bread in the morning. Now, with most of his uniform stained a dull red, he might have been any other carcass, slipped from its hook.

Libush surveyed the great dead bulk in silence for a while. Then she let out a long sigh.

"I did use to think one of you would do for the other," she said. They were talking in whispers, but her voice still seemed too loud to Drozde, echoing round the empty kitchen. "Didn't think it would come out so bloody, though. Jesu, girl, I'm glad it's him and not you."

It's both of us, Drozde thought. But better this way round. She'd lain down to sleep in her own tent, half expecting not to wake, but her dreams had been full of her own dead face. "Almost the hardest thing," she had said: staying back here while the others carried out her plan;

not knowing how it would work out or how many it would save. She'd keep alive to learn that, if she could. Her whole side burned, and she could not stop shaking, but she had walked here and she was still on her feet.

"Help me lay him in the corner," she told Libush. "It doesn't matter who finds him now. And then if you could help bring my trunk up, I'd be grateful."

The trunk was not too badly damaged to close, after all. She laid all the puppets carefully in their places and threw the props and the bolts of cloth in after them. There was room for her shawl and the three books she'd taken from the library: all her worldly goods. She let Libush carry it up the stairs for her. Molebacher's cashbox was where he always kept it, at the bottom of the sack of potatoes. As an afterthought she took out the last two bottles of his good brandy: let the Prussians find their own.

"One for you and one for me," she told Libush. "And this is for you as well—for you and Alis and Ottilie." She held out the cashbox.

Libush looked more astonished than Drozde had ever seen her. "But that's . . . You can't . . ." she said.

And this was hard too. She placed the box firmly in Libush's hands. "Take as many with you as you can," she said. "Be away from the Drench by sunset. And give Alis my love."

She watched as realisation came over Libush, and horror. But she had no more energy left for grief. "I'm staying here," she said. "I'm too weak to move far, and I'm damned if I'm going to die in the dust of the road like a dog."

She let Libush fuss over her a little, building up the fire and sitting her in Molebacher's great armchair. The relief of being able to sit was so great that for a while she forgot the pain. She looked up a little later to find that the light had changed; shadows were gathering in the corners, and Libush had gone. She'd left a glass of the brandy at her elbow, though, and the bottle nearby: a good friend.

The brandy burned in her guts and set little fires dancing in her chest. She took another swallow, and another. She'd never realised how quiet it could be here, without the voices of the ghosts; without Magda's constant chatter.

And where *was* Magda? The child wouldn't willingly leave her alone; not in such extremity. She must be here somewhere. Drozde recalled the way the ghosts had drawn her aside after Agnese's story, to hide her from the colonel and his soldiers. Like pulling her behind a curtain . . . She felt about for that other place now, summoning up the sense of it. Magda was there, standing by the table and holding out a hand as if to touch her. But two of the other ghosts held her back, granting Drozde these last few moments of quiet and solitude. One figure was herself, her arm around the little girl's shoulders. The other was a man: smallish, clean cut and brown skinned. Even serious, as he was now, Hanslo's face was as unguarded as Magda's own.

You wouldn't trust me with him, would you! she chided her ghost self. *You thought if I saw him I'd be distracted, not get the job done. You thought I'd turn soft.*

She glanced over at the mound of Molebacher in the corner.

Maybe you were right.

With an effort, she reached out to pour herself another glass of brandy. Not long now till sunset.

They were all dead. All of them. He'd lost his command, his men, even his guns. And posterity would damn him for an incompetent. This last thought was the bitterest of all: Colonel August physically staggered as he forced himself back up the road, back towards Pokoj.

He should have stayed and died with his men; of course he should. But there had been treachery here: there had been sedition and double-dealing, and by God he would see the miscreants suffer before he died. He would fasten Klaes to that whipping frame and thrash the cur himself. Or better, get Molebacher . . .

He recalled suddenly that Molebacher had not been in the muster that morning. He had remarked on it as they marched off. Mole was a brisk man; a keen soldier, always in the front of the ranks where his commanding officer could see him. Yet there had been no sign of him today. Was he sick, perhaps? The possibility that the loyal sergeant might still be alive, back at the house, gave the colonel a spark of comfort. But then, how could he reveal to that brave, honest man the appalling scale of today's betrayal and defeat?

He had reached the walls of the grounds. He pushed through the first gap he came to, ignoring the damage to his uniform, and made straight for the house, shouldering through weeds and saplings. The campsite was as quiet as the grave: even the women seemed to have abandoned it. Like rats, he thought bitterly: they can tell before the men when the vessel is holed.

Not all the women had gone. As he entered the house he heard subdued female voices from an upper room. Of course, his wife would never desert her post, and the other ladies, he was sure, would be loyal to their marital bonds. But he quailed at the thought of going to them. How could he tell them that three of them were now widows? What would Osterhilis think, when she learned the truth? That her husband, going confidently forth to cauterise a weak spot in their country's defences, had instead laid his command wide open to annihilation, and the empire to invasion?

Almost with relief he let his thoughts fall back into that track: the rout, and the treachery that had caused it. He need not confront the women just yet. First he would get to the bottom of what had happened here: discover who the traitors were and make them pay— for clearly, Klaes had not acted alone. There was a witness to the first stage of the plot, he remembered: the guard, Cunel, who had let Klaes and his men steal the powder. Cunel was even now in the lock-up on a charge of dereliction of duty. With new energy, now that a clear path of action was before him, August headed for the north wing and let himself into the makeshift cell.

A querulous voice came from within as he opened the door.

"Schottenberg, is that you? I'm starving—no one's brought me anything all day!"

"Schottenberg," said August heavily, "is dead." He let the door slam shut behind him, shaking flakes of damp plaster from the walls. "As are you, if you fail to answer me to my satisfaction."

The mere sound of the colonel's voice filled Cunel with such terror that for some minutes he was unable to answer at all. Then he babbled a stream of apologies and self-exculpations, and when August roared at him, lapsed into cowed silence. The colonel was forced to calm himself, to talk quietly and reasonably, before he could calm the man enough to get any sense out of him.

They'd come in the night, a dozen men or more, and threatened him. He'd held them off, he had, until Lieutenant Klaes ordered him to stand down; but Lieutenant Klaes was an officer—and besides, was sticking him with a sword . . . Of the men, he'd recognised Toltz, Schneider and Kuppermann, maybe Haas as well. The others—well, there were so many of them, sir. And they'd tied him up and broken in the door and taken the three barrels of powder, and the horses too.

All the men Cunel named had been absent from the morning's

roster. So August had his culprits to hang—assuming he could find them. And assuming he had a single man left to effect the capture, and could somehow get himself and his prisoners far enough away from the Prussians to hold a court martial.

The private gave him one more piece of information. Talking among themselves as they hoisted the barrels, the men had mentioned the name Drozde. "Her with the puppets—you know, sir?" Bizarre though it sounded, they spoke as if the woman had had some role in the plot, even instigated it. "Not that I'm saying that's what happened, sir, only truly repeating what was said. But you know what the whores are like—they'll take credit for anything. Or rather, I don't mean that you know the whores, because of course you don't, sir . . ."

August cuffed him, and the man sat down heavily on his bedroll. "Enough prattling," the colonel said. "That's all of it?" Cunel nodded in hurt silence, and August turned and left him. The blow had relieved his spirits a little, but he doubted the man would receive any further punishment. Who did he have left to administer it?

Drozde, though . . . Molebacher's whore; the woman he had seen last night. Bloodied; looking and sounding somewhat crazed. What had become of Molebacher since then?

He found himself almost running as he headed for the kitchen.

At first sight the room was peaceful. There was a scent of brandy and something less pleasant; turning meat, perhaps. The fire was burning down, and the whore sat in front of it, seemingly in a drunken stupor. There was no sign of Molebacher. That was, until he looked around once more and spotted the bulky shadow in the corner.

August crossed the room in two strides, but Molebacher was cold: he had been dead some time. And he'd been butchered. The gaping rents in his body were fearsome to see.

The woman stirred at the colonel's cry. She spoke to him without turning, her voice so slurred as to be barely comprehensible.

"I hoped I'd see you. Did it work? Did the river move?"

August could barely speak for shock and rage. It was true then, what Cunel had reported. Somehow this creature was the source of all of it: the betrayal and his disgrace. She was mad, of course; but that would not save her from punishment.

He found his voice. "The Drench is in flood," he said, amazed at how steadily he could still speak. "Lieutenant Dietmar was swept away, and then when we crossed, the Prussians were there waiting for us."

Drozde sighed. "It's done, then."

"You admit to it, woman?" August demanded. "To causing all this?"

She did not answer at once. Instead she turned in her seat, with what seemed agonising slowness, till she could focus on August's face. And she laughed.

"Colonel August, by all that's wonderful!" Her voice was suddenly stronger and clearer. She laughed again, not harshly as she had done last night but softly, as if at a private joke. "Oh, I should be honoured. The commanding officer himself! I was expecting Lieutenant Klaes."

She would never come to trial, August knew. Yet Fate had seen fit to appoint him her judge. She would acknowledge the charges against her before he killed her.

"You brought down my men. You subverted justice, and betrayed this company, which has fed and sheltered you. You—you murdered Mole!"

"Yes," Drozde agreed. Her brazenness astonished him. "I did all that. I had no quarrel with your men, and I'll ask their pardon when I see them, though most would have died anyway. But the town is safe. I've put Narutsin out of your reach."

The words were wild. But her tone was almost that of a rational creature. She had set herself against him, she was saying; and she had won.

August had always prided himself on his judicious nature. But the rage that woke in him then was unlike any he had known: it bore him up and carried him forward like flood water, and he welcomed it. The harpy had declared herself his enemy and he would destroy her.

His sword was already in his hand. He came at her with a wordless roar while she sat unmoving, laughing at him.

There were sudden footsteps behind him, and a voice shouting, "Leave her!" He knew that voice. Knew and hated it. He spun round even as the man rushed at him.

Klaes.

The filthy little traitor had come back after all. Dripping wet and red faced, and as brash and self-righteous as ever. But he was unarmed! As the colonel slashed at him he flinched and leaped backwards. He would not outrun justice this time. In spite of everything, August smiled.

Klaes had left his sword in the equipment stores after disarming Corporal Cunel: he had not wanted to go armed to meet the villagers.

He should have remedied that as soon as he got back to Pokoj. Instead he had run straight to the ballroom and then to the kitchen, leaving Bosilka Stefanu to catch him up. By the time he heard August's voice it was too late.

Drozde was seated in a chair by the fire, slumped but alive: he saw the flash of recognition in her eyes. August reared above her, his sword raised. If Klaes had not shouted he would have murdered her there and then.

The colonel whirled, his face contorted with fury, and lunged at Klaes. He sidestepped and backed desperately, searching around him for anything he might use to defend himself: the poker by the fireplace; a cleaver on the chopping board; pans hanging at the wall. Nothing within his reach. And Bosilka was not far behind him. He prayed that she would not arrive till this was over, however it fell out.

"What are you doing?" he cried. "Would you kill a woman?" The colonel only bared his teeth in reply. He made no more lunges: he advanced steadily now, the hand gripping his sword-hilt white around the knuckles. Klaes feared the man was crazed: there would be no reasoning with him. But for now words were all the weapons he had. He took another step backwards. "Is this how you want to be remembered?"

It sounded pathetically weak in his own ears. But something changed in August's face: a moment of indecision, almost of grief. There was a movement behind the colonel, and Klaes saw Bosilka in the doorway. He wanted to yell at her to leave, but August must not see her, not mad as he was.

Klaes pressed on wildly: "All you've done here: the floggings, the bombardments. It was nothing but mistaking your enemy. They'll say you punished harmless men because you didn't understand them. And now you'd murder the women as well!"

August made a choking sound and took another step towards him. But if Klaes backed off any more he'd be against the wall, with nowhere to run. He stood his ground, willing the girl to take the hint and flee.

"I'll spit you like a capon," August said, as much breath as voice. "You and your kitchen whore . . ." He leaped forward as he spoke, and Klaes ran. The sword nicked his arm, but he reached the fireplace, grabbed the poker and brought it up in a clumsy *en garde*. His first blow was deflected, but August merely laughed and came at him again.

And was met by Bosilka, who had not run away. She held the

cleaver from the chopping block, and she swung it at him two-handed, burying the blade in his chest. August fell forward without a sound. He twitched once and lay still.

They stared at each other over the colonel's body. She had blood on her, Klaes saw, spattering her face and dress; "Jesu!" he blurted. "Miss Stefanu, I—I'm so sorry."

"I'm not," she said. Her voice was fierce. "He was the man who ordered the floggings. He had Anton murdered. I won't shed one tear for him." Her face was white and set, but she stood her ground: she would not faint. Klaes withdrew the hand he had half-stretched out to support her. "Well," he said awkwardly. "I'm very grateful for your intervention."

For a moment he saw a flash of something in her face: irritation, perhaps, or amusement at his absurd formality. Then she was grave again.

"And now I've become what he said poor Anton was: a traitor. And a murderer."

"No!" Klaes said, appalled. "Neither one! The colonel was mad: he'd have killed all of us. You struck him in self-defence. No court in the land would blame you." He was not at all sure this was true, and in his head his magistrate father reproached him. But he could at least spare her that burden. "If there's blame to be given here, it's mine, not yours. I was the one he meant to murder. I blew up the dam, and left my comrades to face the Prussians. I betrayed my commission. This was all my doing."

"Well, I'm answered," Bosilka said. "Though I think you're too hard on yourself, Lieutenant." She gave him a wan smile. "But thank you."

She had used his proper title, Klaes noticed; now when he must set it aside for good.

There was a sound behind them: Drozde. Klaes had forgotten the puppet mistress for the moment. She spoke so softly they had to bend over her to hear.

"That's three of us Gertrude has done for . . . Mole should be proud . . ."

She closed her eyes and seemed to sleep. Her skin was greyish and her hands icy.

Bosilka looked at Klaes in consternation. "But the colonel didn't touch her, did he? How badly was she hurt before?"

Drozde did not move as the girl unlaced her dress and pulled aside the stained shift. For a long moment Bosilka looked down at her in silence.

"I think . . ." she said, and stopped. She closed her eyes for a moment. "Oh, this is bad."

Drozde's wound stretched from ribs to stomach, red-black and suppurating. Her whole side was red, the skin swollen.

Bosilka covered her again, for the moment. They moved a little aside from the hurt woman while they conferred, as if fearful of disturbing her.

"She's not bleeding."

"It's gone beyond bandages. We'd need to use leeches, or cut her to let the infected matter out. But I'm not a surgeon."

"If we could get her to the town," Bosilka said. "Panov is a good doctor. Or Birgitta—she knows remedies."

"But look at her! She wouldn't stand the journey."

"Don't trouble yourselves."

Drozde had woken while they discussed her. Her voice was no more than a croak, but her eyes were clear. "Surgeon won't help. Leave me here."

Klaes well knew her stubbornness; he tried to keep the frustration out of his voice. "Drozde. If we leave you like this you'll die."

"I'll die in any case. But I need it to be here."

It was a plain statement of fact, and Klaes had no answer. But Bosilka had not known the woman so long. "There must be something we can do!" she wailed.

"Could give me some brandy," Drozde said.

A bottle and glass stood by her on the table. Bosilka filled the glass and held it to her lips; Drozde winced as she drank, but her voice was a little stronger afterwards. "Over behind you," she said, gesturing with her eyes, "My trunk. It's for you; take it with you. I don't want them wasted."

It was the big box from which she ran her puppet theatre. "We'll take care of them," Klaes said. It would slow them down: they would struggle to get it across the river. But Bosilka looked as awed as if the dying woman had given her diamonds.

"You have to go," Drozde said. Her voice was slurring and her eyes began to close as she spoke.

Klaes went to fetch the trunk, holding it awkwardly by both ends.

"We'll need to wade through the river," he said. "Unless you know of a bridge further down."

Bosilka did not answer. She was looking down at Drozde, her eyes full of tears.

"We can't just leave her!" she cried.

"I'm sorry," Klaes said. "But she's right. We can't help her. And the Prussians will be here soon."

"But she saved us. We all owe her our lives. How can we leave her to die alone?"

Drozde opened her eyes. A dry, convulsive sound came from her: it took Klaes a moment to realise she was laughing.

"Alone! Oh, save your pity, girl. I'll have more company than I can well deal with. Go, get clear of here. Klaes, see her safe."

The speech had exhausted her, and she sagged like one of her own puppets. "I will," Klaes promised. He shifted his grip on the trunk, took Bosilka by the arm and pulled her away.

Drozde listened till their voices faded, and waited a while to be sure. No sound of marching yet, no gunfire. She was too weary to move: even talking had been too much for her. She'd meant to give the two of them some advice: tell the girl to be a carpenter if that was what she wanted, even give her a tip or two on how to look after the puppets and how to work them. And tell Klaes that the army was no profession for an honest man. But her voice had let her down, and there was no time. No more time at all.

Well, then. They'd have to work it out for themselves.

39

It helped that there was so much to do. Any repining or blame must wait until later.

Stefan Glatzer and the Hohlbaum family had had their fields flooded by the Drench; now both had nothing but stretches of swamp and water. The Hohlbaum brothers were the richest in the neighbourhood, and owned other fields, but Glatzer would be ruined, having lost his house as well. Ten other houses had stood in the path of the flood and might not be habitable again. The colonel's bombardment had killed Pavel Hecht's cow and left the church in ruins. And then there were the newcomers to the town: some seventy men and a dozen women, all of whom, the mayor ordered, must be given hospitality. Most of the men would only stay until the good weather came, and then move on to seek their fortunes elsewhere, but there were still strangers to fill every spare room or space where a bed could be laid, at least for the winter.

Meister Weichorek had set out immediately to visit all the town's solid citizens, while Dame Weichorek went to work on their wives. A heifer was donated to Hecht and new furniture and a bushel of seed promised for Glatzer. Then the real business began: felling the forest for some acres to the south of the town, clearing a field for planting and building new houses. At least the presence of the soldiers speeded the work. Fifteen men were deputed to help Meister Stefanu put together the house frames and another five, led by Private Leintz, who had been apprenticed to a stonemason before his conscription, set to work on the church.

A few of the newcomers had asked for land to build houses of their own once the main work was finished. There were two men whose wives were with them (one of them a girl of no more than eighteen), and, astoundingly, two lone women, Libush and Alis, who proposed to set up together as seamstresses. Some of the townswomen looked at these two askance: who knew what threat women of that kind might pose to their menfolk and children? But Dame Weichorek was adamant. They had all done the town service, she maintained, and all deserved its help and its hospitality.

For their part the newcomers were grateful for their reception, having seen the fate of the comrades they had left at Pokoj. They paid for their billets in storerooms, barns and attics with hard work, and with coin if they had it. That did a great deal to extend their welcome.

Lieutenant Klaes—no longer a lieutenant, he had to remind himself—took no part in the work at first, and in fact wished fervently that he were anywhere but here. He had been offered lodging by the mayor himself, who proposed setting up a bed for him in the back parlour. The Weichoreks had received him with as much courtesy as if he had never wronged them, and even Jakusch, already back on his feet, greeted him with no sign of rancour. But the sight of the boy's stiff walk, and his wince as he sat down, filled Klaes with shame. He protested that he could not give the burgomaster so much extra trouble, and found himself a billet at the town's inn.

He might have stayed at the carpenter's house instead, he knew. Bosilka—Miss Stefanu—had politely offered him lodging as they walked the three miles upriver from the Drench's southern bridge, the night after the deluge. It was the least she could do, she added, after his service to the town. Klaes could not share her good opinion: if his obstinacy had not uncovered the body of Petos, the whole exercise might not have been necessary. Nor Drozde's death, he thought sadly.

Nor his own disgrace, nor August's blood on the girl's head. On the other hand, he had got her safely home and carried her trunk for near six miles. That probably earned him a bed for the night.

She had led him into a workshop and shown him a closet room almost filled by a narrow bedstead. It had been Anton's, she said—and started to cry. She wept for a long time, hunched over the workbench, while Klaes stood by helplessly. He already knew that he could not sleep in Hanslo's bed. When Bosilka's sobs subsided a little he had led her into the little room and made her sit down, finding a blanket to cover her.

Klaes had waited until he was sure she was asleep before leaving the workshop. He had walked about the town till morning, thinking that he could not stay in a place where he had caused so much misery.

But he had stayed: he had nowhere else to go. And to his surprise, he found no one to blame him. Quite the contrary: Meister Weichorek had instructed that the visitors be welcomed, and as their leader, Klaes commanded a certain respect. When he presented himself at the inn he was offered a room without demur, though the innkeeper had been one of those whipped. Possibly the man took some pleasure in his new guest's embarrassment when he was forced to ask to pay for his keep by chopping wood. But there Klaes had no choice: he had barely enough with him to pay for two weeks' lodging; less if he wanted to eat more than bread and beer. All he owned now were his coat, his pen and a few books.

For the first week he ate at the inn and stayed in his room when not carrying out the owner's chores, but one night at supper he was surprised to find himself surrounded by a group of local men. He knew them by sight: they drank most nights in the room next door and had nodded at him once or twice. But now they came up as soon as they saw him, and two or three wanted to shake his hand. It seemed that some of the men working on the new houses had been telling the story of the bursting of the dam to entertain their coworkers who had not been at the scene. Privates Toltz and Schneider, who had seen the fuse being lit, had cast Klaes as the hero of the day; had painted him, in fact, as some kind of reckless daredevil.

"Meister Klaes! Pleasure to meet you, sir," an old man said. "Diverted a river with a stalk of dill, hey?" Someone laughed and slapped him on the back. Two others contended to buy him a drink. The innkeeper himself came over to hear the story retold, and looked at his guest with a proprietorial pride.

People had short memories, Klaes thought.

His newfound popularity did not alter his predicament: he was no longer a soldier, and there was no life waiting for him outside the army. He could not stay indefinitely in Puppendorf as a hanger-on, living on charity or taking what work he could to pay his way. He would have to find a profession of some sort, and quickly. But running through the list of his accomplishments, he could not believe that the town required a sapper or a figures clerk, nor a magistrate for that matter.

He had no skill with his hands, and no great strength: he could not train as a wheelwright or a shoemaker, and would be little use to them in the building. Maybe, he thought, he could find work on a farm. When he was a boy everyone in his village had helped with the harvest. And he could care for animals: he had groomed and fed the horses he rode, though he had never owned his own. There would be ploughing and sowing in the spring, and calving; maybe there would be enough for him to do.

He walked to the north edge of the town where the cows were pastured. A group of children were playing at the side of a field, balancing on the stone wall and taking it in turns to swing from a pair of ropes tied to a tree branch. Klaes stopped to ask them the way to the nearest farm.

"That's my dad's," said one of the boys. "But he won't stop to see you today, sir; he's out fixing fences in the back field."

That fitted well with Klaes's agenda. He asked the boy if his father might have use for a man to help him with such work. The boy, looking at Klaes a little doubtfully, allowed that he might. "But you can't ask him now," he repeated. "He don't like to be disturbed when he's working."

"Maybe I could leave him a note," Klaes said, unwilling to have come out for nothing. The boy laughed.

"Can if you like, sir, but it'll do you no good. There's no one here can read."

"No one?" This was an out-of-the way place, Klaes thought, but still. "What do you children do for schooling, then?"

The boy gave him a blank look. "What's that?"

Meister Weichorek was in favour of the idea, to Klaes's considerable relief. He even suggested a place for Klaes to set up: while the church was being rebuilt, its surviving furniture had been moved to Laslow's empty barn. The services were held there on Sundays, but for the rest of the week the pews and lectern might just as well be used for an impromptu schoolroom. Klaes would charge two *groschen* per pupil for a week's teaching, and would move on to figuring once they knew their letters. The mayor would send away for slates and pencils at his own expense. He could not order the townspeople to send their children, of course, but many of the mothers would jump at the chance. And Dame Weichorek could be very persuasive.

Klaes prepared for his first lessons two weeks before Christmas. Eight families were sending their children: eleven boys and three girls in all. He laid out the pews in a hollow square around the lectern and propped a large slate in front of it, feeling as nervous as when he'd taken his first command.

He heard a step behind him and turned to see Bosilka Stefanu. He had not spoken to her since the night of his arrival, and could not imagine why she was here now, though from her stern expression it was not a friendly visit. He bowed to hide his discomfiture, and waited for her to state her purpose.

"I want to join your class," she said without preamble.

Klaes was completely taken aback. But she clearly required an answer. "You—you mean, to study with the children?" he managed.

"I mean to learn reading; to read better. Drozde left books in her trunk. I want to find out what they say."

"But . . ." he stuttered, and was silent.

"Dame Weichorek has approved it," the girl said defiantly. "I can come in the mornings and work longer in the afternoons. I already know my alphabet, and some words, and if it's more trouble I'll pay extra." She rummaged in her apron pocket as she spoke, and held out coins. Four *cruitzers*—that would be at least a week's wages for her. When he still hesitated she added tartly, "Or don't you teach girls?"

"I do! Assuredly I do," he broke in at last. "But Miss Stefanu . . . these are children—the oldest is fourteen. Will you not feel out of place?"

"I'm nineteen," she said. "If we'd had a teacher when I was younger I'd have gone to him, but there was none. And my father couldn't read;

nor could Anton. I've had to teach myself. Do you think I'm too old to learn more?"

She met his gaze levelly, challenging him to disapprove. Klaes felt his face grow hot. "I'm sorry for doubting you, Miss Stefanu," he said. "I'll teach you gladly." Her grey eyes were almost black in the room's shadows. He pressed on without giving himself time to consider. "But I won't take your money. Perhaps . . . Do you think you might come here as a helper, rather than a pupil? Assist me in running the class, I mean. As—as a friend. I think you could still learn all you'd need."

She hesitated. And Klaes had the sensation that he'd stepped over a cliff.

"I could," she said. "That would work very well. And Lieutenant, my name is Bosilka."

By the new year they had twenty children. All of them could chant the alphabet and write their names, and Klaes had started the more advanced on reading passages from Drozde's chapbooks and his own Old Testament, written painstakingly large on the big slate. At the end of each session Bosilka would teach them a song, or retell an old story with the children joining in at the exciting parts. And in February, when snow would otherwise have kept everyone indoors, they staged a puppet show.

It was Bosilka's idea. She had pestered Klaes for every detail he could remember of Drozde's shows, and then she'd gone to find Private Taglitz, now doing odd jobs in the forge, to question him as well. They had agreed on a short performance for the first experiment: the stories of "Clever Gretel" and "The Cobbler's Son," both favourites of the children, and to finish, a dramatization of "The Moving of the Mala Panev."

Klaes had raised some objections to this. They couldn't tell the full story, he pointed out: they would have to leave out important facts, even falsify. But Bosilka overruled them all.

"We won't lie," she promised him. "But this story is important to them, perhaps the most important of all. It tells them how their town has become what it is. It tells them who they are."

She worked night and day to make scenery: a series of cutouts for the town, model barrels of gunpowder, a long skein of blue and green cloth for the river. She removed the fluttering eyelashes from

Drozde's model of the great gun and replaced them with menacing, reptilian eyes copied from the dragon. And she practised endlessly with the puppets: the overbearing colonel, Drozde, the soldiers and townspeople on their crosspieces, and the gangly officer who would stand in yet again for Klaes.

This was Klaes's greatest objection of all, though he'd been too embarrassed to voice it. His men's lurid accounts of his exploits had gained some currency among the town's drinkers, but the children had not yet connected the hero of their fathers' stories with their well-mannered schoolteacher, and he had no wish for them to do so. But Bosilka had foreseen this problem too. "We'll use your given name," she said.

He did not like his Christian name. He had been teased about it too many times in the past: schoolmates and fellow soldiers informing him, as if he had never heard it before, that his parents had named him after the wrong animal. But the townspeople, and most of his men, had never heard it. So for the sake of the story the hero of Puppendorf, who blew up the dam and saved the town with a reed, would be Lieutenant Wolfgang.

On the day of the show the barn was packed. Nearly a hundred children sat on the pews and on benches hurriedly made by Stefanu the week before, while their parents stood at the back. The press of bodies generated such heat that many had already opened their heavy coats before the performance started. Klaes stood to one side of the theatre booth, welcoming the arrivals and privately wondering what he had got himself into. He was no showman! But Bosilka raised the Drozde puppet and made her wave to him. Taglitz blew a fanfare on his trumpet, as raucous as it had ever been in the old days. And the crowd fell silent.

Klaes took a deep breath. "Pay attention," he began.

40

And now, at last, she is with them.

And now she has always been with them.

And she is poured, for an endless moment, across the centuries, as oil is poured across a skillet. Her mind rushes to the furthest corners of things—the darkness before and the darkness after, the flash of light and life that counts as history, the endlessness of existence. She becomes a film, a thin slick of selfhood, spread far, far too thinly across cold, indifferent acres of casual cause and dread effect.

But then she gathers herself in again. She does it, in part, because she knows it can be done. And in part she does it because she is a teller of stories, which is how the thing is achieved.

And there are others coming and going around her, through her. They know her. They speak her name, and she speaks theirs. It is a benediction, flowing both ways.

And she teaches them, the things she only knows because they told her. She tells them about time, and about stories, and her wisdom is passed among them like the bread of the sacrament.

They come together in a complicated, fierce

embrace. With each telling they become stronger—through endless repetition shore up their borderlands, defend their core. They build, through words, towers and ramparts of themselves. She helps them do it, leads the way, becomes the template and the map for every one of them.

And is the first to realise that these walls, which were a refuge, have by degrees become a trap. Not the walls of the house (the house comes and goes; the *houses* come and go) but the walls of their telling. They have dropped their foundations so deep and reared their walls so high that there is no moving now. They have built their own prison.

She shares her doubts with Gelbfisc and Ignacio, Ermel and Arinak. Most of all she confers with Anton and Magda, who are so close to her that they have almost become her.

"We have always been here," Anton points out.

"So if we were ever going to leave," Gelbfisc sighs, "we could not be here now."

"But what if there's more than one always?" Magda asks.

And Drozde laughs and hugs her, heart against heart and thought against thought, because the little girl has set them free.

Even the smallest part of eternity is still eternity.

She gathers them, and tells them. We've done what there was to be done here. We've become so strong, in ourselves and in each other, nothing can extinguish us. We're like a ball of string so knotted up it cannot ever, ever be untied.

"We are the crown," Father Ignacio murmurs. "The crown of thorns."

"It may well be," Drozde allows. "So now, I say, it's time to leave."

"We can't," Thea protests. "We can't leave Pokoj."

But Ermel at least is nodding. "Yes. I think we should."

And Arinak: "It's where we died. Where all the generations of us lay our bodies down."

And Petra Veliky: "But did we mean to lay ourselves down, too? Or were we only taking off our flesh the way a runner takes off his coat and shirt—so that our souls could run the faster?"

And the questions and the answers and the declamations run between them. The stories of their lives are all told again, sifted for wisdom, combed for sense. Drozde waits, and says nothing more. It is for all of them, now, and she has made her position clear. Repeating herself would serve no purpose.

And one by one they come to it. And one by one they decide. And it grows in them like a seed, like a sense, so they're like birds gathering on a sodden field in late October as the winter prepares to slam its lid in place over the sky.

They have to fly before that happens, but like birds they wait and wait. It will come when it comes. And it feels close. It feels as though it might be any moment now, if there were any moments left.

And there is. Just one.

And it opens within and around them as they fly.

ABOUT THE AUTHORS

Linda, Louise, and Mike Carey are three writers living in North London. Sometimes they write together, sometimes alone. Their previous book with ChiZine Publications was *The Steel Seraglio*.

Louise wrote *The Diary of a London Schoolgirl* for the website of the London Metropolitan Archive. She also co-wrote the graphic novel *Confessions of a Blabbermouth* with Mike.

Linda, writing as A.J. Lake, authored the Darkest Age fantasy trilogy. She has also written for TV, most notably for the German fantasy animation series *Meadowlands*.

Mike has written extensively in the comics field, where his credits include *Lucifer*, *Hellblazer*, *X-Men* and *The Unwritten* (nominated for both the Eisner and Hugo Awards). He is also the author of the Felix Castor novels, and of the *X-Men Destiny* console game for Activision. He is currently writing a movie screenplay, *Silent War*, for Slingshot Studios and Intrepid Pictures.

They share their crowded house with two other writers/artists, a cat, and several stick insects.

EMB
RACE
THE
ODD

THE STEEL SERAGLIO

MIKE CAREY, LINDA CAREY & LOUISE CAREY

The sultan Bokhari Al-Bokhari of Bessa has 365 concubines—until a violent coup puts the city in the hands of the religious zealot Hakkim Mehdad. Hakkim has no use for the pleasures of the flesh: he condemns the women first to exile and then to death. Cast into the desert, the concubines must rely on themselves and each other to escape from the new sultan's fanatical pursuit. But their goals go beyond mere survival: with the aid of the champions who emerge from among them, they intend to topple the usurper and retake Bessa from the repressive power that now controls it. Together, they must forge the women of the harem into an army, a seraglio of steel, and use it to conquer a city. But even if they succeed, their troubles will just be beginning—because their most dangerous enemy is within their own number. . . .

AVAILABLE NOW
ISBN 978-1-926851-53-2

THE BOOK OF DAVID

ROBERT BOYCZUK

The Spheres of the Apostles: an artificial world consisting of massive concentric spheres. A millennium has passed since the Spheres were first seeded by the Catholic Church and few remember the persecution from which they fled; even fewer are aware of the systems quietly functioning and malfunctioning around them. The world is simply the world as God has made it and so beyond their ken. Angels, a genetically modified elite, have trapped themselves in Lower Heaven and can only observe as the world slowly comes undone, while men scratch out a meagre existence in Spheres below, afflicted with the violence that accompanies the disintegration of religious authority. In an attempt to wrest scarce resources from the Angels, the Papacy has declared war on Lower Heaven, while below, an army of the poor and dispossessed gathers, readying to march on Rome. . . .

AVAILABLE SPRING 2016
ISBN 978-1-77148-351-3

THE APOCALYPSE ARK
PETER ROMAN

In the third Cross book, the immortal angel killer Cross faces his most dangerous enemy yet: Noah. For ages Noah has sailed the seas, seeking out all of God's mistakes and imprisoning them on his ark. Noah is not humanity's saviour but is instead God's jailer. But he has grown increasingly mad over the centuries, and now he is determined to end the world by raising the mysterious Sunken City. Only one person can stop him: Cross.

AVAILABLE SPRING 2016
ISBN 978-1-77148-377-3

ALMOST DARK
LETITIA TRENT

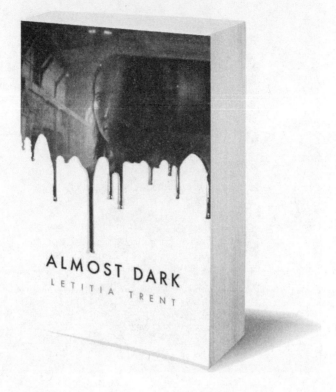

Claire, a private and outwardly content librarian, carries a secret: she is wracked with guilt over her twin brother Sam's accidental death fifteen years earlier. Claire's quiet life is threatened when Justin, an aggressive business developer, announces the renovation of Farmington's oldest textile factory, which is the scene of Sam's death along with many other mysterious accidents throughout its long history. Claire not only feels a personal connection to the factory, but she also begins to receive "visitations" from her brother, which cause her to question her sanity. As Justin moves forward with his plans to renew the factory, Claire, and the town as a whole, discover that in Farmington, there is no clear line between the past and the present.

AVAILABLE SPRING 2016
ISBN 978-1-77148-336-0

WRAPPED IN SKIN
MARK MORRIS

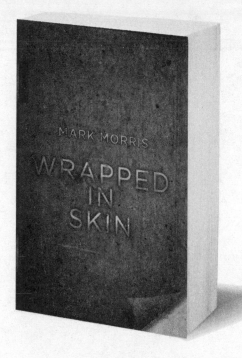

A woman haunted by a mysterious upside-down door . . . a meeting between a famous punk rocker and a voodoo priestess . . . a group of friends who willingly place themselves in the path of bullets that travel through time . . . Mark Morris's stories are wrapped in strange skin. Skin suffused with regret and grief and anger. Skin that twitches with bad dreams and appalling memories. Skin that is so thin it is unable to prevent the terrors of the past from breaking through.

AVAILABLE SPRING 2016
ISBN 978-1-77148-357-5